I0762500

"What happens when youthful dreams and ambitions hit the wall? Emily Nemens's compelling new novel, *Clutch*, is an exploration of long devoted friendships in such pivotal moments. The life-changing situations and choices leave us aware of both a universal experience and the most private and fragile one. Wise, witty, and at times harrowing, Nemens skillfully weaves the lives of these five friends, memorably cemented by time."

—**Jill McCorkle,**
author of *Hieroglyphics*

"*Clutch* is a sharp, heartfelt celebration of modern friendship, positioning it as the backbone of our social lives. Through bold, inventive leaps, Nemens's prose dazzles, elevating the group chat, and the friend bond, to something sacred and vital. A big-hearted and daring novel from one of our finest creative and critical minds."

—**Jonathan Escoffery,**
author of *If I Survive You*

"Finally, we have a collective noun for a group of aging female friends, and only the great Emily Nemens could've declared it. *Clutch* is hilarious, philosophical, anthropological, polyphonic, with a keen eye for the specific foibles of our present American moment. Nemens is an expert chronicler of the subtle ways women wound each other, and also, the ways they offer love. The way a friendship can carry venom and antidote both. These pages made me laugh and broke my heart—yes, it had me in its clutches."

— **Hilary Leichter,**
author of *Terrace Story*

"A sharp, funny, utterly engrossing exploration of the enduring complexity and deep love of long-term friendship, *Clutch* enmeshes you in the particularities, yearning, fears of these five friends, as they try and fail and try again to love and care for one another amidst the endless push and pull, losses and joys of middle life."

—**Lynn Steger Strong**,
author of *The Float Test*

"*Clutch* is a powerfully intimate portrait of female friendship, following five college friends through the turbulent landscape of their forties as careers implode, marriages fracture, and dreams reshape themselves in unexpected ways. With razor-sharp insight, humor, and deep compassion, Nemens explores how these women navigate life's most challenging moments, proving that even when circumstances threaten to tear them apart, the bonds forged in youth can become the foundation for reinvention. This is a bracingly honest and exhilarating novel about the messy, complicated, and essential work of showing up for the people who matter most."

—**Kimberly King Parsons**,
author of *We Were the Universe*

"Witty, incisive, and gorgeously written, *Clutch* is about the friendships that carry us through life's most complicated chapters. The five women in this book, so lovingly portrayed in all their imperfect glory, will step off the page and into your heart."

—**Ana Reyes**,
author of *The House in the Pines*

Clutch

ALSO BY EMILY NEMENS

The Cactus League

Clutch

A NOVEL

Emily Nemens

Tin House
A zando IMPRINT
NEW YORK

Tin House

Tin House is an imprint of Zando.
zandoprojects.com

First US Edition 2026
Manufacturing by Lake Book Manufacturing
Cover and text design by Beth Steidle

Library of Congress Cataloging-in-Publication Data Available Upon Request

978-1-963108-66-8 (Hardcover)
978-1-963108-75-0 (ebook)

10 9 8 7 6 5 4 3

Manufactured in the United States of America

For my mother

Here, you said and say, is
where we are. Give back

what we are, these people you made,
us, and nowhere but you to be.

—from "America," Robert Creeley

In the group chat

Bella 40, corporate litigator, Manhattan; married (Bill), two sons (Gus, 4; Bill Jr., 2)

Carson 40, writer and academic coach, Brooklyn; single

Gregg 39, politician, former actor, Austin; married (Zeke), two sons (Xavier, 2; Zack, 1)

Hillary 40, ENT physician, Chicago; married (Miles), one son (Roger, 5)

Reba 41, homemaker, former management consultant, San Francisco; married (Terrence)

Prologue

Tue, Nov 15, 2022 at 9:03 PM

Carson:

There better be a gd pool.

What is time, really? It can be measured in centuries or seconds, calendar years or costume periods, milestones or metamorphoses. Some quantities we know to be immutable; seconds feed into minutes into hours; light speed being what it is, in midwinter it will take the sun's rays eight minutes and twenty seconds to reach a backyard swimming pool in Palm Springs, California.

But time is also measured more subjectively, the experienced length of things, intensity times duration. Sometimes the days are slow but the years are fast—truisms aren't born on a lark—and sometimes you lie down for a quick nap and wake up to find half your life has passed.

By this idiosyncratic stopwatch, maybe February isn't the shortest month of the year, maybe those twenty-eight days can set a Guinness record for Longest Month Ever; this story's quintet could make the case for it in 2023, given the pileups coming down their collective and respective pikes. Because while these women, the five friends we'll meet in a moment, knew that sometimes the two modes of timekeeping decoupled completely, the milliseconds of the iPhone voice recorder staying steady even as one's life fell apart in slower motion, they couldn't have known that the first quarter of that year was to be the most consequential of their lives. They certainly wouldn't have guessed, as they texted back and forth about their long-punted reunion, that they'd be seeing one another three times in three months, and that after the dumpster fire of late winter, their constellations would be tumbled into wholly different star charts. Bright pinpricks where there had been dim ones, some specks flaring more orange or pink than before, other lights absent entirely. Every aspect of their night sky, of their day sky, of their lives below the dome: different.

No, not every single one. One subjective thing that had become, through duration, objectively true and nonfungible was their friendship. Because the group had been friends for twenty years, more if they were honest about the starting bell, a literal three-hundred-pound inverted brass cup that rang out during their New England college's convocation exercises, then continued gonging periodically throughout the welcome-to-campus activities of their freshman year. As for the five of them being placed along the same residential hall, maybe it had been the college's social optimization algorithm, maybe it had drawn on all the compute power of eenie, meenie, miney, moe, but they were grateful for their forced proximity. Five women from four parts of the country, each with a distinct upbringing and different academic interests; on paper, they'd have been unlikely love matches, yet here they were, decades later, all and still dear and trusted intimates. They'd seen one another through marriages and at least one impending or recent divorce, childbirths and miscarriages, dead-end jobs and big-deal jobs and those deemed once-in-a-lifetime opportunities (some of which had turned out to be very good, while others had just sounded fantastic but became ho-hum, as quotidian and tedious and gray-hair making as the rest of their obligations). They'd been there for all of it.

For a while after graduation there'd been a critical mass living in New York, or if not living there then at least appearing at the West Fourth subway station with some frequency. Reba kept an apartment in the West Village, even if work (management consulting) more often shipped her to corporate apartments in Flint or Columbus or Orlando. During her internship year, Hillary did a surgery rotation at Mount Sinai; she'd hoped for lots of domestic violence reconstructions and asthma mitigation, but during her three months on the Upper East Side she mostly scrubbed into happy-birthday rhinoplasties for the daughters of the city's elite. Gregg, still acting then, might get cast in an off-off-Broadway production; she had inadvertently become a specialist in the role of understudy. If Reba was between far-flung client consultations, the women would turn Gregg's stage run into an extended sleepover, everything but the pillow fights; if she was absent, Gregg would go domestic in Reba's apartment, vacuuming and mopping and taking her friend's mussed and musty suits to the cleaner, things Reba always meant to get to but somehow couldn't manage.

And then, for several years, they'd had the excuse of weddings. Theirs, less Carson, who was either hopelessly self-sabotaging or hiding an affair or truly as indifferent to romance as she claimed to be, and Reba, who was too busy to find love, at least until she did. There were also celebrations feting the next circle of friends; the women had plenty of mutuals among their outer, overlapping bands. In recent years, weddings—and the affiliated showers, bachelorette weekends, rehearsal dinners, recovery brunches—had tapered to zilch; people who were going to find love had done so. Or, if they were late arriving to the land of connubiality, the newcomers didn't think it worth the fuss of mason jars and tea lights and hosting a hundred of their closest friends for steak and salmon. There was a time and place for everything; the time for passed rolls had passed.

Now only Carson and Bella were still in New York. Hillary had joined an ENT practice in Chicago, but between her still starter apartment and the transitional state of her marriage (which was chugging toward *fine*—the musical term, not copacetic), her life hardly seemed settled. Contrast this with Reba, who'd finally quit the consultancy, returned to San Francisco, and, once she'd off-loaded her parents to a nearby retirement community, moved back into the house in which she'd grown up. (Some of the women thought this was the ultimate settl*ed*, while others considered it settl*ing* . . . that wee gerund bore so much judgment.) Gregg had, improbably, wound up in Texas. Improbable because Gregg had been the savviest, most urbane of them upon arrival to college; she had grown up toddling across the Cambridge campus where her parents both taught, she liked Stoppard and Sondheim, she had eaten pâté! So when Gregg sent them all Texas barbecue sauce for Christmas 2015, it was like a pie to the face, that surprising and good tasting. How many missed roles does it take to get to the center of an actor's psyche? We'll never know, but after a dozen heroic years of mostly unsuccess, and close on the heels of the UT production that fortuitously brought her to Austin and introduced her to Zeke Graves, Gregg chomped down on that lollipop and went from theater in the round to the state's Capitol Rotunda and the start of her political career.

And so, spread out as they were, tethered to home by third-trimester travel restrictions and breastfeeding requirements, because for years now it seemed someone was always coming or going from the maternity ward, it had been four years since they'd all seen one another. This was the longest stretch since forever, since the gongs of August 2001, when they'd endured their residential hall's excruciating icebreakers (never mind that those cheesy campus scavenger hunts and three-legged races had worked—the five of them were forever bound in a six-legged race, happily joined at the ankles), though it hadn't been a total abeyance. Bella and Carson still got together, once every month or two, to drink wine on the Metropolitan Museum's roof or along its Great Hall Balcony as seasonally appropriate. Gregg had been through Chicago for a Lori Lightfoot fundraiser and seen Hillary; she thought her friend had looked exhausted but blamed a busy surgery schedule and the sweet menace of Roger (whom they all called the Little Raj for his already pronounced imperiousness, his little boy swagger). Weeks before the lockdown, Carson had flown to San Francisco to catch up with Reba and hear about her new beau, who would become her new husband, and who might yet become her new baby daddy, if the stars and the fertility treatments aligned. Terrence had been out of town that weekend, and so to Carson remained a minimalist Instagram profile, a photo on Reba's living room mantel, a man reinventing himself after two tours of duty in Afghanistan and a dishonorable discharge. (These last points sounded somewhat sinister to Carson, but she set them aside, not wanting to deny Reba her ongoing swoon. And who was she to judge?)

But all of them together.

"Something must be done," Bella had texted the group in fall 2022. Had it been Thanksgiving? A swirl of well-wishes around Carson's fortieth? In any case, that doleful *Something* had stirred the group chat up from its latency. This same chain had chirped constantly during the first weeks of the pandemic, all of them rabid with worry and boredom and manic energy, news gathering and fearmongering and loneliness. Since then, the chain had settled into an occasional chime, a kid doing something cute or some tea. But now, it was churning, churning back to life.

"You're right," Gregg typed in reply. The *dot dot dot* from Hillary's phone was excruciating—it gurgled for several interminable minutes.

Until Reba chimed in. "Palm Springs. 2nd wknd Jan???"

It was a canny strategy. No one did anything the second weekend in January. People binged Netflix or swore off streaming; people regretted their consumption of Christmas cookies or made and froze the low-sodium soups that they'd dutifully reheat into April.

The women's screens filled with cascading replies. A straightforward thumbs-up from Hillary, a GIF of a B-list celebrity with a confetti gun from Bella. Gregg sent a clip of those cartoon kids from *Captain Planet* lifting their ringed knuckles to the sky and summoning an environmentally conscientious hero. Carson, the most deadpan of them—though quiet, earnest Hillary was a close second; she could occasionally unleash a scorcher—wrote, "Lemme check my calendar."

Bella thought about replying *lol*—Carson didn't have a job, just that tutoring gig she'd had forever; and she didn't have a husband or kids or aging parents to consider, the commitments that clogged up the rest of the women's calendars and kept them within a stone's throw of insane.

"Jk jk, im in," Carson added after a beat. Then she sent a short video of a dog walking off the end of a diving board. The creature, a fluffy golden, seemed startled when the mint-green plank turned into air and then into water with a splash.

1

Fri, Jan 13 at 3:08 AM

Carson:

This is yr 3am wakeup call 😆 see you @jfk xx

Bella and Carson were taking a six a.m. flight out of JFK. To fly directly into Palm Springs would've been ungodly expensive, which Bella could have afforded on her corporate law salary, but because she was sensitive to her friend's finances, and knew how much of a stretch Carson's fifth of the holiday rental would be, Bella was the one to suggest they fly to LAX, pick up the weekend's rental car there, then drive to the desert. Besides, she added as cover for them both, the directs would have gotten them into Palm Springs late in the day, and the five women had pledged to one another that they'd show up in time for Friday lunch.

Bella reasoned, as she swallowed her morning pills in the stumbling dark (Bill snoring, oblivious, across the room), that this itinerary saved face for Carson, which was good because Carson didn't have much face left. She could offer up her usual skeptical smirk, or her standard stiff-lipped-and-staying-proud face, which was her default when anyone asked about her one published novel and its middling success. No longer could Carson milk the what-if wistfulness of a potential best seller or a film adaptation starring Miles Teller or Michael B. Jordan or Henry Golding (because each of the women had her type). Admittedly, Bella thought, Carson had more faces in her arsenal. She also had her *fuck you* face, which she swore by for riding public transit. And there was her mildly amused *I have a secret* face (the face she'd made when she told Bella what she'd done with that teenage client all those years ago; it had taken great restraint on Bella's part to keep it to herself, but she had, and sometimes still patted herself on the back for her enduring discretion). Carson beamed similarly Cheshire while *receiving* secrets, and accepted all of Bella's extracurricular confessions as scintillating episodes right up until they disappeared. With the hormonal shifts of pregnancy and motherhood's new exhaustion, Bella's days of polyamory were gone, or at least holed up in a two-star hotel in a hard-to-reach foreign country. The potential of some sexiness, or even just day-to-day calm returning to her life—via monthslong sleepaway camps, maybe boarding school, but only if and when her boys were ready—was a distant beacon. She loved her sons, but sometimes delegating their daily maintenance sounded so delicious.

Bella, now dressed in a comfy traveling outfit, tiptoed into the kids' room. She kissed each boy on his damp forehead—*Goodbye, Mommy loves you!*—then gathered her things, uttering a prayer that, under Bill's watch, they would not require any visits to urgent care. Her husband meant well, but his only example of fatherhood was absenteeism—his late banker father had always been busy earning money enough to support three wives (two former, one current; this wasn't Utah) and the associated offspring—and Bill was still learning how to offer the care he'd never encountered with his own dad. She wished for Bill (for the boys, for herself) bath-time protocols that didn't soak the whole bathroom, a menu of reasonably healthy meals, and no accidents, because really, both of them were old enough to use the potty. But when Bill was in charge, the hallway always seemed to flood with bubble bath, the boys ate greasy things from the diners and delis of Lexington Avenue, and Bill usually managed to get himself strafed with toddler piss.

She slipped quietly out of their apartment and into the antique elevator that could've woken half the building for its pings and pangs. She strode through the lobby. Her car was waiting at the curb, her stomach was arriving in her throat. Why? she asked herself, befuddled by her sudden discomfiture. Bill would be fine; there was a fridge full of tiny Tupperwares with prerinsed, precut snacks; if the boys ate pizza for breakfast: oh well. Was she anxious about seeing the women? These were her oldest friends, her dearest ones. Their bond was so different from the semi-competitive kindness of the nursery school drop-off set, nowhere near the mean-but-said-sweetly atmosphere at work. (There, Bella had absorbed her boss's treatment and started delivering similarly disparaging instructions to her assistant. She hated herself for it, but also didn't stop.) Carson, Gregg, Hillary, Reba—they all, and together, were special.

Bella settled into the back seat of her livery and thought again of Carson's face-saving techniques. She wasn't dating niche famous musicians anymore, which hadn't exactly been an accomplishment, but had offered cred, a kind of coverage. The coolness factor of the hot-slash-renowned indie rock boyfriend, the backstage passes she willingly shared around, the largely nocturnal existence she embraced with smoky eyes and mussed hair (though to think of it, her hair was still usually a mess). In those days, Carson puffed American Spirits like a chimney and did permanent damage to her ears—Hillary had been so concerned about her cochleae. But all of it had been very chic, in its tumbledown way.

Or was the idiom *saving face* about diminishing proportions? Maybe Carson just had a sliver of cheek, one eye and a nostril, an inch-wide swath of lip and chin left, and that's why she was so guarded. No, no; Bella knew that was not what the phrase meant. (She needed coffee.) The point, no matter the expression's literalness or its etymology, was self-preservation, and maybe that was what Bella observed on Carson's face during those Friday night glasses of museum wine, her friend having trekked over from central Brooklyn but talking like she might as well have traveled in from another planet. Because as much as Bella Winston thought all her friends were wonderful, talented, and as tough as freaking nails . . . statistically speaking, not all of them could get everything they wanted. Sure, they each totally deserved it all, and they were all good, worthy people. Maybe they'd made a smattering of mistakes along the road, but who hadn't? Bella was pragmatic enough to know that earnest efforts were not every time duly rewarded. This was life, and in life, unfairness abounded, which meant no matter how hard they each worked, someone would invariably draw the short stick. Maybe it'd be Carson; signs (her perpetual singledom, her sputtering literary career, that she still had *roommates*) were pointing that way.

The car slowed. How could there be traffic at this hour? Bella, short in the trunk, couldn't see much from the Lincoln's deep back bench.

But this weekend was not about doom and gloom, not about Carson's meager bank account or Hillary's anticipated (official? Bella couldn't recall where Hill and Miles were in the process) divorce. Nor would it be a time for passing judgment or being judged, not for the pleasantries of school pickup or the hallway dodge of neighbors forever angry about her children's happy racket. It would be none of the stuff of daily life, instead forty-eight hours of bottomless joy, true feeling, no BS. A weekend just as beautiful and giddy and sloppy as it needed to be. Their beloved six-legged race returned! But instead of ankle binds and a fifty-yard dash, maybe they'd opt for five massage-chairs-plus-footbaths in a row, ten calf rubs and fifty toes painted with precise, pretty polish.

2

Fri, Jan 13 at 4:48 AM

Bella:

Here!

Carson:

No im here

Carson was at the gate, looking placid or bored in the terminal's sterile light. The writer was wearing blue jeans, a stylishly distressed T-shirt of a long-gone band. Atop that was the slouchy, soft cardigan that she donned so often her friends joked that she'd come with it, like the set of dresses and pumps that were packed in the pink box alongside their favorite Barbie doll.

Bella waved, Carson waved back, then looked her up and down with a smirk. "Nice soccer mom getup," she said as they hugged. Bella was wearing a sweat suit in pastel tie-dye, which had looked cute on Instagram, though in real life it was giving off rainbow sherbet vibes. It had been expensive, but to its credit, it was very soft, and earlier that morning—so early the night was still squarely looming outside her window—she'd stepped into the stretchy pants and pulled the pillowy top over her head and exited the room before she could psych herself out of the lilac and mint.

"Did you brush your hair today?" Bella replied, noting the morning's pronounced tousle.

Carson ran a hand over her scalp; her hair settled a smidge. "Guilty as charged."

Bella plucked at the sleeve of her new outfit. "Soccer mom, really?"

Carson shrugged noncommittally.

"Anyway, I thought this was a judgment-free weekend?" Bella added.

"We're not there yet." Carson's smile crooked up on one side. Sometimes they bickered like sisters, Carson playing the junior know-it-all, though Bella was the real-life younger sibling, with a brother, a decade her senior, living out west. But they also shared secrets like sisters, Carson's affairs (after the student and the musicians had been a smattering of married men and divorced women, then a long stretch of nothing) and Bella's (pre-kids, both she and Bill permitted and partook in sex outside their marriage, the only rules being don't get too attached, and no one new in the marital bed; since kids, the idea of cavorting with anyone, Bill included, had, to Bella, withered on the vine).

"I don't think it's soccer mom." Bella smoothed the performance fabric. "And I should know." She was referring, they both understood, to her years as a serious soccer player, a sweeper known among her teammates and rivals as Bella the Destroyer. Varsity for three seasons, which didn't rise to the level of Reba's hooping (she was briefly a starter on the U-19 national team), but Bella's Westchester high school often showed at the state tournament.

Carson nodded. "Whatever you say."

• • •

The three-hour time difference would have been to the women's advantage except that when they landed in LA at ten and got their rental, they still had to contend with the morning rush, all these Southern Californians just now heading toward the office or their life coach or wherever it was they were going. Back in New York, Bella would have done a predawn workout, preschool drop-off, and 2.5 billable hours by eleven, not only now going to her first appointment of the day. And the way Carson was driving—it wasn't laziness, more laissez-faire, as if she were steering a large and buoyant boat—made

Bella wonder if her friend had been drinking Bloody Marys on the flight. (Bella, with her airline credit card's many points, had been upgraded out of steerage.) They stopped for coffee just past Pomona and Bella offered to drive, but then Carson reminded her of what she'd done to the rental car at Gregg's wedding (thank God they'd opted for bumper-to-bumper coverage) and said that she would manage fine, thanks.

They were already up and over the mountains when they got a text from Gregg saying that she'd missed her flight, or her flight was canceled, or anyway, she would be late, very sorry et cetera, but not to worry, a friend was "playing golf in PS this weekend," like that explained everything. Bella dictated the text chain to Carson as she drove, adding air quotes where she thought them appropriate. "Catch a ride," Bella repeated with fingers curling the air. "That means her friend has a private jet."

"I'm not stupid, Bella," Carson said.

"I know that," Bella said.

3

Fri, Jan 13 at 12:38 PM

Hillary:

Landed. Also has anyone watched the latest season of Naked & Afraid?

Asking for a friend

They were going to be five, because that was how many would fit into a rental car, no bother that they'd been upgraded to a three-row SUV. Carson quietly fretted about the larger vehicle for environmental reasons (Gregg, the fervent recycler, would blow a gasket), for economic ones (the gas bill would be massive), and because driving it in LA traffic felt like maneuvering a shopping cart through a subway station, stairs and turnstiles included. She'd gotten her license at sixteen, but subsequently had scant reason to drive, as she and her mother, Sonja, shared a beat-up VW Rabbit; then in college, when Bella had brought the family station wagon to their off-campus house (the five women used it for grocery runs and leaf-peeping day-trips), Reba usually commandeered the keys; during Carson's two decades in Brooklyn the difficulty of parking, to say nothing of negotiating the BQE, dissuaded her from seeking out a car. Now, she saw clearly that driving on city streets in Seattle in the 1990s was not like navigating LA's contemporary interstates. She took it easy.

There was a sixth woman, Amelia, who could've been invited. She was another friend from college with whom three of them were still close, but there was some unspoken animosity between her and

Bella. Not a hatred, nothing as strong as that, but a not-good feeling, a hostility or skepticism that lurked below the surface. The dorsal fin of it would flash up every so often, putting everyone on edge. *Out of the water, kids!* Early in the weekend's planning stages, Carson and Gregg and Hillary had side-channeled about it, and decided the risk of shark bites, of catfights, wasn't worth it. Because they liked Amelia, a figurative painter who had toiled for years before even her first minor critical success (any meaningful remuneration would take longer still), but they liked Bella more. Plus, the last time they'd all been together—they'd converged on Bella's apartment, the prior one, in Turtle Bay (she'd made Bill go to his mother's for the weekend)—Amelia had arrived to the reunion direct from discovering her boyfriend's infidelity and spent the whole weekend requiring hands-on consolation. Plans were canceled, dinner reservations tossed out the window in favor of greasy takeout. Bella bore the brunt of it—it was Bella and Bill's bed getting soaked with another woman's tears, Bella's Resy profile that was marred with no-shows—and she had fumed over it in the kitchen. "I don't see what the big deal is. It's not like he dumped her," Bella said to Hillary, adding that while she preferred the five of them and their six-legged configuration, she was okay with being seven-legged too, so long as she and Amelia were on the far ends. She was less okay with their race team turning into a tearstained group hug, collapsed on the grass, all because of one inconsequential indiscretion. And did Hillary know, Bella continued, what she had promised Bill to get the apartment for the weekend? Hillary didn't, and mumbled some reply about how they couldn't know what Amelia was going through, not really, because each of them was her own mysterious island of nerves and ambition and desire. "What was that?" Bella had snapped, her hands sudsy with the prior night's wineglasses. "Islands?"

Or maybe, Hillary had thought (Bella had, by then, stomped out of the kitchen, leaving Hillary to dry glasses by herself), they were all fundamentally alike: women who wanted peace on earth and a degree of material comfort, reasonable sex lives and good health and some professional satisfaction. But in pursuit of these goals, they'd been placed in wildly different locales, and they were forced to play out their scenarios like their lives were the myriad plots of a reality TV show with very well-concealed cameras. As for their locations, some of them had washed up on lush islands, essentially oases, and ate juicy, sweet fruits all day, while others were dropped onto rocky outcroppings and proceeded to expand their stone compounds, rock by heavy rock. It wasn't a competition, this metaphorical unscripted show of theirs, but it wasn't *not* a competition, either.

One of those hidden cameras cut to Hillary now, these dozen years later, as she rode on her morning flight from Chicago to Southern California. She was nursing a wound on her left hand in the shape of a five-year-old's hard palate. In the rubric of her reality TV/private island theory—which she still mostly believed, especially when things felt dire—she was convinced her island site was all sand, one scrawny palm tree for shade and sustenance and company. That lonely tree was named Roger, and he was in pre-K, again (his birthday had been on the cusp, but his maturity, or lack, nudged him into the younger class), the best thing to come out of her failed marriage to Miles. The best thing, full stop. But the boy had the attention span of a fruit fly, and seemed to revel in the chaos he wrought on the universe generally, his mother in particular. In this configuration of islands and isolation, the camera was always rolling and Hillary was forever waiting for that damn coconut to drop.

• • •

Hillary and Reba stepped out of Palm Springs International Airport concurrently, one exit apart. Each looked past the other, as if the desert light were blinding after their grayed-over winters or the other woman had turned invisible or their appearances had changed so much in these four-ish years that they'd been rendered unrecognizable. The last time they'd all been together was Bella's baby shower, though nobody had treated that as any kind of Last Supper.

And Hillary did look different, having recently lopped off her hair. The stylist had called it a "sleek bob," but he cut it so that a looser, air-dried version would look nice too—he had met Roger and assumed a baseline level of havoc in her life. Meanwhile Reba looked gaunt, skinny where most of them had thickened in the intervening years, owing to neglected Pelotons, an administration's worth of stress eating, pregnancies, and new, beguiling metabolism. Carson had almost kept her early-twenties figure, thanks to an ambitious running routine and not bearing any children, but she'd messed up her knee last summer, and while thankful to have dodged surgery, in her new inactivity she too had gone up a pants size. She'd once told Bella that she'd added the weight in "solidarity" with her mom friends, which made Bella glower.

Bella and Carson now spotted their friends through the windshield and Carson eased the SUV to the curb. "Definitely not pregnant," Bella said of Reba. There had been a chain without Reba, a discussion over Reba and her endless "radical" (her term) sabbatical. Taking time off to have a kid was one thing, but she was going on year five with no work and no baby in sight. The friends accepted her extended "rest" as a privilege few could afford but Reba definitely deserved, though they still periodically asked one another whether she was pregnant yet. "Not yet" had been Hillary's latest reply to the subgroup, spoken with the authority of a doctor. (And she was, in some ways, the team physician, answering calls and texts about maladies that had nothing to do with ears or noses or throats. Carson's patellar tendon, Bella's meds while she was pregnant . . . The reach of Hillary's advice even extended to the women's parents, children, husbands, and paramours. Hillary, for instance, personally wanted nothing to do with Bella's husband's scrotum, but she listened patiently when Bill got a tick bite on his ball sack, offered the advice of tweezers and ice, and sent an antibiotic prescription to the Duane Reade on Eighty-Second. She'd talked Reba through both her father's prostate diagnosis and Terrence's anemic sperm counts, only later pondering, What was it with her and men's crotches? Those were the opposite of the sinus canal.)

From the front seat, the women determined that neither liked Hillary's haircut.

Carson laid on the horn, a syncopation that could've been the hook to a Britney Spears song if you tilted your ear just right. She played the rhythm not as a nod to the #FreeBritney campaign, though some of them had followed the hashtag, watched the documentary, and listened to the podcast, but because they'd all been somewhat earnest fangirls of the singer twenty years before. That era of her career, that early slice of her oeuvre, gave voice to so many of their young adult impulses, the big feels of life before a fully formed prefrontal cortex. That their busty blond mascot had had a very public breakdown, that her life had become a pop-culture punch line and the singer had skittered off the radar for most of a decade, that her music now felt lewd in some lights and wincingly basic in others . . . all that felt somehow appropriate too. *Goodbye, sweet youth*, it said with a shove. *You'd best be moving on.* Which they did. Publicly, at least. Never mind that Bella listened in her workout mix, and Carson still sometimes thought about the prescience and impossibility of the 2001 Super Bowl halftime show, when Britney and NSYNC and Aerosmith had shared the midfield stage. There was Steven Tyler's tongue, there was a baby-faced JT in green leather, and here comes Britney, at the height of her pulchritude, singing in a cropped and corseted football jersey. Oh, how the world had been so innocent, and slutty, and sluttily innocent then.

Pavlov-like, both women turned toward the horn's plaintive bleating.

Then Bella rolled down the passenger-side window and leaned out of the car. "Bitches, hey!" The women saw Bella, then saw each other. On that cue, the organ in the sky, the one in their hearts, hit a big resounding chord. The celestial key player shifted to the fifth, took a step up, then resolved into bliss. The song was Handel's "Hallelujah," right there at curbside pickup.

They were ten minutes into lunch before Hillary thought to ask, "Where's Gregg?"

4

Fri, Jan 13 at 1:38 PM

Reba:

Made it to PS np. Good luck with the deadline. Luv u!

They finished their fancy salads, then went by the grocery for weekend provisions, ping-ponging between the snacks aisle and the wine one, before checking into the vacation house. It appeared as advertised (though the online photographs may have benefited from a fish-eye lens): both sleek and opulent, midcentury modern on the outside and decorated like a Renaissance painter's idea of a Turkish bath indoors. The great room was furnished with low, soft couches, embroidered plush ottomans, antique rugs laid in overlap. Reba saw the carpets and thought, Trip hazard; she was now, thanks to her octogenarian parents, reminded of danger with every rumply floor covering. But she also reminded herself that everyone here had ample, abundant mobility. (Mostly: Carson was still favoring her knee; when they were leaving lunch, Hillary had noticed and questioned her friend's limp.) For Reba, this would be a weekend with no no-step showers, one without grab bars, panic cords, or anticoagulants; here, she could step away from the innumerable concerns that occupied her parents' minds and therefore hers too. It would also be a scoldings-free weekend, Reba thought. Or at least, if her friends picked and prodded at her life's present configuration, she'd face nothing so scathing as Doris Boaz-Becker's level of critique. That woman was remarkably adept at cutting down her only child, even as Reba was a highly functioning, moderately successful middle-aged adult. Or at least she had been all of those things until somewhat recently.

After they'd picked rooms (Reba and Bella obviously together in the king; Carson in one queen, Hillary in the other—Gregg would have to choose to share with one of them), the pool beckoned. It wasn't hot out, per se, but according to Reba the sunny weather was warm for Palm Springs in January, and wasn't that awesome? Carson's head bobbed enthusiastically; she couldn't wait to get in the pool. Once changed, they pulled together assorted deck chairs so they could chat without shouting over the burble of the water feature (there was also a hot tub, covered and quietly gurgling, at the pool's far end). Reba went back and forth from the kitchen, first appearing with a bowl of organic corn chips; then, after checking on everyone's cilantro tolerance and heat preference, returning with hand-mashed guacamole. The homemade guac was new; she was historically reliant on the closest Whole Foods deli and those pre-chopped salads for sustenance. "Terry's recipe," she explained. Apparently, she'd been learning to cook in her unending downtime.

The women discussed, at length, whether they thought Gregg would run for US Congress. There was, as a result of redistricting and Austin's manic growth, a new seat in Travis County. An octogenarian congressman had come out of retirement to claim it in 2022; he promised to serve only one term, just until the party got its house in order. Now, for Dems (which they all were, though Bella's husband was maybe a quiet Libertarian), it offered better odds than most corners of Texas. Gregg, who had hopped from state legislature to state senate in 2018 with apparent ease, had been deliberately evading the topic during public appearances, in press interviews, and even when asked by longtime friends, point-blank, on the phone: Was she going for it? "We'll see," Gregg always replied. "We'll see, we'll see."

But now, the women concurred, there were so many arrows pointing to yes, she was bound to run for Congress. She'd be so good! For all of Gregg's highbrow occasions (and with Charlene Thomas, a famous-for-a-poet poet as a mother, these started early and were many), she was at other times accessible and down-to-earth, able to code-switch as she moved between poetry readings, country club fundraisers, and truck-stop photo ops. Maybe her agenda was tilted toward socialism and net-zero emissions—if she'd had her druthers, she'd disembowel those verdant golf courses' irrigation systems and join the Valve Turners in their campaign of twisting off oil spigots—but Gregg understood compromise and didn't charge in on her high horse too often . . . only when riding that steed was her last or best hope. And so her favorability in Austin was through the roof, even if she was a transplant. (That's where the years of acting came in, Reba thought—she wasn't *playing* Texan, but she could handily pick up the necessary cues to perform it well.) Of course she'd run, and win, and take her savvy agenda from Texas's big granite dome to the slightly smaller marble one in DC. She'd probably even tell them about it over the weekend, when they were all together, Hillary conjectured. Make it a real celebration, like they didn't have enough else to celebrate (life, forty-eight hours without toddlers, desert sun). Thinking about the possibility, Bella started riffing the names of future political action committees—CCF (Citizens with Concerned Footwear), AKM (Alliance of Kickass Moms), CTTYNMT (Committee That Told You Not to Mess with Texas)—until Carson, who still felt at times insulted that Gregg had stepped off the artist's path and ambled into the political arena, sighed a very big sigh and tried to shift the conversation. What did they all think of the resurgence of mom jeans? Hillary was pro, short-waisted Bella skeptical, Reba agnostic.

"What are we going to do tomorrow?" Hillary asked. Reba and Carson swapped knowing glances. "What?"

"Carson brought chocolates," Reba stage-whispered. When the women looked unimpressed, Reba clarified, louder. "*Mushroom* chocolates."

"You flew with those?" Bella questioned. Not that she was a narc, but she was taken aback. Carson had seemed so calm in the airport.

Carson waved it off. "Donny helped me whip some up," she said, referring to one of her two roommates. "He swears by regular microdosing and the occasional mind melt. I thought it might be a fun bonding experience. No one's pregnant, right?" The women nodded yes to bonding, no to embryos.

Carson smiled. "Good. Making them isn't rocket science, but there is some calibration, so I tried to customize for each of us. Reba and I talked about what she's looking for, not like she needs much guidance." When Reba wasn't trying to get pregnant, in those unceasing stretches between fertility cycles, she was something of a pothead. It helped that Terrence knew just what to cultivate, the right mix of THC and CBD to keep her calm-ish. They had a few plants growing in the basement, another in the backyard.

"Hill, for you I made something mellow," Carson continued.

"I appreciate that." Hillary liked getting stoned as much as the next woman, but her husband—her ex—had a "substance abuse issue." They all knew about Miles's SUD to some extent (it had been the subject of a text chain among the women, sans Hillary, after Reba and the then-new Terrence had gotten together with Hillary and Miles in Chicago, and Miles had nearly nodded out at dinner). Hearing those details, and maybe remembering Miles's behavior at his and Hillary's wedding (charming nerves through the ceremony, a totally sociable reception, but sloppy—beer slamming and thrash dancing—at the after-party), perhaps recalling how he was supposed to be on the straight and narrow since the filched pills incident (the hospital had agreed not to press charges if he went into treatment), the texting women had thought it was worth keeping an eye on. When Roger was two or three it had gurgled up into a real problem again, but reticent Hillary wasn't forthcoming about how bad it was and how freaked out she was and how many ultimatums Miles had blown right by . . . That stretch had been awful, they could all admit, now that it was over. Because she'd kicked him out last year, and they were getting or had gotten divorced! Her friends were so happy for her. Well, not *happy* happy, but relieved. "Dodged a bullet," was how Bella put it in one message. Too blunt—Bella had a habit of being bruising—though no one on the chain disagreed with the sentiment.

"I want to trip balls," Bella said.

"I figured," Carson answered. She didn't know the particulars of Bella's current anxiety, that when Bella got home, she'd be heading not only into trial prep (this part Bella shared readily, her all-in case and how she hoped her boss would at last put her up for partner once she'd won), but also into three-times-a-week speech therapy for Gus. The problem was that he still couldn't say his *s*'s, had another problem (related? independent? no one could give her a straight answer) with his *r*'s. Gus didn't have to follow his parents into the law; no one expected him to become a champ litigator. But he needed to be able to express himself, to convey his ideas without his audience curling their mouths into so many derisive smiles. Carson wasn't aware of the therapy plan, but knew generally that Bella needed to keep her life in New York a safe distance from her brain until Monday morning. Until then, Bella's mind should be as blank and as blue as the glinting pool water that lapped before them.

"I got you, girl," Carson said.

5

Fri, Jan 13 at 3:15 PM

Gregg:

You guys better not be having too much fun yet! Kidding! See you soon. xo

After a quick dip, the women settled back into their loungers and turned their attention to the guacamole. In time, conversation drifted to work. When Gus was born, Bella had scaled back and stayed that way, which now meant all her billable hours were for one client, a beverage company facing a slew of litigation over its caffeinated alcoholic beverages. The first of the cases, a wrongful death (some guy had drunk a dozen cans of the stuff and basically exploded his heart), had been settled out of court for an acceptable amount, but now the feds were investigating the brand's marketing practices, trying to make permanent the temporary injunction against its sale. Bella and her team were going full throttle to defend consumer access to the beverage.

She expected, she told her friends, she'd ramp up to three-quarters or full time, maybe more, as they headed into court next month. And she *wanted* to ramp up, to show her mettle. Her trajectory at Cushman was more like a pinball game than any sort of straight path: the bouncing between different teams, the unanticipated chutes of out-of-court settlements, the hidden ball holds of birthing and caring for young children, for a time without day care (the pandemic had been like one of those trapdoors that ate pinballs for supper). But she'd be up for equity partner soon, or she should be, or she feared she never would get the opportunity. The rest of her associate class had moved up or out years earlier. For Bella to meet the challenge she just had to be organized, strategic, ruthless—and utilize their nursery school's after-school program. She'd promised her boys—and especially herself—she'd be the type of mom that picked them up right at the end of the school day, and she loathed the prospect of more time apart, but this flex up at work and downshift of momming was totally temporary. And while the extended school day was suboptimal, it wasn't so bad as getting a nanny. Bill had been pro in-home help, pushing since before there was a vaccine, but for Bella bringing in a helper had been both an existential and, for a time, a viral threat. They were her children, and she'd take care of them, please and thank you.

With but the lightest tap of encouragement, Bella continued talking, outlining the scenario of her upcoming case. The product in question was stronger than a spiked seltzer, more caffeinated than a Red Bull, and came in flavors like neon-green candy apple and hot-pink berry blast.

Carson winced at the garish descriptions, while two loungers down, Hillary's brow knitted. "Do you believe in the product?" Hillary pressed. "Like, is it justified to defend them, to keep this . . . beverage available?" Hillary had thought, when picking her medical specialty, she'd focus on trachea surgeries, cancer removal, and windpipe reconstruction. But she had entered the field in the nadir between smoking-related throat cancers and whatever all these vaping teens were going to get next. Probably more throat cancers, but who knew? For now, everyone's throats were safe, glistening, and nodule free, and so she'd shifted her focus within ENT from neck parts to noses.

"Oh, it tastes like shit," Bella was quick to say. "Better than Red Bull and vodka, in my opinion, though that's not saying much. But the case isn't about artificial strawberry flavor, it's about liberty," she continued, watching her friends' faces for agreement or disdain.

"Freedom of choice," she added, her posture shifting higher in her chair. "An individual's right to have a kick-ass time." Her cadence changed, her volume increased. The women braced for litigator voice.

"And a hangover," Carson said, mostly to herself.

Hillary wasn't sure she agreed with Bella's constitutional tack, but remembered how they'd fought about the Sacklers—one of Bella's firm's clients for a while—the last time they'd all been together, and it had been unpleasant. Sometimes history declares a victor, and Hillary had clearly won that argument. She would not mention Oxy now, not utter *Wrong again* on the topic of this stupid drink. It wasn't like Bella could pick her clients; she was beholden to the partners for assignments.

Whatever restraint Hillary thought she was demonstrating, to her friends she seemed spiky or tender or both, like a tiny puffer fish on the verge of inflation. Reba, for one, noted that their friend was exuding a weird vibe, the energy of which was being funneled toward an unjust grilling of Bella. And Hill, she saw, kept rubbing her hand, which was taped over by bright Band-Aids. There were yellow cartoons on them, SpongeBob or the Simpsons, something sunny.

When Hillary followed up with a question about Red 40 Lake, Reba had had enough. She sat up straight and snapped, "We've all got to earn a living," which was objectively true, but silly coming from her, who, if she managed her money right (previously earned income and ongoing trust distributions and the slated inheritance), could stay out of the workforce until 2065, and by then they'd all be dead or bedridden or bionic. But what Reba meant, what she was indicating toward, was that work would never be righteous, it was forever a capitalist exchange, and your best hope was that it wasn't too exploitative. The women had each heard her speechify from this soapbox before—her decampment from hustle culture was relatively recent, and she bore a convert's amount of zeal—and they now let her run out her rant.

When she was done, Reba settled back into her chair. She had not wanted to sermonize poolside, while they were having such a nice time; she just wanted Hillary to back off poor Bella. She and Bella had a special bond—they had shared a dorm room on campus in years two and three, then they'd sublet a place in New York together, the summer between their junior and senior years. Glorified gofers they'd been, sixty-hour weeks of document formatting and Excel sheets and slide decks for their downtown firms (bespoke management consultants and corporate lawyers, respectively, and both portals into their futures). The rest of the women knew that *something* had happened that summer—Bella came back to campus senior fall a touch withdrawn; Reba, always bossy, no longer tried to restrain her high hand; and the two were even closer than before. To see them together again now was to be reminded of whatever had happened that summer, to be made aware of their language of eyebrow lifts and nostril flares, to be shown that friendship wasn't a competition, but if it were . . .

The tightness of their alliance, even among such close friends as these four, made standoffish Carson a touch uncomfortable, and caused the trombone of Hillary's loneliness to honk a little louder. Hill wasn't inherently a loner, but work had been relentless lately, and just as soon as she was warming up to the other moms at any given playground, Roger was liable to be "asked" to leave (they meant kicked out, but politely), and Miles's side of the bed was cold. Underneath all this, and it'd dawned on her soon after Miles left for his new studio apartment, was the realization that virtually all her friends from Chicago, from med school, from the last fifteen years effectively, had been *their* friends, guys and girls and couples who, at the end of the day, liked Miles more. He was the center of attention in any room, attractive and appealing and good at hiding his troubles from all but the most observant. She observed it all!

But, she reminded herself, Miles's loquacity and his entrancing eye contact and how *hot* he was (Hillary was pretty, but Miles turned heads) did not sway these women's loyalties, and for that she felt gratitude. Even if Reba and Bella's closeness made her feel a tad left out, and Carson was so cool that an observer might deem her aloof . . . Dwelling on relative rankings—who were the tightest friends, who had the easiest time losing weight, who was doing the most good for the world (would that be one of the mothers, raising respectful sons, or was it Carson, with her compact life and its tiny environmental footprint, her contributions to *the canon*?)—such thinking was not helpful. Hierarchies were bullshit; they were all doing the best that they could.

Looking around the patio, she reminded herself she was a thousand miles from Chicago and the cold feelings there. Here it was just the sun on her skin and the reflected warmth of these women, their long-standing and unconditional friendship. Those various furnaces made her feel delectably toasty on this January afternoon. She closed her eyes. She, Hillary Koenig, would absorb all the heat she could.

6

Fri, Jan 13 at 3:30 PM

Mom:

Got Roger. Said today was 'so-so' & teacher said it went better than last week, so that's good! Have fun with your friends, sweetie. Love you.

The conversation drifted farther into the pool, the ladies splashing around such topics as deviated septa and Gregg's husband Zeke's Twitter presence, how he wasn't as bad as Elon, but was often mentioned alongside him, given their physical proximity (both in Austin), their tech products' adjacency (foundationally useless, but very addictive), Zeke's investment in rockets (not as big as Elon's, but not insignificant, and wasn't he too vying for government contracts?), their similarly canny if erratic business strategies. When did the women think Zeke would IPO? (He'd been dodging a date for years.) Bella said six months, Carson said never. And did any of them think he'd really get a rocket to Mars? They looked at one another. No one said yes, but it seemed shortsighted to pronounce *no way*.

They moved from Gregg's husband to speaking about their own spouses. When it came to Reba's thoughts on Terrence, she had few criticisms, other than that her husband was possibly taking his health tech start-up job too seriously. (There it was again, her newfound conviction against late-stage capitalism, popping up its head like a hungry groundhog.) But, she was quick to add, she could understand his near-desperate want to play catch-up, to prove himself. Terrence had been a bartender when they'd met; it was only through her encouragement that he finished his credits at Portland Community College—which wasn't about her interest in academia so much as trying to build a bulwark against the disdain she anticipated from Doris, knowing her mother would *hate* the prospect of her daughter living with someone without any sort of college degree—then went to one of those coding boot camps, which he reported was a cakewalk after boot-camp boot camp. She was, she said now, glad he was out of harm's way and the armed services (making no mention of his unceremonious split), but as far as she was concerned, he could still be making martinis. Though she'd seen how he felt better about himself with the buzzy, name-brand company, entry-level as his role might be. The ego was as real a thing as that beach ball floating at the pool's far end. Besides, she added, the firm covered 100 percent for in vitro—and here the women held their breath, to see if Reba would say more about her pregnancy journey and its most recent swerves; she did not.

Next, Bella had more express complaints about Bill, regarding his parenting skills, his snoring skills, his enviable metabolism, his clumsiness while dining in expensive clothes. The extent and frequency of his spills felt, to her, willful. Was this a response to her plunging libido, which had fallen through the floor and settled at subbasement levels? (There was a hormonal reason for this, Hillary knew, but she held her tongue. Bella didn't need a biochemistry lesson, she needed a pat on the shoulder.) While Bill outwardly acted supportive of Bella's changed moods, he'd recently spilled red sauce on his light gray Brooks Brothers blazer and put a plateful of pesto on his nice winter suit. Was this retribution?

Then they plied Carson and Hillary for updates on their dating lives, which were spare. Hillary hadn't gone on a date with anyone but Miles since 2007, and Carson purportedly hadn't seen anyone for months—with her, it was feast or famine; her twenties defined by the former, her thirties, the latter. The start of her forties? Reba egged. Carson made a face at the prospect of dating that suggested her voluntary absenteeism would continue.

And then, like a chime had rung at some moms-only frequency, Hillary and Bella were in their phones, checking to see whether their kids had been picked up from school or day care or wherever they had eaten their lunches and listened to their story times and taken their midday naps. This led to a great sharing of pictures—oohing and aahing and chortling as appropriate (even Reba clucking at the cuteness, though her posture perceptibly stiffened)—which led to complaining about RSV and how tired they were of wiping tiny asses, at what age did a kid figure out how to do it for himself? Which led to Carson slipping into the the water again and Reba abruptly leaving the group to attend to something inside. She returned with a bottle of white wine, four glasses, and a glint in her eye.

"How's writing going, Carson?" It was Reba asking, holding out a stem.

So they did remember she was there, Carson thought, kicking toward the edge of the pool and a cool glass of sauvignon blanc. Sometimes, when conversation veered into child-rearing and husbands, she had her doubts. It was so hard to pull them out of their photo timelines, the pride and nostalgia and self-righteous exhaustion of having created a miniature human and kept it alive. She could've argued that she'd made a book, and maybe that was even harder than cooking a baby. Look at the baby versus book population—there were so many more of one than the other. And only one could be made with a bottle of red wine, a sloppy ninety seconds of missionary, and nine months in the oven, while the other took . . . But she was too good a friend to make veiled comments about Bella's descent into lame, very infrequent sex with her husband. The story of Bill Jr.'s conception had been shared in whispered confidence across a café table during one of their nights at the museum, and in confidence it would remain.

And how was writing going? For years, Carson had been working on a historical epic about a penitentiary island in Washington State, an hour's boat ride from her hometown. "Imagine Alcatraz with ferns," was her default reply; she didn't like getting into the weeds of a work in progress, never had and likely never would. Consequently, five years into the project, her closest friends still didn't know the storyline or even how she felt about incarceration. Bella, before she'd had kids, had given many pro bono hours to bail reform legislation. "I mean, are you more Hammurabi or live and let live?" the lawyer had asked the writer more than once. Regardless of how many glasses of red Bella bought Carson on that museum balcony, surrounded by Ming dynasty porcelain, she never got a straight answer. Ditto for Reba, who, since meeting Terrence (who'd done two combat deployments, then one to the military prison at Leavenworth for pot possession, though the amount of weed in his infraction would have struck most civilians as laughably small), had many thoughts on the criminal justice system vis-à-vis drug reform. Her entreaties to Carson had gotten similarly nowhere.

"Have you solved capital punishment through literature?" Bella said now, sliding from her chair to the edge of the pool. She sank her legs into the water, and her skin turned greenish in the water's blue tint.

Carson thought she should give them a crumb; the book was done, after all, out of her hands and onto her agent's desk. But she wasn't ready to tell them everything, not how its story and her life's intersected. Intertwined. Because for all their liberal bona fides, Bella's bail reform and Reba's decriminalization campaigns and Hillary's apologist approach to Miles's illicit substances, none of them had stared down profound, true violence. How a room changed when premeditated murder stepped through the threshold—*bam*! It was like someone cut all the lights. And she didn't want to do that here, not now. To kill the lights would do away with their pleasing late-afternoon sun. Carson looked around. Bella was splashing in the pool, and Hillary, after one-third of one glass of wine, appeared blissed out. These women were still so perfectly ignorant; they didn't know a thing about her father. Or they knew one thing, that he was out of the picture, which was true—but they had no idea why. She'd prefer to keep it that way for the time being, maybe forever if she could manage it. So, she offered a deflecting crumb. "Well, in one scene," she started, lifting her sunglasses, "I have them throw an electric chair into the sound."

"Okay!" Reba said, slapping the side table. The guacamole jumped. "Now we're getting somewhere."

Fri, Jan 13 at 8:00 PM

Gregg:

Wheels down! See y'all soon!

Gregg had told them to go to the restaurant; she'd Uber over once she landed. So they did, and were reaching the clinking ice cubes at the bottom of round one, commenting on how strange it still sounded when their friend deployed her Texas twang (even by text, the contraction *y'all* was a shock), when Gregg arrived alongside their table, wearing what looked like a flight suit. But it was magenta, and had subtle tailoring—darts at the waist, tasteful tiny knife pleats at the hips—and rhinestones at the collar, which was channeling late Elvis, but not in a tacky way.

She made beauty look so easy, Bella thought. And she was getting better with age, if that was possible? Bella had heard about this phenomenon; some women peaked in high school or college (that had been Bella, suitors stretching around the dorm block), some hit their prime in their twenties (like Hillary, doe-eyed and lovely enough to nab the heartthrob of her med school class), and some became more beautiful in their thirties. Case in point: Reba, because even in her more gaunt present, California Reba looked way better than her prior work-worn iteration (Reba's specialty at the consultancy had been "efficiency," which meant mass firings). There were women like Carson, naturally attractive, who didn't ever try, or at least not much, and consequently never did reach their full potential. Some days Bella envied such women, on others she felt sorry for them and their obstinacy, the missed opportunity looking back from every mirror. And then there was one last, special category: the woman who became more beautiful at forty. That was Gregg, except she'd been gorgeous at eighteen too, showing them how to put on eyeliner, lecturing them (though it didn't feel like a lecture) on why August Wilson deserved the Nobel Prize. True, since becoming a politician, she'd had to don dowdy pantsuits sometimes, but when she wasn't stomping around the statehouse in the pastel blazers and wide-legged slacks required by America's post-Hillary progressivism, she wore things like this bedazzled flight suit. That she wasn't quite forty—hers was a late birthday, the last of the friends'—was a technicality. Bella shook her head. Thirty-nine and looking fine!

The waiter came with Gregg's drink. "Vodka tonic?" He said it like it was a question but maybe he already knew the answer. Gregg raised her hand demurely, wiggled her fingers. Her nails matched the jumpsuit. My word, Bella thought.

The waiter suggested they have another round; they concurred. How about food? The women were suddenly ravenous, or they were often ravenous, but tonight they were permitted to admit their growling hunger and solve for it with enthusiasm—it was, remember, a judgment-free weekend.

Once the waiter had sauntered off with their orders, liquid and comestible, Hillary leaned toward Gregg. "Did he just wink at you?"

"Did he?" She shrugged.

As they drank their drinks and ate their food, the friends bounced between topics—here was the story of Gregg's ambitious manicure, there was Carson eviscerating a cocksure editor at some magazine launch party, next Bella and Reba were comparing their insufferable mothers' latest antics. (Marianne and Doris were polar opposites, but each made her daughter's life very difficult.) Listening to the prattle, Hillary remembered when they had first started piling into dining hall booths together, the five squishing into a space made for four. How thrilling and disconcerting that new proximity had felt. She had grown up with not a lot, but in her shrinking Wisconsin town there was always *space*. An underpopulated high school, streets cut wide enough for snowbanks, an apartment that wasn't big but was so spare of people (just her and Sheila, the undynamic duo) and possessions that it felt roomy. The chirping cacophony of those mess hall meals, several people talking, and fast, was so different from the slow volley that she'd had with her mother, but once she'd grown accustomed to all their crowded energy, it transformed into a current of swirling, surging affection. What had been overwhelming became normal, stayed that way until they'd gone their separate ways, and then Hillary missed it.

Now they didn't chirp, but instead squawked and hooted and howled, swapping stories and debating policies and showing, on their fingers, how many times they'd each contracted Covid. Bella held up three digits, which was the most among them, and blamed her boys' fancy nursery school. Preschools were germy cesspools, the women agreed, but when Bella suggested that rich New Yorkers thought health and safety protocols didn't apply to them, not really, that many had found self-isolation an undue burden, the urgent inquiry of contact tracing somehow rude, no one around the table was surprised.

At the end of the meal, an ice cream sundae appeared, five spoons. On the house, the jovial waiter explained. The women said they couldn't possibly, or please, after you, or maybe just a nibble. Hillary and her sweet tooth did not participate in such posturing; she picked up her spoon and boldly, happily, took the first bite. The dam was broken, the other spoons were lifted, and the bowl was licked clean in ninety seconds flat.

• • •

Upon their return to the rental they called it an early night—the East Coasters, Reba suggested, must be wrecked. And perpetually tired Bella was sleepy; Carson, not so much, but she was fine to turn in if that was the consensus. They hugged and clasped hands and kissed one another on the cheeks.

As they drifted off to sleep, the women with children worried about their kids or were glad to be multiple states away from the slobbery goblins or felt both things in one wobbly moment. The married women missed their husbands' warm bodies or were happy for the respite from their disruptive respiration, while for Carson, it was simply sliding out of one empty bed and into another. Gregg had elected to sleep with Hillary, which stung Carson just a touch; another reminder that Gregg had left her creative side. She, Carson Larsen, was the last artist standing—and on nights like tonight, alone in her bed, she felt as though she might as well have been the last lonely rhinoceros, solitary of her species. Maybe there would be some miraculous intervention yet—cloning or a conspecific discovered deep in the bush—but otherwise she had to get used to this feeling, to recommit to looking out for herself and her project of art making.

This bed was firmer than her mattress in Brooklyn, she thought. It wasn't a bad thing, just unfamiliar.

And so, all across the house, the women slept well or slept fitfully or accidentally spooned as the clock spun its circles.

8

Sat, Jan 14 at 8:03 AM

Carson:

Mornin. Any mail for me yesterday?

Carson was up early, as she was programmed to rise and write: at her desk by six, six days a week, so she could get in a day's work before her midday run and afternoon tutoring. (At least that'd been her schedule pre-injury; now she did thirty minutes of low-impact Pilates on YouTube before a late lunch.) Six was three a.m. California time, and though she was wide awake then, she willed herself to stay in bed until five thirty and spent the two intervening hours staring at the ceiling and its punched-tin light fixture, closing her eyes, then staring at the fixture again. When the palm tree outside her window emerged as a black silhouette in the navy sky, she got up, put on a pot of coffee, and opened her computer.

On the screen, she reread the first page of her manuscript. She'd sent it to her agent, Tina, twelve days before—she'd had the tact not to send it on a federal holiday but waited until the 2nd, when everyone was recovering from their merriment. There'd been a quick and cheery "confirming receipt," then, crickets. Why? Was it because she hated it and was trying to figure out the "right" way to respectfully end their relationship? This book was so different from the last. Carson was proud of the new project, all the effort it'd taken to eke out. Water from a stone, she'd thought sometimes; at other times she'd felt like a strung-out detective with her corkboard, yarn, pushpins, and Xeroxes… She'd never claim her process was an orderly one. But in certain lights, like the first light of this winter morning, the book felt meek. No, not meek, she corrected herself. *Quiet.* Restrained. Four hundred pages of whispers, the electric chair's splash notwithstanding. Extra hushed, given that her debut had been full of screaming, shouting, and waving crowbars around. A portrait of 1990s New York, featuring a group of twentysomethings who were not averse to yelling mean, irrational stuff at one another, because the characters had reached the ends of their ropes. "Mary McCarthy but coked out," one reviewer had quipped, and while Carson had initially been flattered by the snarky comparison, the line ended up getting more mileage than she'd have hoped. Whenever a podcast host or review made mention of it, she wanted to (but didn't) point out that she hadn't done coke in years.

And prison stories? People wanted Anna Delvey, *Orange Is the New Black*, or an old-timey George Clooney on a pratfall-laden jailbreak, not something so severe as what she'd written. She had the atonement angle going for her, but a reader had to be very patient for that payout. This felt conceptually correct, given the durational aspect of a prison sentence, but in doing so, she'd created a slog of a read. What had she been thinking?

• • •

In two hours of scrolling through the manuscript and surgically removing predictable adjectives, Carson had made no real progress on her draft or quashing her doubts about it. She retreated to her room and fished a slender box from her suitcase. Inside was a tray of a dozen irregular, glossy chocolates. She admired her work. Well, it was not *her* work—she was sous-chef to Donny, who knew how tiny to dice the mushrooms and the precise temperature at which to temper the chocolate; it had been Donny who had carefully measured out doses according to Carson's description of each woman's temperament and need, then sunk their corresponding portions into tiny molten bonbons with the fastidiousness of Jacques Torres handling fondant. (Donny had taken an online confectionary course when he was stuck at his parents' during the lockdown; when he'd moved into

Carson's Sunset Park loft, he brought his accoutrements, saucepans and spoons and those tiny muffin liners meant for peanut butter cups.) Before they'd poured the chocolates, on the bottom of each morsel's petite paper cup, Carson had written a woman's initial in gold marker. Now, she lifted a chocolate (this one was *H* for Hillary) and held it an inch past her nose, inspecting it. The look, the smell. She sniffed again, then touched it with her tongue.

9

Sat, Jan 14 at 8:45 AM

Gregg:

> Hi Maggie, I will be offline for 12-14 hrs. Pls update me on Sun sched by email, will confirm by midnite PST. Thanks!

"No phones!" Reba barked. When the women had lived together in college and were moving too slowly toward a meal or a party or their morning classes, Reba had been the strident one, known to clap her hands and bellow, "Let's go, go, go!" like they were so many lazy point guards. It was her basketball training—she had been one of the most talented players to come out of California in a generation, and had done a gap year with the junior national team—and her mother's strict rules before that, that made her such a disciplinarian. To get them moving, she'd encouraged her friends with everything short of a coach's tweets (though she had distributed rape whistles when they'd moved to the creaking five-bedroom Victorian off campus, because safety was paramount). The women found it sometimes grating but appreciated that for Reba, having been barked at for so many years, it was hard to loosen up.

At work, when she'd been working, this default toward command and control had meant Reba could make the most complicated reorgs and draconian downsizings look like easy lay-ups. She'd lasted fifteen grueling years at the firm, a place known for its exhausting pace; a dozen years there was akin to four dozen at any other job, whether measured by wear and tear or by their regal compensation packages. Her friends, her family, Terrence—they'd all been quietly relieved when she at last decided to quit. Even if pulling the plug, approached with ample foot dragging (she wanted to close things out with one client, then thought she might just wrap up with another), felt, to her, like a dunk tank or that dog-on-the-diving-board GIF Carson had circulated. She had been so good at laying down the law; a part of her was sad she'd have to stop.

Now, at least, Reba wasn't oblivious to the fact that her insistence on establishing rules and implementing standards—what had made her good at work, great on the court—could be off-putting to those around her. But there is cognizance, and there is self-regulation, and sometimes, despite the former, her bossiness still showed up like a flash of gold in the back of her mouth. Such as that Saturday morning, as she rounded up her friends' cell phones. She couldn't help it—when she knew what was best in any given scenario, she had to see the optimization through. And now, she knew a screen-free Saturday was in everyone's best interest.

She snatched Carson's phone from the counter, then grabbed Bella's from her hands as she entered the kitchen. "Hey—" Bella began to protest, but saw something in Reba's expression that made her stop.

Carson stood to begin a second pot of coffee; the dregs of the first one had gone cold.

"For Shabbat?" Hillary asked, handing hers over. Roger grinned up from the lock screen. Her in-laws were Jewish, but she'd made only the most cursory of efforts to follow along.

"No, for the drugs," Reba said. She was raised Jewish, and her levels of observance had fluctuated over the years. Her family liked Dungeness crab too much to keep kosher, and her firm's work-through-the-weekend ethos hadn't encouraged keeping the Sabbath. If she had taken a Saturday off, it was due to exhaustion, not God. "Screens are always bad for you, but they're especially icky with psilocybin on board. Why do you think Tim Cook created that Screen Time report?"

To make us feel inadequate anew, Bella thought. She was aware she spent too much time on her phone. She'd feel less guilty about it if her hours were spent on FaceTimes with friends or flirty texts with her husband, but most of the log was scrolling social media, comparing herself to acquaintances, measuring her kids' cuteness against that of other children, and buying things she did not need. The daily tally—three hours, forty minutes; three hours, fifty—always felt like an indictment. Four hours a day, and she hadn't even read the news. Her New Year's resolution was *less* of all of it. She was two weeks into the project and not doing very great.

"Can I keep mine till I shower?" Gregg asked, weaving around the kitchen island, staying a step ahead of Reba. Even her pajamas were fabulous, Bella thought, silky blue and embroidered with constellations. She'd seen a similar pair online, been tempted to buy. That algorithm knew her so well. Better than Bill, anyway, who kept gifting her frumpy jewelry, expensive but far from her style.

"Fine. And hurry up. Carson." Reba looked toward the computer at the breakfast bar. "Laptops are even worse for the altered mind."

"Understood," Carson said, closing the device, only a dash miffed by Reba's take-charge directives, given that they were about to trip on *her* chocolates. What could she accomplish today anyway? The ad infinitum revising of her chapters' last sentences could wait. (It was a compulsion, trying to get the lines to land like they were gymnasts coming off a balance beam: full-rotation backflip, tuck, and stick the landing.) Reba was holding out her hand, ready for the laptop. "Not necessary," Carson said, tilting her head toward the doorway. "I'll put it in my bedroom."

"No cheating," Bella said and winked. Bella, who had gamed the LSAT and her kid's pre-kindergarten placement exam, who'd even had a fling with one of her summer associates the week of her wedding (that she and Bill had an open relationship was one thing, but shouldn't she have been focused on her fiancé that week, of all weeks?). It took not many sips of wine for their museum catch-ups to turn confessional, Bella talking about the ways she was a fraud and a cheat, and how she could never decide: Should she feel horrified by her dupery or proud of her cunning?

Carson winked; she understood her friend, knew that all the fundamental and good things about Bella overpowered any encroaching ick. Bella had chosen the law as a profession; clearly she'd find ways to bend it. "Never."

When their devices had been properly stowed, and those who were going to shower had done so, they reconvened in the kitchen. Before Carson could reach the box of chocolates, Reba had lifted them from the counter. This felt more pushy than the phone collection, but it was not worth the wrestle, Carson decided, and she leaned back against the island to watch Reba dole them out. "Here, Bella," Reba said, checking the bottoms as she went. "You get one, two, three."

"I hope I can't feel my face." Bella popped her first candy in her mouth and chewed.

"No," Reba corrected. "I hope your face feels awesome."

"I still can't believe you flew with these," Hillary said, inspecting her bonbon. Was that the one Carson had licked? Carson couldn't tell.

"It's not going to bite you, Hill," Reba coached. "You bite it."

Carson nibbled at the first of her two; she'd done this with Donny not long ago but had mostly forgotten the beat-by-beat, including this first toe into the ice bath. "Ugh," she said, her face screwing up. "This tastes disgusting."

"Coffee," Reba said, wincing through her own mouthful. "Drink a mug quick. There's sugar on the counter, cream in the fridge." That was the thing about being bossy: Usually she was right.

Gregg, meanwhile, peeled the paper from her first chocolate and smiled at the group as she slipped it into her mouth. She let the morsel melt on her tongue. "Mmmm," she said.

10

Sat, Jan 14 at 10:45 AM

Bill:

Gus says he has 🏀 on Sats. Does he have 🏀???

How to describe how it felt? Quotidian, or euphoric. Slightly strange, or a total epiphany. *Ho-hum*, muttered under one's breath, or *Hoo-rah!* as a full, guttural cry. It was all that, everything in between, a spectrum that stretched from one woman to the next to the next, not in a straight line but as many arcing ones, reaching from the crown of one person's head to another's pinkie toe, rays bowing from finger to finger, belly button to butt crack to crook of the elbow, innumerable loci, a spider's web of enchanted feeling.

Or, that's not how it felt, but the true and accurate record of each woman's experience is not as important as acknowledging that it happened, that these five women gathered one Saturday in a borrowed house in the desert, unwrapped their chocolates, linked their arms, and stepped, united, off a ledge. The drop was two feet, just a big step really. The drop was two hundred feet, a veritable cliff. They would land like feathers or like Wile E. Coyote in a big cartoony puff, rest for four beats, and emerge no worse for wear. The specifics, the difference between their experiences was irrelevant. What mattered was that they were doing this thing together.

"Juntos," Bella muttered. She so rarely used her Spanish anymore. The bodega by her doctor's office, teaching the boys to count. *Uno, dos, tres.* Gus was a good counter, even if he sounded like Shakespeare with his *doths*.

Carson linked her arm with Bella's. Most of the time she was convinced she was a recluse. Now she remembered what it felt like to be joined with her friends, the psychic bond and touch-feel.

The woman with the fastest metabolism (Reba) felt the effects first, but she also had the highest tolerance, having spent much of the pandemic in a cloud of homegrown pot smoke. And her regular toking had helped; it was the best method she'd found to manage the near-monthly letdown of the brownish spot in her underwear. Reba had learned that along with her cycle, her body had another meaningful threshold: If an egg did embed, as several had over the past few years, her uterus would hit the ejector-seat button at approximately six weeks. These disappointments took more than a spliff; they took a full court press of flowers from Terrence and to-go soup from her favorite ramen restaurant and a mouthful of those lozenges that claimed they were high-wattage THC but felt more like ayahuasca.

Bella did indeed trip balls, and at one point that morning, as they absorbed vitamin D in the backyard, she was insistent that there were giant porcupines descending from the hills. These were barrel cacti, and stationary. Once the women had put her at ease about the quills, she started blabbering, then blubbering, about Gus's lisping, how scared she was that her sweet guy might be anything less than utterly capable. The women gathered round to comfort her. Hillary, as she back-rubbed her friend with a soothing clockwise palm, attempted to dial up her med school training on disorders of speech, but her brain was moving slow, like a canoe on a molasses canal. A shallow molasses canal; the oar kept scraping the silty, sticky bottom. Her hand went round and round on Bella's back. Hillary felt fairly stoned, then mostly lucid, then largely confident of her recall, remembering that one colleague who spent every day clipping frenula. To Bella she narrated what she knew about ankyloglossia.

Carson's limbs felt blissfully separate from her body, her mind a puffy cloud taking an aerial tour of the block. She floated away from the curving streets of the neighborhood, toward the scrubby edge of town—there went Bella's porcupines, there went the rattlesnakes sunning themselves in the midmorning heat—and up the mountain, not that zigzag trail they could see from the patio but straight up, like God was pulling her on a string. Then there was a golf course spread out below her, a dimpled ball rising. The ball got so close she could touch it, and then it was gone, reaching for the vaster blue.

Gregg fell asleep on a lounge chair, big floppy hat over her face.

11

Sat, Jan 14 at 11:34 AM

Mom:

Hi Hill! Just checking in. Roger is being an angel.

Well, an angel for Roger. Hope you and your friends are having fun! Love, Mom

After some time—it could have been minutes, it could have been days, it could have been the subsequent January 14, exactly a year later—Reba roused the women from their reveries with a soft but steady clapping. "Let's go!" She smiled with big, straight teeth. Their ringleader, their bossy-pants, their poster child for adolescent orthodontia. They rose unsteadily, the five of them Rip Van Winkled into a new universe with sparkling blue water and smooth teak loungers and a house that slipped from minimalist to sumptuous through a broad glass slider. Carson went back and forth several times before Reba took her by the arm and said again, more gently, "Honey, let's go. It's time for a nice little walk."

Bella and Hillary had their heads thrust back, watching the sky where the contrails of a jet were slowly spelling *Melissa, will you marry me?*

The women checked to see if there was a Melissa among them. There wasn't.

Before she'd locked away all their phones, hers included, Reba had mapped a route through the neighborhood, hitting the area's architectural highlights—this part of town was known for its modernist icons. What many considered Richard Neutra's best single-family residence was two blocks west; they'd go there first. A few blocks north of that was a prefab house made solely of steel, which was weird, but maybe interesting? Also, entirely recyclable, which she thought Gregg would appreciate. A quarter mile, maybe a third beyond that sat Elvis's famed honeymoon bungalow. They'd take a leisurely stroll, she figured, eat up the architecture and the xeriscape, end their design tour with an al fresco lunch at a place regionally known for its fresh and healthy cuisine. All of them should be reasonable enough for a seated meal in two hours, she thought, and even if they weren't, who cared? This was their weekend, in a town full of strangers, retirees, and retired strangers. The day held every possibility, and no consequence.

They walked slowly, looking at the low-slung buildings and stacked-rock gardens. The women, as attentive to the skin on their arms—how it freckled or pinked or turned a more chestnutty brown, how it grew warm to the touch—as to the ambitious landscaping, seemed underwhelmed by the midcentury modernism. Or perhaps they were just more stoned than Carson had assured them that they'd get. Reba, feeling a bit loopy herself, glanced at her hand-drawn map, scrawled on the back of a receipt for airport coffee; it looked like a bunch of squiggles. The lines did not correspond with the world before her, which was a wide, curving lane, a median plugged with a hopscotch of succulents. She knew there was a more direct route to Elvis's hideaway, if only she could decipher her drawing or pull it up on her phone.

She pushed the thought away. She didn't need GPS right now—she needed her friends and a general sense of direction, both of which she had. The sun rises in the east, the mountains are to the west! With that, she was oriented again, or enough, and after bellowing, "Straight ahead, ladies!" she joined Carson and Hillary's conversation, the two speculating aloud about how many of these homes had interiors with a similar sort of Moorish magic as theirs; azulejos and ruby velvet and quite possibly the ghost of Jean-Auguste-Dominique Ingres. Who could say what was inside any of them really? Hillary posed the question in a slow, sonorous voice. Reba scanned the street's windows for quizzical faces, but all she saw was glass that showed the sky. Hillary continued, "Maybe one holds an ornate carved wood screen, an overstuffed chair, a throbbing heart . . . Or maybe one holds a young girl, wanting, waiting to be loosed on the world?"

Carson's eyes grew wide as she imagined this small and curious person. She described her pigtails and big hazel eyes and scrawny knees. The child would, if she could, Carson continued, her voice just a whisper, run out her front door and straight up the mountain. Or maybe, she posited, the girl would turn the other way and sprint down the middle of the town's busy main drag, yelling, "The world was made for me!" Carson ran into the middle of the present, quiet boulevard, yelling the line, trying it on for size.

Reba's eyes met Hillary's; neither had heard Carson raise her voice in decades, save for wooting at a music venue. But maybe Carson was right about that conjured girl, who could say?

Bella, listening quietly, could practically see the girl running alongside Carson; she let out a mewl. She had really, really, really wanted a girl, but not so much as to have a third child. She'd had a C-section with Guston, and a second for Bill Jr., which she thought would be easier but ended up being worse—and recovery had been so brutal. Slip-on shoes for months; bright, persistent pain whenever she even thought of moving her trunk; the seeping wound. For weeks, she couldn't pick up a gallon of milk—forget about touching her toes or lifting Gus into his baby swing or stroller. Reba had pushed back her move out west to help after Gus, but she couldn't come back for Bill Jr., and why should she? She lived in California and was busy with her own life. That stretch, with the huge incision and the impatient, clingy two-year-old, the husband who blanched upon seeing just the shape of her bandage under her maternity pants, forget about helping her bathe . . . that had been when Bella needed her mother most.

Bella did not want to dwell on negative thoughts, not while she was so floaty, but her mother truly was a selfish bitch. Declaring she wanted to "live her life," which was code for moving to some sunbaked retirement town—but wasn't her life also Bella and her grandsons? (Bella's brother was and would remain a confirmed, childless bachelor.) Wasn't happiness basking in her progeny and helping them thrive? Her parents had said they'd "split their time" between Westchester and West Palm Beach, that they'd "be around" if Bella needed them. Lies! After one week of house hunting in Broward County, they decided they'd need additional capital; their Scarsdale house was sold within the month. This was four months before Gus was due, and Bella mourned a version of his childhood in which they'd go up for the weekends, frolic in the yard with its beds of jaunty perennials, all those daffodils, then tulips, then irises. Apparently, for Marianne, joy was not watching her grandsons grow; it was a midafternoon wine spritzer by the pool, swapping out her tanning bed for authentic sun. Bella wished she'd been surprised by the move, but even when they'd lived under the same roof and it had been Marianne Gomez's legal obligation to care for young Bella, it had seemed a low priority. It'd been the team's other soccer moms, the choirmaster and church youth group leader and her junior high civics teacher who had buoyed Bella through the thick of it. Not Marianne.

Let it go. Bella didn't know who was whispering at her, but when she turned around, her friends looked at her like she had three heads. "Who said that?" she barked.

"Who said what?" Hillary asked, confused.

"We didn't say anything," Carson added.

"You okay, sweetie?" Gregg said.

Reba kept frowning at the scrap of paper in her hand until they turned a corner and her face opened into a beam. "There it is."

Reba told them the home was known as the House of Tomorrow, as the place where Elvis and Priscilla went on their honeymoon, as where Lisa Marie was conceived. They approached with awe, stopped at the property line, marveled at the notion of staring into tomorrow's bay windows. Reba described the design principles of the cantilevered dodecagonal living room. Bella, partway listening, enjoyed the strange word, *do-dec-a-gon-allll*, on her tongue. Mostly, she was grateful to get selfish Marianne out of her mind.

Then it was lunchtime, but Reba ascertained they were not ready for a sit-down meal, and so she opted for something more casual. They walked to a drive-in and crowded around a picnic table in the restaurant's AstroTurfed backyard. There they ate greasy burgers out of paper bags (there was even a veggie burger option for Hillary), licked their fingers ruefully, slurped at milkshakes, and thanked God for providing a world that had such magnificence as malted chocolate.

When they were done with the meal they wandered onto Palm Canyon Drive, where they talked too loudly and inadvertently blocked traffic and caught themselves staring at their hands, which were continuing to freckle, tan, or toast. They walked right off Reba's map, which made her squeamy, but then she reminded herself to trust the universe.

Not long after, they came upon a humongous and fairly realistic sculpture of Marilyn Monroe.

The women stopped in their tracks. The three-story starlet rose above the surrounding buildings, her shoulders brushing nearby palms, her ass and undies on easy view to normal-sized passersby. The women gravitated into a clump and held one another, the pulses in their palms thudding. What in the world? Why Marilyn, why here, why so big? They then split up for closer inspection. Hillary scoped out the butt cheeks, the line where ass met undies not pinched or puckered but two smooth spheres, a piece of fruit cut in two and smooshed back together. Bella looked at the statue's significant cleavage and was reminded of her own measly breasts, still puny despite all the breastfeeding. Reba stared at the statue's feet and the painful-seeming heeled sandals. Reba's feet still held the muscle memory of so many eighteen-hour days in work-appropriate pumps, shoes that always felt comfortable enough in the morning but descended into blistering and burning by midafternoon. Since quitting she'd worn chunky sneakers and Birkenstocks, almost exclusively, and here was poor Marilyn, never able to quit her heels. Carson went to find the sculpture's label, a slab sunk into the nearby sod—it was called *Forever Marilyn* and was by someone named John Seward Johnson II.

They walked on, passing a modernist gas station that was a gas station, then a modernist gas station that had been converted into a tourist information center. Everywhere there were beautiful cars, meticulously restored Mustangs, candy-colored Lambos, a fleet of glowingly white Teslas, straight off the lot. Gregg slowed by the vintage vehicles, admiring. She hated oil's impact on the environment and hoped for a gas-free future. But for all her morality and earnest commitment to the cause, some part of her hindbrain still loved the particular vroom of a muscular engine.

The women paused before antique shops that they had the good sense not to enter, not while their thumb pads and the tips of their noses still felt numb. Instead, they studied the wares through wide storefront windows as statuesque older women placed themselves onto the sleek furniture, trying out different pieces' firmness, the texture of their upholstery and leather.

Someone (an older gentleman, bolo tie and blazer) stopped Gregg on the street, and she was instantly, stunningly lucid. Her friends, trying to make themselves inconspicuous around a mailbox, watched captivated as she spoke at the right volume and speed about some recent Austin City Limits concert they'd both seen. Gregg and the stranger talked for another minute, then said goodbye in a totally normal fashion. When she returned to the group, starting to explain about an Austin neighbor but seeing her friends' aghast expressions, she stopped midstream. "What?"

Next, Reba guided them to a bus stop, where they boarded a bus that would carry them to the northern edge of town. There, the lower terminus of a funicular sat squat like a turtle, waiting. They purchased tickets and rode a cable-strung pod up the slope, the fishbowl cab shuddering in the wind. At the top of the ridge the air was ten degrees cooler and the light ten percent stronger. They stepped to the ledge.

The city had transformed into an ant farm. They watched its dinky, determined inhabitants moving this way and that, carrying things and being carried. They moseyed (Reba herded) toward the bar, where they drank cocktails around a patio table right next to the rail; here they laughed and griped and further contemplated the view. The sun was setting and the sky's pastels, the blues and blushes, shifted one notch, then another. They swore they'd get the next funicular down, or maybe the one after that. Didn't they run every fifteen minutes? The light changed again, briefly an electric, zapping yellow before it went dusky lavender. Their hands, their teeth, turned gray with twilight, and the temperature dropped precipitously. Soon they wouldn't be able to see anything, and it would be very cold. But they wanted to hold on to this, the hot pink and periwinkle, the taste of juniper on their tongues. This, this was perfection.

12

Sat, Jan 14 at 2:06 PM

Donny:

Hi, C! Having a few folx over but don't worry won't touch yr rm.

No mail!

On the way down, Reba pulled a baggie out of her purse and from it, distributed diminutive yellow candies.

"What's this?" Hillary studied the Day-Glo orb in her palm.

"Lemonhead," Reba said. "But not a regular Lemonhead. More of a hangover helper, something I read about."

Carson unwrapped hers and popped it into her mouth, feeling only briefly put out that Reba had thought of another thing to steal her thunder. Not that she wanted her friends hungover, but the drugs were her idea. This was *her* trip! As she sucked the hard candy, it tasted like lemon, like a sunshiny morning. Like this morning, those dulcet minutes by the pool when she'd forgotten about her book and the worry there. Wait . . . she'd forgotten about her book and the worry there for the whole day—she'd been so centered on the sun, the city, her friends, rabid cacti and truffle fries and monumental sculpture. She'd even forgotten about the letter and paperback she'd sent to her father, which had unsettled her just as much as emailing Tina the manuscript. What would he say? Would he say anything? Would he help her? He had to, right? The questions were endless, except today, when they'd ended abruptly, a blank spot where her anxiety had been. She wanted to kiss her friends then, for being such delightful distractions. Donny too, for sharing his mycological knowledge with them, for dousing them with a fire hose of happy. She was so appreciative!

An elderly couple, with matching windbreakers and wrinkles, were scooched up against the car's far window, acting like they were admiring the view. Were the women behaving oddly, Carson wondered, somehow menacing with their giggles and puckered mouths? Maybe so, but there was nothing to do but keep dropping out of the sky, and so they did.

In the process of unwrapping her candy, Gregg dropped it on the floor; the ball scuttled into a crack in the bottom of the cab. "Whoopsies," she said.

• • •

They took a car back to the rental, then frightened a pizza delivery guy with their various states of undress, swimsuits and cover-ups and Carson, plainly plodding around the living room in her underwear. They devoured the pies, artisanal sausage and mushroom, pineapple and heirloom ham, one with organic artichokes for mostly vegetarian Hillary. Reba produced a beautiful cake from thin air, chocolate with a gooey-looking frosting. "Happy Birthday," it said, in red cursive icing. It was none of their birthdays, though they'd all recently turned or were soon turning forty, an occasion they'd approached with various levels of pomp and parade and agitation. Bill had thrown Bella a birthday party; Carson had gone, as had a dozen colleagues from Bella's firm and Bill's, and some of Gus's friends' parents. (Bella's parents had declined to make the trip, which was disappointing but also typical.) Carson, keen to avoid any reminder of how much older she was than her present roommates, had hoped her natal day would pass without remark, and as it was, she got only a passel of well-wishing texts, flowers from Reba. (Zariah and Donny were chill enough but also, she suspected, quietly judging her life decisions—surely she must've blundered something to still have roommates at forty and to be asking them to help her dose her mom friends with psychedelics.) Reba had had sex on her birthday, but that was not so much celebration as calculation; she was within ninety-six hours of ovulation. Gregg was not forty yet—hers was a March birthday—but she had designated, perhaps arbitrarily, the early spring day that began her forty-first year as the one on which she'd officially decide if she would run for US Congress. It gave her a few more months to punt the pronouncement; it gave her some time to focus on other big things first.

They elected to let their food settle before they divvied up that beautiful chocolate disk, and after dinner, Carson sneaked into her room, nominally to get another layer, but really to take a quick look at her computer. No important emails, and from her laptop she could check her texts; her phone and the others' were still sequestered. Just a message from her roommate, something about a minor party. Her heart sank a little, sensing they'd taken the occasion of her absence to host. She texted him a thumbs-up and thanked him again for the chocolates.

Then, in atonement for her communications transgression, she set about cleaning the kitchen, which had, over the course of the day, slipped into disarray, chocolate wrappers strewn across the kitchen island, detritus from avocado toast and DIY cucumber water on the cutting board, microscopic cubes of garlic-knot garlic dotting the counter like stinky glitter. Did the house compost? She didn't know. She'd make a pile first and later investigate.

As Carson gathered the wrappers from the morning chocolates, she noticed that one of them was heavier than the rest. Gum? She tested it between her forefinger and thumb. It didn't feel squishy like that. She couldn't help but peek.

She was flummoxed by what she found. Someone had sucked the chocolate off the minced mushroom and spat the fungus bits back into the wrapper? She turned it over. The initial on the bottom: "G."

Gregg. She crumpled the wrapper again, cleared the rest of the kitchen with a low dose of rage, or confusion, or jealousy—the Lemonhead, sloshing in her stomach, kept her from sinking her teeth into one feeling fully; instead she gummed at them all. She loved Gregg, but what the hell?

13

Sat, Jan 14 at 9:15 PM

Mom:

Hill I need you to call me asap Roger is having a grand mal meltdown

Gregg was lying on the same poolside lounger she'd sprawled across that morning. Carson stood above it, her hands on her hips. Gregg was dozing, or acting like it, so Carson moved her friend's pedicured foot and sat down heavily. Upon impact Gregg opened her eyes and gave a dreamy, slow smile. "Hi, hon. What's up?"

Carson bit her lip. "I know about the—" She made a spitting motion into her palm.

Gregg sat up, sniffed, more attentive.

"Why?" Carson continued. "Are you worried about your career? I mean, I know Texas is more conservative, and you wouldn't want anything to get out about illicit substances, but we'd never tell. Besides, your husband." Zeke had been an early and vocal proponent of experimental psychotropic treatments, frog-licking retreats and intravenous ketamine. For that, and a hundred other reasons, people thought he was zany, but also probably brilliant, and so his antics were tolerated. He might soon be licking frogs in space, and who wanted to get in the way of that?

"It's not that."

"Then what? Do they make you pee in a cup at the statehouse?"

She shook her head, no again. "Texas has way too much personal liberty for that."

Carson could feel her anger like a sheet of baby bubbles across the bottom of a saucepan. "Why can't you just go with the flow for once?" Carson may have presented as laid back, but she was her own breed of control freak—she could never have written two novels, with all the deprivations and organization they entailed, if she weren't. She had never before uttered *go with the flow* unironically, and she cursed the Lemonhead again, for making her imprecise. She wanted to feel her anger's edges, to squeeze them and have them cut into her palms.

Gregg placed a hand on her friend's knee and checked that Carson's trembly glare had stilled before she spoke again. "Don't tell anyone, but I may be a little bit pregnant."

The air caught in Carson's throat. "What? Just a little bit? Just maybe?"

Gregg wrapped her arms around her knees. "Eight weeks. And for sure."

"Wow." Carson felt like she'd been slapped, like she'd been punched, like she'd been pushed right into the pool, but that couldn't be, because her clothes were bone dry and quaking. It didn't feel as bad as it had when she'd learned Gregg wouldn't be acting anymore. When Gregg had shared that news, Carson had first flipped through her mental Sondheim catalogue before understanding that *Politics* wasn't the title of some obscure musical—it was the name of a life-altering career shift. How could she do it? Carson had been sure that, as the rest of their friends continued along more conventionally affirming career trajectories (i.e., steady paychecks), she and Gregg would stay the course, commit their lives to capital-A Art, become old lady artists together. But then Gregg'd gone to Austin, met a tech millionaire (the women guessed that Zeke was now a tech billionaire, but Gregg would neither confirm nor deny it). After that, it was like dominoes, a chain reaction. Within months, the one-time actress was a full-time resident of Austin, engaged, and mulling a career "evolution"; then she was a wife and running for state representative. Every tile made such a satisfying *clack* as it hit the table, but as they went down they were gaining speed. She was elected, she was elected again, she was pregnant, she was pregnant again. The impositions of early motherhood, the friendship neglect that could stretch for years—none of it was as disagreeable to Carson as Gregg's decision to walk away from their joint project. But she still wasn't excited to hear Gregg would be largely out of commission for another stretch with the demands—or were they indignities?—of a newborn. And would this one be born when the Texas senate, which met every other year, was in session, like Xavier? Or, like Zacky, would Gregg be spared the challenges of having an infant on the floor? Did it really matter? It'd be grueling, regardless.

Gregg interrupted Carson's internal rant. "I didn't want to say anything. I mean, with Reba and her treatments." When Reba had begun her fertility journey, the injections and retrievals and fertilizations were a backup measure; she said she wanted to cover her bases as she was getting a "late start." But as things went sideways—the bewilderingly spare follicles, the literally bad eggs, Terrence's slow-swimming sperm—each cycle became more fraught. At this point, they all knew how many fertilized embryos Reba had left. It was not a good number.

"How old are your kids now?" Carson tried to track her friends' offspring, but there were so many among these women and others, a veritable clutch of kiddos at or under five. It was difficult to keep straight who was precocious, who was missing benchmarks, who was going into pre-K or 3-K or if it was still just called nursery school.

"Too young. I swear, it's like I look at Zeke's crotch and it's the annunciation, zing."

"Definitely don't say anything about *that* to Reba."

"No kidding. Jesus. Have you seen the needles?"

Carson had. When she'd last visited San Francisco, Reba was prepping for another retrieval and very candid about the whole ritual of morning and nighttime injections, a second fridge in the pantry dedicated to syringes and vials. Terrence was away, so it fell to Carson to jam those nightly needles into her friend's belly.

"How are you going to run with a newborn?"

"I don't know. I don't know if I'll keep it, but I wanted to—"

"Keep your options open." Carson finished the thought, noting that Gregg hadn't said *I don't know if I'll run*. Carson had to admit that as blindsided as she'd been by Gregg's decampment, Gregg was very good at this other thing, her fallback plan. But maybe it shouldn't have been such a shock? At the time of Gregg's reinvention, in a text chain sans Gregg, Hillary reminded the rest how Gregg had, before college, been the debate queen of Greater Boston. Reba added—Reba's memory was like an elephant's—that Gregg had canvassed for Obama during his first campaign. They'd all assumed at the time that she'd blown a series of auditions and needed a quick paycheck, but now . . . In any case, her actor's training and font of emotional intelligence, overlaid with a policy wonk's embrace of the budget allocation process, made her an ideal fit for the new role. Still performance, but hardly art.

"Bingo." Gregg said softly, then looked up at the sky. She pointed at some clump of stars, and Carson squinted after her friend's finger. (Carson needed glasses—or, she had glasses, but she needed new ones, a stronger prescription.) What did Gregg see in that fuzzy cluster?

"There's Jupiter," Gregg said. "My astrologer says it's in retrograde."

"Is that a good thing?" Carson's roommate Zariah was also into astrology and tarot (her Sunday evening readings took over the dining table for hours each week), but soon after moving in, she'd asked for Carson's birthday, then her birth year, then looked alarmed and never brought it up again.

"Jupiter is the planet aligned with good fortune and wealth," Gregg continued.

"Okay?" Carson wasn't sure what to make of that, if a planet in retrograde meant minus or extra.

Gregg's eyes were still on the sky. "This stuff with Jupiter means everyone's going to get a little less lucky."

"Oh, great."

Gregg closed her eyes tight, like she was trying to shut something out, then opened them and locked her gaze on Carson. "We'll just have to ride it."

14

Sat, Jan 14 at 9:38 PM

Mom:

HILLARY CALL ME!!

It was just then that they heard a song, at first quiet. Tinny and compressed, but the chord progression was familiar, the lyrics vague to start, then clearer.

It couldn't be, but it was. Louder now, the hook of ". . . Baby One More Time" was unmistakable; the song had been their anthem for much of college. Then came a bellow from inside the house, something startling in its fury, and the patio slider pulled open. Hillary ran out, hurrying in her bare feet to the far side of the pool, a phone to her ear. "Just a sec—" she said.

A moment later Reba appeared, holding a knife. The blade had been sunk into the chocolate torte; the frosting's black ooze looked lurid in the moonlight. At some point between the kitchen island and the pool deck, Reba's grip had shifted from cake cutting to thrusting, and upset was flaming in her eyes. She bellowed again; the women flinched.

"I said no phones!" she screamed. "Did you *sneak* into my room and *take* it out of my suitcase?"

"Carson was checking her email!" Hillary shouted across the pool. The water rippled at the revelation.

"What?" Reba stopped in her tracks and her glare flashed to Carson, who showed her palms, somewhere between not-me innocence and self-defense.

Hillary's whispering into her phone drew Reba's attention again. "But you're on your phone now! Can't Miles just wait till the morning? For fuck's sake, you decided to marry him and spend your life with him! So what if you got divorced, or are getting divorced, or whatever you two are doing, he's still the father of your son! He can manage your child—it's his child too!—for forty-eight hours without your help!" Reba moved toward her.

"It's sixty!" Hillary hollered back and started running. The women lapped the pool, once, twice, the manic energy of a Looney Tunes chase, but with beach cover-ups and still the knife. "Two and a half days!" On her next circuit, Hillary found a side gate, struggled briefly with the latch, and pushed it open. She ran into the side yard and over the river stones of the drainage ditch.

Carson could hear Hillary say, "Hi, I'm here now—" into the mouthpiece before she moved out of range. Carson was waiting for the neighborhood to respond—barking dogs and motion-activated floodlights—but the dark night stayed still and quiet. Quiet except for Reba's heaving breath—now she was puffing audibly as she continued spinning around the pool.

Sleepyheaded Gregg was no longer so. She was up, stepping into Reba's path with her hands out. "Whoa, cheffie."

"What?" Reba shouted. Her nostrils flared wide, and her eyes looked crazy in their darting. The knife glinted. "She had no right to go into my suitcase and sneak out her phone."

Gregg showed Reba her palms. "Calm down, baby. Calm down. Breathe. I know she broke the rules, but it was probably for a good reason. Right?" Gregg looked to Carson for affirmation; Carson nodded as her cheeks burned. Because Hillary probably did have a good reason, but she, Carson, had not had a valid excuse to check her email. Just an insatiable itch.

Reba's breath was ragged. Gregg approached slowly, her hands aloft. "Give me the knife."

Reba made a humming noise that sounded like a kettle set to boil.

"I know you're mad, girl. I get it. She messed up, but that's it. It's over."

"I said no phones."

"You did." Gregg reached and touched her arm—the softest tap. And with that pinprick, Reba was deflated. The knife clattered to the pool deck.

"You did say no phones," Gregg said again. "I heard you. It's a good rule." The fingers pressed, the hand wrapped, and the distressed woman was pulled into a hug. Gregg rocked her gently. "I hear you."

Carson quickly bent down and collected the knife.

"I just want my friends back for, like, one day," Reba sobbed into Gregg's shoulder. "I want living, breathing humans, who think about the composition of the Supreme Court and sad, serious movies and don't care about the consistency of their kids' crap. Who think about themselves, who think about the world, and who maybe even think a shred about me."

"I know." Gregg hugged her tighter. They all knew that what Reba wanted more than bear hugs or a critical conversation on John Roberts was to have a baby of her own to coo and kvell over. She wanted to channel her fierce energy away from course-correcting hapless executives and toward one teeny, gurgling thing who genuinely needed her. Desiring a baby as the world burned was impractical, choosing *flesh of my flesh* over, say, an egg donor or surrogacy maybe a touch godly, too strident, but that was how she felt.

Reba sniffled. "I mean, what happened to you guys?"

Hillary was sneaking back into the yard, looking abashed. "I am so sorry about that. Strawberries," she said. Like that explained anything.

The women stared at her blankly.

"Roger won't eat them, and Mom forgot. He was apoplectic. Like, End Times terror. The neighbors threatened to call the cops. Again."

"Wait, *again*?" Carson asked.

"Your mom?" Reba added, wiping her eyes. "I thought he was with Miles this weekend."

"Roger's actually"—Hillary paused, doing some internal calculation, a risk assessment or damage report—"with my mom, who's staying at my place." Another pause, long enough for the night air to fill with the pool's gurgle. Hillary's face changed, her mental Band-Aid pulled off. "Miles is in rehab."

"Talk about burying the lede," Bella said. She was listening from the doorway and stepped onto the patio. "I just checked my phone too, Reba, if you want to stab me."

"Oh my God," Carson whispered; then, louder, "Are you, is he . . . okay?"

Hillary crossed her arms. "I hope he kicks it this time. For his sake, and because joint custody, what we provisionally settled on, would be, just, like, very helpful. Two days a week, I'd take one night a week, or one every two, like my dad did with me. Some amount of time when I could get a break?" She shot a glance at Reba that wasn't mean, but wasn't quite forgiving, not yet. "But for now, I can't think about that."

"You have to think about strawberries," Gregg said, and Hillary burst into tears.

They all joined in, despite their stiff upper lips or because they welcomed the catharsis of a group sob. They shed tears for Hillary, the double vision of her future—one view had Miles present for Roger, another had a Miles-shaped hole. Cried for Reba, how frustrating it was that she'd traded in her big career for this one tiny want, and all she'd gotten was a fistful of beans and a hard patch of earth. They cried for Carson's knee, which had started to throb with the day's walking—had she known they were going to hike clear across the city, she'd have put on that ugly, cumbersome brace. They cried for Gus's tied-up tongue and Bella's court date, and without mentioning it outright, Bella shed an extra tear for the sparking, dangerous electricity she experienced not when she took Donny's chocolate-dipped psychedelics but whenever she *didn't* take her meds, a five-pill cocktail each morning. That was the secret of what had happened that college summer in New York, her and Reba clutching each other as they discovered just how fragile the mind could be. How fragile it was for Bella, and how precarious it would stay, even as she willed, as she prayed—drawing on the liturgy of her Catholic girlhood (she could still dredge some up), pulling from the Episcopal church she presently attended (they'd joined for the day care, but the priest was okay)—for things to be different. To get better. They would not get better, she knew, but she had to keep believing they might. Hanging on was her one option.

They did not weep for Gregg's election uncertainty or for whatever might happen to the cells dividing in her belly; she acknowledged neither in the pool's fluttering blue light. She didn't talk about the rocket her husband was building with his friends out on the Gulf, how she prayed he'd swing back toward public education and a socially responsible fiscal agenda before one of those spaceships crashed into the moon. Those concerns were just for her.

Then red-eyed Reba served chocolate cake, and they ate it, their cheeks still damp. Hillary and her sweet tooth were mollified.

Later, as they flossed in the shared hall bath, Carson asked Gregg how she'd managed to calm Reba down so effectively. "Live shooter training," Gregg said, adding that everyone in the capitol complex had to do it, along with modules on sexual harassment and anticorruption.

Gregg spat into the sink before she continued. "I know how to identify nepotism and avoid getting stabbed in the neck."

15

Sat, Jan 14 at 11:45 PM

Carson:

Hi D. Hope you have/had fun tonight. Also: any mail for me?

Sorry to keep asking... but waiting on an important doc. Hopeful 🤞

Before bed, Carson opened her laptop again. It didn't count if she was mostly sober and on her way to sleep, right? It couldn't count, not after the showdown they'd just had, the strawberries and screaming, the knife-wielding chase around the backyard. Reba had gotten over her rules, let go of her rigidity for the night. Anyway, it was Sunday on the East Coast, and close to it here.

Still, and again: nothing substantive in her inbox. She couldn't tell if she was more wound up about her agent's reply or her father's. One might come by email, any time—but probably not on a Saturday night. Tina had boundaries, professional decorum, a life outside of work. The other could only arrive by post, if at all. Carson asked herself again, for the hundredth time, Which had been scarier to send? After she'd emailed the manuscript, she'd gone into the bathroom and retched; but walking her package to the post office, a route that should've been seven minutes on foot, had taken her twenty, given how often she'd needed to stop and drop her head below her heart. She wasn't one to get vertigo, but there she was, dizzy at the prospect that she might have a father. Or, she'd always had a father, but with this package, she might *get* one.

Her inbox's closest thing to book news was a literary newsletter. She opened it. A recent novel was being hailed as one of the best of the year. Already picking winners the second week of January? Carson was dubious, but she clicked over to a text preview, scanning the novel's first page. The narrative voice was endearing right away, but the tone felt challenging to maintain for any distance. She scrolled to the publishing information—not even two hundred pages. She sighed. Her fondness for long-winded Russians, for doorstops that took a committed month to wade through, was stronger than most readers'.

Her brain bounced around her skull, a pixie in pogo shoes. Fucking Reba, Carson thought. That Lemonhead had tasted good, and likely was preventing a major morning headache, but it had dropped her, hard, back into the plastic seat of her roller coaster, and right as she was about to exit the ride. She had enjoyed the hazy, hallucinatory day, but now she wanted to get back to herself, to stop swerving and zooming along. She loved control, and missed it.

But thank God for Reba too, imperious and vulnerable and probably still blubbering in the hot tub. Did she regret losing her temper? Carson considered it. She knew that Reba was rightfully frustrated and livid about her last few years, that she was unsure where to direct her ire. Though Carson also knew the meat of Hillary's thigh was not the correct target.

Of course Reba had regrets. They all did, and more would invariably come. Steering clear wasn't the project, it was accepting their regrets and finding ways to make them productively dissipate. Theirs was a long-term project of regret management, supporting one another as each tried to control her remorse like it was the water level on some persnickety reservoir. They each had access to a series of spigots, inflows and out-, and had to factor in evaporation. That they might have total control of their emotional lake was as likely as claiming the control of nature, which was unattainable; Carson had known that since long before reading the McPhee book of the same name, since way before she'd seen the city's subways flood. But still. They had to try.

A dry chill had arrived after dark, and she pulled up her covers, closed her eyes. On her eyelids she saw the skywriter, and pondered whether Melissa, whoever she was, had looked up at the right time and, if she had, what she'd said. She saw that giant Marilyn again, looming over them. And she saw her friends, how they'd changed, how they hadn't. Gregg the performer. Hillary the earnest. There was scolding Reba, more like her mother than she could see, and bipolar Bella, who seemed better than at their last visit, but Carson knew Bella's moods rolled in and out like the tides. (Carson had guessed at the diagnosis years ago, and Reba, under duress and at the end of her second martini, had, after pinkie-sworn confidentiality, confirmed it.) Carson was so grateful for these women, their flaws and foibles, their self-awareness and completely blind spots.

Carson was also grateful that they accepted her, that they forgave her this morning's stoned shouting and her noncareer career and her long-vacillating but always fickle approach to sex and relationships. And that maybe, probably, hopefully, if they learned the truth of her family, they'd forgive her the lie she'd upheld for these last twenty years. Good friends would forgive almost anything, so long as you promised to be better in the future. Just like Reba, who swore over tear-speckled torte to work harder at emotional regulation, and Hillary, who affirmed she would be more forthcoming about the situation in Chicago going forward.

But Carson didn't know that that last ominous *would* would be coming to pass so soon, that the bat signal would be sent up from Hillary's Addison Street apartment in just three weeks' time. No, that night, alone in her borrowed bed, she was only aware that the Lemonhead was at last mellowing, and her skin was still pleasingly tingly with the day's sun, and, with her glowing laptop open beside her, she was finally falling into the shushing arms of sleep.

16

Sun, Jan 15 at 8:50 AM

Reba:

Good morning Ter. Did u sleep? Good luck w/ deadline!

They slept in on Sunday, even Carson in her big, firm bed.

In the master suite, Bella woke before Reba, swallowed her morning meds, then returned to the fluffy king to watch her friend sleep. Poor Reba, Bella thought, stymied for so many years now. She would be such a good mom. Maybe, given the follicle situation, she should start considering adoption? Bella weighed this against how much she loved that her boys looked like Bill, especially when they all dressed in their navy blazers for Mother's Day brunch. She didn't blame Reba for wanting to make someone in her own image. Her image was fantastic, smart and generous and very, very tall.

The woman stirred, opened her eyes, and smiled up at her friend. Bella smiled back. They both believed in pushing hard all the way to the finish line; it was one of 6,027 reasons they were friends. They understood it wasn't over until the curtain dropped or the hook came out or the fat soprano sang her solo. Where Reba was now, this wasn't the end; it was simply looking bleak. They could handle bleak. They had and could and would.

The morning was sunny but cool, and when everyone was up the women decided to take a short hike before their inevitable, regrettable reentries into reality. The sweat suit that Bella had been wearing Friday made sense in the Sunday light—Gregg told her she looked "exceedingly stylish." Gregg felt queasy but didn't say so; instead, she put on a T-shirt for Beto O'Rourke's failed 2022 gubernatorial campaign and sucked in her stomach. Carson was wearing a literary magazine logo T, a prestigious place that had published a story of hers once. (Bella, who made a point of tracking down Carson's occasional stories, had found this one on the Barnes & Noble magazine rack, read it, admired it. Mostly understood it, except for that detail about the agate on the fireplace mantel. Was that hunk of rock a metaphor, and if so, for what?) Carson also put on her mean-looking knee brace, which got a round of upset questions. She offered deflections and assurances. She was healing, she lied. She hoped.

They stopped at a quiet luxury café, got nitro coffees or mushroom coffees or decaf—Gregg ordered last, and said it under her breath. If her friends heard, so be it. Maybe they'd think she was still breastfeeding—her show of nursing on the statehouse floor had been such a thing—though she hadn't pumped all weekend, had shown no wet spots on her bikini. So maybe not.

• • •

The trailhead lot wasn't totally deserted, but as they set out on the rising path, they couldn't see other people, beyond a couple drinking coffee in their backyard at the edge of the parkland. At a clearing on the trail, only moderately winded by the climb, they took a picture of themselves, glowing faces pressed together. It was muscle memory, but they were unthinkingly replicating a pose of twenty years before, when they'd clustered before Bella's boyfriend and a clunky first-gen digital camera, grinning like idiots.

"Say cheese," Reba instructed, reaching out her long arm. They did.

They kept walking, following a trail with no signposts or markers, no indication beyond the encouragement of prior tread. They probably should've started to think about the distance; the first of their flights was in two hours, and no one could predict anything about the traffic getting back over the mountains, not on a Sunday afternoon. But for a stretch of minutes, up on that trail, none of them thought of any of that, not of the phones in their back pockets, the contents of the uteri, the docket for Monday, the emails and mail mails that would arrive or wouldn't, that might say something that they did or didn't want to hear.

Somewhere, down in the town, a church bell was pealing; it sounded like cotton balls shot out of a copper cannon, tiny *pum, pum, pums* floating up the slope. As they counted the strikes or didn't, as they looked up toward the pure blue or down to an edge-of-town solar array, its gray-blue parallelograms tipped toward the light, as they scanned for that couple flipping through the Sunday paper or closed their eyes, the women thought of the sun on their skin and the quiet wrapping them—cut through by that soft, soothing *pum, pum, pum*—and how nice it felt to be alone up here and together again.

17

Sun, Jan 15 at 4:45 PM

Bella:

Hope you boys had a fun weekend! You're getting them ready for school right?

When Bella had initially suggested the red-eye return to New York, Carson didn't argue with an additional six hours in California; she envisioned visiting the ocean or perusing a local indie bookstore, taking Bella to the Getty or LACMA—they could ignore the art there as well as they could at the Met. But it turned out that Bella had other ideas, namely an early dinner at a trendy Venice restaurant, her treat. It was nearly on the way to LAX, she explained as Carson maneuvered their SUV through stop-and-go traffic, a restaurant she'd been dying to try, the kind that Bill, as conservative in his eating as he was in his fiscal policy, wouldn't touch with a ten-foot fork. He loved a century-old steakhouse with tuxedoed waiters and was skeptical of almost all else.

As she drove, Carson listened to her friend rant about her husband—nothing new in the food stains and metabolic resentment, but were Bill's politics getting worse? Bella brought up the in-house thing again; Carson settled in for the familiar story. Several years back he'd opted for corporate counsel at a private equity firm rather than run the gauntlet of partner track at Cushman, and it still made Bella livid. How could he raise the white flag when he was not yet at the battlefront? Carson, having heard the saga from both Bella's and Bill's perspectives (the way he told it, he was poached by the PE firm), was unsure of whose version was correct. Maybe it was a betrayal of Bella and their shared commitment, as Bella suggested, but maybe Bill was shrewd? A third possibility was that his ability to fail up was the world's unfairness, illuminated.

The conversation shifted, as it often did with Bella, to money. She was already thinking about the pay bump of a promotion, how she'd invest if she was given partner equity. They were well off, Bella recognized, but there were so many fixed costs in her life: condo maintenance fees, the boys' preschool just the tip of the iceberg in a giant floe of tuition. All would change with Bill's inheritance, but when the Winston patriarch passed in 2017, Bill's pledged pile of cash had been detoured to Bill's mother (Wife #3) and would remain parked there for any number of years; the old crone was in excellent health.

Carson was so tired of hearing about money. She cut off a Mercedes convertible and silently said farewell to the prospect of putting a foot in the ocean. "So, where's this restaurant?"

• • •

With traffic and Bella's bad directions, they arrived thirty minutes late to their reservation. After some light groveling they got seated anyway, a dim and noisy table by the kitchen. Bella had voiced concern about their dusty hiking outfits but need not have worried. There were T-shirts everywhere, athleisure that was even more casual than Bella's matching set. LA continued to mystify her.

Carson ordered the fish, which scared Bella off with its accompanying onion rings; she had had misgivings about fitting into her courtroom clothes before the weekend. After a cheeseburger, pizza, a *milkshake*? Her suits might need alterations. And so she selected the sunchoke salad, and when it arrived she felt virtuous. But as Bella forked through her grilled little gem and jabbed at her sunchokes, she had some buyer's remorse. Across the table, Carson's moist and flaky fish gleamed like it had come from an alternate universe where fish were abundant and lived happy, mercury- and PFAS-free lives; one where, when they'd had enough swimming and kelp and hide-and-seek with apex predators, they'd throw themselves into the holds of ruggedly handsome fishermen's waiting boats. And the onion rings looked delicious. Her friend's eyes rolled back as she gummed on another loop. But fried and breaded FOMO wasn't bothering her as much as this other thing. Bella cleared her throat.

"I'm sorry I talked down to you the other day, Carson."

"Bella, you talk down to me, like, every day."

Bella chewed her lip. Did she? "I mean, about the airplane. Gregg's. Obviously you know some people fly on private jets."

"It's okay." Carson took another big bite of fish. At one time, when they were just starting out, the span between them (smaller then) had been a positive thing. Carson's otherness, her future-slash-possible literary career, was so intriguing. A writer, with a musician boyfriend! (And she wasn't a groupie, more of a muse.) Bella would invite Carson out with her new law school friends, big Saturday nights in NoHo or the Lower East Side. The future lawyers always paid for everything; in exchange, the writer played the free-spirited artiste, a scion of the creative class that was New York's beating heart. Carson and her writerly ways offered an antidote to their weekday tedium, the Murray Hill and FiDi studios they only ever saw in the dark. To the future JDers—still too young for the staid and stable patronage of Broadway tickets and ballet subscriptions, still too optimistic to acknowledge how stultifying wealth could be—supporting the arts meant buying this friend of their friend a steaming bowl of moules-frites at Lucien and keeping her in cocktails all night. But then Bella'd graduated and started working at Cushman and met her future husband, an associate several years ahead of her. With Bill, Bella's social world flipped again, and she was trying to make a good impression on his friends, all old-money Manhattan types, young guys who'd briefly aspired to edginess (the rebellion of weeknight coke and vintage Burberry, rather than drugs on the weekends and trenches straight off the Barneys rack). When Bella had met Bill, his friends were already sliding into muckety-muck territory, having obtained bespoke tailors and entered the arms race of Hamptons summer rentals; it was all Bella could do to keep up. She and Carson started spending less time together.

"And it's not like you're always nice to me."

Carson's eyes jumped from her plate to her friend's face: the lowered gaze, the verging-on-petulant pout. The gray hair, just a few and only a couple of millimeters, showing at her part. Bella could be such a baby, but she could also be right. Carson *did* talk down to her, about Bella's center-left politics that she was so proud of but were tepid anywhere south of 60th or north of 110th, about all the meaningful books and music and art Bella wanted to consume but didn't have the bandwidth to seek out or the critical faculties to really get. Bella was just curious or excited, maybe an itsy bit jealous of Carson's access to cultural production, her capacious vocabulary and unfettered attention span. Because Bella's life, the one she was working doggedly toward—equity partner and a classic six, a designer couch and the boys' matching outfits—risked predictability, boredom, even monotony in its polish. Both women saw that brewing on Bella's horizon, even if neither would name it outright.

"Fair point. And sorry about that. Do you want an onion ring?"

Bella nodded, she did.

18

Sun, Jan 15 at 10:24 PM

Bella:

Boarding. I assume no news=good news? 

Bella thought she'd sleep on the flight and had a cocktail plus wine at dinner to speed things along. She *needed* to sleep onboard, to get through the boys and Bill and a Wednesday deposition about her client's beverage's potential toxicity. How unsafe was it really to get caffeinated and drunk at once? And what did that say for the future of the espresso martini? Counsel's strategy was not to dwell on health outcomes because there was the dead guy—but he'd had coke in his system too, and whose fault was that? There was also one possibly damning study, not about alcohol content but concerning cancerous chemicals, that red dye Hillary had mentioned. Instead, Bella would focus on free will.

But once they were airborne and Bella pulled out her cashmere eye mask, sleep would not come. She tossed and turned in her Comfort Plus chair, fussed her short legs around the extra legroom, but only managed to doze, lightly, as their plane hurtled east.

Carson, by contrast, knew she couldn't sleep on flights—she learned that as a young adult, flying back and forth to Seattle—so she didn't bother trying. She poked through the movies in the seat-back player, stopping at *Everything Everywhere All at Once*. She'd met the directors, two friends each named Daniel, ages ago. Their circle and hers had overlapped for a time (not the women she'd just seen, but another friend group), and the Daniels threw good parties. At one, Carson'd made out with a guy who she thought went on to be the Daniels' go-to editor; all these years later she could remember the way he'd bitten her lip out on that fire escape. But when she saw him speak at an awards ceremony (okay, at the Oscars; she had made out with someone who had won an Academy Award!), he looked different, and sounded unfamiliar too. Had her memory betrayed her in its capacity for heft and hue and mouthfeel? Or had he changed that much in the intervening years? And if that was the case, was that what success wreaked—it made you unrecognizable? Her mind flicked to another possibility: Were there *two* Daves who were both film editor friends of the two Daniels? Maybe she'd had nothing like a brush with cinematic greatness; maybe her Dave had said he was a *sound* editor and was still adjusting crunch levels on chicken sandwich commercials from a tiny studio in Brooklyn. Another prospect: He looked unfamiliar because she'd stayed stubbornly the same, as stuck in her rut and her old cardigans as Michelle Yeoh's character was mired in her laundromat.

The first time she'd seen the film, she'd bawled like a baby; tonight she cried silently, not wanting to disrupt the white-haired stranger who was slumped over and sleeping on her shoulder.

They arrived in New York early but spent an eon on the tarmac—up the aisle Carson could see Bella's eager head rise and start bobbing, at least until a flight attendant chastised her back into her seat belt.

In the terminal at last, Carson and Bella walked together down the concourse. Bella looked sidewise at her friend. She'd offer to share her ride, she said, but they were going in different directions. Carson agreed and acted like this was not a problem. The A train operated at six in the morning, she pointed out. They stepped out of security. There, the livery drivers with their iPad signs were lined up alongside parents, children, and lovers, who, for reasons related to mobility, aptitude, and desire, insisted on being as close to arrivals as legally permissible.

As the friends passed the baggage carousels, Bella looked more troubled. She was weighing the veracity of her friend's statement and its no-big-deal assurance versus her own true and pervasive fear. Bella was loath to admit it, but she was scared of the subway. Especially when it was empty (late nights, early mornings), particularly since the pandemic (the whole city had become strange). She knew someone who knew someone who'd been sliced with a box cutter on the 2 train—and not even a robbery, just for demented glee. What was wrong with people, one; and two, what sort of New Yorker did her fright make her? A bad one, she suspected.

They reached the point where they were meant to split—taxi line to the right, subways to the left—but Bella hesitated. How could Carson be so casual—was she really not scared? Carson, chin up and watching the signage, did not seem at all bothered by her upcoming commute. "Let me pay for a car," Bella said, reaching for her wallet.

Carson stopped her with a scowl. Bella meant well, but she'd apologized for acting pompous what, twelve hours ago? And she was still, again, talking down to Carson, like Carson was looking for alms. She wasn't! But those three puny words, *Let me pay* . . . Like money could keep you safe. Bella's blind spots were so disappointing.

Carson slung her shoulder bag over her shoulder. "I'll be fine. Have a good one, Bella." She walked quickly away.

Carson was already out of earshot, beyond sight, when a somewhat stunned Bella hollered goodbye in her direction. "See you soon!"

19

Mon, Jan 16 at 10:55 AM

Bella:

Hi Darcy, can u pls cancel my 11? Thx/sorry for last min/no notice. Will be in soon.

Bella made good time—no traffic on the GCP, none in the tunnel this early—and as she rose in her building's elevator, she prayed that her kids might still be asleep. Or maybe, she thought, looking at her watch, they'd be gone already. Not disappeared, nothing so sinister, but dropped off early at the nursery's before-school program, because Bill had anticipated how zonked she'd be after the overnight flight.

It wasn't that she didn't want to see Gus and Bill Jr., she did. But she yearned to settle and regroup, to rest a beat before the chaos of her life began anew. She wanted to unpack the argument(s) with Carson—why had they cut each other down all weekend? Carson making fun of her outfit; all that stuff about imagining little girls, when she *knew* it was a sore subject; Bella reminding her often how broke she was. (She knew she shouldn't, but money was a scab she couldn't stop picking. Also, Carson could've signed on to a real job years ago. With no kids in the picture, no current or future tuitions due, she could have even worked in nonprofits.) Bella also wanted to spend some time remembering the way her face had felt with those chocolates on deck, the way her heart had felt to be with her dearest friends and disregarding the rest of her life. Those seventy-two hours away had been like looking into a mirror that wasn't a mirror, one where the reflection moved independently. It ate fried foods without consequence, it chortled as often as it cried, it didn't care a whit about diaper supply levels. (Bill Jr. was about to turn a corner on potty training but had accidents often enough that they kept a pack of diapers on hand and sent him to school with backup clothes.) In the desert she didn't care about her husband's blood sugar or how many hours she could bill before pickup.

No such luck.

The boys were revving their engines at the first tinkle of her key in the door, and as soon as it swung open they went for her legs with hugs and pinches and weird soft slaps on her upper thigh (where had Gus picked that up?). Maybe they'd been ready to spring since the rumble and ding of the elevator; maybe they'd been arrayed around the door, poised to pounce since four, her plane still five miles above western Pennsylvania. Who knew? Gus slapped her ass again and made a slurping noise into her thigh. It was odd, what he was doing.

After she'd greeted her sons, squatted down and made meaningful eye contact with each, telling them *how very much* she had missed them, she looked around the apartment. The place was so thoroughly trashed it could've been burgled. Her husband acknowledged as much with raised eyebrows, a sorry smile from the far end of the foyer. "The good news is everyone is alive, and we only needed three Band-Aids." Three Band-Aids was an accomplishment for him—both that it was not a larger quantity and that he had handled the sight of any amount of blood without passing out.

Bella, still squatting, tried to reciprocate his toothy grin. Bigger, she told herself. She felt her cheeks creaking, she felt her knees ache. "I'd mark that as a victory."

"Me too." He looked left and right. "Sorry about the mess."

"I'll see if Olivia can come early." The maid—no, they were domestic workers, she corrected herself—typically didn't come until Thursday, scheduled that way on the off chance they might host on the weekend. It seemed laughable now, her earlier ambition to entertain amid young children.

Gus had wrapped himself around one of Bella's shoulders, a squishy, squirmy monkey. His miniature sweatpants were on backward, she noticed, his little shirt inside out, and he smelled like he hadn't bathed all weekend. He extricated himself from her neck and backed up. She was bracing for the impact of another full-speed hug when she spotted that he was limping.

"Gus-gus, what's wrong?" She looked into his face.

"Nothing, Mama." He tugged on the hem of his shirt. The ghost of Clifford the Big Red Dog stretched pink across his belly.

"Does anything hurt?"

Gus said no. She studied him, moving from the top of his head downward. She wanted to cry—so much was wrong, or could prove to be wrong, could yet become wrong with her firstborn. The lisp was just the start of it, the first of a million challenges he'd have to wrestle, because even privilege—and he had the trifecta of whiteness, maleness, money—didn't protect you from all the world's shittiness; these days, it covered maybe 60 percent.

It was when she arrived at his feet that she saw the problem. He'd have stomped out of the house with his left shoe on his right foot and his right on his left if she'd let him. (Bill would have let him.) "Gus, do your toes feel pinched?"

He looked confused, glancing from her face down to his feet.

"Do you remember what we learned about left and right?" She held up the two L's of her forefingers and thumbs, but realized they were backward for Gus, and maybe even more confusing. She dropped her hands and crawled toward him.

The child allowed her to slip off the shoes; he stepped into them correctly. "All better."

When she rose, her husband kissed her on the mouth, relaying a puff of coffee breath, and handed her a travel mug. "Can you do drop-off? I have a breakfast meeting downtown." Since going in-house, Bill had become a lawyer who took schmoozy breakfast meetings with other general counsels. Bella imagined they just gossiped and ate bacon for hours.

She hadn't offered to do the morning run, but she could see how her crouching by the door, with the boys climbing all over her, could be misconstrued. Then she spotted the book bags and coats shoved against the wall. Had they even been unpacked, cleaned out since Friday? She was scared to look. *Welcome home!* the stinky Tupperwares would shout, and *We missed you!* the damp, snot-streaked mittens would chime in.

She quietly fumed as she gathered the boys' things (mercifully, the bags had been cleaned and prepped for school). What if her flight had been late or she'd never stepped onto that plane—what would Bill and his "breakfast meeting" have done if she'd stayed in Venice or caught a ride with Gregg to Texas to become campaign counsel? (And why hadn't Gregg told them whether she would run? Even if it wasn't official, they could keep a secret!) Or she could've flown home with Hillary, shown up in Chicago and scared Miles straight—*If you hurt my friend one more time* . . . Hell, she could've taken the subway with Carson to Brooklyn, eating crow all the way.

"How was your trip?" Bill shouted from the kitchen. So he had thought to ask, a beat late.

"Fine," she said, straightening. Once Gus had figured out his shoes, she peeled off his shirt—*pop, pop* over his ears—and put it back on, right side out. Now the dog on his belly was bright red and grinning. The pants, loose and without a fly or pockets, she decided would be fine remaining backward. She heard her husband clanking in the kitchen, so she spoke louder. "It was nice to see the girls."

• • •

After drop-off, Bella came back to the house she'd hoped for. Somewhat. Quiet, but the disorder was even worse than she'd realized. Her poor kitchen—Bill meeting her in the hall with a travel mug of coffee had been, she now understood, a strategic cutoff. She dialed Olivia and the call went to voicemail—Olivia was probably vacuuming and couldn't hear the ring. Bella looked around at the sticky counters, the heaped sink, the milk spills on the floor. Thursday was a lifetime away, inconceivable. She would have to do it herself. She would do it herself, or triage at least—she didn't need to be to work until eleven—just as soon as . . . Before Bella realized it, she was horizontal, splayed in the center of their bed. She spread her arms, reached her legs like a starfish. She'd only be a minute, she thought.

20

Mon, Jan 16 at 11:32 AM

Carson:

This client keeps writing me about scotus and affirmative action/ legacy admish like the sky is falling & im like hello dobbs??? Sky already fell lady 🙄

Anyway rant but thought youd appreciate. Keep killing it in tx xo

Carson opened the loft's door and blinked, thinking it was her imagination, the angle of the morning sun, some afterburn of the mushrooms. Whatever the cause, the apartment looked as though a tornado had blown through. No, that wasn't right. The upset stacks of magazines and tilted plants could've been the casualties of a cyclone, but that didn't explain the massive amounts of refuse—empty cups and full ashtrays and half-full cups that'd been volunteered as ashtrays, abandoned bottles and paper plates showing the splatter pattern of greasy pizza.

"You're here!" Donny shouted, his voice sounding strained in its attempt at cheer. "I thought you weren't back till tonight." She liked Donny, his Pooh Bear–bellied crop tops, the haircut–facial hair combo that evoked an eighties East German punk band.

"And I thought the party was Saturday?"

He gave a feeble laugh. "It ran late. Or long. Dunno."

"Got it. Celebrating anything special?"

The younger man shrugged. "A friend's magazine unionized."

Carson was glad. Even if these Gen Z white-collar workers acted as if they'd invented the wheel and not simply picked it up from the side of the road, patted it off, and watched it roll straight and true . . . more labor was more labor. Her mother had been her grocery store's rep for years; Carson had been quick to assist when campus food service workers struck their sophomore fall. She'd also been the one to speechify to Hillary that Roger could go public or private, but for the love of God and the AFT, he could *not* go charter. Hill'd opted for an extra year of preschool (she cited some new study about juvenile brain development), so the point had been punted.

"How's your head?" Carson closed the door as quietly as she could.

"I can move it today." Donny's feathered hair floated this way and that. He winced, and Carson was glad again for Reba's citrus suckers—even if it had been presumptuous of her to dole them out.

"Good luck with that." Carson picked her way across the living room. The furniture was indestructible, or had been wrecked and repaired a great many times. One couch, missing a leg, was propped up with obsolete dictionaries (her 2001 *Webster's Collegiate* still thinking *scroll* was primarily a noun, as in Dead Sea); her dining chairs were beyond mismatched. The furniture in her room—plenty of it used, but some of the more recent acquisitions nice (antique rather than vintage)—was another story, but her space was off-limits during gatherings, no ifs, ands, or buts.

"This'll be gone by evening," Donny said, indicating the welter. "Working from home."

"Fine." Carson had had a dozen roommates over the eighteen years she'd lived here, and Donny was the most conscientious by a mile. He'd make a mess, but then clean so thoroughly the loft would be better for the disaster. He *liked* cleaning, he confessed one night as he scrubbed behind her meal prep, practically taking the cutting board from her hands. Plus, as an editor at a prestigious if limping-along fashion magazine, he often came home with goodies. Zariah, who'd been a college pal of Donny's, got first dibs, but as a stylist, she had access to freebies too, and was exceedingly discerning about what she brought into her life. This meant Carson had a shelf of lavish face creams, a stack of designer hoodies that the other woman had turned down.

Zariah, bleary with sleep, wandered out of her room. "Hey." That Zariah came with Donny almost excused the tarot shutdown, the woman's eye rolls and snootiness. Carson didn't understand the disdain being directed her way. It wasn't like being an elder millennial was the mark of the beast—age was just a number. And even if age was consequential, Zariah would be forty herself before too long, and Carson couldn't wait to see how she felt about her thighs and finances then. At least they didn't share a bathroom.

"Hey," Carson replied, equally flat. She opened her bedroom door and she shut it.

Carson's room looked pristine, but she inspected it nonetheless. The big bed and dresser, a petite dining table she used as a desk. Matilda the jade plant, which was as close as she'd let herself come to having a pet. It seemed they'd respected her privacy. Except . . . She sensed something was askance, and scanned her wall of books, the floor-to-ceiling shelves that a carpenter/paramour had built for her a decade ago. (The relationship was brief and had sucked, but the shelves remained sturdy and delightful.)

And then she landed on it: *Crime and Punishment* was missing. She went a second time, spine by spine, through the D–G shelf, scanned the books clustered by her bed, those stacked on her desk. Nothing. "Shit," she muttered.

The book wasn't materially valuable, with its stodgy translation and unattractive cover, the cheap beige paper going brittle. But she'd purchased it soon after she'd learned the truth about her dad, as she was trying to understand what *life in prison without the possibility of parole* really meant. She'd thought the novel would offer more punishment but found in its pages mostly crime, its motivations and psychological costs. These costs were another form of punishment, of course, but she'd been looking for a literal sentence, the time behind bars. That Dostoyevsky saved this part for the epilogue was not a problem; she'd just gone in with the wrong expectations.

When it came time to write her novel, she studied Solzhenitsyn and Bryan Stevenson, binged *Orange Is the New Black*, then cycled through *Dead Man Walking* (the book, the movie, and the bootleg recording of the opera), then turned to Dostoyevsky again. On her second read she was still trying to wrap her head around its psychology of violence, examining how Raskolnikov's reasoning might give her access to the mind of a murderer. She was disturbed and fascinated by his bouts of euphoria and guilt, how they oscillated like a sine wave. And his hubris! Had her father felt so self-possessed, then so scared, in the days after his crime? She couldn't know; even after examining the evidence, newspapers and newsreels and her mom's unnerving scrapbook, she had a lot of questions. *Crime and Punishment* had helped her imagine answers.

By now she had something like a spatial memory of her edition, whether a line appeared verso or recto, near the front of the book or close to the end. The marginalia too, the notes she'd made at twenty-two, when she was first attempting to come to terms with her father's trespass, and those she'd made weeks ago, as she searched for the ideal epigraph and plotted what she'd say in that long-postponed letter. It had felt so important to do one thing before the other, to stay out of the way of her chugging imagination, to keep whatever she would discover about her father from intruding before she finished the book, but now that the other—reaching out to him—was bringing up the rear, she couldn't stop that teensy voice inside her head from asking: Why? Why did she have to know him and make herself known, after all this time? She wanted a parent's affirmation, yes. The occasional calls from Gregg's mom (Charlene had taken a writerly interest in Gregg's most literary friend) were buoying but hardly enough.

Also, frankly, she hoped for a good edit. An insider's eye could help zhuzh it up.

Carson allowed herself a surge of vitriol over her missing Dostoyevsky but then willed it to abate, to float away like a toy ship on a smooth-skinned pond, leaving just a ripple of wake. Maybe she could find her edition online. Her notes would be gone, the forensics of what she'd thought when erased, her crazy-lady marginalia, goodbye. But she had the results: the manuscript, the letter, and the future both might bring.

21

Mon, Jan 16 at 11:35 AM

Reba:

Good morning, Mother. Leaving now, see you in 30 assuming okay traffic.

Mondays, ever since they'd been vaccinated, Reba had a weekly date with her mother. Lunch and a manicure, errands as needed. That Reba had gone from being scheduled into meetings twenty-seven days a month to acting like a retiree at forty-one, watching paint—okay, nail lacquer—dry, still felt perplexing. She wasn't irrevocably retired; she'd gone as far as taking an occasional recruiting call, her Zoom background a blurry version of her childhood bedroom—nor was she committed to *not* working, i.e., free labor, as her mother had been with her various roles on the PTA and across community board subcommittees, the brief stint (appointed, acting) on the city council. (While Dianne Feinstein was a touchstone for Doris, Doris quickly learned she was no DiFi, and declined to run for a full term.) Doris's civic engagement and eager volunteerism were as much as one could hope to fit into a week. More.

They went to the same café as ever, forked through the salads they always ordered. Doris, still vain at eighty-four, insisted on dressing on the side of hers, and grimaced at Reba's glistening greens, how she buttered her bread. Then the older woman cleared her throat. "Are you pregnant yet?"

Reba stopped chewing.

"Wait, don't answer that." She squinted through her trifocals, her drawn-on eyebrows jumping up and down. "You're not."

"Thanks for the vote of confidence, Mother." Reba set down her fork and dabbed her mouth. "I'm having my curse, if you must know." The term was her mother's, and wildly anachronistic, one of a million ways Reba was reminded that her parents were dinosaurs.

"I thought the car smelled funny."

"Christ, Mother."

"I'm just being honest. And I'm sorry to hear that. Again."

Doris had always insisted that for her and Hans, becoming parents had been a late-breaking change of plans, but once the choice was made, it'd been easy. Doris liked to remind Reba that they'd called her "Grandma" on the maternity ward (the current euphemism, *geriatric pregnancy*, was more clinically accurate but stung worse); she was quick to add that though she'd had a decade plus on all the other new mothers, she'd birthed a hale and healthy baby, the longest to enter the UCSF system all that month. Reba's early height became an advantage in youth basketball; as an adult, she found that her physical stature helped "steer" clients toward her strategic recommendations—she was excellent at the cross-armed lean-in—even if it meant some difficulty in finding well-fitting pants. (When she did, she'd buy them in triplicate.)

Doris credited her easy late pregnancy, fast delivery (they'd made it to the hospital with fifteen minutes to spare), and quick recovery to her years "in the fields." The nurses had, apparently, chuckled at the declaration—how could this posh woman, who wore *pearl earrings* into L&D, have done agricultural labor? But she had; her 1960s flower-powered rebellion had been to spend most of a decade abroad at a collective farm, harvesting beets and ignoring her trust fund. During that time—which was also when, not inconsequentially, she'd met Hans—she'd had plenty of experience with other women's pregnancies and their young children, learning the milestones of gestation and babyhood as well as she'd internalized the stages of a bean's growth from zygote to stalk to bloom and, eventually, glossy green bean.

With her sample size of one, Doris was convinced that their family was good at having children late. That Reba, too, could wiggle her nose, and like the lady from *Bewitched* (another mark of advanced age: references to television shows fifty years retired), she'd be pregnant. Everyone had assumed Reba's inherited size—Doris was taller than average, but Hans was genetically Teutonic—and her athleticism would translate to easy childbearing, a baby bump like a basketball, childbirths like a luge course, *zip zoop*. (And it'd be *births*, plural, because Doris was already anticipating two or three grandkids.) Hence Doris's disappointed sigh, her dainty stabbing of a cherry tomato.

Reba wanted to explain to her mother that she'd been very fortunate to become pregnant after forty—Doris had been forty-three, and in the prenatal care prehistory of 1982. That she'd been luckier still to stay healthy, no preeclampsia or gestational diabetes. And that she, Reba, had turned out okay! Another blessed turn. Contrast this with what her generation was up against, trying to get pregnant in the 2020s. There was better science now, but for all they knew about chromosomal abnormalities, there still wasn't enough data on genetic mutations and medical complications among the most recent post-forty pregnancies to know heads from mutated tails. These newest old mothers, in addition to being subjected to all the documented perils of getting pregnant late, were being cooked or nuked or otherwise harmed by high concentrations of forever chemicals and cellular rays, toxic particulate and TikTok's mind-melting algorithm. The air quality alone—thank God she wasn't pregnant during the wildfires, she'd told herself as she watched the orange skies of 2020. That consolation worked, at least for one summer.

"So what have you been up to then?" Doris nibbled on a green.

Reba refocused her attention on the ginger-haired woman across the table. Today, as usual, every dyed curl on Doris's head was placed just so, secured by hidden pins and a quarter can of hairspray. Her mother's makeup, similarly strenuous, did a thing to her wrinkles, smoothed them out or filled them in. The effect was to confuse the viewer, even at this close vantage. Doris Boaz-Becker didn't look a day over seventy-two. "This weekend was Palm Springs with the girls."

"Oh, how is everyone?" It had been Doris, though she was the farthest from their New England campus, who visited most frequently, showing up for a long weekend each semester, spending plenty of one-on-one time with Reba but also on each trip treating Reba's friends to fancy off-campus dinners, appetizers and desserts, wine whenever the waiter didn't have the gumption to check their IDs. Doris basked in the energy of the young women, all but vibrating with their newly discovered knowledge and sense of possibility and righteous indignation. What they told her about the Triangle Shirtwaist Factory, and macroeconomics, and mitochondria! (There was no indignation regarding mitochondria, only a fawning awe at nature's complexity.)

These meals may have seemed like grand gestures to the young women, accustomed to dining hall falafel and moms who rarely came around (Hillary's intimidated by the airs of campus, Bella's self-absorbed, Gregg's tied up with state poet laureate commitments, Carson's too dying and then too dead), but that was hardly the case. Boaz Mercantile had been around since the 1849 Gold Rush, and while they weren't the richest of San Francisco's old merchant families (Reba had cousins who were great-great-grandnephews of Levi Strauss), the Boazes were well off.

No, the price of those meals was never an issue, though money, for Reba and her mother, did pose another, more fundamental quandary. If finances weren't a consideration, why hadn't Reba also chosen to fight the good fight? Her father, once he'd married into wealth, had become a mechanical engineer, responsible for a few teensy but vital components upstream from modems. Instead of keeping up a breakneck pace his whole career, he filed a patent, let off the gas, and found ample time for beach cleanups and neighborhood composting campaigns. Meanwhile, Doris perennially topped out their congregation's mitzvah counter (the aforementioned PTA committees and Feinstein fundraisers, but also early childhood literacy campaigns, hospice help, support for Israel). Doris had been quietly disappointed when her daughter went corporate for that summer associate job at the management consultancy. She'd clucked a louder cluck of disapproval when, days after graduation, Reba signed her soul over to those high-flying consultants.

Over the years, Reba had tried to explain to her mother her complicated feelings about inherited privilege, but Doris stared dumbly at her daughter every time she brought up generational wealth. Similarly, Doris's eyeballs flashed *cannot compute* whenever Reba spoke about the asymmetrical power dynamics and toxic dependency that philanthropy engendered. What did Reba mean when she said that Doris's volunteering perpetuated unsustainable hierarchical structures? All she knew was that she'd been doing good for six decades.

Hans had watched his daughter's trajectory and his wife's refutation of it, understood both angles, and tried to stay out of the fray. Until he too had had enough of Doris's badgering, her unwillingness to acknowledge her emotional cudgel. He finally persuaded his wife to let their daughter be. "Life's too short," he reminded Doris, which was ironic when presented by one then-late septuagenarian to another. When Reba at last quit the firm, her mother, glad but not totally over the base betrayal, chose not to quit her sanctimony.

"How's little orphan Carson?" Doris considered Carson one who had stuck to her guns, eschewed the pull of creature comforts and the empty affirmations of a big paycheck. A degree from that college offered identical credentials to all the girls; Carson could have been a banker, a doctor of the unseemly nose. But she'd used her energy for *literature*, even if Doris thought her first novel was a whit nasty—by which she meant both mean and lewd. She'd slogged through to the end, wincing at the curse words.

"Please don't call her that. We'll all be orphans, sooner or later."

"If you're lucky."

"Mother!"

Doris speared a cucumber. "I always felt so bad for her. Scholarship girl to start, like that wasn't enough, and then to get such a blow."

Carson and the public school kids had scraped by with their loans and work-study jobs. One kid in Gregg's econ cohort even ended up with a show on MSNBC. So what, Carson'd bought used textbooks, shopped at the vintage store and tried to pass it off as a point of style (and it was commendable that, in college and after, she could take Reba's and Bella's discards, the stretched-out sweaters and dresses too long or too short for her frame, and make them look great). She'd done fine. She was doing fine, even as, Reba assumed, her royalty checks had dwindled to a trickle. Carson had been offered full-time work on multiple occasions—in the English department at that prep school, college counseling with a bigger firm—and it was always: No thanks. She was too busy writing. Reba had built a career out of maximizing efficiency; she respected Carson's ongoing repudiation of such pragmatism.

"It *was* terrible. But it was two decades ago. She's fine. Just done with a new book, in fact."

"Oh, really?"

Reba described what she knew—the island, the jail, the ferns. From there, they discussed Gregg's potential political future (Doris cut a check whenever asked, which was kind of often) and Gregg's husband's latest product launch. Doris wasn't a tech maven; her iPhone still gave her trouble. But she'd lived in the Bay Area long enough to understand that what started in a garage thirty miles down the highway could one day drive the world. Not that Zeke was going to run the universe, but he had had a few prescient product launches, which had kept him relevant for longer than most. Reba hurried over Hillary's updates, spoke in the most general ways about Bella. Bella, she said, seemed to be doing fine.

"You're sure about that?" Doris's eyebrows arched. She'd been the one to show up at the Manhattan hospital that summer, when Bella's folks couldn't figure out a way off of their Mediterranean cruise. ("It's easy enough," Doris had fumed as she and Reba huddled in the ward's hallway, where Bella couldn't hear. "You go to the captain and say: 'Let me off this godforsaken boat.'") For the first years of their friendship, Reba had thought Bella was exaggerating her parents' disengagement; after her breakdown, Reba was positive that Bella had *under*stated the situation. Skipping her high school soccer games was one thing, that they missed regionals and the time Bella sprinted up from sweeper and scored . . . even that could be explained or excused. But she was hospitalized. In a psychiatric ward! And they were somewhere around Sicily, twirling each other's pasta like Lady and the Tramp. Indelible in Reba's mind was the conversation Bella had had when she finally got her mother on some land-to-sea line. Bella'd said, her voice wavering, that she needed Marianne to stroke her hair and feed her chicken soup. Marianne, on speakerphone (Reba holding her breath so as not to be detected), had responded that she'd only ever used bouillon cubes; couldn't Bella get herself some of those and an electric kettle? No, Marianne had said, there was no need for her to ruin her vacation with Bella's "minor emergency"; Bella just needed a nice-nibbed hairbrush and to not take herself so seriously. She needed to "buck up."

Now, Reba looked up at Doris. "I'm sure."

22

Mon, Jan 16 at 2:15 PM

Reba:

Need anything at the real pharma, Dad? I have Terry's RX for you 😉

After lunch Reba took her mother to the pharmacy. The groceries would be delivered, but Doris had a prescription waiting, and mentioned wanting a specific skin cream she'd rather pick out for herself. Reba quietly relished the time roving the aisles of the suburban CVS, as the drugstore by her had closed for "safety reasons." (For her, it'd meant lots of online ordering, accidentally buying miniature tubes of toothpaste and giant bottles of Tylenol.) Then, mother and daughter made their way to the manicurist, where Reba got a grassy neon green this week; her mother picked a pale pink that almost matched last Monday's shade. Then they headed home, or to Doris's *new* home. The old house, the bright, beloved Victorian on Steiner Street that Doris and Hans had restored from near decrepitude, was Reba's now, an all-cash purchase at a fair-enough price, given capital gains and the flexible terms that Reba offered her parents.

Those terms: They took what they needed to Marin—regular-rotation clothes and kitchen essentials, their bed, the house's one comfy couch (the rest were lumpy antiques), a TV, and the kitchen table. They left rooms upon rooms of mostly sound, fairly valuable heirlooms (which Doris made Reba swear she would not sell or discard), abandoned closets full of stale-smelling coats and 1980s-era eveningwear (so many sequins, and the beadwork!). Her father's dusty tools remained in the garage, and the kitchen was jammed with fifty years of hazy Tupperware. Reba and Terrence considered consolidating all the fusty furniture into one crowded room and visiting the Knoll store for something swish, but then the supply chain snapped and they had their answer. Instead, they bought what they absolutely needed online and dealt with the frowsy floral prints and overelaborate woodwork of Doris's aesthetic. There were claw feet everywhere.

To talk about her parents' relocation now made it sound like things had neatly slotted together, but the real-time unfolding of the move was anything but easy-peasy. Reba had started campaigning a decade ago for her parents to age in place—to relocate to a *safe* place, with no stairs, no gutters, no steeply pitched porcelain bathtubs. This was back when Hans and Doris were simply undifferentiated old (osteopenia and bad hearing) and not yet their present, acutely old (osteoporosis and prostate cancer). Their first concession was a gutter service when her father turned seventy-five ("No more ladders, Daddy!"), but then and for several years, they'd tolerate no other recognition of their advanced and advancing age. Doris had fumed when she noticed a laminated card magnetted to the fridge boasting their prescriptions, allergies, and preexisting conditions; Reba had surreptitiously placed it there during one of her visits. How dare she! But then Hans had fallen in that slippery second-floor tub and Doris wasn't strong enough to pick him up, let alone get his drippy, soapy body down the stairs, and that in-case-of-emergency card on the fridge had come in handy to the first responders. Doris didn't admit to her daughter that Reba had been right, but after that she allowed the conversation about single-floor living to proceed. Reba began spending her scant off days flying into San Francisco to tour facilities—*communities* was the term on which Doris insisted, and it was fine with Reba to let her hang on to that sliver of pride. Some of them were neighborhoods more than facilities, though the assisted living wing, the dementia ward, and hospice care were always within arm's reach, the next stage of enfeeblement another floor of the high-rise or hidden behind a hedgerow.

Reba found these trips tedious, but a silver lining emerged when Terrence became a stop on her West Coast sweeps. They'd met while she was on assignment in Portland, halving the corporate ranks of a legacy outerwear company, and what started as a flirty night at the bar (him behind it, her leaning hungrily over) quickly became more. A whirlwind weekend was followed by a long-distance courtship, which swung between scintillating sexy time and drudging weeks apart. Sometimes she'd do a night and two days in California, then fly up to Oregon for dinner and a romp; other times she'd bring Terry down to the Bay and put him up in a hotel not far from her parents' place, sneaking over just as soon as she'd done the dishes and put the old folks to bed. Doris was suspicious of Reba's furtive texts at the dinner table, her inconsistent stance on being a houseguest (some visits she insisted on not inconveniencing them, at other times she was quick to let herself in and raid their fridge). But Doris kept her theories to herself. Everyone was waiting for Reba to change her life, and maybe this was the start of that.

After several seasons of touring antiseptic modernist towers and sprawling low-profile complexes, they'd settled on a spot in Marin, bungalows that parroted Sea Ranch on the outside; inside they were ADA compliant with extra-wide doorways and voice-activated lights.

Reba sorted the property sale, vowed to keep alive her mother's vegetables (heirloom varietals from Doris's farm years, squashes and beets and cucumbers), and made plans to put in her notice. Her want for a kid then wasn't knife wielding or even at the level of that dancing baby from *Ally McBeal*, but it was present, an infrequent but unsettling *thunk* coming from under the hood. The check engine light wasn't yet on, but every time the baby clank clanked, Reba braced herself, waiting for her muffler to fall off or an axle to snap.

Hans was pleased with the place, its professional landscaping and level footpaths, the backstop of twenty-four-hour on-call staff. He was glad for the ready access to nature and, soon, his beloved daughter. Doris remained wary. She hadn't wanted Reba to make a life of management consulting but also felt Reba should not quit outright—she just needed to "set reasonable boundaries." The advice made Reba livid. This from a woman who hadn't worked a day in her life, unless you counted the beet harvest and the three months she'd filled in on the city council. But Reba put the snub aside, too frenetic with quitting and Bella's baby and orchestrating three moves at once.

Reba had hardly unpacked her parents and moved herself in and relocated Terrence to California when the lockdowns happened. She introduced her parents and Terry over Zoom, though Reba did not tell her parents the whole truth about where Terrence was living until much later; the need to create a bubble made such a good justification for why he was forever hanging around the house. The part about how he'd spent his twenties they didn't discuss until later still, and when they did, Doris had been vocally, visibly aghast. Reba couldn't tell if her mother was more distressed by his service—she and Hans were longtime pacifists—or by his drug charge, though neither was warmly received. Reba was not in the mood that day (or any) to start a foreign policy conversation with her mother, but did state that Terry's "drug crime" was overblown, hardly a violation at all. He'd been holding maybe three spliffs, and now there were THC oils and joints and gummies everywhere. They even had CBD for dogs! (She didn't go so far as to explain her own self-therapy routine, the balm that pot had lately offered her addled heart, but she was thinking about that too.) Listening to Reba's justifications, Doris had remained skeptical. Hans, sitting quietly next to his snapping turtle of a spouse, had seemed more ecumenical about it all; he was glad to have another man around.

"Where's Daddy?" Reba asked now. She put her mother's purchases on the kitchen counter. When Hans's treatment started, it had been Terrence who really saved the day. Hans felt wicked after his initial round of chemo, then a hundred times better after getting lit. Doris started to feel more warmly toward Terrence then—so long as their grow operation remained within California's personal use provisions and didn't disturb her raised beds. Reba assured her their plants were legit and all indoors, endangering no heirloom vegetables whatsoever.

(Most of them *were* under grow lights in the basement, but one hardy varietal was outside, where Doris's cucumbers once had been.)

Hans's prognosis was good; he was not in remission yet but heading that way. His progress was a relief, but still, this Monday and every Monday, Reba wanted visual confirmation that he was not too weak from the chemo, or feeling so spry as to attempt a dangerous activity. Not that he'd skydive—at eighty-six, Hans had some sense of his limits—but after switching to a recumbent bike, which distributed his weight more comfortably, he continued to avail himself of local bike lanes. Reba was glad he stayed active, but there were so many threats out there, things that could challenge his balance, his strength, his success at coagulation (he was on a heavy dose of blood thinners after a prior clot event). The chemo had knocked his white blood cell count into the single digits, so infection was another hazard.

"Out somewhere." Doris gestured vaguely toward the hills behind the complex.

Reba removed the vial of joints from her purse and set it on the counter. "These are for him," she said, tapping the lid. Terrence had even printed out a faux prescription label, instructions so basic as to be cute. "Take 1/day. DO NOT operate a motor vehicle under the influence." Neither of her parents was supposed to drive, whether they'd ingested THC or not, which had been another good thing about moving them to Marin. Security guards checked visitors in, but the nice people in the gatehouse also ran interference for the facility, stopping those without "current credentials" from hitting the open road. (This was Doris's preferred designation; *suspended license* sounded so harsh.) "Tell him to stay out of trouble."

"Yes, sir." Her mother gave her a soldier's salute, which was shorthand for Reba being bossy again. It was a thing she'd done since way before Terrence, but now it seemed newly awkward. They had a real soldier, or former one, in their midst. Was it disrespectful, or cavalier, to equate Reba's imperiousness with Terrence's service? Probably, but that didn't stop Doris from continuing her shtick.

23

Sun, Jan 15 at 2:06 PM

Gregg:

This might take a while... so good to see you ladies!!! xoxo

Was it a deception? Maybe a small one, or maybe it was two tiny fibs. A pair of white lies—one to her friends, one to her husband—though they were the most innocuous variety. Gregg believed in telling the truth, no question. But sometimes the truth could be bent or dodged for the greater good. And she knew, in this case, her reasons for fabrication were sound.

The first fib: After Bella and Carson had dropped Reba, Hillary, and Gregg at Palm Springs International and the three women had walked into the building, Gregg, knowing she would not get on her flight to Texas—she had no ticket—made some excuse for the other two to "go ahead" (she'd debated feigning a phone call or suggesting she needed the toilet, and decided on a belly rub and a *who knows how long this'll take?* look). Everyone had promised to put work aside this weekend, to ignore their inboxes and be indulgently inefficient for once in their adult lives. So while the idea that she was multitasking her time in California wasn't generally awful, in this instance it was not aboveboard, either. Once she'd offered a round of *maybe I'll see you in a few, but in case I don't* hugs and the women were out of her sight line, she doubled back out onto the sidewalk and scanned the cars waiting curbside. She checked her phone, looked up again, and like magic, a large black SUV materialized. Gregg waved as the car rolled to a stop. As ludicrous as it was to be the car's sole passenger—a pre-K class could have fit inside, the whole state environmental subcommittee (which was a comment on the size of the car and the group both)—there was something nice about its hush, its comparative height, the anonymity of its darkened windows. She liked the concepts of public transit and commercial flights, enjoyed open and untinted windows, but no politician who'd spent time in Texas could be blamed for preferring bulletproof glass, a private plane, fewer opportunities for gawking. She wasn't so hubristic as to consider herself JFK's second coming—given her leftist agenda and chamber-floor theatrics, she acted more like a junior Khrushchev than an aspiring Kennedy—but since gaining local prominence she'd received her share of social media death threats and doxes. That being said, she *had* missed her American Airlines flight on Friday and was bailed out by a quick-thinking staffer and a donor who was flying west. She hated what the trip had done to her carbon footprint, but he'd have burned all that fuel with or without her, so in that sense it hadn't been so bad.

Her advance team had done a great job—the Ray-Banned driver knew where they were going, knew to call her Gregg rather than Mrs. Thomas-Graves or Senator or ma'am, and the car was stocked with her favorite brand of sparkling water, granola bars, various device chargers, and a miniature plastic-lined garbage can, no questions asked.

Once they hit the freeway, Gregg settled into her neglected inbox. Did she see when her driver—aggressive but not hazardously so—overtook Bella and Carson in their SUV? Probably not. She'd moved from email to a manila envelope by then, packed with printouts festooned with stickies and the inks of three highlighters, and was reading about a director whose filmography she knew by heart. What she hadn't yet committed to memory, but what had been comprehensively researched and annotated by a staffer, was his impressive history of political donations (he only engaged big-D Democratic campaigns), his third wife's social causes, the couple's pet projects and pet names. The new wife (Gregg clocked the handwritten, underlined note: "Don't mention the second") was interested in German shepherds (theirs was named Hilda) and early childhood education, and flipping through her dossier, Gregg thought the woman looked like she wasn't very far removed from her own early childhood education.

Be generous, she chided herself. She knew what it was like to be on the receiving end of strangers' skepticism. Opponents on both sides of the aisle had called her a carpetbagger during her early legislative runs (not untrue, but so many in Austin were transplants, what of it?); tech bros had called her a gold digger when she and Zeke tied the knot—again, not untrue, but her prospecting had been happenstance. With Zeke and his money, it was like she'd been hiking, put her hand in a mountain stream, and unintentionally pulled up a shiny nugget. She was only interested in the stream's cool flow, but what was she to do, throw the hunk back? (And it was evident those naysayers hadn't seen the phone-book-sized prenup; while Zeke made Gregg's life very comfortable, his side of the ledger was as secure as Fort Knox.) And the friends of Zeke's first wife, people Gregg had never met, gleefully, spitefully spread the gossip that she was a homewrecker, even as Zeke had sworn up, down, and sideways that he was already moved out of the house and well on the way to a divorce when they'd first met at that Austin cast party.

"Why the split?" Gregg had been curious, not fishing or thinking of her own self-interest, though he was attractive, in that lightly disheveled, too-smart-to-care way. She was simply trying to make conversation with a stranger who wasn't a part of the cast but was attending the opening night cast party, which meant he'd done something substantial on the play's behalf. (He'd underwritten the advertising campaign.)

"No kids," he'd said, and he'd looked so forlorn that she could fill in the rest—that he had wanted a family and his ex had not. Zeke hadn't in that exchange explained wanting three kids or three dozen or enough to populate Mars, just *kids*. Seeing his brief but bald-faced sadness, Gregg felt her heart muscle give an extra-big whoosh. For a while, kids had been an abstraction to her, a *later* that stayed a long time off, but that night she'd moved one square closer to *soon*.

The SUV exited the freeway, rolled down a West LA arterial, and turned onto a residential street filled with eight-figure homes. She had met this guy—now a prospect, not a filmmaker—once, at an audition in Culver City, though she doubted he'd remember that encounter. Her agent had cautioned her that the part would be a long shot, but that didn't mean Gregg hadn't hoped for it—she'd binged his films for weeks, studied his scripts, trying to understand what he was drawn to in his female protagonists. Her assessment: They were often antagonists, antiheros and double-crossers, which was problematic, but at least they were complicated. No one was passing the Bechdel Test, but she appreciated that the women in his films were often smarter than the men.

She'd jumped right in with a juicy, vulnerable scene from the film, in which she monologued about her deflowering. He'd watched it without interest and cut her off before she was through. Officially, the casting director had been the one to say, "Stop, that's enough, thanks," but Gregg wasn't dumb; she'd seen the flick of his wrist, partway under the table.

After, Gregg had stepped into the bright morning and ugly cried, right there on the sidewalk. Not because she'd wanted this part so badly (the script was misogynistic at the end of the day), not because the process had been very bad—it was a long flight for a short audition, but she'd burned more greenhouse gases for other opportunities, and on the jerk scale, this guy was moderately low—but because she'd seen a hint of something in the director's eyes. He'd been so sanguine about what he wanted, and she was not it. She, by contrast, had never known so decisively what she wanted. Or she had—she wanted to be an actor, to land the best parts!—but she'd never been self-assured enough to not prostrate herself at the feet of the next opportunity, whatever it was, even if it meant incremental progress or lateral movement or a bit of backslide, career-wise. That he could be that casual, knowing in time he'd find his fit. What did that kind of self-assurance feel like? She couldn't say, but that morning she understood that, as much as patience was a virtue, it was also a privilege, and one she'd never had. She was so far back in the crowd, she grasped at whatever she could get: Sex Worker Number Two, Crazy Sister, Star of a Cottage Cheese Ad.

Tears in her eyes, she'd scanned the street for some sign that she was doing the right thing with all these luckless auditions. A thundering El Camino rolled by, a city bus slowed but did not stop, an unhoused man humped his shopping cart along the sidewalk, humming loudly. She saw no divine signal but was instead reminded of the massive disparities of this place, Hollywood but also America—and of her relative privilege. Even as she'd been made to feel like a bug below the man's foot, she'd been able to reach a position where she might be squashed by a very *nice* shoe, Italian leather and a hand-carved sole. That was something, right?

In her second career as a politician, she still didn't have the advantage of patience—for all intents and purposes, it was forever election season; she was perpetually trying out. But at least now her fate didn't depend on one person's self-regard and was instead in the hands of a plurality. There were still a great many thumbs on the scales, party favorites and unmatchable campaign coffers, powerful people who thought they knew best. But it was a vote of constituents, with whom she'd prevailed, first in her limited legislative district, then in the larger state senatorial one, and maybe next in Washington. Somehow convincing several thousand people of her value was turning out to be easier than convincing just the one. How did that work?

As she walked into the director's Santa Monica home and saw the look on his face at their greeting, she knew he had no recollection of her long-ago audition. Just as well. She said hello to his wife and pinched the chubby thigh of the baby on her hip; the child vanished into the nanny's arms soon after. Far off, she heard a dog woof.

She had thought the call would take twenty minutes, maybe thirty, but the director and his wife wouldn't shut up. They talked about his latest film, which Gregg had thought was so-so, but she spoke only of its strengths. She asked about a striking painting above the fireplace and talked to his wife about the benefits of cloth diapers.

Gregg, too, had hired a diaper service for environmental reasons. She didn't mention that she'd reverted to disposable more often, because really it was so much more convenient.

And at their request, she recounted the story of her expulsion from the statehouse.

Was it the thousandth time she'd told it? She'd memorized her telling as well as any Wilson monologue. The saga wasn't so different from your standard Hollywood plot—the cliff at the end of act one, the bootstraps and training of part two, a harrowing victory delivered in the third—and the couple loved it, even as (also like Hollywood) they already knew the ending. How they gushed at her triumph, complimenting her on her fortitude and strong sense of duty. And what good-looking boots they'd been, the wife tutted. She'd gone and ordered herself a pair.

At long last, he withdrew his checkbook. Gregg explained there was an exploratory committee (still under wraps) that could accept funds at levels much higher than the standard individual max. He listened along, chin on his fist. Then, in smearing, jet-black ink, he wrote a large number, one that might persuade the state Democratic party that she knew what she was doing. Not that she needed anyone's blessing, but blessings helped.

As Gregg walked down the director's front path, she waved back toward the happy couple. They waved too, pleased with themselves and their munificence.

This time was so different from the last. Gregg had been in control, patient and plotting and very clear about what she had wanted from the man across the room. She'd gotten it.

Ahead of her, the big black car was waiting, its engine a quiet purr, and the sun was nearly sunk.

24

Sun, Jan 15 at 4:45 PM

Gregg:

Having so much fun decided to stay another nite. Will coordinate w/ Gis about boys+dogs AM dropoffs xo

Back in the car, Gregg texted Zeke. Not about the check, which was part of a larger conversation that would come after they had addressed her pregnancy. Clearly the idea of a congressional run and what was happening in her uterus were related, but the whole universe was related. She didn't want the order of information to imply causality; it wasn't so cut-and-dried. As much as she needed the bandwidth and not to be derailed by pregnancy brain for the upcoming election cycle, she needed that bandwidth and full presence of mind to thrive in *every* cycle, be it moon or sun or season of *The Bachelor*. Why couldn't Zeke understand that? He acted like being pregnant was as easy as setting a kitchen timer, T-minus nine months.

No, for now, she was just telling him about a change in her travel plans, which wasn't a change so much as the second of her eensie untruths that afternoon. She'd be a day late, she typed, but the nanny could manage it. Giselle already always took the boys to their Monday music class (toddler percussion), and dropped off the dogs (four from a litter of show-winning Cardigan corgis, named after characters from *Saved by the Bell*) to their weekly obedience session. The dogs would never be well-behaved, but these regular tune-ups kept them from nipping at the children.

Zeke didn't text back immediately; she hoped it was because he was playing with their sons. She doubted it.

While Gregg was inside the director's house, Giselle had texted. That afternoon she'd led the boys through toddler yoga, she reported, then gotten them both to meditate. Meditate! This was unique from napping (though the schedule accommodated that too); it was developing a capacity for conscientious focus. In the photo Giselle shared, the boys were sitting lotus-style, their eyes closed, small smiles curling the corners of their Kewpie mouths. They'd stayed like that, Giselle wrote, for fifteen minutes.

Gregg shook her head. It was remarkable what that young woman could do. And while she was grateful, it made her failures at anything approaching Zen with her boys feel that much more pronounced. Even if Gregg had been home and reading baby books and mommy blogs rather than reviewing prospect lists in the back of a tank two time zones away, she'd never have figured out how to make them so calm. She wasn't resentful of the nanny, but she was not *not* jealous. She knew a part of it was that the kids were hyperresponsive to the energy around them. They meditated with Giselle; with her they had unexpected bursts of strength and indignation. A few weeks ago baby Zack had close to bitten off her nipple with his three baby teeth and already muscular jaw. After the chomp she had looked into his face and it was fixed back into an angelic expression, even as he had her blood on his lips. What had gotten into him? She had no idea, but understood in a new way that while she'd never be Giselle, with more face time, more focused attention, perhaps her boys would not be such ciphers. She also saw clearly that she was done with breastfeeding.

Zeke pinged: "Fine." She'd have thought he would put up a fight, some guilt-trippy *I miss you* or *The boys are asking for Mama*, but zilch. She shouldn't have expected much of anything; he'd been so distracted lately with congressional hearings and his rocket launch, the tech recession as ominous as a bank of black clouds on the horizon.

As the car glided through LA traffic, she considered that "fine" some more. What were its implications? She tried to put aside her worry as nothing more than anxiety, or pregnancy brain, or denying-it's-really-pregnancy-brain brain, which is even more scattered. Would it also be "fine" to Zeke that, after the boys' FaceTime bedtime and her late dinner with Karen Bass, after an early-morning flight to San Francisco and two breakfast meetings (coffee at the first, muffin at the second), her last appointment of this California swing was with one of his closest tech rivals? It felt a tad turncoaty to call on the executive at his home, but coalition building was essential if this campaign was going to have legs. And it wasn't like they were rivals on this, which was her progressive political agenda, which wasn't hers but all of theirs, and really the only way forward if they wanted to restore a woman's right to choose, if they wanted to preserve a safe and sustainable planet on which to live, if they wanted to save little-d democracy for future generations. They all wanted that, right?

25

Tue, Jan 17 at 10:35 AM

Reba:

Going 4 a walk be back in a couple hrs

Reba woke to a quiet house, Terrence's side of the bed empty. She sat up and stretched, mindful of her fingers. The injured ones—slammed in a car door at nineteen, ending her basketball career just as it was beginning—always tingled in the morning. From there, she followed her energy up her arms and into her shoulders, the vim of her life-force moving down her back, through her trunk and into her haunches, around her pelvis and toward her middle—where it shorted out on a spot below her belly button, a forever reminder of her failure. Her "not yet success," Terry would kindly correct, whenever he could hear her discouraged mutterings or see her scowl. After her last six-week ejection—being pregnant had been their Thanksgiving surprise, followed soon by their not being so, the blood-soaked pads stretching from Cyber Monday through the following weekend—her doctor told her to take a month off, which made her as enraged as when Hillary had answered that call on Saturday night. She was so sick of waiting.

She padded to the toilet, pulled out her tampon, and looked at the red drip in the bowl. That she had her "curse" was a good thing actually: a sad reminder of her vacating womb, but it also meant she was getting back to normal, to a time and an ovulation cycle during which her doctor said they could try again. That was something.

Terrence was, as she suspected, already or still in front of his computer, the glow of his double monitors bathing the room in blue.

"Good morning," she said. He grunted. He handled work stress fairly well—better than she had—but if she got too close, asked too many questions, lingered too long in his doorway, he was liable to get snippy. And that wouldn't help anything—not him and his deadline, not her and her loneliness.

She walked into the kitchen, made herself tea. Terrence hadn't yet recognized his employer's pattern of undoable deadlines (which were always miraculously met), but she had, and was sure that his firm—that all firms, this was a problem of late-stage capitalism—would milk him for every ounce of sweat that they could, lap up every drop of blood they might squeeze from his veins, collect his tears and snot in vials. (Here she imagined her desiccated husband, those gorgeous thighs dried to beef jerky.) He'd been glued to his computer last week; judging by his smell and the precarious pile of empty takeout containers that greeted her on Sunday night, he'd worked straight through her weekend away as well. She knew he just wanted to make a good impression, was still playing catch-up for the big blank space on his white-collar CV, but it was slightly pitiful to see him kowtow to a middle-manager tech bro a decade younger than them both.

Not that she was one to talk. Setting sensible boundaries, fostering humane and respectful work environments—these things had not been a part of her working days. Indeed, all her understanding of professional limits and decent work-life divides and the merits of quiet quitting had come in the years since she'd unquietly quit. (Her exit: She'd made a thoughtful two-month transition plan to address the needs of her clients, which HR took one glance at and said would not be necessary; her email was off by the time she was back at her desk; twenty minutes later she was escorted from the building with a cardboard box of personal effects.) Soon after, Carson had started Reba on a reading list of anti-hustle-culture screeds, the sociology of work, Marxist aesthetics, and books about our bad desk posture. At some point, Reba didn't need Carson's recommendations anymore—the algorithm knew what to do, feeding her more and more titles about how to do nothing.

Now that she could readily identify corporate toxicity, she sensed a healthy work culture wasn't present in Terry's health tech start-up, and what an irony that was. But she had to remind herself that he was still inhabiting that nervous place she'd resided in fifteen years before, across the first seasons of her career: trying to make a good impression, extending that first win into a second opportunity, leveraging it for a third. She could remember how hard she'd worked to persuade people she was worth their investment, and not because she was preternaturally tall and came with a good pedigree. Sometimes she wanted to share with Terry what she'd learned in her recent reeducation—namely, that work wouldn't love you back—but she knew he was far from ready for that speech.

Instead, Reba drank her tea and puttered around for an hour, then decided to head out. She texted her husband in case he might look up and wonder where she'd gone, though she knew he would not.

The day was gray and cool, the city quiet. How many miles had Reba walked at this point? San Francisco was a seven-by-seven-mile square, and she'd crossed it . . . hundreds of times? A thousand? About as soon as walking without a dog was permitted again, she'd started crisscrossing the city, desperate for something to do as the rest of the world Zoomed into virtual workplaces and remote schools, as the hospitals filled and emptied again. She walked by herself, but she wasn't alone. Some days she headed toward the ocean with David Graeber's ghost; other days she'd walk through the city's desolate downtown, listening to the midday call-in show on KQED.

Today she was halfway through an audiobook about the social, political, and economic history of Palo Alto, which felt at once damning—the Boazes' long relationship with the region meant they had helped light the fires—but also so satisfying, as it explained *cause* and *effect* quite cogently. If Leland Stanford hadn't come west, if the Bank of Italy had not changed its name to Bank of America . . . The author worked himself into a lather, explaining the million ifs and thens that had carried them to their sorry current state.

She walked west, thinking about the city and its evolutions. In some ways, her twenty years back east were a blip, warp speed or a wormhole. Except that everything outside her house's blue-shingled walls had changed. In the version of San Francisco she encountered in 2019, the city felt newly icky, overrun with tech bros and oozing privilege. Lambo traffic jams, loud voices and secret speakeasies, so much posturing from the affluent and the ambitious. And the poverty, it was everywhere. Unhoused people sleeping in tents on traffic islands, in parks and parking lots, on the stoops of businessmen's second homes. She knew it was an oversimplification to say that the city had bifurcated into two places, Disneyland and dystopia, but that's how she perceived it. Two universes, forced to share one hilly peninsula.

Reba recognized the pandemic had brought the anguish of death and dying, real and profound suffering for so many, but when Covid hit San Francisco, there had also been a valuable upside. Namely, the city emptied out. Some techies decamped to the suburbs, while others picked random tracts of Montana forest as sites for their new log-cabin mansions, and a whole cruise liner's worth sailed to Miami. It was like a magnet had been dragged over the city, pulling out the jerk-offs and fair-weather friends. Yes, there had been some new and newsworthy crime: A car was stolen with kids inside; that start-up guy'd been murdered in the middle of the street. For a while everyone was in conniptions about the crime spike, panicking that San Francisco was going *Mad Max*, but it turned out to be overblown. The tech bro killing was some frenemy situation, which made more sense than a random, brutal act; the property crimes were generally covered by homeowner's insurance. Homelessness and drug use were difficulties still, but the city was starting to have more productive conversations about accessible mortgage terms and rent control, Narcan distribution and needle disposal.

Reba, if pressed, would admit some pleasure in seeing how the city had emerged from its lockdown gauntlet. Not the still empty downtown, the blank storefronts that'd been favorite restaurants unable to adapt to contactless delivery. But the city's newfound sense of humility . . . She wanted to hold on to it now that things were "normal" again, but the jury was still out on just where things would land. A proportion of the population had come back since the vaccine, and some companies were talking about mandatory returns to the office, but she'd also heard that tech companies were beginning to quietly hemorrhage jobs. A tech recession would bring a different manner of hush to the streets, and she didn't know how the city might react to a second, reeling blow. On the other hand, what did they expect? The industry had exponentially expanded, capitalized on the pandemic's uncertainty and busted supply chains. Everyone knew that what goes up must come down. Did gravity not apply to the California coast?

She reached Outer Sunset and continued onto the Great Highway Trail, heading south. Reba searched for the offing, the horizon line so faint it barely registered. How had she gotten here? Not physically, to the ocean on that Tuesday—she knew she'd arrived on foot, walking because in year two of trying to get pregnant she'd demoted herself from running and other high-impact workouts in the hope that if she treated her lower trunk with extreme care, things might go better. But how had she gotten, existentially, here? Alone, on a wind-whipped winter afternoon, staring at the Pacific, brooding on the future of her city and her life?

She stopped the audiobook, which was talking about weapons research at Stanford. Why had she drunk the Kool-Aid for so long? She'd always been determined not to turn into regal, self-righteous Doris, but the route she'd picked, corporate optimization, was hardly better. How had she missed its underlying flaws? She'd dug the problem-solving, especially when she kept things abstract, more about improving numbers than ruining people's lives. She was good at amelioration, and she really liked being good at something.

She watched the horizon for another minute, then turned around.

• • •

The return always went faster, even as Reba willed it to go on forever, or until Terrence was ready to pay her attention again. As she turned the corner onto Steiner, there were still hours until his quitting time, an empty stretch she'd fill with chores or audiobooks or dread. Reba went up her front steps, thinking about what she'd cook for dinner and when she could start clattering the pots, which was Terry's cue that he should stop working, or at least take a break to acknowledge her existence.

But no pot banging would be needed. As she stepped inside, she saw that her husband was standing silently at the kitchen island, staring at a cup of water. Or was it vodka? As Reba approached, she got a whiff of something strong.

"Did you finish?" Her face was full of expectation. If he was already drinking, he deserved it. This deadline had been extreme, even for his go-hard-or-go-home team.

He nodded, looking grim.

"Why so sad?" She wrapped her arms around him. "You've pulled plenty of all-nighters." She looked at the pleasing spot that cleft his chin. "Was this one that much worse?"

"I was just laid off."

She didn't mean to recoil, but she did. So she pushed into him again, more deliberately this time. This job had been a big step for him—the much-hyped company, the stock options, the validation that a community college–educated veteran could compete with so many Ivy League brats. She looked up into his eyes. His eyes looked so sad!

"Well, fuck a duck," she said, trying to recall the sequence she'd gone through in her decoupling. Had Carson started her with a podcast about core beliefs, or did that come after dissecting and being disgusted by toxic corporate culture? Had she first read that book about how to articulate goals for her new freedom or begun by drafting a list of work-related accomplishments? When did the capitalist critique come in? In any case, it'd taken a long time, and a lot of work, to untangle her knot of emotions. And she'd come into the exercise after having pulled the plug herself, with her extensive track record (her client cost-savings calculator, tallied across years of efficiency audits, was approaching $200 billion when she'd called it quits). Terry's track record was eighteen months. Three inconsequential product updates, including the one he'd filed ten minutes before getting canned.

"Correct." Terrence was taking it well, she thought, or at least he wasn't bawling. The straight vodka was concerning—usually he'd be drinking something more interesting, a dirty martini or a copper-mugged Moscow mule, because once a bartender . . . This, straight booze, meant he was desolate.

She hugged him tighter, nestling her head into his chest. She heard his heart thud through his stinky shirt. Work might not love you back, but she would love him always, she wanted her arms to say. She hoped the press of her hips conveyed that his labor needn't be his identity; that her nose against his breastbone reminded him that identity was who he was, deep down, when he woke up in the morning, before any to-do list could be set, that it was him when he stood in the kitchen in midafternoon and cried. That person, whoever he was, was enough. She needed that to be true, just as much as he did.

26

Sat, Jan 21 at 9:35 PM

Bella:

How's everyone doing with those resolutions? 

In the weeks after Palm Springs, time passed quickly or it slunk slowly along. It was unseasonably warm or very goddamn chilly. There was an ice storm in Chicago, there was an atmospheric river in California, and in New York there was no snow at all, which led area forecasters to declare: This was the most boring winter ever.

All around the women, people were keeping their New Year's resolutions or breaking them with aplomb. Carson was doing okay—not great—at being more patient; it was embarrassing how many times a day she scuttled downstairs to check the mail, even as she sensed his letter would not be there, not yet. (She was, she realized, worse than even her most high-strung high school seniors waiting for word on their college applications.) Bella was not doing great at her goal of quitting her phone—she was up thirty-two minutes a day on average—though now she was mostly Googling speech disorders and trying to see if anyone on TikTok was talking about her problematic beverage. She had memorized its sales curve, which was slow at first but then climbed steeply upward; it stuttered and nose-dived when that coked-up kid had died. As she scrolled TikTok, she found sparse evidence that the booze remained in the zeitgeist. Not like in Q1 of 2022, at least; then, it had been everywhere.

Time would tell whether the women's resolutions would be resolute, but as the clock was so bendy, sprinting and creeping and speed-walking along, none of the women felt good about making any bets. That was why Carson wanted to crack Zariah's frostiness and finally get a tarot reading (a part of her needed to know who'd draw the sun, who'd draw the fool), why Gregg had her psychic to help her connect the starry dots, making shapes out of the darkness between bad feelings and good. (The psychic and her star charts had assisted the Thomas-Graveses in buying their house and picking an auspicious wedding day. When Hillary, the most pragmatic among them, had asked Gregg if she was perhaps overvaluing this woman's advice, Gregg had a two-word rejoinder: "Nancy Reagan." That'd shut Hill up.)

In San Francisco, Terrence had stayed in bed for three days straight, watching his phone, then moved from the bedroom to the living room to continue watching his shows on a bigger screen. He made it through *The Sopranos* start to finish; Reba would dip in and out, and noticed how Tony's swinging countenance—from sad to enraged to briefly optimistic, then sad again—mirrored her husband's own rumbling moods. Then *Succession*, which Reba had no patience for. Why did anyone want to gawk at very rich people behaving badly toward one another? *Trust me*, she wanted to yell—thinking of Doris and her sternness, the nastier of her blue jean cousins—*it happens all the time!* But the show kept her husband occupied, and while Terrence was distracted by lavish melodrama, Reba made some calls. First to Bella, to check on her big brother, who'd been out in Menlo Park since the late 1990s, to see if he might have some leads on work. Bella, busier than ever with trial prep, did not call her back. Reba got a hold of Gregg next. Did she think Terry would be able to move from biotech into tech tech, and if so, might there be a role at Zeke's company? She knew how ridiculous it sounded, to go to the boss's wife and beg for a job, and not even a good one—anything in engineering would do. And Terry was a veteran, didn't that hold some sway in Texas? Gregg listened sympathetically and told Reba to thank her husband for his service, then promised she'd ask around. Gregg wouldn't let anyone she cared about work for her husband—she loved Zeke and knew how to manage his moods, but in the office he had the reputation of being a tyrant. In this situation, all that was beside the point; what was required was a kind and open-ended *Let me see.*

No one was hiring. Terry, it seemed, had been on the front edge of a big wave, and not long after, the thundering crash of a sector-specific recession surged through the Bay, flooding first floors and basements, metaphorically pushing foundations askew. The tech bro party houses on Alamo Square, which had gone quiet for 2020, then come back to life after the first shots were available and been roused to rowdy by late 2021, got sedate again, all except for the AI incubator across the park. Reba hated what tech had done to the city over the past quarter century, but this recoil—fifty thousand jobs cleaved from tech and its adjacent sectors, most of those in or within fifty miles of the city—was gnarly. Meanwhile, hoping for other routes to Terry's healing, she left Jenny Odell on the coffee table, nudged its spine toward him with her toe. "Oh, look at that! *How to Do Nothing*. Hmmm!"

In other arenas of Reba's life, it rained interminably, and they got some not-metaphorical puddles in their usually dry basement. She spoke to their IVF clinic, learned what treatments would cost without Terry's company's health insurance footing the bill, and cursed under her breath. It wasn't that they couldn't afford it; they could. But what an absurdity, the sticker price of motherhood. And that was to get to the starting line; childcare and educational resources introduced a whole second bassinet of expenses, which also brought along another tranche of inequities and barriers to access. It enraged her, and so she walked farther, faster across the city, despite the rain. She could feel her body pushing to run; she willed herself to slow down.

Her father fell off his bike again, but while hardly moving at all, more like tipping over than a crash. He bled profusely, owing to the blood thinners. Her mother didn't mention the incident over their weekly salads; instead, and for several weeks running, she had a real bee in her bonnet about what the national media were calling San Francisco's "doom spiral." The crux of her argument: The Boazes had rebuilt after the 1906 earthquake; San Francisco could handle another round of knocks on the chin. Reba thought Doris was right that the reports were hyperbolic; however, Doris had not been south of Market for a decade. Regarding Hans's injury—what they should have been talking about this whole time—Doris didn't deign to acknowledge it until Reba came over and saw Hans on the couch, his feet on the coffee table, one shin replaced with a shin-sized scab. ("What the literal fuck," she said; "Language," Doris replied.) After Reba chewed them out for hiding the accident and not being careful and not soliciting her help, her mother spent the rest of the afternoon, and most of the subsequent week, watching the atmospheric river fall outside her new, triple-glazed, efficient and expansive picture window. What was Doris thinking? Was she bothered by the urban decay eating away at the city? The state of her former garden, tucked into the slope between their block and Fillmore? In this weather, the backyard and her beautiful beds—and this she knew without needing to see them—would be a slurry of sticks and sludgy mud. She prayed they would recover.

27

Sat, Jan 21 at 9:37 PM

Carson:

I regret my ambition.

Meanwhile in Brooklyn, Donny was sliding a hand-drawn invitation under Carson's door. When she inquired about it, that evening in the kitchen, he explained he was throwing a cocktail party, caviar themed because he'd gotten a sponsor, by which he meant a friend from Moscow via Crown Heights whose family's fish egg import had tanked since the war in Ukraine. "The invasion," he corrected himself before Carson could. She'd instructed him on how to speak about the conflict, how to spell Kyiv. Carson tried not to be schoolmarmish about her roommates' self-indulgent self-care routines and profligate dating (she'd been similarly promiscuous at their age, and while she wouldn't recommend it, she understood the draw), but when the topic was important enough—and international conflict was—she wasn't above a sermon. If he'd had his way, Donny would rely on his socials' algorithms for news. He knew that one day he too would be a loyal NPR listener, but for now, all that felt so middle-aged.

As for his Russian friend, Donny described how Nikolai had evaded arrest in Moscow after making some cheeky anti-Kremlin comments on Facebook. His parents forced him to relocate until things cooled down; now, with mandatory conscription of men between eighteen and thirty, Nikolai couldn't even think of returning until Putin was dead in the ground or he'd turned thirty-one. (Still so young, Carson thought.) Nikolai was not trying to cut in the international sympathy line or take anything away from Ukraine and its struggles, but like leftist Russian ballet dancers and agnostic tennis stars and even their dear, dead Dostoyevsky, Nikolai had taken a hit to his reputation, and he thought he might rehabilitate it by doling out fish eggs to an attractive young crowd. Plus, he had to move some product. The shelf life of caviar was, according to Donny, quite limited.

As Donny described the party's genesis, Zariah, sitting across the table, sighed heavily. She was not exhaling in acknowledgment of the complicated sociopolitical situation for progressive Russians who wanted to support Ukraine (a Venn diagram that, according to Carson, should be waxing gibbous but was instead two adjacent full and contrary moons), but because she'd be away on party day. She took this personally; she and Donny had been two peas in a pod since freshman year. Carson recognized in their bond her own long friendships and valued it on that merit—you stood by your ride-or-die, even if she was slowly werewolfing into a jerk—though she'd have loved to cut Donny loose of his adjoining paper doll. Had she been able to, the mood in the loft would be much more felicitous.

As they talked, Carson admired the invitation's handiwork, Donny's looping calligraphy and his ample use of glitter. She stuck the paper to the fridge. Donny didn't mention how he'd scanned the same sheet before slipping it under Carson's bedroom door, how he'd emailed the JPEG of it to three dozen people, though she assumed he had. He also didn't say the recipient list included Carson's future boyfriend (the last future boyfriend, but nobody knew that yet), how he was a scientist whom Donny'd not seen since before the pandemic but was newly returned to New York. No, on that night, why would that Gmail address be notable among the thirty-five others?

Aside from that blip of glitter, the days of late January proceeded normally in Brooklyn. Carson's agent dodged her for another week, then two—Carson was miffed, but saw in a publishing newsletter that Tina had meanwhile brokered a big deal for a writer acquaintance whose book sounded even less commercially viable than Carson's.

After a shot of splurge bourbon (something Japanese and smoky from a bottle shop on the more gentrified side of Prospect Park), she reminded herself of her resolution—*patience*—and picked up a used copy of *War and Peace*, as if to test her commitment to the cause.

Also: One of Carson's students got into Brown early; another didn't and threatened to jump in front of the G train. Carson expressed empathy to the girl's mother but also reminded her that emotional regulation was way beyond her pay grade; she'd be glad to suggest some resources. One mother continued fretting about SCOTUS and legacy admissions; another asked Carson how eliminating test scores was beneficial, considering the decade her family had spent improving their son's performance in high-pressure test environments. Carson made up something about character development.

And: A former student slipped into her DMs. She tried not to have much contact with past pupils, but former tutees might write with news about graduation or master's program acceptances, a Fulbright or fancy job. (This was not any of those; this was a thirty-two-year-old accountant in Connecticut who wanted to reveal his long-ago crush and send a dick pic.) She deleted it immediately. One of Carson's former boyfriends (from her musicians era) slid into her comments; when, a few clicks later, Carson discovered he was now in Jon Bon Jovi's backing band, she quickly closed the app. It was too depressing—the comparative accomplishment (she wasn't in the backing band for New Jersey's second most famous singer) but also its lameness. After you played "Runaway" one hundred times, did you pass into another, more interesting dimension? Probably not.

28

Sat, Jan 21 at 8:40 PM

Hillary:

Have made/froze many soups. Tbd if rog will eat

In Chicago, no one heard from Miles, but no one was supposed to hear from Miles. His was to be the driest of Dry Januarys, not a drop or a sniff or a poke, not even a quick missive, any communiqué with the outside world—house rules. All contact with family was generally embargoed at this facility, but when he'd inquired about keeping in touch with Roger, and after a round of closed-door discussions, his care team thought the five-year-old might "boost morale," so they made an exception. Not for real, live children (too many variables) but for recordings of one. This meant Hillary took on the task of video production; she sent Roger's daily dispatches to a facility administrator, who sent them along to a PA on Miles's floor, who watched them once at the nurses' station, so as to screen for potential harms and also to note the cutest turns. That way, when she watched the clip again with her hunky patient, standing close so they could both see the tiny screen, she'd be ready to giggle in just the right spots. Here was Roger tying his shoe, there was Roger jumping off a swing and eating a mouthful of wood chips. Roger deciding that he liked strawberries with such aplomb that he ate a whole clamshell of the fruit. (A pound of berries, and after the whole thing with her mother and Reba and the knife! Hillary tried not to take the boy's 180 personally.) Roger drawing a picture of their family—Mom and Dada and Roger, with

Grandma Sheila (who was frowning and somehow still portly, even as a stick figure) lurking in the back.

When Hillary got a curt automated message that her phone's memory was almost full, she thought it apropos. Because it was true, on the phone and in the larger, metaphysical sense—her memory *was* almost full. With ninety-second videos of Roger, and also overloaded with medical data, and stuffed to the gills with the good times and bad times and downright awful stretches of life with Miles. It held the hysterical fear she'd felt when Miles passed out with Roger and wouldn't answer his phone. She'd been in one surgery that morning, scheduled into two more that afternoon, and had tried to reach him between each procedure. She could still hear the ringing, ringing, ringing, then the automated voice disconnecting the call. She remembered the dial tone, and asking herself how she could have married someone who never set up his voicemail.

That bad day took up a lot of memory. So did their wedding (fun until the end), so did their last Passover in Omaha. Eight days without leavened bread was fine for Miles, but apparently he couldn't go the two nights of seder without a fix, and while Hillary was horrified at his stupefaction at the dinner table—he'd drunk Elijah's wine! even she knew not to do that—she was also glad that her in-laws saw just what she was up against.

Her memory also held their lovemaking. When Miles was sober he was stupendous, and the floaty-feeling oxytocin of their coupling would carry Hillary pleasantly along for days. He remained a decent lay up to and including five drinks or one pill.

Other than Miles's stint in rehab, and her wondering wondering wondering if it would work—saying she was suspended across a bed of nails would be understating her emotion—those first weeks of the year were typical for Hillary and young Roger. Miles had been out of the house since the summer, living in a studio ten blocks away (which he'd forfeited before they checked him in), so his absence from the apartment was nothing new. Roger had a good stretch at pre-K—no bites, minimal disciplinary action required, and he learned ROY G. BIV a second time, but the duplicate curriculum didn't seem to bore him. Hillary's work was fine, her schedule a mix of slip-and-falls, car crashes, and new-year-new-you nose jobs. She made and froze a lot of soup. Miles had been the chef in their house, but she could do sensible if bland pots of lentils, a passable tomato bisque.

At night, alone in her bed, Hillary would let her doubts splash around her like the tide coming in. If Miles didn't get better, if the waters that wrapped her tiny island never stopped rising . . . what then? But then she would close her eyes and open them and light would be streaming into the bedroom and her pajamas would still be dry and Roger would be jumping on the mattress, imploring her to wake up and play! And so she would rise, thankful anew for her dear, bouncing coconut.

29

Sat, Jan 21 at 9:42 PM

Bella:

Same same (not about the soup, what Carson said)

Way before New Year's resolutions were declared or discarded, Bella had made herself another promise. In 2023, she would try for partner. Not like she could snap her fingers and be nominated, clap twice and have her packet approved by the voting partners, whistle a high C and get an office with a door . . . but she could insinuate and push and suggest she was eager "for the opportunity." She'd started her quiet campaigning in 2018, but back-to-back babies and the pandemic had put a stop to any forward momentum.

Cushman was all equity, which meant making partner was that much harder, but her situation was, and not just in her opinion, approaching shit-or-get-off-the-pot. Bella was good at Monday-morning quarterbacking her years at the firm, analyzing how and why she'd kept missing her mark. There had been the early flush of Bill and his courtship, which distracted her—not that she was complaining, but she began her tenure at Cushman with divided attention, even as she pulled seventy-hour weeks. There had been her first, creepy practice-group leader; after watching her flirtation with Bill, he thought he might have a shot too, and when she made it clear that he didn't (he was as bald as a cue ball and a blowhard besides), he made her life very difficult, staying just shy of behavior that could be deemed quid pro quo. The internal transfer had been awkward, but doable. Her second boss, an austere woman who specialized in corporate accounting, was polite enough, but then Bella'd gotten pregnant, and her new boss became decidedly icy, staying just shy of behavior that could merit a sex discrimination case. Then she had Gus and wanted to work part-time; then, with no childcare owing to the lockdown, she'd requested to step down to quarter. Her boss had been fine with the drop, though Bella felt that there was a target on her back. Announcing her second pregnancy had elicited another big sigh from her group lead, but she'd managed her account fine. The beverage company's criminal charges were dropped, the civil case with the heart-bursting boy settled, and now they were heading toward their last hurdle, the showdown with the DA's office.

Bella had broached the subject of promotion again in the fall, told her boss that she was interested in trying for partner. Only if she thought it appropriate, of course. The older woman agreed, but Bella was unsettled by her offhanded "It's getting late, isn't it?"

And there was one caveat, the older woman added. Bella would need an additional, noteworthy win to make her case "solid." Given the slate of upcoming clients and court dates, that win would have to be with the alcoholic caffeinated beverage case. Bella thought this was propitious, as the beverage conglomerate's in-house counsel loved her (without prompting, or at least with the gentlest prod, June had put in a call to Bella's boss to say how *invaluable* a team member Bella was, wasn't she due for a promotion?), but Bella recognized the challenge. She was required to produce not just a happy client but a public win. Actuarial success aside (they all knew that sometimes it was smarter to settle), the firm had been folding many hands of late, and in the court of public opinion and biz dev, Cushman was starting to get a reputation.

"Understood!" Bella was louder than she meant to be in her affirmation, but point taken. She hurried back to her desk and circled the case's adjudication schedule on her personal calendar. She had this.

For months, the court date remained far away—or not far, but there was so much to do between here and there. The fall's preliminary hearings were intense but mercifully stretched by religious and patriotic holidays. It wasn't that people drank a lot of alcoholic caffeinated beverages on Veterans Day or Thanksgiving, but if Bella didn't win, they'd never be able to again, and what were we thankful for if not our freedom? Over to-go turkey from Citarella, because no one had the energy to deal with extended family, she'd tried out this argument, the roughest draft of her opening statement, on Bill; he was encouraging. More depositions, more prep, and suddenly 2023 started and she went to Palm Springs and came back and court was just weeks away. There was still so much to do.

Hurtling into the homestretch, Bella pushed herself into the style of work marathons she'd done early on, back when she was trying to impress her boss and Bill both. Goodbye to exercise, so long to meal prep. The boys bathed not nearly as much as they used to; they arrived at nursery school ninety minutes earlier than their previous routine and often stayed until closing, or after, until someone—Bill and Bella locked in a cross-island staring contest to see who would answer the call from the pissed-off preschool manager first—conceded to retrieve them. (Not without penalty; after six the school charged an additional four dollars per minute.) Bill was occupied at work, his company acquiring some health tech start-up; even more, he was averse to solo parenting, ill-equipped as he was. When he'd ask Bella, *How do I do this?* or *Where do I find that?*, she wanted to scream, *Weren't you paying attention?* His answers were meant to flatter: *Why would I, when you had it on lock?* A blue flame in her heart would surge at the compliment, but she'd quickly move to tamp it out—she'd had to learn every mundane detail of how to keep their boys alive, clean, and content. Over time, bedtime routines and snack preferences had displaced her knowledge of Shakespeare (tenuous at best) and algebra and some stuff she really should remember from her torts class. Bill should be subject to the same little-kid curriculum, be put to the toddler tests rather than always pssting her for answers.

As Bella focused on the upcoming trial, Bill's pleas for her to *please come home* morphed. Where before, Bella had heard in them the Pavlovian ding-a-ling of her family's need, now she just heard the clang of hassle. "Let him do bath time," she cackled as she gave herself a French shower late one night in the firm's women's room. "What's for dinner?" he texted, and she replied with a shrugging lady emoji. They could go to that awful pizzeria on Lex and get orange grease all over themselves, for all she cared. "Bill Jr. had an accident." Boohoo, she thought as she checked her phone under the conference room table, her colleagues dissecting a beverage executive's deposition atop the mahogany surface. Did he really want her to get in a cab and come clean it up? Fat chance. She typed: "Pullups in the closet."

In Bill's messages, in the late-night greetings and early-morning goodbyes they did manage to exchange in person, she heard how he struggled. But she didn't note any acknowledgment of the fact that they had *cut her open. Twice.* And like that wasn't enough, she'd given one boy Bill's name, the other his father's (and grandfather's and great's; they had Gustons going back to the founding of the nation). This passing of the baton, from her to Bill, was only fair.

There was enough chaos brewing at the office besides. The icy paralegal who thought he was not being fairly compensated. A co-litigator who liked the sound of his voice too much. Her assistant, Darcy, who typically had the patience of a saint, had been grouchier lately. Bella battled to secure the opening statement, and when she did it felt like a victory, though she knew the win that mattered was not this but a notch under W in the firm's ledger.

And there was the client rep, June, whom Bella would call a friend after their two years of working together. In the first weeks of the year, June seemed cagey, slower to return Bella's calls, not as chatty on the phone. What was going on? Bella asked, point-blank, one afternoon while the women discussed the DA's office. The way June hemmed and hawed and blatantly made up some vague line about personal issues (like this woman hadn't heard all about Bella's personal issues, mastitis and her withered sex drive and the last time she'd done coke, which was maybe inappropriate but also totally relevant to the discussion) . . . Bella was shook.

Were they thinking of settling? she asked. June did not say yes, but she didn't say no.

Bella did not want to settle, because she was a litigator, pugnacious, at her best while waving her arms in front of a jury and judge. She'd been preparing her opening for months, and it was great, the sort of thing Carson could've written, that poetic and incisive, something Gregg could've delivered from the stage or statehouse floor. She'd prepped their witnesses and studied potential cross exams, could call up each person's stat sheet and vulnerabilities in a split second. And there were her outfits—she had three weeks' worth planned, and they all fit too. Each looked assertive and intelligent and chastely sexy, with enough repeated separates so as not to seem extravagant, but not so many as to appear thrifty or absent-minded. Instead of saying any of that, she reminded June that they were probably going to win, maybe even launch a countersuit for reputational damage. Wasn't kicking ass worth the diminutive chance of loss?

When Bella's boss got wind of that pesky word coming up, she reminded Bella that even if the bev co's actuary's risk assessment was sound, even supposing this was why God made liability insurance . . . settling, after Cushman's string of necessary but not ideal "resolutions," would be "suboptimal." Bella said nothing beyond "yes" and "I understand" and "of course," though she bristled at how her boss used the term *roll over*, like there was nothing worse in the world than being a submissive dog. Bella had grown up with a meek Italian greyhound rescue named Sonata, and there'd been nothing wrong with her, except for whatever three years of constant breeding had done to her psyche and bladder control.

As much as she disagreed with her boss, Bella shuddered to think of the alternative, another year—another decade?—in the associate pool. Soon promotion to partner would not even be a possibility; she'd be shunted over to the has-been track, training the summer interns, managing the paralegal pool, being forced to smile like she enjoyed watching younger lawyers climb right past her, waving ta-ta as they went. The idea of it made her want to wail, to punch Bill in the stomach for being so canny about his own career trajectory, to reach for an extra-large can of that caffeinated alcoholic carbonated fruit punch, and chug.

30

Sat, Jan 21 at 8:43 PM

Gregg:

Less interested in New Year's resolutions than making it to the end of the month 😬

As for the last voice in this five-part round, deep in the heart of Texas, Gregg had a few more weeks in the January legislative session, a few more months in her thirties, a few more clicks righty-tighty in her fortitude before she blew a gasket. Each day was excruciating, the queasiness and mounting conviction about what she had to do; knowing it would not get easier even as she moved, one floor debate and procedural vote and hallway argument at a time, toward the end-of-month break during which she might feasibly follow through. She burst into tears in a committee meeting, she couldn't keep down anything but saltines, and eighteen men—twelve of them in the statehouse, while she was wearing credentials around her neck—called her "darling." At home, she tried to avoid sex and attempted to persuade Zeke that she, too, was doing that Dry January thing. "A month without merlot?" He sounded skeptical but did not push further. He was so busy across those January weeks, his mind already halfway to the moon, that it was easy enough for Gregg to dodge and weave and not look him in the eye for anything more than a glance.

She thought about calling Hillary—it was still legal to terminate in Illinois, and Hill's team doctor status could be helpful in navigating her care—but Hill's apartment was tiny (it could've fit into Gregg and Zeke's master suite). Also, Roger was a maniac—the Koenigs' place wouldn't offer a restful recovery. She thought about calling Bella, but Bella was preoccupied with work. She thought about Reba—California had also protected women's rights—but going to Reba for help terminating a pregnancy as she endured so many fertility treatments would be cruel. Could she *give* Reba the baby? Gregg turned over that idea for all of a day, trying to decide if it was brilliant or bonkers before coming to the conclusion that Zeke would never ever go for that.

That left Carson, which was where Gregg should've started. That Carson already knew about the pregnancy was reason enough to go to Brooklyn. The fewer things Gregg had to explain, the better. Also, Carson didn't have or want children, and this was an advantage. If Gregg went to her mom friends with her situation, they might also, and maybe inadvertently, convince her against going through with it. Because while they'd readily affirm she was spread too thin, maybe they'd also mention how much they had loved the cooing baby phase. Gregg felt susceptible to such entreaties, because she had loved it too. She had loved it and had wanted it to go on, for her children to forever be discovering their feet and triumphantly holding up their big, fuzzy heads. But *forever* was different from wanting it to start over *again*.

Gregg's logic was fighting an uphill battle against eons of human development; intellectually, she knew it was a feat of evolution that babies smelled so good (except for when they didn't), that there were hormones that made mothers feral with love (except for when they weren't). She understood that, biologically speaking, human life could function with very little sleep, even as she felt dysfunctional, glitchy for the first six months of each boy's life. Zeke had offered to help with overnight wake-ups, but had also noted that nine times out of ten, the babies were crying for milk, and so he'd posed the question: If she had to be up anyway, why should they both lose sleep? They were both logical this way, cunning and careerist even at two in the morning, and that was part of what she loved about him. *Had* loved? No, that was her residual sleep deprivation, wiggling in a way that just looked like doubt. She'd agreed with Zeke's reasoning at the time—he was so busy, in the middle of a string of can't-stop-the-train product launches and funding rounds—but watching his mummy-like form, how he'd seal himself off (eye mask, earplugs, moisturizing mittens) for eight hours every night, sometimes it was all she could do not to smother him with a hypoallergenic pillow.

During those first weeks of the year, her babies, now sixteen and twenty-nine months, could sense her distraction even as she tucked them into bed each night. They were sharing a bedtime, which everyone told Gregg would make things easier, but she'd not seen much improvement. Their new ritual was three stories; each boy picked one, the last was dealer's choice. "What's the matter, Mama?" They looked up from their picture books, happy fire trucks and cowboys and multicultural families. And what was it, really? These tiny humans were so precious, the best thing in her life. Didn't she want more of that? She had the hips to carry a pregnancy (if she could get through the morning sickness of her first trimester); she had the resources to give them a good life (Gregg wanted to employ Giselle until Zacky was eighteen). What was the matter, indeed?

Between the kids and work, she had shaken every penny out of her emotional purse, smashed the piggy bank and gathered all the nickels and dimes of waking consciousness. It wasn't like she was foreclosing on mankind's future by stopping now—she'd made two humans in three years' time. But a simple majority—two of them, one of her—felt different than staring down three, the four or five or fifteen Zeke wanted to merrily roll along. Too many kids and they'd have to get a special big car, and how would she feel about her fuel efficiency then?

And also, maybe glowing the brightest among all her protests, was the sheer perpetualness of these last few years—pregnant, then pregnant, then pregnant again. With each, she felt her personhood, her ideas and ambitions and bodily autonomy shrinking, being supplanted by an identity more like a farm animal or an incubation machine, maybe that sad woman on TV with nineteen kids. She wasn't sure which metaphor was most apt for her situation, but none of the comparisons made her feel great.

• • •

And so the women, who had so recently been spooning and hugging and threatening one another with knives, each followed her own path farther into the new year. They thought of one another, cheered and chafed and talked a little trash—but then felt bad about even the well-meaning criticisms and thought up something nice to say. Mostly, they pursued their individual lives, their singular paths, their own tines on the five-pronged fork. Some studied the upcoming topography in advance and stepped forward with dread; some plowed ahead solely with the compass of her nose and hoped for the best. They all, at some point, thought about *how* and *if only* and *what if* they might work together, in concert or collaboration? It'd be Gregg's *Captain Planet* Planeteers, *Our powers, combined!* Together they could lift all roadblocks and throw them at the land mines in their paths, clearing the way and neutralizing the threat in one fell swoop. Then, their leftover rubble could be poured over quicksand to fill in those pesky sinking pits. Presto chango, every route would be rendered utterly passable.

But as much as they loved one another, offered advice and hooted from the sidelines (as if to make up for Bella's indifferent parents, the friends had regularly attended her soccer matches through college, which was overkill for coed intramural but also fun, to scream full-throatedly for Bella the Destroyer to *Destroy, destroy, destroy!*), they knew they could only do so much to intervene, to hop onto another woman's silvered tine, to prop her up or redirect her around her individual dangers.

When they had all lived under one roof, the dorm and then the off-campus place (a firetrap, and frigid all winter, but charming in its way), they moved through life together—eating matching meals, PMSing concurrently. Throwing their dirty laundry together into the hamper and washing it with high, absolving heat. But that was so long ago. Now, except for those rare convergences—their faces all pressed against the funicular's glass, Lemonheads melting on their tongues—they were far apart. From a distance, a friend could offer some things: meal delivery, flower delivery, the delivery of gossip about a college beau that would send them all cackling. But none of these five were saints (as Reba had noted to Terry, it was difficult *not* to be self-absorbed by the fifth decade of one's life). None was so selfless as to sacrifice her own journey for that of another. Ahead of each woman lay too much sparkling possibility and, importantly, too many things to get done.

Unless, unless. Unless that is what friendship really is—undoing the fractal, doubling back down your tine, muttering "Fuck the fork!" because your friend needs you. Traversing parallel paths through everyday life is fine and well until it is not, until you're running through the underbrush from your trail to another's in an all-out sprint, blackberry brambles and hidden stumps and squelchy ground be damned. Your shoes might get ruined, but there are more shoes. Running like that: Some situations call for nothing less.

31

Sun, Jan 22 at 10:01 PM

Reba:

Hi Gregg! Ter & I just saw you on SVU! Your corpse looked great!

Sorry just realized it's midnight in Texas. Sleep well!

When Gregg was acting, her primary (first and most serious) focus was on the text, whether the script was Pulitzer worthy or purely bingeable. She'd seen her mom's process for birthing a poem and had, in playdates and teatimes with other poet-moms, peered into the lives of Charlene's writer friends, their messy desks and cluttered kitchens, citations from the Poetry Society hanging proudly on their walls. How hard they worked to eke out fourteen lines; clearly they deserved her esteem. Charlene taught Gregg about the Black Mountain poets (the family had made not one but three pilgrimages to the North Carolina campus), about remembering her breath and how, with breath, the words would follow. On top of that, or after it, Gregg had spent so many late nights talking about writing with Carson. Carson, who was a devotee of duration, had an iterative drafting process that became, through persistence, more of a chrysalid one. Gregg *believed* in Carson and her painstaking process of metamorphosis. She believed in butterflies!

So, it started with someone else's expression. She wanted to acknowledge the effort of the playwright or screenwriter; she wanted to understand their intention for the role, then explode it to new and unthinkable dimensions. That was collaboration—creating more than one person believed they could achieve on their own. It was the multiplier effect, the *Captain Planet* phenomenon IRL.

However, she wasn't so theoretical or aloof that she'd not acknowledge the audience as the third leg of her stool. Was it Jimmy Stewart who said, "Don't treat your audience like customers, they are always partners"? Someone said that; someone said, "To have great poets you need great audiences" (that was her mother, paraphrasing Whitman). To state the obvious: If she was lucky, there were people in those seats or in front of that screen, and she had better treat them right. Some audience members, like Carson, and Gregg's mother, and even her dad (he didn't always like her roles, some of which were pretty unhinged, but he respected her performances, the physicality and intelligence required), knew what to expect from her (anything and everything). Carson had memorized several of Gregg's scripts herself (whatever it took to get Gregg off book; Carson even read scenes in the bathroom as Gregg showered, and could remember Gregg's shouts of "Line!" over the plinking of water on tile), while Charlene had written an entire book of sonnets about her vagina (you could not astonish that woman). But others of Gregg's friends, like Bella, like Bella and Bill . . . Gregg could still recall when they'd first started dating and come to a downtown show, Bella so proud of her artsy friend. (Gregg had gotten used to her unintentionally patronizing compliments long ago.) How Bill had blanched at the play's cursing, the nudity (much of it by Gregg's character). Both of their faces had shown their consternation, but Bella was short enough to get lost in her seat, while Bill was tall in the torso and had such a big head. Not *big* arrogant (though he was pompous, the women later concurred), but physically large. Gregg could see him from the stage; they were in the second row or third, and with his wide shoulders in that crisp white shirt and his square jaw, he was as broad and bright as a lantern. And he'd looked horrified.

Afterward, the couple had come backstage. It was so impressive how she was able to flip a switch and bellow, Bill said, adding, "Bella tells me you're usually such a nice, quiet person." He meant it as a compliment, so Gregg smiled politely. She knew if she raised her voice, if she moved too quickly, even here in the dressing room, her frizzy wig resting on its stand, her makeup partially removed, they were liable to jump right out of their skin.

And how did she do it, transform herself alongside the text? It was her training, high school drama club and college productions and Alexander Technique workshops, the foundational *yes, and* of improv theater. It was also a small secret; Gregg understood that inside her was a tiny but vital but dangerous creature, a violent and self-certain aspect that usually resided, curled into a ball, just behind her breastbone. She let it out onstage when the role required it; she released it when she'd taken a certain dose of a certain type of hallucinogen or had three ounces of premium tequila in thirty minutes; she allowed it to escape in bed some nights, Zeke holding her hips hard against his and begging for more. But mostly, now that she was retired from acting, the creature stayed out of sight, snug back in its resting place, deep inside her chest.

Emphasis on *mostly*.

Often, in those first Texas years, as she learned her way around the capitol complex, its subterranean corridors and the huge, soaring rotunda—she always stopped by the portrait of Ann Richards to pay her respects and was also figuring out the place's written procedures and unspoken norms, she wondered, Could people see it pulsing through her blouse? Plenty of folks eyed her warily; maybe they had spotted her miniature fury, or maybe it was because they weren't comfortable with a youngish woman clomping down those grand halls, heading determinedly toward her very own seat of power.

Did it give off a scent, her creature? She asked herself this as, back at home, one child, then the second latched to her breast, Zacky practically shoving Xavier out of the way. Could they sense the feral creature, curled so close to their noses?

She thought of the creature again that January, as she lay awake night after night, stirred not to comfort her boys but by her own uncertainty. She tried to push down the day's worry, and the next day's, and the next. Instead, she asked herself, Did it have its own heartbeat, a *lub-bub* thudding at a pace different from her own? She listened for its presence on those lonely nights, but only ever heard Zeke's soft snoring.

32

Mon, Jan 23 at 8:04 AM

Maggie Leonard:

Hi Boss, sent you draft text for gun legis. Tldr it's f'ed up, but looking forward to your thoughts.

Once she moved to Texas and swapped out her acting spurs for custom-made cowboy boots (she got an early, helpful piece of political advice: a pair of Luccheses would go far with her new crowd), Gregg returned to the text. Now, instead of scripts, the state budget was her muse; she scrutinized firearm regulation proposals, looking for her cues. As she read the documents, she brought her own energy and ideas to the proposed legislation and, thus prepared, marched into the chamber, ready to perform. Sometimes she entered with a spirit of collaboration propelling her step; more often, it seemed, she found herself approaching the floor with a tailwind of roil and rage.

As she transitioned into this new chapter, she had, for a time, feared that someone might make a reel, not of her career highlights but of her most *most* moments from her acting days, TV clips and some of those theater publicity shots where she looked deranged. There were enough syndicated reruns, theater reviews, documentation out there that if opposition researchers took things out of their original artistic contexts and put them into nefarious new ones, they might sink her nascent political career. (Zeke's optimistic take was that it would simply boost her residuals payouts.)

She shouldn't have lost sleep over it, as in due course, her shouting on the floor supplanted her theatrical highlights for vim and vigor.

Gregg was halfway through her first senate term when she became a mother. After Xavier, Gregg found no provisions at the statehouse for proxy votes or Zoom participation. She had to be there, present and persistent, to have her voice heard and vote counted. So Xavier started coming to work with her at two months. She could afford childcare (they even had a nanny, Giselle's predecessor, whom Gregg left at home watching daytime talk shows while Gregg's staffers passed the swaddled baby around the office), but Gregg had a point to make. The very politicians who celebrated their "mascots"—headshots of the kids and grandkids of legislators were featured in the photo display of each elected class, going back a century—could not bend to the exigencies of those same children's existence. And so Xavier's presence became a cutie-pie symbol of congress's duplicity. Gregg's voting situation come the January legislative session (Xavier all of four months then) was unique to elected officials, but she saw there was insufficient support for new mothers all over the state. Maternity leave was permitted because of the federal Family and Medical Leave Act, and a few weeks of it came with compensation, but it was hardly enough time for most new moms to bond with their babes and recover from the trauma of childbirth.

Relatedly, in service of the lactating women of the state capitol and her own aching breasts, Gregg converted a large janitorial closet in her office into a lactation room—the statehouse's first. Obviously the capitol's union plumbers were behind Gregg; they got hot water and cold hooked up within three days of the work order. The place was often in use with staffers from both sides of the aisle.

Between word and deed, Gregg became a hero for the mom, mom-adjacent, and mom-appreciating communities of the state capitol. But while one group of colleagues went out of their way to say thanks, another group, the ones old enough to be inattentive grandfathers to boys like her son (and they were all grand*fathers* in this huffy group; the senate's one geriatric woman, a gallerist from Marfa, absolutely loved Xavier and brought him a Chinati Foundation onesie), were upset by the child's presence and annoyed that the lactation room's new plumbing reduced the water pressure in the second-floor men's washroom. Things came to a head one day when the baby interrupted a budget vote with his big-lunged wail, and Gregg, unwilling to miss the vote by ducking into her repurposed broom room, unbuttoned her shirt and unhooked her nursing bra and brought the child's mouth to her breast, right there on the floor. This grabbed the livestream cameraman's attention; he quickly swiveled his camera and refocused his lens.

The baby's outburst, and Gregg's solution, had driven the geezers crazy. What a breach of decorum! The lieutenant governor, aghast at his dais, gaveled assertively, called her out of order. Gregg's cold stare and even-keeled clapback—Xavier still attached—had been superb, and the internet had a field day with the footage. Memes were made; that same clip was picked up by MSNBC and Fox News. Anchors introduced her segment with lines like "Take a look at this firebrand" and "Here's one hot mama." They were reductive, but it also got Gregg's point across. She was a force to be reckoned with.

Her city loved that flash of boob, her seething ferocity. People began stopping her around town, thanking her for her service. It was flattering to be recognized at the farmers market, but Gregg's new status as local celebrity took some time to embrace. For so long she had assumed she'd attain recognition as an actor—*didn't I see you in* arm touches at the grocery and *you look so familiar* squints across crowded restaurants. But because of her chin shape and the slight asymmetry of her eyes, a hundred minor deviations from standardized American beauty, her star never did rise over LA. She would just have to pivot to her strength and second major (economics) and enter the zeitgeist via Texas. More local news stations, then cable, began to set up their tripods in the chamber, waiting for another performance.

Her next reprimand—and her next popularity boost—came when they were still in the proposal stage for SB 8, that legislation that offered $10,000 checks to anyone who ratted out their possibly pregnant neighbors. It was early days, the sponsoring senators testing the waters, the handful of progressives in the chamber struggling to pick their jaws up off the floor. Even as her colleagues were still sputtering their disbelief, Gregg gathered herself, got a staffer to bring her a print copy of the bill, and speed-read the text. She was aghast at the five-figure bounty, appalled at the idea of criminalizing abortion after six weeks. Who even knew she was pregnant by then? Not everyone.

Sure, as she took off her left boot, it looked as though she might throw it. She remembered the shoe thrown at Bush II, as did some others in the chamber; she saw, as she raised her arm, a few senators duck. But instead of sending that delicious leather airborne, she shifted her grip around the toe and the boot came down hard against her desktop.

She hadn't meant to pull a Khrushchev; it was more convergent evolution, a snap-judgment idea for how she might get the chamber's undivided attention. And she needed all eyes on her, all ears listening to what she had to say, because what she said next was "This is immoral!" *Rap, rap.* The thick wooden heel made a satisfyingly loud sound. She pushed the desk's blotter out of the way, the noise grew. "You should be ashamed of yourselves!" *Rap, rap, rap.* Her banging produced a cluster of tiny dents in the desk's polished wood. "Hunting down your neighbors like they are criminals for making decisions about what is best for their families?" *Rap, rap.* The blotter fell to the floor, as did her pens. "I am enraged and you should be too!" *Rap, rap, rap.*

When she was done, she felt a trifle sorry about the dents, so many waxing moons, but regretted nothing else of her percussive performance. She slipped on the shoe again and collected her writing utensils from the carpet.

For her outburst, she'd been censured a second time. Later, in the lieutenant governor's chambers, she was given a stern warning about her breach of decorum. "A third strike, Senator Thomas-Graves . . ." The older man cracked his knuckles. She didn't like baseball and could hardly follow the game when she'd go to meet and greets at Dell Diamond. She knew to shout, "Express!" when one of the guys in white hit the ball, but that and what she'd gleaned about the sport from *Fences* was it. Even still, she knew what this man meant with his "three strikes" and his knuckle pops.

Gregg called her mother to recount the latest. Charlene patiently waited for her daughter to talk herself tired, then reminded her that she had ample fortitude and could get this job done. But Gregg didn't have to do it alone. "There are bad people out there, no doubt about it," Charlene said. "But there's good too. Trust your constituents. They've got your back."

Her constituents. Gregg represented Austin, a bright blueberry in the state's strawberry puree. And she loved the place, having fallen fast and hard for Zeke and his hospitality (after the cast party was a candlelit dinner, was a dance hall, was a late-night dip at the springs, was a moonlit drive in his midnight-blue Ferrari; every night of the production, he'd pick her up at the stage door and show her a great time), but also for the town itself, its taco stands and moonlight towers and that bucolic mid-city swimming hole. The love feeling, as indicated by her string of easy elections, was mutual.

Another reassurance: federal backstops. Because that bounty rule, wicked as it was, had initially been hypothetical; America's women had national abortion protections that would override any harebrained state law. Her health policy analyst advised that if the bounty law went forward, the circuit court or the Supreme would rule it unconstitutional. That was a comfort, like the bump-bump-bumping of the lane-edge rumble strip.

But then the Supreme Court did review the Texas law and punted it back to the state, meaning her colleagues' draconian measures could go into effect. "At least we still have Roe v. Wade, amiright?" she texted a progressive colleague after thirty seconds of screaming into a couch cushion in her office. But then, after *Dobbs* won at the Supreme Court—fifty years of precedent, gone in a day—Gregg skipped screaming into upholstery and went straight to wild sobs, right along with most of her staff. Word was that an 1850s abortion law would go into effect in thirty days. Gregg had thought topping out at six weeks was ludicrous and civil penalties were uncalled for.

But those dumb rules were better than zero weeks, better than criminal prosecution and six-figure fines. Plainly put, they were screwed.

The Supreme Court decision, the ancient abortion ban (it had been written in cursive—they didn't even have typewriters then!) were not texts she could work with. First, she tried a rational approach, dismantling the prose. Across several special sessions of the Health & Human Services Committee, she brought in experts (including her own gynecologist, head of obstetrics at the university hospital) to explain why women still deserved the right to make decisions about their bodies. This had, despite their persuasive arguments, no discernible effect; *Roe* was still gone, the bounty still bountying, and the trigger ban's start date (late August 2022) was approaching like a runaway train. It wasn't until weeks later, another special session—mere days before the ban went into effect, and while her colleagues were discussing some particularity of care for women with ectopic pregnancies (ovarian ruptures, catastrophic blood loss . . . none of the gynecologist's gimlet-eyed points were seeming to budge the pro-lifers from their stumps)—that Gregg spotted her next move, clear as the fifty-yard line at Texas Memorial, high noon on a sunny game day. Rather than dreading censure, tiptoeing around the warned third strike, she had to go barreling toward it, tits out and screaming. The need for reproductive freedom hadn't embedded itself in her uterus at that point, but it was still her issue, because it was 52 percent of the population's issue, which made it everyone's issue, because everyone had a mother or a daughter or a sister or a cousin, someone in their life who would have to make a choice at some point. Gregg suddenly understood that a woman's right to choose was going to be her Sputnik or her Cuban Missile Crisis, her launchpad or her burial plot. She was fine with that.

And so, as her colleagues discussed "acceptable" mortality rates for expectant mothers with congenitally deformed fallopian tubes, Gregg took off her left designer cowboy boot again and then she took off her right one, and clutching the two hand-cobbled hardwood heels, she started playing her desk like a set of timpani. The boots made such a nice, resounding bang. Whatever fear she'd had that people might label her *too* progressive, that political operatives might dig up the more lascivious episodes of her acting career, whatever concerns she had about anyone or anything else in the world were shoved off. This was happening.

The senator from Beaumont stopped what he was saying about fetal tissue—he called it "a mother's unborn baby," even if it was going to explode the woman's abdomen months before becoming viable—and stared in astonishment as Gregg explained, in syncopation with her improvised mallets, that "If." *Bang!* "We." *Bang!* "Do." *Bang!* "Not." *Bang!* "Protect." *Bang!* "The lives." *Bang!* "Of women." *Bang!* "In this state." *Bang!* "We will." *Bang!* "All." *Bang! Bang!* "Have." *Bang! Bang!* "Blood." *Bang! Bang!* "On our hands." *Bang! Bang! Bang!* Her desk was dented beyond the reaches of sanding and refinishing, her throat was burning with strain, and she just kept going. "Tell me." *Bang!* "Senator." *Bang!* "Do you." *Bang!* "Want your." *Bang!* "Daughter's." *Bang!* "Fallopian tube." *Bang!* "To rupture?" *Bang!* "Do you." *Bang!* "Want her." *Bang! Bang!* "To bleed out?" *Bang!* "With." *Bang!* "This." *Bang!* "Bill." *Bang!* "You'll have." *Bang!* "Your fetal tissue." *Bang!* "And your." *Bang! Bang!* "Sense." *Bang!* "Of." *Bang!* "Morality!" *Bang! Bang! Bang!* "But no more." *Bang!* "Daughter." *Bang! Bang! Bang!*

The live-stream cameraman was on point that day, quick to find Gregg, then just as fast to wheel from the flecks of spit leaving her mouth to the senator from Beaumont's ashen face and sputtering reply. "Are-are-are you th-th-threatening me and my-my family?"

Ad-lib as it was (those high school improv classes' *yes, and* still such a useful tool), Gregg was ready with her line. "No, sir. But you are threatening me and my family, and I." *Bang!* "Cannot." *Bang!* "Let." *Bang!* "That." *Bang! Bang!* "Stand!"

There were maybe twenty pro-choice protesters in the gallery that day, and they cheered when she was through, banging their own sneakers and pumps and wedge sandals against the balcony's brass rail. There were two dozen pro-life senators on the floor, and they looked at their sock-footed colleague as if she'd been percussing not on her desk but running around the room, popping each one of them square on the forehead.

The legislature booted her for breach of decorum that afternoon.

33

Tue, Aug 30, 2022 at 3:45 PM

Gregg:

OMG someone just sent me a meme of me. Does this make me internet famous?

Carson:

Youve been internet famous for like 2 yrs

Before the expulsion, or maybe as it was heading toward its inevitability, Zeke had covertly planned a party for "a few friends" in the Thomas-Graveses' capacious backyard. He said it was a Labor Day celebration, because he knew she loved labor (Carson had rubbed off on Gregg, and even though Texas was a right-to-work state, Gregg would make sandwiches and pour coffees for any picket line in her district), and because he was courting some AI engineers, trying to woo them from the Bay to Austin, and they, he said, would be visiting. She'd offhandedly okayed his plan, initially still devastated by *Dobbs*, then distracted by the incoming trigger ban, then so disturbed by the stinging slap of her dismissal that she hardly paid attention to the gathering's catering order or its invite list. Once she'd been booted, she wanted to cancel the party, to slink into the gully of a dried-up arroyo and die, but Zeke cajoled her to keep the party on the books, asked that she just "make an appearance." Added, "For me." She'd grudgingly agreed. It was a joint project, their world domination, and understood between them that they'd alternate who was in the driver's seat. For the Labor Day party, it was Zeke's stretch of miles, and even if she felt low, she wanted it to go well for him. Said another way, they were partners in all things (or nearly all, per the prenup), career boosting included. So all right, fine. She'd make an appearance, meet these engineers, act like the world wasn't collapsing all around them.

The veritable roar of the crowd when she stepped onto the patio with a fresh bowl of guacamole, the corgis surging around her ankles, had scared her near to death. She'd had no idea she was stepping into a fundraiser and a media event (she'd have worn different shorts, done her hair, maybe), but between Zeke and her staffers and their quick reframes, it'd become both. The AI recruits from California were in attendance, sure, but so were a range of local luminaries, there to wish her well and hand her checks. Someone had even brought a backup pair of Luccheses, in case she "wore through hers while fighting for her constituents." Zeke had flown down her parents, who, miracle of miracles, had slipped away from campus the first week of the semester, and few things had ever felt as good to Gregg as her mother's arms around her that afternoon. Though Matthew McConaughey's arms, big and strong and squeezing across her back, also felt nice.

That celebration had been the boon that got her through the subsequent week, which was both pretty good and very bad. The district council had reinstated her in an emergency meeting that Tuesday night; she was back to the statehouse on Wednesday. That was the good part; the bad was that abortions were still illegal, criminalized, and impossible to obtain within the state. And so she got back to work through the fall, endured that brutal midterm. (She'd done fine with her reelection, but poor Beto!) Zeke had consoled her on election night, but that evening's attentiveness may have been what got her pregnant; her math was iffy. Thanksgiving 2022, Gregg knew there was a lot to be thankful for—her husband and toddlers and fur babies, her still healthy parents, an electorate that would vote her to the moon and back. But as she carved their organic, free-range turkey, she felt not grateful (which was different from *un-*) so much as despondent.

Christmas came on the heels of Thanksgiving, as it always seemed to do. The kids got an elaborate play structure for the backyard; the dogs did too (apparently Zeke *had* noticed when Gregg binge-watched reruns of the AKC agility competitions on late-night cable). But while kids and dogs squealed with joy, Gregg and Zeke just got through it. They were both beleaguered by work, both busy thinking about Washington. Gregg was analyzing the demographics of the new Travis County congressional district, considering if it was viable to run for the seat in 2024. Might she make things better *here* from *there*? She dreamed of dreamy federal legislation: national abortion access, guarantees of equal pay for equal work, expanded parental leave. Zeke, meanwhile, had a more immediate question about Congress, namely whether he might get called before that governing body for questioning. Lawmakers were worried (again, and perpetually) about teenage mental health and the internet, and his company, if not partially responsible, was at least party to the mudslide. Gregg tried to support Zeke through his anxious waiting, but in her heart, social media accountability seemed like the tiniest of small potatoes compared to bodily autonomy for half the populace.

In the end, the invite never came—there went Zuck, Elon, the guy she'd visit in SF (his check would pay for a six-month contract with a top political strategist, whom Gregg would file in her phone under "Anne-Stylist" because she couldn't be too careful until she was ready to announce her run). Zeke's exclusion was a relief, but also its own brand of insult; getting bumped from the program was, according to Zeke, not an absolution but a comment on his company's comparative triviality. Gregg felt differently but didn't say that; when she asked him if he wanted to talk about it more, it was like he could see her skepticism as plain as a toucan sitting on her shoulder. He made an audible *harrumph*.

The couple rang in the New Year at another tech exec's home, a palatial place down the street from their own. The party was jammed with rich ranchers and Houston oilmen, the Cowboys' defensive line. At the midnight countdown, Gregg couldn't find Zeke. This gave her an eerie feeling, but she pushed it aside, kept weaving the crowd until 12:12, and voilà, there he was, on the far side of the pool, in rapt discussion with someone she didn't recognize. As she approached the men, she picked up something about agave futures and succulent varietals, but there was music blasting from a balcony, and as far as she was concerned, all tequila was good tequila. She waited for a break in the conversation. A late New Year's kiss, even one that tasted like an overpriced cigar, was better than no New Year's kiss, so at a pause in the men's patter she smooched Zeke, smiled at the swaying stranger, and excused herself, humming "Auld Lang Syne" on her short walk home.

The sitter was watching television on low; as Gregg stepped into the room, she vaguely recognized the man on the screen. Did he resemble an old lover, was he a former colleague with whom she'd shared a stage for a few passing weeks? No. She squinted. That shaggy blond mustache was what had thrown her off—it was a young Matthew McConaughey, Richard Linklater's *Dazed and Confused*.

The sitter said the boys were sleeping; Gregg cracked open their bedroom door to check. It felt strange for them to be in their own space, not in a bassinet at her side or co-sleeping (which she'd preferred once they were sturdy enough not to be crushed under Zeke's elbow). Strange for them to be eating un-mushed vegetables and organic chicken nuggets, to be slurping cow's milk rather than suckling at her breast. Her boys had been such *hungry* babies, and she had loved that—their coiled need and their happy, satiated release, even as their insistence drained her so literally.

Gregg gathered the monitors from the sitter and sent the young woman home with a hundred-dollar tip. Then she sank onto the couch, her children glowing on their screens, as some strange, time-warped version of her adopted city spun out across the TV. There, she watched teenagers in muscle cars, Parker Posey in a mint-green truck. There, she saw elements of Austin she recognized, but other parts of the film felt like they were set in another world, some sunken Atlantis. Then everyone was heading to the Zilker Park moontower—that she recognized, even if the shots of the structure, the boy climbing its rungs, were plainly filmed on a set. The view from the top—that was real too, although it seemed *un*real, how small Austin was then. For over a decade, Austin had been the fastest-growing metro area in the country, and it had the gentrification and homelessness, the bad traffic and shiny towers to prove it. She was a part of that problem, directly responsible for three of the city's new inhabitants. But could she fix the problem too? Maybe with the new district . . .

A text pinged from Bella. "Happy new year's bitches!!!" A montage of Britney Spears spinning, spanning from some preteen dance competition to a lockdown selfie, her eyes smudgy with liner. "I love you all," Reba replied, with a GIF of the pop singer blowing kisses to a crowd. "You, too," Carson wrote and sent a GIF of the singer bald and calm and smiling prettily.

As Gregg typed her well-wishes to the group, she hypothesized about what the new year would hold. She wanted it to be good for Austin and those boys, now men, on the screen, who were looking out on their twinkling city. At least she wanted it to be better than 2022's pearl string of catastrophes. But for that to happen, for her to be a functional lawmaker and decent human, for her to be a good mother to those two cherubs sleeping down the hall, she first had to take care of this one thing.

The one thing was really a third thing, her third pregnancy in three years. She just didn't have it in her. Or, her uterus could do it, physiologically speaking, but the rest of her—her head and heart and parasympathetic nervous system—could not.

One of the boys stirred in his bed, flipped and flopped over to his side with a groan. Gregg sat up, ready for a cry that did not come, then slowly eased herself back into the sofa.

34

Mon, Jan 23 at 8:07 AM

Gregg:

Thx Maggie will review. Could you pls schedule an appt w/ Dr Renner?

Maggie Leonard:

👍 Legislative or medical?

Eleven weeks pregnant, her doctor confirmed. Dr. Renner also told her that the embryo, or fetus—it depended on whom you asked, what it was called—looked normal.

"Thank you," Gregg said. And she was grateful, for the doctor's plainspoken medical evaluation, which was followed with a reminder to avoid sushi and unpasteurized cheese, then the pushy encouragement to *sleep*.

Gregg was also thankful for the doctor's neutral face, which did not show hope or disapproval or any judgment at all, even as Gregg spouted about physical discomforts—how nauseous she'd been feeling, the swelling in her hands, the radiating pain in her lumbar spine, which couldn't be baby weight because she hadn't gained any yet—before enumerating her psychological symptoms. She was uncomfortable with the idea of having another kid so soon after the last, both for her body's resilience and her boys' emotional development, how much work they still required and which she manifestly did not want to further delegate. Even with a lot of help—and Dr. Renner had met Giselle, thought the young woman tremendously capable—Gregg was barely keeping her head above water. Sometimes, she confessed, it felt like she was blowing those nose bubbles that happen right before you're sunk.

The doctor nodded sympathetically, while privately noting that Gregg had quite a number of metaphors for what it felt like to be a progressive public official in Texas with two kiddos under three: last time it was treading water in the middle of the ocean and draining a lake with an eyedropper, today it was blowing bubbles and moving a mountain with a teaspoon. They tended to be like the plots of Werner Herzog movies and were not, in Dr. Renner's estimation, very productive comparisons. "Anything new at home," Dr. Renner asked, "besides the obvious?" She was eager to change the subject from Gregg's fatalism. The patient shrugged a *not really* shrug. She was, she said, grateful for Giselle, but she hardly saw the boys, and really, she wanted them to know her, and for her to know them. How could they do that over the span of three board books a night?

The doctor nudged, "Things with Zeke okay?" Gregg admitted she similarly hardly saw her husband; they were sometimes no more than roommates who shared a wide bed. Some of that came with the territory—she knew that marrying someone as ambitious as him, alongside her own crazy striving, meant they'd both be busy for long stretches, but it was still discouraging that they spent so little time fully present, totally together, not snoring or tapping at their phones. What she wouldn't do to watch a bad rom-com with him, no phones in the room.

When they were done chatting, Gregg watched her doctor fill out the last pages of her chart. She looked tired too, undoubtedly worn down by patients with more questions than ever, the normal qualms about development (women who'd memorized those inane mommy blogs and their what-fruit-is-my-fetus timelines) multiplied by a myriad of new and difficult factors. Gregg couldn't stop thinking that it was all her fault—the doctor's fatigue, the dour mood in the reception area, the rising blood pressure of every pregnant person in Texas. This guilt was irrational—her vote was one of thirty-one, her chamber one of two. But she was there when SB 8 was passed, and she hadn't stopped it. Couldn't stop the antique abortion ban from triggering either. In that sense, this was a mess of her making. Now, what were they going to do?

The doctor finished, sighed, smiled. She'd done such a good job when Gregg had invited her to speak to the HSS Committee, Gregg thought, had cogently explained why spontaneous miscarriages were quantifiable dangers to otherwise healthy Texans. You could be a God-fearing and baby-loving woman, but that didn't protect you from an unexpected hemorrhage, chromosomal abnormalities, so many things that doctors were no longer legally authorized to address. No one wanted a worst case, but worst cases were happening every single day.

Now, Dr. Renner capped her pen. "I'll see you in four weeks. Or I won't."

Gregg slid off the exam table. This open door . . . Gregg was grateful for that too.

35

Mon, Jan 23 at 8:05 PM

Gregg:

ETA??

8:28 PM

See above.

Most nights in the Thomas-Graves household, food was fuel. They did not rotate through favorite recipes or various cuisines as much as respond to who was on what diet, who was teething, and what was seasonal at the Barton Creek Farmers Market. But that afternoon, a large cooler showed up on their stoop. Gregg was stumped until she remembered how she had paid in advance for a quarter cow before the calf was even born (which was also before Zacky was), with the assurance that the beast would be sustainably raised, humanely butchered, and conveyed, in choice cuts, to her front door. She had been given the option of driving to the ranch and looking the animal in his Moon Pie eyes, petting him on the fuzzy forehead before he got zapped in that same spot. She declined the invitation.

Now, fresh from her visit to Dr. Renner, she peered into the cooler. Atop a bed of ice, glistening ruby-colored slabs were arranged small to large, the largest being the size of a Frisbee. It was like the world had predicted this, or willed it to happen: that Dr. Renner would say she'd gone borderline anemic, that Gregg would need an occasion to sit down with her husband and talk, that their Whole

Foods order would have gone awry (there was no record of this week's groceries; she'd sent Giselle and the boys out for tacos). She thought of her astrologer's silky, smooth touch on her forearm and tried to remember her most recent chart. Had it pointed toward this convergence? She drew a blank. It was fortuitous regardless, so she put the kids down early and returned to the patio's outdoor kitchen. Over a proper meal, like one of those moonlit dinners that had started their courtship—maybe even with a glass of merlot—she and Zeke would talk, really talk, about recent developments and near-future plans.

Would her pregnancy even be news to him? She doubted that Zeke had really not noticed that her period was two weeks late, then three, then four—though he was so distracted these days, the Senate committee and all the tech sector's post-pandemic, pre-recession churn. Look at what was happening in the Bay. Reba's husband was one of what, three hundred to be let go at his firm? Zeke's company had thus far dodged layoffs, but Gregg couldn't tell if they were thriving or white-knuckling it or in denial. (By contrast, she was positive the recent rocket launch they'd tried to paint as a success was a case of full-blown kidding themselves.)

The rocket. It hadn't been his rocket, but Zeke had put so much of their savings—*his* savings, per the prenup—into the venture, no wonder he was obsessed. This was another thing that'd happened since Palm Springs, and while she was upset about it, she didn't want tonight's conversation about her body and their children to veer into her feelings about that giant metal phallus. But the fact of it was that he'd driven (dragged) the whole family to the Gulf Coast to watch the launch, and it'd monopolized one of the few free days they'd all been together in months. Once they'd arrived at the viewing location, Zeke had peeled off immediately to hobnob with rocket scientists and their spouses, offshore investors and local businessmen, all looking so preemptively pleased by the test flight. Gregg assessed the well-heeled attendees and thought about how she wanted them to invest in Austin's affordable housing before building colonies on another planet, but out of deference to Zeke, she spent the hour chasing after her children rather than telling these people that their priorities were demented. There were astronaut-themed snacks—the freeze-dried ice cream she recognized from childhood trips to the Air and Space Museum, but also hot dogs shaped like rocket ships and an ice sculpture rocket that functioned as a fountaining centerpiece for a giant punch bowl of lemonade. (Someone on the party committee had a sense of humor, Gregg thought, looking around for the culprit.) Then some guy with a bullhorn told them to look at the launchpad and count down from thirty, and right on cue, the rocket had fired its jets and slowly lifted. The sound, which took a strange breathless moment to reach them, was huge, unlike anything she'd heard before. Then the heat reached them and was, briefly, a solid wall. Zacky, in her arms, recoiled into her chest, and she checked her eyebrows to confirm they were still present. They were.

After liftoff, the rocket had gone from being the size of a building to that of a bus, to a toy bus and a tiny toy bus, to the size of her thumb, the nail of her thumb, then to that of Zacky's baby pinkie. Maybe ninety seconds in, it started spinning. It was clear from the titters around the platform that the rocket wasn't supposed to move like a drunken bumblebee; someone made a joke about popping a wheelie. Before anyone had a chance to think of more quips, before ground control could switch to its contingency plans, it'd blown up. The explosion was likely a scorching, tooth-rattling detonation up in that part of the stratosphere, but from where Gregg stood, thirty feet above sea level, it was a quick set of mini-marshmallow white puffs, a flash of gold flame. Silence.

The platform slowly replied with polite claps, some reserved whoops, a two-fingered whistle.

As the applause died down, the countdown guy lifted his bullhorn again. What they'd witnessed had been an "indispensable step," he shouted, "an unqualified success" that would change the future of space travel. Was it? Gregg wondered. Tens of millions of dollars, maybe hundreds, literally just went up in smoke. Xavier tugged on her hem and asked when the rocket was landing on the moon. She looked over to Zeke, who was still staring at the sky and the split contrails of his former rocket. "Ask your father."

The following Monday, a colleague had come to her office in tears. Hundreds of shorebirds in his district had been scorched at the launch. Heat waves and sound waves and sooty exhaust had blackened the marshland surrounding the pad, a blast radius of a quarter mile. Gregg swallowed a lump in her throat, remembering how her eyebrows had felt—and that was a mile away from liftoff. Her colleague couldn't have known that she'd been there, could he? That she'd clapped?

It wasn't like, he went on, the Gulf Coast didn't have enough problems with its entrenched oil money and the industry's offshore pipelines, belching container ships and their destructive canals. The state senator was oblivious to Gregg's internal turmoil and the pinpricks of sweat across her forehead—it became clear he didn't know about Zeke's investment or her affiliation, he just knew his outrage. Now, he continued, these impoverished, polluted coastal communities had to bend over so some billionaires could play space camp? She smarted at the truth of it. If only there'd been another round of environmental review, he opined, if only the community hadn't been so eager for the expanded tax base, if only billionaires didn't feel so entitled to move fast and break things. In this case, Mother Nature's things!

Gregg, listening to his jeremiad, felt more awful by the second. But he'd come to her as a friend and as the leader of the state senate environmental concern; for now, all she could do was let the senator tire himself out, offer a Kleenex and a cough drop at the end of his tirade, and tell him she'd look into it. Ten minutes later he shuffled out of the office, sniffling still, and feeling marginally better. A charred, fuming piece of shorebird flesh had been pushed off his plate and onto hers, and he couldn't understand how much she deserved it.

Now, she tonged her steaks aggressively. *That* was the rocket. And the situation was far from resolved; she might have to recuse herself or resign from her favorite subcommittee or take draconian actions against all those pleasant, arrogant people on the viewing platform, her husband included. But she'd do nothing about that tonight. Tonight, no rockets.

The flames on the grill surged higher, high enough to hurt if she hadn't leaned back in the nick of time. She lowered the gas. Would Zeke even eat? She'd at first thought the addition of Ozempic to his fitness regimen was funny-vain, assumed it was due to the possibility of the Senate committee (if the camera added ten pounds but he was down fifteen, he'd look svelte for C-SPAN). But the DC window had closed, and he was still nibbling four carrots a day. Was it training for space camp? Judging by their last demo, the rocket company was far from recruiting living, breathing astronauts. Maybe they'd incinerate a dog or monkey soon, but until they'd passed through the proof-of-concept stage, she'd steer clear of the volunteer queue.

And if not that, what else could be spurring his new vanity? Another woman? She'd not seriously considered his infidelity, given their hotness differential (she ran circles around him, even with her widening hips, the post-baby circles under her eyes). She'd felt secure in this, grateful that she'd aged as well as she had. But something about Zeke was changing. He was growing more distant, and more hot.

Meanwhile, in these last weeks, he'd been making her hot, and not in the sexy sense—more mad-as-hellfire. That was new. They were often too busy to connect at length when they first met he'd been in the middle of a $1.5 billion funding round and she'd been doing six shows a week, and their lives had only become more hectic since—but rarely were they at each other's throats. Now they were arguing about everything. Even taxes! Last week his accountant had run some numbers, working Zeke's company's 2022 state bill down to $48.57. Oh, she'd railed at that. Texas didn't have state income tax, and for that to work, corporations had to pay their fair share of gross receipts. How would they fund education, transportation, without a tax base? Did he want to go without paved streets or the electrical grid or mail? He had made a good point about the postal service being federal and increasingly obsolete; then reminded her of the ice storm, the state's already woeful grid. But still. If he truly thought he'd be better off in space than contributing to the society they had, well, he should just go see about that. By himself. No way she'd let her kids fly through the cosmos in one of his machines.

She prodded the meat again, listening for a sizzle. Behind the tax thing, and why it set her boiling, was a basic, recurring disconnect. That Zeke could support her career and promote her agenda but deny the means to fund it . . . It was parallel to his appreciation for health in general but his snaky shortcuts to achieve it; just like his wanting a hundred kids but then spending zero time with them. Ditto on his desire to "improve" society but literally trying to leave the planet. He was such a hypocrite.

She stepped away from the grill and took a deep, centering breath, remembering her mother's lesson: The breath was central to the poetic line but also to life. She told the monster in her chest to sit. To wait. To lie down and stay. She wouldn't get distracted by her anger, not let it pull her in a hundred incensed directions, adjacent conflicts that were big deals (the poor seabirds, the woeful education budget) but that had no bearing on what they needed to talk about tonight.

Tonight they had to talk about the embryo, and what she wanted to do about it. What she was going to do about it, in New York or Illinois or California because she couldn't do it here, and how terrible was that? She wanted to hear his thoughts, because they were a team, in good times and bad, they'd sworn to that in front of their friends and family and Willie Nelson (what a stunner that had been, when he'd come out with his guitar and serenaded the newlyweds, but then again Zeke was a sucker for grand and surprising gestures). But it was also her body and her choice, and she chose to preserve what life-force she had for her boys, her marriage, her career, her country, herself. Could he really resent her for making that decision?

She already knew that the answer was yes—he wanted to have a big family, environmental resources and hours in the day be damned. She hated that he was so casual about outsourcing their boys' development—yes, they found the best that money could buy, but she believed that they, the parents, should be in charge of bath times and meal planning and their kids' grasp of the solar system, not some fleet of well-paid experts. It was the difference between self-driving cars and manual transmissions—Zeke was happy to tell Alexa his destination and then go hands-free (checking his email, taking a quick nap), whereas Gregg would keep one hand on the wheel, the other on the gearshift for the whole drive. She wanted to know the limits of every gear, exactly how sticky the clutch might be.

Before Xavier's arrival she had thought three kids would be okay; maybe she'd said she'd consider four. But seriously. What had she been thinking? Her vagina would revolt. After having done this twice and clocked the wear and tear on her body, but also gauged the fullness in her heart, she now knew she wanted her two kids and no more. More corgis, maybe (she'd have to work on Zeke, who was mildly allergic and always tripping over them), but no more children.

Her dogs—Zack (the dog came first, but Zeke wouldn't budge on his preplanned list of boy names), Kelly, Slater, and Screech—had caught a whiff of the meat and made their way out the doggy door and to the grill, curious at her project.

Gregg turned down the gas. The steaks needed to rest; they'd be ready right at eight, when Zeke said he'd be done with whatever it was he was doing. She poured herself a glass of wine and sat down to wait, scratching one dog after another. This was what couples did. No, not wait on the patio, petting their dogs—they worked through their differences by hashing them out. Talked over disagreements until they found a middle ground, or everyone felt okay about the spread between their respective posts. She and Zeke were more strong-headed than average, but even that shaped their mutual regard; they were both as driven as subway rats after their pizza. They loved that about each other, even if it made their conflicts more electric.

Zeke eventually stepped onto the patio, much later than he'd said he would. The dogs scattered, knowing the man of the house arrived with more risk than reward. By then, the meat was cool, coagulating.

Gregg, wrapped in a throw, told him her news, her decision. Her reasons.

He remained quiet, his face darkening.

"Well?" she said into the silence. Sure, she poked the bear. But did she have a choice?

He did, he finally replied, not think it was the right decision. His voice was tight, and his dismissiveness sounded like a slur, as if the many plates she kept spinning weren't accomplishment enough. She could do more, he said. *Should* do more; they had the means. Giselle and her yogi instructions were great, Gregg countered, but she wanted to make the most of what they had. And not *most* like optimization or efficiency, private chefs and nannies who were better with kids than she was. *Most*, like joy.

He didn't have a response to that, only a dead-eyed stare that turned her stomach.

The argument continued on from there. He said he thought their family should be bigger; she raised her steak knife in the air, offended on Xavier and Zack's behalf. They were enough! In what universe were those two boys not enough?

When the conversation was done, both of them disappointed in the other, Zeke stalked back inside. Gregg, alone again, noticed a new chill swirling the patio. Zeke's steak sat untouched, and so those dear, short-legged dogs of hers, they had a feast.

36

Mon, Jan 23 at 11:42 PM

Carson:

> Matilda's leaves shivered when I told her you were coming. We can't wait to see you xo

In Brooklyn, Carson's phone lit up. It was late, but she was awake, staring at a document on her computer screen. No news from her agent, none from her father, but ever since she got back from California she'd been starting stories—and getting nowhere. She tried beginning with character, then the launchpad of a witty conceit. She wrote from first-, second-, and third-person perspectives, tried the royal *we*. Nothing was holding her interest. Her head, before the phone's interruption, had been stuck on a strange loop, a conveyor belt carrying the word *next*, *next*, like so many empty cardboard boxes. "Gregg. What's up?"

"I'm not going to keep it." She was talking quietly, and the way the wind garbled the phone's mouthpiece suggested she was outside.

"Okay." Carson closed her laptop. The conveyor belt could wait.

"I can't take care of it here."

"I've heard." There'd been a text chain without Gregg when SB 8 went into effect, the others sharing freaked-out messages and fresh memes of Gregg and her boot intercut with Beyoncé, with RBG, with the queen and her dogs (this was before Her Highness's death, so the pun was cute, not foreboding). So many Texans were mad about the ban; Gregg was their lividity, embodied. Then, when she'd protested the trigger ban with both boots, there'd been another chain, this one including Gregg, filled with exclamation points and encouragements like "You got this" and "Fuck men" and Bella chiming in with "Remember the Alamo." Even if that moment in history wasn't particularly applicable here, in terms of matching contours, the feeling was right. You did *not* fuck with Gregg. She'd be the last one standing, every time.

"Can I come stay with you?"

When Carson had needed an abortion, they were both twenty-three, exceptionally broke, and everything was a possibility—everything but having a kid. Carson couldn't fathom it. Not emotionally, and not the logistics. She was already at the loft then, but at the bottom of its pecking order, living in what was now Zariah's puny room. There was no way the others—a straight-edge metalhead, a guy finishing a PhD on Zola—would abide a squalling infant.

Carson could still recall *getting* pregnant. She'd experienced some worry the morning after, but she was hungover, and too enamored with the guy to hop out of bed, head to the pharmacy, and make herself sick with Plan B. He wanted to take her to brunch, and Bloody Marys meant the relationship was going somewhere; later that day he had a show at the Bowery Ballroom, a backstage pass with her name on it. Their two-day date became two weeks of Velcro hanging out, then the guy went on tour, their texting tapered, and scene. The ghosting part was expected (cell phone etiquette back then was the Wild West), but the sperm-meeting-egg stuff, the cells dividing and the surge of hormones, that it'd happened, even after every health teacher since middle school had suggested it might . . . all of that came as a blow.

Because she was a good friend, Gregg had offered to go with Carson to the appointment. She was in the city for a play, cast in a major but not lead role, and sleeping in Reba's empty flat. Gregg, so often the understudy, had the singular experience of being the one to call in sick, and what a thrill it'd been. She claimed food poisoning, a bad clam.

As the women entered the clinic, Carson absorbed every detail of the place, equal parts self-loathing and scared and relieved and journalistic, already guessing that maybe she'd write about it someday. (And there was an abortion in her first novel, the protagonist's revenge against her deplorable boyfriend and his infidelity.) Carson had also noted that Gregg seemed very comfortable navigating the situation. She handled the paperwork in a snap, knew what to ask during intake and in the recovery room. Carson had assumed it was her friend's forever confidence and thorough preparation, that it was because Gregg was plain *good* at everything. But Carson, who at that point knew Gregg as well as anyone, save for Charlene, didn't arrive at the most logical explanation for Gregg's competence: that she'd been here, done this. That would also explain her familiarity, why she knew to query about co-pays and extra-absorbent pads.

Because as close as they were, Gregg had never mentioned that she'd been there before. Well, not *there* there, but a very similar clinic in Boston, identical linoleum and font for the signage. ("This is a safe space." "All are welcome." "Gov. ID required.") And that she'd done the same *this* this. It'd been just after high school; she'd gotten pregnant on prom night, cliché as that was. There was so much buildup around losing one's virginity, and that night, with its clumsy corsage pinning, the preposterous limousine (had her date rented it from a funeral home?), the awkward slow dance (him whispering about how nice it felt for their bodies to be close, even as his dick wasn't whispering but shouting and jumping and mashing into her stomach through the fabric of his tux), seemed as good a time as any to pull the plug.

Charlene had taken the news in stride; sexuality was, in her eyes, a blessed part of life. She sat Gregg down at their kitchen table and asked, "Do you want this to be you?" She could get through college with a baby; she'd have to transfer to somewhere local, defer a year or start part-time. Probably she'd have to pick practical economics over theater, because double majoring would be a challenge, and how would she go to auditions with a baby on her hip? Charlene knew that Gregg could make it work, even with a diapered handicap; that was never the question. No, what was up for debate was something more nuanced: Was this how she wanted to define herself? The teen mom, the uphill? Gregg thought about it, about what she already knew she wanted to do in this life. The answer appeared in glowing neon. *No*.

Gregg had been thinking about that time again recently, as this second unwanted pregnancy settled in her abdomen. That first one would've been twenty-one now, and while she'd never asked the sex, she'd felt sure it was going to be a girl. Had she stuck around, that girl, that young woman, might right now be getting drunk at frat parties, flirting with the wrong sort, spending up her credit cards, taking classes and skipping classes and figuring out her dreams. When Gregg realized her first not-child was old enough to be a parent herself, it seemed like a magic trick, but as Gregg turned it over, she saw it wasn't miraculous, just a woman's body, its indefatigability and relentlessness.

Back in Palm Springs, around the pool with her friends, everyone had talked about going through peri- and full-on menopause as a catalogue of frights: hot flashes and dry vaginas and saggy boobs, the terror of losing something vital. But when Gregg thought of running out of eggs, her body shutting down in that way, she had a different response—a big, relieved sigh. She'd take an industrial furnace's worth of hot flashes to be done with reproductivity, to close out this conversation with Zeke once and for all.

Carson didn't skip a beat. "When do you want to come?" Gregg could hear a tiny siren braying somewhere past Carson's Brooklyn window.

"I have an appointment for Monday."

37

Sat, Jan 28 at 11:25 AM

Carson:

Remember Zariah: not a peep

Donny and Zariah were in the living room when the front door buzzed. Carson sprinted to the intercom, waving off her roommates. They watched with curiosity—Carson rarely had guests. A noise on the stairs, then a dainty knock, and Carson opened the door quickly. As her friend appeared and the two embraced, all the oxygen left the room. Some zipped out into the dim hall, some sprinted through the cracked window (the loft's steam heat was feast or famine, and this morning it was sweltering), and a portion went into Zariah's lungs; Carson heard a distinct gasp from the couch.

Carson took Gregg's weekender from her hand and spun around. "Guys, this is my friend, uh, Charlene." Gregg shot Carson a questioning look. They'd cooked up a story to deflect attention from Gregg's presence and purpose, complete with a pseudonym. What had they decided on? Not Gregg's mother's name, but that's what had popped into Carson's head. The odds that Zariah and Donny knew the poet were slim; they were too cool for the Best American Poetry anthology and likely had not noticed the shelf of Charlene's titles, many inscribed to Carson, in Carson's room. "She'll be staying with me for a few days. For work," Carson added.

"Nice to meet y'all," Gregg said and offered a pageant wave. The roommates sat up straighter, and Zariah even smiled. Already Carson could sense their suspicion, their interest.

Carson and Gregg made a beeline for Carson's room. It was still configured as Gregg had seen it a decade ago, its big windows looking out on the neighbors' backyards. Those yards were bare now, but come May, they would bloom with all sorts of lilac bush and wisteria vine, lavender things. The room's contours were as before, but Carson had upgraded, bit by bit—an appealing light fixture, a new desk (a Shaker-style table) in the corner. Her own domestic ship of Theseus, Carson quipped as she showed off her new ergonomic chair.

"Make yourself at home," Carson said, patting the bed, then returned to the living room, where Donny and Zariah were on the couch. Addressing her roommates, Carson kept her voice just above a whisper. "You guys'll be cool about this, right?"

Zariah nodded like her head was on a spring. "I am trying to keep it together. It's an honor to have . . . 'Charlene' under our roof. I'm extra bummed I have that wedding today." Zariah was soon departing for the Hamptons, a socialite's nuptials that required an on-call stylist, even though the outfits and accessories were selected months ago.

"Nothing online, you understand?"

Donny raised his right hand, palm out. "Scout's honor."

Zariah scowled at her friend. "You quit the Boy Scouts after, like, two weeks."

"I did. But I promise. Zip." He made a lock-turning motion over his mouth, then tossed an invisible key behind the couch.

"I can't believe you *know* her," Zariah said. Carson sensed a dig burrowed beneath her compliment, and wanted to point out that she knew plenty of cool people. That film editor from the Oscars, maybe; the string of musicians she'd dated, some of whom had become famous before flaming out. Her friend Amelia, the painter, had had a show recently that received great press, was even mentioned in the "highbrow, brilliant" quadrant of the Approval Matrix. (That the gallery was on Staten Island and hadn't sold a single painting was irrelevant. Amelia was *cool.*) Maybe Carson didn't see her friends often enough; people moved away, got busy with babies and work, and who had a social life after Covid, really?

"You know she caused, like, a massive run on Lucchese boots? I heard her style is back-ordered for over a year." Zariah was excited.

"What are you talking about?" Carson tried to look vacuous. "My friend was wearing sneakers." She knew about Lucchese—the supple leather and elaborate, elegant stitching; the solid, resounding wooden heel. But she relished getting under Zariah's skin.

"Right." Zariah flashed a crooked grin. "She is such an inspiration. I mean, how she's advocating for women in that dystopian state. Jeez, bounties? I'm not setting foot in Texas till the law's repealed. Unless it was for, like, the perfect gig. If Mr. McConaughey needed someone to unbutton his shirt to here." She touched her own breastbone and stared into the distance.

Donny rolled his eyes and cleared his throat, pulling Zariah out of her fantasy and back into their Brooklyn Saturday morning. "We won't say anything," he said.

"But what about the party?" Zariah asked.

Carson glanced at the younger woman. "Party?"

"Caviar with Nikolai tonight? 'The Gilded Twenties,' or whatever you're calling it?" Zariah eyed the fridge, where the glittering invite for the party hung, and continued, "I don't like the mouthfeel of roe, too slimy. But you know, it'll be a thing. I hate missing things."

"Damn, I forgot." Carson's eyes pinged from Zariah to the invite to the front door, which would soon be receiving forty strangers and five pounds of roe. "It's fine. Fine. We'll work around it." The door buzzed, and Carson jumped. It was only Gregg's bagel—Carson had ordered her friend's favorite sandwich and spread.

Carson returned to the bedroom with their bagels and began to apologize. Gregg listened, trying to parse what Carson was so worked up about. Some people, fish eggs, and an *anti*-anti-Russian agenda? Carson offered to get them a hotel. They could eat a seven-course dinner, go to one long movie or two regular-length ones. They could go clubbing, they could take sleeping pills, they could . . . What she meant was they didn't have to partake in the Gen Z party that would shortly be unfolding on the other side of the wall. As Carson talked through the multiplexes in Downtown Brooklyn (who was showing Marvel, who might be showing anything besides superheroes), how they could get rush tickets or go bowling or—Gregg cut her off.

"Carson, sweetie, shut up. It's fine." She explained that the parties she went to now were all political fundraisers or tech bro bashes or toddler forward, with lots of jolly but still creepy clowns. Sucky, in short. A loft party in Brooklyn, populated by the sorts of comely and creative people she used to hang out with in the before times? Her mouth curled up in the corners as she thought of her former life.

Carson crossed her arms. "They're more artsy than artist, FYI. Copywriters, not writers. You know the type."

Gregg brushed it off; she was unbothered by Carson's designations. "I don't care, that's ten stripes better than Zeke's doofy engineers. Do you think anyone will recognize me?"

Carson shook her head no, even as she thought, Absolutely.

"Good," Gregg said, and unwrapped her bagel. "You gonna eat?"

Carson lifted her sandwich but was still thinking of Zariah, how she'd looked lovestruck at her friend's unannounced appearance.

Gregg wiped a dollop of cream cheese from the corner of her mouth, inspected and swallowed it. "Is caviar pasteurized?"

38

Sat, Jan 28 at 4:56 PM

Carson:

Hey b— coming to bklyn tonight? Caviar etc & ive got a surprise 😉

Donny suggested he confiscate everyone's phones for the evening; that would protect their special guest. Carson appreciated the concern for Gregg's privacy, but wouldn't that put a wrench in Nikolai's planned social campaign? He'd wanted to photograph the fish eggs, and hip people eating them. It would, Donny said, but always the problem solver, when Nikolai came to set up, Donny encouraged his friend to take some unpeopled snaps before guests arrived, to pose Donny and Carson as hand models with the edible offerings. And the spread was photogenic, bowls of jewel-like roe cascading across the table, a big vase of sunflowers right in the middle. This was a nice touch, Carson thought, for color and political messaging. Hopefully the foodie corner of the internet would respond with enthusiasm.

When Nikolai was done with his documentation, Donny pulled him aside and explained who their first guest—that one on the couch with the striped top—actually was, and once he did, Donny's unanticipated cell phone protocol made total sense. Nikolai had seen the videos. He wouldn't admit it in mixed company, but he'd played the breastfeeding clip a few times on his laptop, pausing the video at a frame that afforded a decent view of her boob, appreciating it for a moment. When Nikolai inadvertently made eye contact with Gregg, Donny still whispering about how she and Carson were friends from college, which was saying a lot, because they'd graduated *decades* ago, the Russian turned borscht red.

• • •

"Where's Bella?" Gregg asked an hour into the party. Carson checked her phone, which was not in Donny's stash but charging in her room. No word, which could only mean one thing.

"She chickened out," Carson said when she returned to Gregg, perched prettily on the living room's better couch. Bella hadn't come to Brooklyn since before the pandemic, at least not to see Carson. And they hadn't entirely made up after Palm Springs, the volley of insult-apology-insult that left them both smarting. If Bella really wanted to make amends, she'd have gotten on a train tonight.

"Did you tell her I was coming?" Gregg pressed. Carson hadn't. For one, she wanted Bella to make the effort, independent of the prospect of an out-of-town guest. And if she had mentioned Gregg's presence, Bella would have wanted to know why Gregg was in the city; she'd poke at Gregg's story until she found a weak spot, then keep prodding until she uncovered the truth. (She was great at cross-examination.) Once she had, she'd keep going, with real hurt in her voice, *Well, why not a third?* Bella was still pining for a girl, but her body couldn't handle another pregnancy; the second delivery, with its rapid blood loss, had almost killed her. Carson could remember one museum get-together in which Bella had ranted for twenty minutes about Gregg's childbearing hips. Could Carson believe that she'd delivered Xavier naturally, no meds? The universe was so unfair! To atone for talking shit, and to thank Carson for enduring the tirade, after Zack arrived—and his was another easy vaginal delivery—Bella sent a big "Welcome, Baby!" bouquet to Gregg and signed it from them both.

What Carson had mentioned was caviar, a menu of beggar's purses and blinis, to which Bella had laughed aloud and typed a *ha-ha* emoji into the thread. "Classing up Brooklyn?" would have been a fine amount of snark if they hadn't just fought about their relative wealth. Carson took several days to reply to that text.

"Too bad." Now Gregg was rising to do another loop of the caviar buffet. She heaped her plate with black, red, and gold, then she noticed Nikolai hovering, his insecure smile. "What kind is this?" Gregg held up a spoonful of glittering red eggs.

"That's not technically caviar. It's salmon roe, which is more pedestrian. True caviar"—Gregg plopped a small pile onto her plate and kept moving, but Nikolai was not deterred from his spiel—"is made from sturgeon."

"So why do you slum it for salmon?" Carson was still listening closely, watching him make his amped-up pitch. The desire to be liked, to land in the proper grid of one's individual approval matrix, felt so petty in the face of geopolitical violence. His country was at war, depriving another nation of its sovereign rights, and he wanted to win a popularity contest with fish eggs?

Of course he did, Carson thought. Who didn't want to be liked? We all wanted approval, whatever was happening on the rest of the planet. Or possibly, especially, because of it.

He met Carson's eyes then, and she nearly gasped. What loneliness lay there. She was still pro-Ukraine, still wanted Putin's doughy chest to get trampled by his own draft horse, but just then she became a little less anti-Russian.

"It looks pretty," he said with a shrug.

• • •

Gregg and Carson returned to the sofa and tucked into their second round of snacks. Gregg turned to her friend. "Is it fucked up that I'm eating all these eggs?"

Carson glanced at her loaded plate. "A bit."

"What's fucked up?" Donny was upon them, apprehensive. He'd already chased off one guest who recognized Gregg and asked her, sotto voce, about the new district.

Carson's mind went racing, and snagged on absent Bella. That'd work. "Our friend stood us up. We think she's scared of Brooklyn."

"She's gone yummy mummy on us." Gregg, always able to carry a story along, chimed in. "Upper East Side. White-shoe law firm. She worked for the Sacklers," she stage-whispered.

"But she's a lovely woman most of the time," Carson added.

"Oh absolutely," Gregg agreed.

Donny considered this as he collected empty glasses from the coffee table. (Already cleaning, God bless him, Carson thought.) "Could she get me some Oxy? Kidding. Maybe."

Even as they cackled at Bella's despicable work and unreasonable dread, at her comfy co-op and cute boys in their matching blazers (Carson had put the Winston Christmas card on their fridge and all had hooted at the preppy plaid), Carson felt a pang. None of them had done it right, not consistently, not totally. Carson had been selfish in so many ways: no kids, no conventional career, no long-term relationship that might get in her way. Gregg was blind to the gotcha of promoting progressivism while being inextricably bound up with the latest (last?) stage of late-stage capitalism; she couldn't see, or wouldn't acknowledge, her normie marriage, the patriarchy of her prenup, how her big-shouldered and bruising careerist tendencies, cloaked as they were in pastel blazers, were only nominally better than Zeke's cutthroat business acumen. Donny was paid by a sputtering media company to fetishize consumer culture, and was it even ethical to print magazines anymore? Admittedly it felt good to have the glossy pages open across your lap, but why fell all those trees when there was the internet? Were Bella's trespasses, her blind spots and toddler blazers, the pill money and her frank admissions of fear, worse than anyone else's trespass? Of course not.

39

Sat, Jan 28 at 10:14 PM

Bill:

How's the party? Looking forward to later 😀

If Carson ignored the champagne headache that was starting to form behind her eyeballs, she was having a good night. Conversation came easily to her; she was charming and funny, without the anxiety that plagued so many of her social interactions. (After her first book, people expected her to talk like the novel, all fast rejoinders and witticisms. It was annoying; in truth she'd be more likely to play with the unattended five-year-old manhandling the crudités at any given cocktail party than to stand center stage and charm on demand.) She knew it had to do with being proximate to her friend; with Gregg nearby, she became a better version of herself. Even if she didn't have eyes on Gregg—and they did split for a time—there was some pheromone she gave off, a high-frequency ping that set Carson at ease.

Carson recognized a few of Donny's friends from previous parties, others from moderate levels of internet fame or notoriety. She avoided the guests who were waving their arms around like they were skydiving—attention monopolizers—and gave a wide berth to the most "creative" looking ones, as their zany outfits more likely indicated large clothing budgets than meaningful self-expression. (Everyone appeared interesting in a $400 blouse.) Tonight, however, she promised herself she would not let loose any diatribes, knowing better than to dress down these well-dressed young people on their self-aggrandizing poses and corporate complicity.

Or, she knew better now. At the last of Donny's parties she'd attended, she'd told a cluster of creative directors that, fundamentally, they were full of it. She had a bone to pick about the wastefulness of their campaigns ("Do you know how many public school art programs you could fund with the budget for one of your stupid thirty-second spots?"), another about copywriting ("Do you think you're solving anything with your pithy slogans? Gimme a break!"), and she'd torn them a new one. The next day she'd been tag-team tongue-lashed by her roommates. She was lording over the block with her righteousness, they said, just a couple of miserly stoops away from Oscar the Grouch. Carson was duly chastened, unsure when she had become so ghastly, so un-fun. Of course they'd thrown their last party while she was in the desert. Served her right.

But she was in town tonight. And on her best behavior, no stridency at all. Gregg was mingling effortlessly with the Gen Zers, into and out of Carson's line of sight, winking like the two of them were in on the world's biggest joke. And things did turn hilarious, or maybe more hidden-camera comical, when Carson all but smacked into the clavicle of a former student.

Julian. She studied his face, which was floating above her, noticeably higher than the last time she'd seen it. Had she stepped into an alternate universe? Gone back in time, teleported to his parents' Cobble Hill brownstone? She checked her surroundings, looking for a tear in the space-time continuum. She was still in her apartment, still in 2023. Gregg's laugh, a magnificent tinkling, lifted from somewhere in the crowd.

A simpler explanation, the correct one: He was a friend of Donny's. It made mathematical sense, that Carson was old enough to have tutored her roommates' peers. She remembered then that Julian had gone to Vassar, same as Donny and Zariah.

To see a student in the wild was disorienting. To see one that had grown a late six inches and into his chin was also a mindfuck. Julian was handsome; when had that happened? Carson thanked him when he complimented her blouse (a Donny freebie) and her place, which in low light did look nice, the dimness and some strategic draperies hiding its most egregious stains and scuffs. She told herself that Julian was safely distant from his stint as a client, she could let down her guard. Or at least, she could accept his compliments without actively frowning.

They spoke briefly about his mom, a musician who'd had one big single in the late nineties and clung to its success for years (to the song's credit, it had become fairly anthemic to a generation of fed-up women). He covered college and his biochemistry doctorate in a single sentence: Vassar was a roving wide-angle lens, Harvard was a single, high-power microscope—literally, but also in terms of his academic interests. With a smart NSF application and a bit of serendipity, he'd been granted seed funding to start a lab, and moved back to New York that fall. "Already?" she asked, not trying to sound dubious. She knew not a lot about scientists' timelines, but to be under thirty and running your own lab at Rockefeller University seemed precocious. He admitted, after a pause, that it was, then described some of his science, which was looking at the behavioral and environmental factors of late-onset Alzheimer's. He used a metaphor that involved rotting lemons, which Carson found gross but clear and effective.

She expected him to keep on about his new lab, but the conversation made a sharp, unexpected turn. He'd bought her book, he said. She tried to respond but felt dizzy. He'd read it. "Loved it." He touched her arm then, and inside, Carson screamed. Gregg, watching from the next conversation circle, made a quiet yipping noise.

Gregg, swiftly at her arm, was introduced as Charlene, but Julian made a face like he recognized her. Gregg ignored the skepticism in his voice as he said "Nice to 'meet' you," then complimented his forearm tattoo, which looked like a butterfly but was, he explained, a drawing of a photograph of a slice of the coronal plane of the brain, something to do with his research. After he'd succinctly described his work again—Carson noted he did not resort to talking like he was addressing seven-year-olds; they were all adults, just conversing about unfamiliar topics, and maybe they did need some help with the technical terms—Gregg began hyping up Carson's writing career. Did he know that she'd been long-listed for one of those under thirty-five prizes?

He nodded enthusiastically, he did know that. Carson almost choked on her spit. How could he, unless he'd taken an active interest in her writing? In her? That young author prize was six years ago, but also six years after she and he had worked together. He'd been thinking of her, periodically at least, for a dozen years? She felt the floor was collapsing, the whole building falling into some sinkhole. She braced her knees.

Her mission accomplished, Gregg made herself scarce, which caused Carson to panic anew, but as the conversation swung into literature—not hers—Carson's nerves calmed. They talked about Katherine Anne Porter's version of the Spanish flu, the future of pandemic literature. What did she think of the new Ali Smith, he wanted to know. Then, out of nowhere, he asked, "Do you have kids?"

"What?" Carson looked fast around the apartment, like they might be hiding somewhere. Then she glanced down at her stomach; maybe the answer was there. And it was, in a way: her tight and unused birth canal, still a unidirectional avenue for dicks and fingers and dildos and tampons. Well, those things did travel in two directions, as ultimately they all came back out, but nothing originated up there, save for the blood she shed each month.

"Don't have any," she started, noticing his eyes noticing hers. "Don't particularly want any either. Writing," she added. In her fluster, she'd lost any semblance of eloquence.

"Right," Julian said, in a voice like he didn't believe her. The conversation petered out shortly after that.

40

Sat, Jan 28 at 11:30 PM

Gregg:

Good nite & love u Z hpe u get 2 spnd som tim w boys wknd xo

The party hadn't quit, but it was getting late, so the women excused themselves to Carson's room. After texting Texas and showing Carson a picture of her dogs, then a second of her sons, Gregg stepped out of her sneakers and pulled off her top. Her limbs were loose, and she swayed as her skirt dropped into a silken puddle. Her belly, now exposed, was maybe a touch rounded? Carson tried not to think about its contents or what they were about to do to it.

"I'm so grateful for you, Carson," Gregg said, extending her arms.

Carson waved off the hug from across the room. "Oh, whatever. You'd do the same for me. You've done the same for me, remember?"

Gregg waggled her head and pulled on a nightie. "No, I'm not grateful for that. Or I am, but. What I'm trying to say." She stopped, pursed her lips, started again. "Is. I'm so grateful for *you*. You, you, you." She made a gesture like an infinity sign, or maybe it was an invisible lasso wrapping around Carson's shoulders. "My literary namesake sister!" Gregg was named for Charlene's best poet friend, Linda Gregg; Carson after McCullers, her mother's favorite writer. (Whether at the hospital young Sonja Larsen was too tired or too stoned on pain pills or too set on her homage to think through the almost rhyme of first name, last name was unclear, but Carson had endured the primary school ridicule like a stoic.) "I hope you never change."

"Thanks, buddy." Carson hugged her friend then, feeling Gregg's warm skin against her own. Did Gregg realize how that stung? Because what she was really admiring was that Carson had held up her end of the bargain. She had committed to that life they'd sworn to each other meant more than anything. But when the going got tough, Gregg sought validation elsewhere—turned out, it was easier to get your name on a yard sign than a theater marquee. Even if her off-ramp was objectively a good cause, challenging and worthwhile . . . she'd jumped ship.

Carson listened to the echo of Gregg's words. Was her compliment tinged by regret? Carson knew that Gregg could've stuck it out, if only she'd had more mettle and a rent-stabilized flat. Also, less pride. Because the rejection, the waves that surged by or somersaulted you or crashed overhead and held you under . . . Well, the whole process could be relentless, especially for someone who thought and wanted to continue thinking highly of herself.

As Carson hugged her friend, she sensed she was holding the old Gregg, the one she'd embraced after shows in those stage-entrance alleys, the Gregg who'd believed so much in herself that she'd stay belly-down on her surfboard for days on end, floating through the Doldrums without a ripple in sight. The scarcity hadn't fazed her, nor had the fact that when she'd eventually encounter a swell, it rarely broke her way. Then, the set would be too big or her timing would be off, or, most often, someone else in the lineup sprang up just right to catch the approaching crest.

Wait, was that how surfing worked? Carson tried to remember *Point Break*, to dredge up her favorite William Finnegan. Carson hated how the champagne had made her fuzzy. No, she couldn't blame the booze—it was her impatience, her inability to do anything other than rush forward and pounce on her feelings. She reminded herself of her resolution. Patience. She needed to sit with her uncertainty, whether in the realm of emotional indeterminacy or figurative language or bibliographic recall. She had to tick through her options calmly, reason through them till she landed on how she really, truly felt.

Carson extricated herself from the hug. "Hang on. Lemme get you some water."

As Carson ran the tap, waiting for cold, she watched herself in the bathroom mirror. She had changed, and would keep changing, but it was a different means of renovation from Gregg's shape-shifting, actor to state rep to mother and senator to maybe, soon, congresswoman. Gregg's transformation had been so public, while Carson's evolutions—in self-respect and creative ambition and hourly tutoring rate (now $200 an hour)—were so minutely incremental as to be invisible to the naked eye. Nothing was static, not even Carson!

Gregg was sprawled across the bed, asleep already when Carson returned, so she took a sip from the glass and set it on the nightstand by Gregg. Carson was happy with how the party had gone. Not that she'd been aiming to get Gregg wasted, but tonight she had seen some ethereal energy in her friend that had been missing in Palm Springs. A truer version of Gregg than she'd encountered for a while. Was it playing at "Charlene," some minor version of acting, that had made her vibrate with vitality? Or was it that, for an evening, she could live the life she'd thought she'd have, the one that Carson had stuck with?

Carson changed into one of Donny's free sweat suits—by the maker of Bella's travel set, but in a more sedate color scheme. It really was so fuzzy and warm.

As she lay back on the bed, the party sounded loud through the wall and then it sounded quiet and then it merely sounded like the night. Nearer, farther, she heard her friend's breath and the occasional passing siren, a racing motorcycle, a couple sharing a cigarette in the adjoining building's frozen-over backyard. Nearer, farther, Carson heard the building sigh and a toilet flush and someone, far away, laughing.

41

Sat, Jan 28 at 11:45 PM

Bella:

OMG I fell asleep by accident! So sorry for unplanned zzzz what was the surprise???

Bella awoke with a start. Something was off. She was lying in her bed, but the floof of down rising around her head and shoulders was wrong; she was on *top* of the comforter, rather than cozy under it. Also, the lights—next-generation LEDs, which Wirecutter had said were best for circadian rhythms—were glowing down on her made-up face. And she was fully dressed—she wiggled her toes—save for shoes. She tilted her chin to look: a sparkly top, black jeans—and it had been a miracle that they fit, thanks not to exercise but to the skipped meals and adrenaline of her recent marathon weeks at Cushman. These were not work clothes. Out the bedroom window, usually a view of a brick wall, a shaftway, someone else's bedroom window, she saw all of those things, but it was presently pitch black and unusually quiet.

Then she did hear a noise, slipping in under the door. It was the mumbling sound of a television on low, the hushed tweets and dull thuds of sports being played.

She looked at her phone—it was close to midnight. Last she'd checked, it was just after eight, Bill was putting the boys to bed, and she was jumping into her favorite pair of jeans. The sitter, they'd heard at five, was sick, and in her desperation not to bail on Carson again, Bella'd offered Bill a blow job, if only he'd skip his fantasy league get-together and stay home with the kids. After a poker-faced beat of consideration, after Bella threw in bath duty for a week, he'd acceded. With that victory notched, and after the boys were fed, she'd sat down on her bed for a minute, lain back for a second . . .

Was this narcolepsy? Did she have a disorder, or was she simply supremely tired? Because she'd lost a few hours to unplanned sleep that Monday after Palm Springs, and last week, she'd fallen asleep in a work toilet stall. Twice. She wanted to look it up on WebMD, but she had a self-imposed moratorium on the site—too many scary *maybes* lurked in their vague diagnostics. (She didn't need the internet to confirm she had a medium-level case of hypochondria on top of everything else.) She wanted to ask Hillary, who served as her own personal WebMD, sans the pop-up ads and paranoia, what it might be. Bella calculated the time in Chicago and decided against it. Hillary was an early-to-bed type; she should already be tucked in, fast asleep.

Bella considered her options. The party was probably still going, but even if she ordered a car and it pulled up this minute, she wouldn't get to Carson's part of Brooklyn until twelve thirty, and she wouldn't get home until, what, three? Four? Four wasn't late, four was early. Four was when she left the apartment for one of those first-of-the-morning flights, when she rose if she wanted to use her bike in the corner of the bedroom before the boys got up. Her downstairs neighbor, a real pill, had complained about the machine's noise, even as Bella insisted it hardly made any. How bad could it be if Bill snoozed right through it, she wanted to know. She didn't add, while making her case to the super, that Bill could sleep through a military assault.

There was no way she could go now, and after she'd even convinced herself to take the train. Bella hadn't been looking forward to the hectic transfer at Atlantic/Pacific, but doing so at eight thirty in the evening, when the ratio of reasonable people to un- was still in the former's favor, she could've managed. (That she'd take a car service home was never a question.)

She texted Carson apologies, followed by a GIF of a sleepy kitten. She stared at the screen, hoping for an instant reply, a quick reassurance that it was all right that she'd flaked, that all was forgiven.

The way they'd been bickering lately was weird—both of them were stressed, she knew, and money was a perennial wedge issue, but what was actually happening? Their wildly different existences were generally an asset to the friendship. Bella had no interest in writing stories—she could hardly get through the short fiction in *The New Yorker* without checking her phone, and she hadn't finished a novel since 2018 (a shame she blamed on her children). And Carson, by and large, had scant interest in lawyerly concerns or material ones, other than as a sympathetic listener to Bella. There had been that one stretch where, every time they got together, she asked random questions about criminal sentencing, which Bella hadn't thought of since 3L. At some point she'd become so annoyed with the barrage that she'd given Carson her Lexis password.

Bella loved the group fiercely, but what she had with Carson was special. With Reba it was so lopsided, Reba looking out for her like she might face-plant at any moment (and when she'd only really lost it once . . .). And with Gregg there was a hint of competition—not that they were competing on anything directly, but there were enough echoes between their lives: the two boys, the fetching and successful husbands, the careers that required a lot of performance, some gavels, real or impromptu. It was like they were constantly sizing each other up. (At least Bella hoped the feeling was mutual; if it wasn't, and Gregg wasn't also considering Bella's diction and handbags, that'd be embarrassing.) With Hillary, too, there was a competitive streak—not for who was most stylish, or the best public speaker (Bella won both by a mile), but in other metrics. Who had the more handsome husband (Hillary), the cuter boy (it'd been Roger, though Bill Jr. might come from behind; one of the nursery school moms recently said he looked like a baby JFK Jr.), who had the more devoted mother (Hillary by a landslide; Sheila would drive from Wisconsin at the drop of a dime and sleep on that lumpy pullout without complaint, while Marianne acted like it was a huge imposition to come up for major grandchild-related events, even when they offered to put her up at the Carlyle). Who was more righteous, which was also Hillary, her moral compass so strong that the arrow of it sometimes pointed into moral*izing*.

Carson was just Carson. Sardonic, smart, too cool for school by ten long blocks. Beloved. And she'd disappointed her friend tonight.

Bella stepped into the hall. The TV got louder, but not so loud as to wake the kids.

"Where'd you come from?" Her husband was lying on the couch, one hand resting lightly in the waistband of his sweats. Four beer cans were lined up on the coffee table.

"I fell asleep," she said. Bella looked at her husband, at his hand—she couldn't remember the last time she'd slipped her hand down there. Had it been December? Thanksgiving?

She glanced at the screen. Was this game important because Bill cared about the teams in real life or because they impacted his fantasy team? That he even had time for a fantasy league seemed like an affront, but she reminded herself that fostering male friendship was a worthwhile aim; her husband needed a support network just as much as she did.

Well, not *as* much. But he deserved something, some hang time with folks to whom he was not contractually or genetically obligated.

"I thought you'd gone hours ago."

She shook her head. "I never left."

"Oh," he said. He scooted his legs to make room for her on the couch, and she sat down. "Whatever, you've needed the rest, the way you've been running."

"Mm-hmm." She sent Carson another apologetic text and reached for the last can in the line, hoping there'd be a slug left. There was more than that, and she took a big swallow.

Her husband was watching her, noting the purse of her lips around the can's mouth, the movement of the muscles in her throat. "Do I still get that BJ?"

42

Sun, Jan 29 at 8:23 AM

Carson:

Next time, Gadget...

In the morning Donny cleaned, Gregg slept in, and when their guest was up, Carson made eggs of the chicken variety, scrambled with shallots and Gruyère; they'd all had enough of the aquatic kind the prior night. Donny retrieved the Sunday *Times* from the corner bodega; they split and swapped its many sections. The news was bad—the war in Ukraine, civil rights violations in the South, violent cops and baying politicians—but they cackled together over a ridiculously puffy piece on Elizabeth Holmes. How had anyone ever believed her? They read the paper until their thumbs were gray, discussing the interesting headlines, pushing around their toast. They drank two pots of coffee, Carson refilling their mugs from her bedroom brewer because she was too snobby for Donny's grocery store beans. Throughout the meal they found a handful of desiccated fish eggs in the cracks of the table. Hadn't Nikolai used a tablecloth?

• • •

That afternoon, Carson and Gregg walked around Green-Wood Cemetery, which was just a few blocks from the loft. There was Basquiat, there was Bernstein, there was Boss Tweed. On their second loop—Carson's knee was feeling good today—Gregg asked Carson to tell her about the cemetery where Sonja was buried. (Gregg, like the rest of them, knew not a thing about Carson's father.) As they walked, Carson described the Seattle graveyard, its sloping lawns and fir trees and views of the lake, how an anonymous gift—she knew it was her friends, even as no one would confess to it—had secured her mother a luxe coffin and tasteful headstone and prime spot on the green hillside, Bruce Lee and Brandon a few plots away.

She didn't say it'd rained at the funeral, though it had; didn't say that there had been only a dozen mourners, though there were (none of the women had made it, the funeral being in the middle of finals). To Gregg, Carson described some of those present: a checker from her mother's shift at the grocery, Carson's high school English teacher, the neighbor from their apartment complex who'd often watched Carson when she was young. She didn't say how, when she'd returned to Seattle fifteen years later and visited the grave, she'd hardly recognized the place. Lake View Cemetery itself was familiar, if a decade fuller of bones and stone, but the view was disoriented by new construction, looming apartment blocks that edged up to the wrought-iron gates. The beloved, eponymous view of Lake Washington was mostly blocked by recent condos, reduced to a thin slice of water.

"Do you miss her?" Gregg asked. Carson thought about the question. She missed how Sonja and she were often more like girlfriends than mother and daughter, Sonja's eternal patience and banter and kindness. She missed her cooking; Sonja rarely had the time, but when she did, they'd feast. How she'd read and encouraged drafts of every silly story, all the way back to kindergarten. But Carson still held so much anger. About her mother's magical thinking, ignoring her symptoms for so long. If she'd been given the chance, Carson would've nursed her through rounds of chemo and radiation, dealt with a dozen recurrences. But instead, there was just the diagnosis and the quick, steep decline. Did Sonja genuinely believe that by postponing treatment until there was effectively none left, she had spared Carson some difficulty? That by rushing straight to palliative care, they'd avoided the awful part? Carson wanted decades with her mother, not months. As for those months, Sonja had fought vituperatively against Carson's taking a leave of absence—she hadn't wanted her to miss even a week of class. Instead, Carson did the registrar's paperwork, drained her bank account, and bought a one-way ticket home. She'd finish up the incomplete credits over the summer, she told herself. They were both operating under the assumption that Sonja wouldn't live past June.

And why had Sonja been so oppositional? Maybe she'd not wanted to get in the way of Carson's education after the scree of her early years. Carson's childhood had been a latchkey life, city buses and countless hours at the library, so many reheated meals and days she'd had to get herself to school. Despite all that, she'd made it to a prestigious college. Sonja knew her daughter would do great things; she told her that often. But soon after Carson's first publication—just a story in the campus magazine—which coincided with Sonja's diagnosis, Carson spotted the flaw in her mother's logic. Didn't she want to be there for the next one too, to celebrate together? The small landmark of a story pub, the monument of her book. (Her *books*? Carson had dared, even then, to pluralize.) Sonja's decision to leave when and as she did—its shortsightedness frustrated Carson still.

That was the optimistic take, the magnanimous one. Carson's ungenerous read was that Sonja knew that if Carson came back to help with her terminal days, she would find out about her father, and Sonja would stop at nothing to prevent that. As it was, when they'd swapped out Sonja's regular bed for a hospital one and Carson had found the binder among the boxes stowed under the old bed frame (and right next to Carson's baby book, how messed up was that?), Sonja had had the gall to play dumb; when Carson wouldn't abide the act, Sonja had tried the line that the pain meds must be causing memory lapses (which they were, but not about this).

Finally, finally she'd confessed. Yes, the man in the scrapbooked binder was her father. Yes, Carson had a father—and he was the worst type of man. A killer, locked up in Monroe Correctional in Eastern Washington since 1983. With the *Post-Intelligencer* clippings, Carson could plot the timeline—he was arrested six months before her November birthday, in court for her mom's last trimester, sentenced when Carson was two months old. Had Carson and her father ever met? Her mother swore up and down that they hadn't—she hadn't even told him she was pregnant. But because she'd felt a strange connection with him, she'd been compelled to follow the case, to reply to his jailhouse letters, to separate his seeming affection for her from his documented violence. Carson could see a flame of belief in Sonja's tired eyes, but after so many lies, she didn't fully trust it.

After the reveal, they'd fought like dogs (one of them a stoned bulldog, lethargic with hydrocodone); it was useless, but both were unable to stop themselves from swiping. At first Carson wasn't angry at her father or his vile act (double homicide, first-degree murder). No, she could only feel rage for Sonja and her deception. How could she have lied for so long? She'd sworn it was a party hookup, that she couldn't remember even his first name. But there were love notes in that binder! Full names and addresses!

Now, walking around a Brooklyn cemetery on the last Sunday of January, nearly two decades after her mother's death, Carson wanted to explain to Gregg her complicated feelings about Sonja, but she did not want to get her family's blood on her friend's hands. How would that help anything? So she said, "It's . . . complicated." Then, keen to change the subject, she asked, "How are you feeling about tomorrow?"

Gregg snorted. "Leave it to a writer to ask about killing your unborn child while walking in a graveyard."

"It's not a—"

"I'm giving you a hard time. I know it's the right decision for me, but Zeke . . ." She studied an ornate headstone, a rose carved into its front. "It'll take him some time."

"He was pissed?"

"When I said I wanted to focus on the kids we have, he looked at me like I was speaking Greek. I think it's part bullheaded, part a sincere incapacity to compute—that guy never taps out. It's a thing I admire in him usually, or formerly. I wanted to be like him, Carson, until I got so damn exhausted."

"He also got to sleep through the night for these last two years." When Carson had heard about his mummying, she'd wanted to punch him in the neck.

Gregg chewed her lip. "What do they say about founders? They never say *no*, they say, How do we get to *yes*?"

"They also have a tendency to be narcissistic, delusional, and sometimes psychopathic."

"Same could be said of politicians." Gregg smiled ruefully.

"Don't beat yourself up for recognizing what you need to do and getting it done. It's why I love you." Carson squeezed her friend's hand. "And he might be mad now, but it's why he loves you too." She had no idea if this was true.

• • •

When they got home from their afternoon stroll and an early supper of steaming Malaysian soup, Zariah, back from her wedding, had her tarot deck out on the dining table; she was giving Donny his weekly reading. When they were done, she turned to Gregg, her voice high with excitement: Would she like a turn?

Carson smirked at the largesse; in more than a year as roommates, she'd never been offered one. Gregg gamely slid into the seat across from Zariah. As Zariah turned out card after card, Gregg smiled, encouraging her progress. With the last card, Zariah was buzzing with energy. Given how she was speaking to their visitor—she gushed that every card was remarkable, very advantageous, so exciting—she still had no idea why Gregg was here, Carson thought. That part of their secret had stuck, even if no one believed "Charlene."

After the women were through—Gregg thanking Zariah with a tight hug, some whisper in her ear—Zariah turned to Carson. "Want a spin?" Carson, stunned and grateful, settled into the waiting chair.

Zariah looked faintly apologetic as she flipped over the death card. Carson examined the skeleton on horseback. He was facing her, not Zariah, which apparently added further nuance to her fate. "That looks ominous," she said nervously.

Zariah clucked sympathetically. "Not necessarily. The death card is about transitions, transformations. New beginnings. Spring follows winter, right?"

Carson grinned. "Correct." She and the blooming backyard had turned Zariah into a wisteria fan last spring.

When the whole grid was spread between them, Zariah studied the configuration quietly. "Two Major Arcana. Something big is coming." Her brow furrowed. "It looks like you'll get tough news this week," she said. "But this one," she added, pointing at a glowing sun, "says that you'll get answers too."

43

Mon, Jan 30 at 3:43 PM

Amelia:

Of course I'll tell the others. So sorry for your loss, Hill. ❤

The Manhattan office of the national nonprofit reproductive care provider was typically swarmed with protesters and counterprotesters; it had been that way for decades and become even more so in the seven months since *Dobbs*. But this early on a cold late-January Monday, there were barely any picketers outside the women's care center in central Queens, just a handful of sleepy-looking Baptists, signs on their shoulders, standing at the court-mandated distance from the entrance. Carson would have managed the angry throng of Manhattan for Gregg, but she appreciated how Gregg had thought of the relative ease of an outer borough, the lower profile of a local clinic, and the peace of mind that a six-foot buffer offered. Not that there was ever an ideal abortion, but Gregg had done her homework.

Per Gregg's request, Carson was allowed to sit in on the consult, which confirmed that a dilation and curettage would be required (the pills stopped being effective at ten weeks); the doctor described the procedure as "easy" and "routine," but also requiring general anesthesia. She asked Gregg if she understood the risks and consequences; Gregg said she did.

Did Gregg have any other questions?

Carson looked at her friend, who seemed a thousand miles away. And she was—back in Texas, replaying the argument with Zeke, how stony he'd been, how he'd acted so dismissive of her feelings and her organic beef. Where was the man who'd wooed her, the one who'd made her swoon with his epic gestures of affection, who'd sworn he believed in her, whatever she wanted to try next? Gregg was realizing that in Zeke's eyes, maybe *next* went in only one direction: toward bigger, grander, more. Furious growth fit with his ethos, it even fit with his rockets. They hadn't started to design the landing gear yet; were solely focused on upping their propulsion. Why think about the return trip when there was still so far to fly?

Remembering their conversation and that evening's unexpected chill, Gregg shivered. Then she blinked calmly at the waiting doctor. Once an actor, always an actor. "Plenty of questions. But none for you."

• • •

Carson hadn't brought a book to read, but it hardly mattered—the waiting room had a loud TV, a stack of appealingly vapid magazines, and a small girl who was trying to assemble a complicated puzzle. Carson asked if she could help, and the girl solemnly scooted over so Carson could sidle up to the coffee table too. More women came in, more women went back to the exam rooms, more women left looking exhausted or relieved or both. Carson pondered where this girl's mother might be. She knew that physically she'd be in one of the many exam rooms lining that long hall. But big picture? She didn't know if this little person, staring at the table for some detail she might recognize, would become a big sister, or if she'd not.

In time, the girl's mother waddled out, largely pregnant. She shook her head. "Hope she wasn't bothering you." Carson and the receptionist assured her it'd been no problem. "Look at the edge," the girl said proudly, indicating to her mother a span of blue sea and sunsetting sky that faded from purple to pink. The mother rubbed her child's back. "Good work."

The front desk staff put in an order for lunch and offered to let Carson tag on. This sounded better than facing the crowd outside, which had grown in size and volume since their morning arrival. Carson offered cash for her sandwich, but the receptionist refused it.

"You're a good friend, being here." Also, she explained, a donor had covered the clinic's lunches for the fiscal year. "Everyone wants to do something now," the woman said. Sometimes, *something* was a tuna melt.

Carson ate her sandwich and watched the clock, listening to Maury Povich shout about paternity. "You are the father!" She thought it might've been tactful to change the channel, given their general circumstance, but no one else seemed to notice the rerun or be bothered by its screaming.

Just before four, her phone lit up. It was Amelia, the painter friend who had ruined Bella's bedspread with tears a decade earlier. Had Gregg told her she was in town? Carson doubted it; Amelia lived in Philly now, and it would have been a hassle to coordinate their schedules, to deal with the New Jersey Turnpike. "Hey, Amelia. What's up?" Carson stood, thinking she'd step onto the street, but at the front door, seeing the shapes of the protesters through the frosted glass, she thought better of it.

"He's dead," Amelia said.

"Who, what?" Carson backed away from the door, trying to find a quiet corner in the lobby. Whichever way she turned, the TV seemed to get louder. "You are the father!"

"Miles. He's dead." Amelia let out a whimper.

"Huh? Hillary's husband Miles? And do you mean dead to us or, like, *dead* dead?"

"*Dead* dead." Amelia was bawling now, but managed to add, "Some kind of overdose."

"Wasn't he in rehab?"

"Jailbreak." She blew her nose. It sounded like an elephant in Carson's ear.

"Shit," she said.

"Right? Poor Hillary, she's a wreck. Can you tell the others? I think Hill called me because I'm first in her contacts, but I don't even have Bella's number anymore. The funeral is Wednesday."

"So soon?"

"A Jewish thing, apparently."

Carson had forgotten that about him. Then she remembered the huppah at the wedding, how Hillary had smashed a napkin-wrapped glass under her heel. She'd looked so happy stomping, even if, according to Reba, the crunch was meant as a reminder of the fragility of their union. Oh, Hillary! Carson's heart sank for her friend, for fatherless Roger.

Amelia was still sobbing. Someone entered the lobby; the voice of a protester shouting about mifepristone surged in with them. Carson swallowed hard. "Thanks for letting me know."

• • •

Carson started a text chain before she was back to her seat. She included Gregg, even though she was holding Gregg's phone; her friend's satchel was slung over her shoulder alongside her own canvas tote. She felt the phone buzz through the bag's smooth leather.

"Guys, bad news." She shared what she knew about Miles.

"Hillary didn't ask us to come—not yet. But we should be there," she typed.

"If we can," she added, knowing about Bella's kids and her court date. Had the trial started already? Bella had texted multiple times to apologize for missing the party, but hadn't mentioned anything about the trial. Knowing about Reba's fertility schedule—well, not knowing the specifics, but understanding the tight window for implantation and the anxiety of those first tenuous weeks. Knowing Gregg would still be recovering from her procedure. Might any of them make it to Chicago?

"Oh. My. God."

"This is so sad." Bella sent one message, then the next.

"Thanks for letting us know," Reba pinged from California. "I'll be there."

So she wasn't pregnant, again. Or still, Carson thought.

She knew she had to call Hillary, to express her condolences. But what would she say? After what Miles had put Hill through, her friends all partway hated him; they had, at times, wished he'd disappear off the face of the earth. But they'd not imagined he'd literally go *poof*! Carson texted Hillary to let her know she was in her thoughts; she could call anytime but didn't have to.

"What about you, Gregg? Can you make it?"

Carson had hoped the others wouldn't notice Gregg's conspicuous quiet on the chat.

"Gregg???" Bella pinged a long line of question marks. They all knew Gregg to keep her phone on her hip, to be the fastest draw among them.

"Maybe she's in a meeting," Carson tried, stalling for time.

Just then, a nurse came out.

"She did great," the woman said. "She's resting now, but you can see her."

Carson tried to settle her face into placidity as she walked down the antiseptic hall.

In the recovery room, Carson beamed down at her friend. She felt so unconvincing in her cheer. "Hey, babe. How are you feeling?"

Gregg smiled back, her face still woozy, and asked, "What did I miss?"

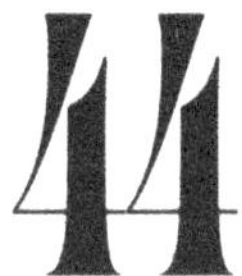

Mon, Jan 30 at 2:45 PM

Hillary:

Mom can you give me a call when you have a sec?

Hillary had seen dead bodies. Her grandparents, both sides, though she'd been too young to remember those well. Her dad's much older brother, back in Wisconsin, in the days when her dad was present enough in her life that she'd do something so kind as attend her uncle's funeral. She'd only seen Uncle Jay among the living twice (her dad's Thanksgivings, which meant days spent at the bowling alley, the three of them alone on the lanes, gutter balls and strikes, so many soda pops and grilled cheeses she thought she'd be sick). Her mother had refused to attend the funeral (Sheila refused to share any room with her ex, the quarter century's one exception being Hillary's wedding), so fifteen-year-old Hillary had put on her band slacks and a dark sweater and ridden the bus downtown, walking into Watertown's old funeral home alone. Uncle Jay in his casket had looked like he was made of wax.

And there was her medical school anatomy lab. There she'd been focused on logistics, the titillating scalpel in her hand. She'd noted the eventual give of the skin (tougher than anticipated), and of muscle (less tenacious than expected, at least after a dose of formalin). Their cadaver was named Larry, and every day, he looked up at Hillary—his bluish skin, that bubble gum smell—and asked, *Are you sure you want to do this?* Yes, she did. With Larry she learned the way a lung felt in her hand—spongy and so much heavier than she'd expected for a thing full of air. She'd even lifted his heart—how assertively it had clung to its aortic root—and cupped it in her palm. Understanding the density of that muscle, the power in her grip, reaffirmed her decision, absolutely. She wanted to do this, she did.

Some students suffered gastro-chemical reactions to the formaldehyde—despite the gore and the lab's bouquet of harsh smells, they would get outrageously hungry, famished like they'd not eaten in days. For her, it was like the room was dosed with aphrodisiacs. During her and Miles's three-hour sessions of careful or assertive or sloppy incisions, she wanted to ravish her lab partner, to rip him asunder, to lick his body and bite. Good news for her, the appealing young man across the metal table usually agreed to her post-lab entreaties. (These days, she tried not to think about how certain she'd felt about her lab partner back then, as if one wrong conviction might call into question every other choice she'd once been sure of.)

And she'd encountered plenty of dying bodies. All bodies are essentially dying ones, all of us on the moving sidewalk that ends at our maker, but Hillary meant the more rapidly extinguishing flames, the acutely dying: inoperable cancers, eating disorders, drug addictions. As much as she complained about her practice's workaday patients—and there were so many nose jobs, owing to vanity or car crashes or hard-kicked soccer balls (even Bella'd had hers reconstructed, and minutely improved, after a misjudged header smashed her bridge)—there was tragedy enough to go around, and Hillary could list many, many consults with patients who were readying, willingly or not, for their exits. The worst was a tumor in the sinus canal, those always made her feel awful. She could offer patients a surgery as inexact as a melon baller, but could make no guarantees they'd scoop out all the malignancy on their first pass or second. And while she saw them less frequently now that she was focused on noses, she also hated examining the esophagi of bingers-and-purgers, how those throats were a few burps away from blowing out. Esophageal bleeds were a bad way to go.

Though she'd chosen to specialize in the disasters of the nose, she held fast to the catastrophes covered in her general medical training. Now she was twelve years out of school, seven out of residency, five past her rhinology fellowship and last round of boards, and she could still spot the jaundice of a failing liver in a passing stranger, could still pick out the crick of an osteoarthritic hip ready to shatter—even at a block's distance, even wrapped in the bulky coat of a Chicago winter.

And she could spot dying at closer range too. Her father had a bad and worsening heart; her mom was hovering at the cusp of diabetes. Bella nearly died in childbirth, Gregg was asking for hypertension (the stress of that job was obscene), and Carson might well be carrying the BRCA gene, given what had happened to her mother. Hillary was aware of her own mortality, the weight gain that had wrapped her menopausal mother already trying to swaddle Hillary too. She'd had gestational diabetes with Roger, which had been a bummer but she'd managed okay with seven puny, sugar-free meals a day. She'd consumed a full field of kale, Miles had joked. Her reward on the toughest days of her last trimester was two glorious strawberries before bed.

Hillary could see death everywhere, but addiction, which she had pathologized in med school and watched in the news, which so many pharmacists had turned a blind eye to and which Bella had defended in court, was the category of dying with which she was most familiar. Even if no symptoms were visible, the patient "high functioning" and well-versed at covering his tracks, she always found a tell. She'd had plenty of practice with Miles.

Miles's version of dying hadn't been so scary at first. More of an embarrassment, behavior that was a little cringe. On sloppy weekends, when their med school cohort would cut loose, he'd cut even looser, and go wild with whatever recreational substance was at hand. Go big or go home, right? That had never been Hillary's modus operandi; she was more tortoise than hare. But enough of their classmates were like Miles—competitive and tightly wound and highly motivated in all things, including getting blasted as the exam schedule allowed—that his behavior fell within a normal range. But then he'd suffered a broken collarbone during pickup basketball—one of those driven peers, driving too hard into the paint—and the doctor had given him pain pills. This was right around that fraught noontime of Match Day, the two of them, a couple since year two, praying and hoping that they'd be placed in the same city. And they had been—Hillary and Miles had gotten the luckiest break of being matched in the same hospital, three floors apart. Hooray for Northwestern Memorial, hurrah for Chicago! In the hustle of their interstate move the prescription had run out, but he could get the meds another way. That he hit a wall at PT, the pain not as bright as when the bone had first fractured, but present, persistent, interrupting his thoughts as he made his way through his hospital days . . . Honestly, she was too busy to notice. Med school, as intense as it had been, was nothing like her first sixty-hour week on the floor, scrubbing into ten surgeries, trying to graft her textbooks' anatomical drawings onto these patients' cut-open heads.

Then, they became lucky a different way. "We're lucky they didn't press charges," he'd told her when he confessed his theft and summary dismissal from the surgery program. She'd thought then, Who's *we*?, even as she twirled the engagement ring around her finger. Her mother would've said *Get out now*, but Sheila wasn't there that night in their Chicago apartment, the Wrigley Field crowd cheering through the open window, and even if she had been, Sheila was not allowed to say squat to her daughter about what was best for her future. Hillary loved this man. So instead of running for the hills, she'd reached for Miles's hand and said to him, "I know."

At the time of his booting, a hundred of their friends and family were readying to gather in an Omaha ballroom—the wedding was only two weeks away. So Hillary had discreetly emailed the best man, Miles's younger and more buttoned-up brother, to explain what had happened, and asked him to recruit the groomsmen to quietly spread the word: *Ixnay on the edicinemay.* She wanted no well-meaning childhood pals pressing for residency gossip, no nosy aunts prying for his ten-year plan, and definitely none of his mom's recitations of her optimistic-slash-delusional script. Irene Koenig was so believing that it'd all been a big misunderstanding; he was going to be Chicago's top orthopedic surgeon still. The guys had done a good job—not as good as her bridal party, Reba and Bella and Gregg and even Carson, in her awkward way, executing a damage control campaign that would've impressed a veteran political operative.

Hillary had read about people making the jump from prescription to street pills, street pills to heroin, but it was still stunning to see it happen up close. Not that close—he never used in front of her (in the next room, in the washroom while they were out at a restaurant, once in the shoebox bathroom of an international flight, which had made her livid, but better to use up the product than try to get through customs with *that* in his pocket). She came to note how there was a smell to it, how his sweat went acrid. And Hillary noticed other traces. Some, like the rust-colored stains at the bend of the arm on his dress shirts (which she spot-treated without comment for years), were just unsightly; others, like how he could be looking right at her but not hear a thing, were more menacing.

He'd tried to hide his first bad injection wound, an abscess in the crook of his arm, but then the infection had hit his bloodstream and turned the whole vein, wrist to shoulder, an angry red. The skin was hot to the touch, and he was clammy with fever. So she took him into their bathroom and lanced and drained and rinsed the wound, as they'd been trained. "What did you do?" was what she said, but she knew what he'd done, and that he'd promised he wouldn't do it again after that business at the hospital.

She'd squeezed the wound from both sides, smiled up at pale-faced Miles like everything was under control. But when the infection's white goo went red and smooth and quicksilver—that had made her dizzy. Larry hadn't done that. Bled.

She'd been rattled by how vivid and insistent it was. Rattled by her rattling—she was not meant to be squeamish, not Dr. Koenig, MD. So she'd said, "Sorry." It was a knee-jerk habit, apologizing for her proficiency, and easier than stopping to consider how she really felt, which was unsettled and frustrated, startled and scared. "It's okay," Miles had said. He'd already forgiven her. Now it was her turn to forgive him.

She did.

The wounds paused after that, save for one or two hiccups. He was good all through her pregnancy (on threat of death; the hormones multiplied her pent-up frustration to morph her from Wisconsin polite to Linda Blair). Either he was not using, he was safer, or he was sneakier, utilizing the spaces between the fingers, between the toes. Hillary had thought, optimistically, this period was the two of them turning over a new leaf, that on this season of the reality TV show of their lives, they'd settle on a new deserted island where they'd find a baby and coconuts, but also where her husband would be solidly sober and wear a sexy palm-frond sarong. She could see him marching into the interior each day (on this island, there was a whole forest and not just the one measly palm tree) and returning with meals he'd caught and killed and cooked over a fire. (When Miles was cooking, she was more cavalier about her vegetarianism, because he was thoughtful about sourcing and could make anything taste delicious.) It was a nice notion, and not short-lived—for fourteen months, he was clean or very good at acting like it. For that same duration he was suggesting and subsequently dodging a return to school. A PA program was starting in the fall; it also offered spring enrollment. He kept saying he'd sign up . . . but couldn't he stay home with Roger just another few months? He claimed it was for bonding and she wanted to believe him, to trust the scrape on his arm was just that, but she wasn't born yesterday. That was Roger, mewling or screaming or burping from his crib.

Miles's blood and its spilling into the sink, as powerful as witnessing that had felt, became entirely inconsequential the first time she saw her child bleeding. Roger had scratched himself, his baby nails tiny razors. Those crimson beads weren't dying, she knew that—kid cells regenerated in, what, forty-two minutes? But the drops were so brilliant she thought her heart might stop. This was whom she was meant to protect, not some grown-ass man whose medical specialty was ortho-disappointing her. So when Miles tumbled off the wagon again with a big *plop*, when he got a new round of infections and requested her assistance cleaning out his crusting sores, she told him he could help himself to the hydrogen peroxide; he knew where the effing Band-Aids were kept. It was around then that she started carrying Narcan, because even as she knew Miles was too smart, too in control to let that happen, she had to admit that it might.

So maybe she did periodically curse him with such venom that if she'd had any of Gregg's psychic's witchiness, had she possessed a portion of Zariah's capacity for prescient tarot readings, she might have thwacked him lifeless on any of several occasions. But she didn't have such skills, and she couldn't have predicted that for all the dead and dying bodies she'd encountered over the years, facing her own dead would be a lot more difficult than seeing fresh blood on her beloved's arm, and much, much harder than slicing down the middle of a stranger's sternum. The things we learn.

• • •

Hillary happened to be between patients when the call came. She recognized the hospital prefix but not the number itself, and seeing that string of digits, she immediately thought, Something has happened to my son.

And something had happened to Roger, though indirectly. His life had changed forever, though in the near term it might've seemed like a series of unremarkable shifts: a late pickup from day care, an impromptu visit from his Wisconsin grandma, a strange reunion with his dad's family (how do you explain shiva to a five-year-old?). His absent father would still be absent, but somehow his mom was suddenly more available and more distracted, fast to smother him in hugs, quick to burst into tears.

She listened to the voice on the phone ask about Miles Koenig's spouse—she was still listed as his next of kin everywhere—and tried to keep her face calm. When the speaker told her what was needed, she said, "I'll be right down." She looked at her watch. She had fifteen minutes until her next appointment, two hours until she'd have to pick up Roger from day care.

45

Mon, Jan 30 at 3:25 PM

Hillary:

Hi mom sorry I missed you will call back in 10. Got your go bag?

Hillary left her office via the side door and looped back to the main elevator, hoping no one might see her exit. "I'm so sorry to let you know," the voice on the phone had said. That was her line when she'd seen something bad on an X-ray; what was she doing on the receiving end of it? The call came from some tech who didn't know the first thing about her, obviously not that they were calling a number that rang twelve floors up in the very same building. And by the way they kept calling her Miles's spouse, they didn't know about the Koenigs' separation, how he'd moved into a cruddy studio but then moved out of that for rehab, how the things that used to take up too much space in their apartment were back there now, his vinyl records and vintage Nikes boxed up in a corner of the living room. In the fall they'd both found reasonable lawyers (they'd be civil; they wanted to do what was best for their son), and she'd spotted a negligible insurance advantage at the facility if Miles stayed enrolled on Hillary's policy. It was still costing an arm and a leg, but Hillary could offer Miles this one last generosity.

And so they'd kicked the divorce can farther.

In recent weeks, her lawyer's secretary had followed up more than once—Miles had signed the paperwork before he went in, and was waiting for her to execute her set of documents. At first, Hillary told the woman she was having "trouble with her schedule." Then she wanted to "review" everything one more time. In truth, she wasn't finalizing the divorce because, for all the poise she'd mustered when speaking about the split with her mother, however decisive she'd sounded to her girlfriends alongside that desert pool, she was still a softy for him, holding out hope that all this could be undone, if only their Control-Z command could be typed into a giant, omniscient keyboard. They made those, right? She thought of the big red Help buttons—even if that was an advertising campaign for an office supply store . . . surely they could conjure a life-sized Undo? For a long time, it'd been an inside joke between the two of them. When he screwed up—"Control-Z!" he'd say, palms up. Shorthand for *I'm sorry*. She and Miles had even been the keystrokes for Halloween once—he'd painted cardboard boxes, cut and reshaped their seams to taper at the slope of an old-school PC's keyboard. (She'd been the Control button, clearly.) But then he'd started throwing his palms up so often. "Control-Z!" became a cup that held less and less water. She pushed the elevator call button. What he'd done now—this one had no Undo.

The hospital's always slow elevator arrived very quickly. Hillary was grateful for this—no colleagues or patients had seen her duck out—until its descent also went much faster than expected. Never had she dropped so swiftly, a stone out of the sky. She wished she could tell the mechanism to slow, to ease her down into the subbasement in one-inch increments, but instead it plummeted, then settled, then pinged. The doors opened on −2. Straight ahead of her were big double doors that said *MOR* and *GUE*.

And how could Miles be here? She tried to puzzle it out as she stepped forward. Because he was supposed to be at rehab, the place that was reaming her bank account anew (med school debt, his and hers, was already oppressive). The place to which she had posted videos of her son every day—and they did not even have the courtesy to text back a confirmation of receipt. *Is this thing on?* she'd wanted to message. *Anyone home?*

She'd not wanted to sound skeptical, but always the pragmatist, at check-in she'd inquired (quietly) about success rates and in-case-ofs.

"No," the mean-looking administrator had snapped. There were no refunds for failures, for the folks who stepped out of rehab and waltzed right back into a bar, not for those who sneaked to the alley behind the bar to find their next score and shot up right there, their backs pressed against the blissful brick. And there were, Hillary would discover, no refunds for jailbreaks, just a prorated bill and a stiff-sounding apology. At least they didn't offer anything more in cases of charismatic, close-to-former husbands who sweet-talked pretty, young PAs; not for guys whose escape routes included fingering said PAs in the supply closet, men who coaxed the gullible PAs not to let them out, strictly speaking, but to not *not* let them out. If only she didn't lock that one door at that one time of day on that one day of the week when the patients were least supervised, he'd have a forty-five-minute head start before anyone knew he was missing...

"No refunds" was written in tiny font on page 7 of the intake forms. Hillary had also missed a clause on page 12 stating that the facility had twenty-four hours to notify the emergency contact of any "developments with patient status." Twenty-four hours was important, because in that window an escapee could be found, an OD could be reversed, so much could be Control-Z'd. For one thousand, four hundred forty minutes—which included the agonizing thirty seconds it took Hillary to walk down that subbasement hall—in the eyes of the the rehab place, Miles was still within the realm of not-definitely-missing; during that time span he stayed a might-still-be-around-here-somewhere patient, sneaky and elusive but maybe not gone. (The facility's notification, the call that started, "We're so sorry to tell you," wouldn't come until she was on her way home that evening, shuffling down an icy sidewalk, saddled by her work bag and her son's school one. They'd say, euphemistically, that her husband was "temporarily absent from the facility," to which she would let out a barking laugh loud enough to stop Roger, and a half-dozen proximate strangers, in their tracks.)

She opened the heavy door and followed signs to reception (their term). She said Miles's name, and the guy at the counter asked for ID.

She showed her hospital badge—his eyebrows went up—and then he said, "Government issued," and she apologized, digging her driver's license out of her bowling-ball bag of a purse. The disaffected young man sifted through papers until he found the file—hadn't it been in his hands when he'd called, minutes before? "Sign here," he said, pushing a clipboard forward.

Stepping into the morgue itself, she could feel the cabinets radiating their refrigeration. She thought of Larry and his awful, intoxicating smell. "You've got this," she muttered, reminding herself of all her previous death and dying, the dissections and sutures and open cavities to which she'd become accustomed. She could handle one more body.

The tech from the front desk appeared at another door and looked down at his hand. He was holding a Post-it note, neon pink. She was taken aback by the casualness of this gesture, his nonchalance, right up until he located the proper shelf and heaved it open. Then, as she stepped forward and lifted the sheet, she was really, truly bewildered.

She knew every inch of Miles, the icy-lake blue of his irises (his eyes were unsettlingly open), his slightly crooked teeth, his impressive, circumcised penis. He was, hands down, the best-looking guy she'd ever been with. Not that she'd been with many—she'd been late to splash into the dating pool (Bella practically had to push her into the water, insisting Hillary not leave college a virgin; to wait longer was not modest but idiotic), and the first of their friends to commit to Real Love. She could still remember making the calls, telling the women about Miles's romantic proposal soon after Match Day. It had felt like a grand gesture, but in retrospect was fairly easy to execute, some rose petals and champagne and an unlocked rooftop. The wind had scrambled his plans, lifting the petals before she arrived, but even that was a happy accident, how the fuchsia-colored leaves had poured down from the roof, falling to the street before her as fragrant confetti. (Miles was often fortunate that way, able to play off slipups as intent.) They weren't going to rush the wedding—no, no one was pregnant, and they had a round of big exams to prep for—but they couldn't wait to start their lives together.

Now, here was her husband. She heard the tech's retreating footsteps; a door shut somewhere behind her.

She scanned his face. He'd scraped his cheek—not a gash, but a stippled pattern of dried blood, a skid or drag on concrete or brick; below the scab, the skin had started to bruise. She touched his lips, first with a tender finger, then more assertively, lifting them apart, noting their stiffness. The charmingly horsey teeth she knew so well were interrupted by a new chip on his right front. Next she registered the tiny blue star-shaped bruise at the crook of his right elbow. She looked at the chart, which she probably wasn't supposed to, but the tech had left it unattended at the end of the bench. Overdose, a lethal amount of fentanyl, with a significant volume of heroin in the bloodstream. She placed the file back where she'd found it, then walked over to a window, behind which the tech was at a computer. She knocked, and the young man took off his earphones, slid open the pane. "Yeah, that's him," Hillary said. "Where do I sign?"

When the paperwork was done, the tech glanced back toward the slab. "You wanna spend more time with him?" She knew it was a pro forma question; he didn't care. This was a normal day for him, Miles the normal dead.

Hillary glanced back at the body, then down at her watch. "No, I'm good."

46

Mon, Jan 30 at 4:45 PM

Mom:

ETA 7:37 pm

The news rippled out into the universe. When it reached Gregg at the clinic, she and Carson were at first both too startled to do anything more than blink at each other across the recovery room. In time, those blinks turned to tears, and Gregg was wetting her paper gown with them.

When Carson and Gregg returned to the loft, eyes red, and explained they were heading to Chicago in the morning, Zariah was confused. "Chicago?"

"A funeral for a friend," Gregg said.

"He wasn't our friend," Carson corrected.

"No, but she is," Gregg said back, her voice pushing toward testy.

"Right." Carson, instantly deferential, had taken her friend's coat then, pulled out a chair at the dining table.

Was Gregg limping? Zariah sensed her gait was off; she was carrying her weight weird. She told Carson and Gregg she was sorry for their loss, then ordered everyone pizza.

• • •

When Bella got the news, she was at the office; she was forever at the office now. She excused herself to the bathroom, allowed herself to cry in a stall for ninety seconds, flushing whenever she felt a sob coming on. The toilet whirled and whooshed. At the end of ninety seconds, her phone dinged, she straightened her lapels and stepped out of the stall.

There was a young associate whose name Bella couldn't remember leaning over the sink, spitting and rinsing.

"How far along?" Bella asked.

"Six weeks, I think." The woman was not wearing a wedding ring, and Bella resented herself for checking, for being so heteronormative. She tried to smile, even as urging her face into that shape made her want to wail all over again. Miles was dead! Poor Hillary, and bitty Roger! Roger and Gus, born not even a year apart, had never met in real life, but they'd seen each other on Zoom often enough that Gus regularly asked about his friend in the computer.

She looked at herself in the mirror and was grateful for the invention of waterproof mascara. Her eyes had some puffiness but no one would notice. No one would notice anything about her until trial, at which point her bosses and clients and the jury would expect her to look like the Hollywood version of a high-power corporate attorney—she'd already scheduled her seven a.m. blowouts. For now—she continued her inspection—her shirt was fine, a few teardrops on the collar.

"Hang in there," she said to the woman at the sink, who was still rinsing her mouth as Bella stepped to the exit. "The puking gets better, the pregnancy brain gets worse."

On her way back to the conference room, Bella calculated travel times. The funeral was, Carson said Amelia said, Wednesday at eleven, downtown Chicago. Bella could say she was working from home, take the first flight of the morning on Wednesday, and return on the eight p.m. She'd be home by midnight, back in the office early Thursday. Wednesday drop-off would be an issue, but maybe the new girl could spend the night? Their "guest room"—former maid's quarters, wide as her wingspan—had devolved into a cluttered storage space, but it'd work in a pinch, she just had to move some boxes, put fresh sheets on the twin bed. Bella had recently ranted against such arrangements—she'd acceded to weekday pickups, not to a live-in nanny!—but she'd eat her words this week if it meant she could make it to Chicago for ten hours on Wednesday.

The new girl. Bella had readily sprung for Olivia the cleaner; she dialed up Taskrabbit and called contractors for all manner of household jobs, but she had resisted outsourcing childcare, mostly because she'd been so readily farmed out by Marianne, and even as a young girl could feel the perfunctory kindness of hired help. (Hers was an old Irish woman named Edna.) Bill, also raised by nannies, had no compunction about paying for domestic help, and often suggested they should. A full-time nanny? A part-time sitter? Bella, in these recent marathon weeks, had at last caved. After all, it was newly him addressing the bulk of the children's care, and if he needed help, he should be able to get it. Free country and all that.

Bella was skeptical when he said he'd had to interview only two candidates and, even more fortuitous, that his first choice had accepted and was ready to start ASAP. (Bella: "Did you even check her references?" Bill had looked aghast; was he speechless at her lack of faith in him or because doing so hadn't crossed his mind?) Bella recognized it was hard for him, matching shoes with boys with backpacks; the present winter accoutrements—there was still no snow in New York but it was very cold—made it that much more difficult to get out the door. So she grudgingly welcomed the new woman, this Jill, into their home. She was from Ohio? Studying literature at Columbia? They'd talked about her grad program for five minutes one evening last week, but as soon as Jill had left the apartment, the details of her reading list slipped from Bella's mind. This wasn't the time for second-guessing what Bill said he needed, or for arguments about their emotional availability for kids who were likely still too young to remember any particular effort or lack. It was a time for being glad that they had a proficient and kind-seeming backstop to help them through a busy stretch. Bella said she had every intent of firing Jill by April 1, one week after the trial's estimated run, which Bill did not protest.

Bella spun past her desk to check that no one had dropped anything on it, and realized in a bolt that "working from home" wouldn't work.

Everyone knew that she hated remote work; they'd seen the hellscape of her Zoom background. (The problem with squirmy toddlers was that you couldn't always blur them out of the webcam.) When the office had reopened after the pandemic, she was the first person back at her desk. Maybe she could tell them she was here, holed up in some out-of-the-way conference room? Nope—they reviewed who was swiping in each morning. The managing partner had, at the last all-staff meeting, said it was for "data," but Bella knew that HR was checking attendance, as assiduously as roll call in seventh-grade homeroom. The in-person contingent were team players, groveling and bossing as their rank required; those who opted for remote were quietly demoting themselves.

She thought back to the puking associate. Food poisoning. Yes! Or a twenty-four-hour bug. Even better! Toddler cooties were usually such an inconvenience, but this week, they'd be just the ticket.

Carson texted again. "I know everyone is slammed right now." Where was Gregg? Bella wondered, and just as quickly thought, Was it snowing in Chicago? What if she got stuck? She checked Chicago weather—snow was predicted—and chose to ignore it. She'd run the risk for Hillary.

She texted back to the chain.

"The trial's not till next week. I'll be there."

• • •

Reba put down her phone on the nightstand and muttered, "Shit."

"What is it?" Terrence was next to her, spread out on top of their tangled sheets. This had been one upside to his unanticipated unemployment: their frequent, athletic trysts, middays included. He knew the vigorous sex wouldn't last—not because of fatigue; they were both in great shape. But Reba'd get pregnant and insist on being very careful. Or she wouldn't get pregnant and be pissy, freezing him out and stomping around the city on her restorative "walks" until she was ovulating again. Or he'd get a new job, in person or with an in-person amount of surveillance. (His health tech company monitored keystrokes, and had figured out how to detect those mouse jiggler devices that were supposed to be indetectable. Under such surveillance, even a quickie felt perilous.) Now there was no peril. Just exertion, and duly earned languor. Which the pinging of Reba's phone had interrupted.

"We have to go to Chicago." Reba was frowning.

He propped himself up on his elbows and looked at her. "You're buying the Bulls."

She rolled her eyes and rolled out of bed, started pacing the bedroom carpet, cursing under her breath.

Terry flinched. "Not the Bulls. The Sky?" Usually she liked this banter, but now, she looked at him as though she might burst into tears. "Too much?"

"Miles died."

"Damn." Between the army and bartending, Terry had spent enough time around substance use disorders to have heard the warning bells the first time he'd met Miles. Prepossessing, charismatic, but also one of those guys who thought he could get away with most things. He'd lost his job, been kicked out of the residency program, dashed those long, hard years of studying and apprenticeship—in this, Terry could relate. He had done nothing so dangerous as stealing Schedule II drugs, but he'd also blown up his future by getting high. But Miles . . . Christ, he had used on their double date—his plate of lasagna went untouched while everyone else forked through their entrees, awkwardly chitchatting. Terrence followed Reba's lead, who was following Hillary's, who was enjoying her gnocchi and sweeping Miles's misbehavior under the rug (he was "wiped out," having spent the previous night up with the baby), but if it'd been up to Terry, he'd have dropped that plate of lasagna into Miles's lap and taken him to rehab that very night. Upon waking, Miles had ordered dessert for the table like none of it was any big deal.

"I'm so sorry. What can I do?"

"Come with," Reba said. According to her fertility app, she would be ovulating by Friday, and she didn't want to miss the cycle. "And don't you dare tell Hillary you were right."

It was Terrence who had given Hillary her first doses of Narcan, right out of his blazer, as they said their goodbyes that night. (Ever since someone at the bar had OD'd, he carried it always.) Hillary had shoved the dispensers into her purse without even a thank-you, then said they were in a rush home to relieve the sitter. Terrence hadn't taken the snub personally; he knew what she was going through.

"I mean, you were," Reba was saying now. "Right, I mean." She stepped into her underpants, pulled on a sweatshirt, and walked toward the door. "I'll find us a flight."

Tue, Jan 31 at 4:30 PM

Gregg:

Hi R. We r at the hotel. U?

Gregg and Carson arrived in Illinois on Tuesday afternoon and offered to visit Hillary, but also understood when she politely declined. Instead, after settling into their shared hotel room (Gregg had sprung for a suite), they turned their attention to Reba. Was she available to hang? What they didn't text was that they were eager to meet, in the flesh, this mysterious Terrence. Reba and Terry, who had flown in early and already copulated twice in their hotel room—Reba was taking this cycle seriously, because she was forty-one and her follicles were shit, because there was only one frozen egg left waiting at the clinic, because she'd read somewhere she might get pregnant up to five days in advance of ovulation—said they'd meet at the lobby bar in thirty. They did, and upon arrival Reba was too forlorn about Miles and flustered by her and Terry's latest quickie to remember to ask Gregg what she'd been doing in New York.

Once they were settled into a booth and had let themselves all be sad about Miles for a few minutes, the women turned their attention to Terrence.

"The man, the myth, the legend." Gregg grinned, but not in a way that made him uncomfortable, more flattered. Carson was smiling too, thinking he was more attractive than they'd realized, and plenty tall for Reba. And hadn't Reba said he was five years younger than them? None of them were young anymore, but he looked like a baby, flush and fresh from a high school pep rally.

But he also seemed skittish; they could feel his foot tapping under the table as he tried to sound charming but not too gregarious, given the circumstance of their meeting. They couldn't know that on the inside he was trying to keep it together, to not be too intimidated by Reba's two semi-famous friends. Gregg was objectively more well-known than Carson, but he remembered seeing Carson's book in the window of Powell's years back. How could you forget a name like Carson Larsen?

Thank God the waiter showed up then; they put in a happy hour order and tried at conversation again. Gregg asked about Reba's parents, the house. She'd spent six weeks as Doris and Hans's houseguest while doing a production at the SF Playhouse; she loved their home. Reba wanted to know about the book. Any news? "Carson is writing about prison," she added for Terrence's benefit, and his eyebrows rose. "We think," she tagged on for her own satisfaction. She loved Carson, but why couldn't she talk about work in progress like a normal human? It wouldn't jinx her to acknowledge what occupied her thoughts all day. Reba understood NDAs and noncompetes, but this superstitious secrecy was baffling.

They continued talking in hushed, deferential tones, and drinks turned into dinner turned into Gregg and Carson's stealth fifteen-point inspection and four-part interview of Terrence. Over the course of the evening, he told them about growing up in Ohio and his first deployment but declined to discuss his second. He spoke plainly of his brief lockup and dishonorable discharge—with that designation went any hope of GI Bill tuition waivers—and the shocking-but-still-slow process of becoming a civilian again. But he'd done it, gotten back on his feet, moved west, met Reba, and . . . When he got to the part about recently being knocked down again, Gregg gamely commiserated, assuring him there were layoffs happening everywhere in the sector. Across the evening, his speech loosened into a kinder, more authentic lope. He expounded on gin versus vodka martinis, on next-gen blood testing that wasn't a scam, and spoke at length with Carson about the merits of Phil Klay.

Throughout, Reba was radiating, despite the occasion's sadness. She loved him *so much*. And her face, even more than the kind and witty and prescient things coming out of her husband's mouth, was what elevated Terrence from passing the women's exam to doing so with flying colors.

48

Wed, Feb 1 at 10:10 AM

Bella:

> Hey Darcy, everything ok @ office? & hope everyone else is feeling 👍. I would hate to have given this bug to anyone!
>
> 🙏 its 24hr virus

Despite Bella's prayers to the contrary—she did everything short of stopping at church on the way home from work; it would've been closed anyway—it snowed in Chicago on Tuesday night. Bella's early Wednesday flight was delayed by eighty minutes, but still, if she rushed—and now she'd be cutting it very close—she might still make it. The taxi driver who picked her up at O'Hare did a good job of balancing Bella's implorations to *hurry* with the iciness of Chicago's roads, and when he pulled up to the downtown funeral home, ten minutes before eleven, she gave him a big tip. As she hurried inside, unbuttoning her coat as she went, she felt kind of like a character in *The Big Chill.*

The first thing she saw in the sanctuary was Amelia teary in the center aisle, which reminded Bella of the girls' weekend ruined over a minor trespass. She smiled weakly at the woman, waved hello. They all felt like crying right now, but did Amelia have to be so dramatic? Gregg was the actress, and even Gregg—Bella saw her now out of the corner of her eye, gesticulating to a black-suited stranger—was dry-eyed. A part of Bella wanted to shove Amelia, to tell her to button it and buck up, but instead she signed the guest book. While she was writing, Amelia came over, and Bella, basically cornered, offered her a tepid hug. Bella had heard from Carson that Amelia, married and divorced since Bella'd seen her last, had recently turned a corner into promiscuity. *Welcome*, Bella wanted to say. Instead, she asked, "Have you seen Hill?"

The woman shook her head no. She had not worn waterproof mascara and already, ten minutes before the service, she looked like a raccoon. "The family is sequestered in some room, they said. Until the service."

"Got it. I gotta—" She tipped her head toward the front of the room and the casket. "Pay my respects." She stepped quickly away, then hesitated, some animal instinct against approaching death. Keep going, she told herself, and pressed forward.

Bella was both relieved and disappointed to find the casket closed. "Some Jewish thing," she heard another mourner say. Next to the casket was a poster board photo of dashing Miles from—was it their wedding? Bella squinted. The wedding party had worn a silky violet fabric, long dresses and cummerbunds, which had seemed like a good idea until the bridal party photos, when everyone squished together and smiled. The shots looked like glistening grape jelly on unevenly toasted toast. Bella couldn't get that dress to the thrift shop fast enough.

Bella stood before the casket, hoping her downcast eyes looked sufficiently sad, like she was recalling good memories about her friend's former husband. But what she was really remembering then was how Hillary had met Miles *after* Bella and Bill became a couple, but Hillary had gotten engaged first, married first, pregnant with Roger first—in each case, only by a wink, which made Bella's life planning difficult. How much time did her friends need to replenish their bank accounts before they could comfortably book more flights and pay for more hotels? (For Reba it was zero days, but the rest of them were broke in their late twenties. Carson was still building her tutoring practice, Gregg mostly got paid in meals, and Bella had so many law school loans, which her parents could've helped with but didn't.) How frustrating it had been, to worry about following so close behind. The first wedding among their friends was going to be amazing no matter what, simply by being first—and it had been, despite Nebraska, despite the grape jelly. But the second would require a nicer cocktail hour, cuter bridesmaids' dresses, better speeches to keep the delight up. By the time of the baby boom (they might as well call it what it was, a boy barrage—were they physically incapable of birthing babies with two X chromosomes?), they were more financially secure but everyone was also much busier. How much time did she have to wait after Roger's shower to have Gus's? It wasn't an outright race, but there was a special feeling about being the first of their friends to fill in the blank. And Hillary got to each of their watershed moments a nose before Bella.

Bella, standing at the casket, was also remembering how Hillary, with her cold feet, had locked herself and her billowy wedding gown into the bridal suite bathroom just before the ceremony. Amelia tried, unsuccessfully, to coax her out, then recruited Bella, who was getting her makeup finished across the room and had been oblivious to the whole drama. Looking up at panicked Amelia, past her toward the locked door, Bella had had the flicker of an idea. *What if I didn't, and Hillary couldn't, and . . .* Naturally, she'd pushed the thought away, chastised herself for its selfishness. She and Bill didn't need to get married first—that was ridiculous. As soon as her lipstick was set, she'd crossed the suite, coached and cajoled through the keyhole, and slowly talked her friend out of the toilet and down the aisle.

Bella straightened. Now this was another first, and not one she'd wish upon anyone. She glanced from the dead man's glamour shot (had Hillary been in it, and they'd cropped her out? Bella thought she saw the knob of a familiar shoulder) and spotted Gregg and Carson concluding a conversation. She walked up to them, wrapped both in a wide-armed hug. "This sucks."

Then, same as the last time they'd served as Hillary's advance crew, they fanned out, determined to spread their message, which was Hillary's message, which was thank you for your sympathy. They circulated through the room, (re)introducing themselves to other mourners, thanking people on Hillary's behalf for their condolences. They noted how everyone was reading from the same script: unspeakable tragedy, not his fault, culpability with the distributors, drug culture in America, yada, yada, yada. The women were agreeable, then stopped being so kind when a couple of Miles's high school friends, yuppies who'd stayed in Omaha, whispered that maybe it was a robbery gone awry. They'd heard about this crime circuit in New York, where dealers were selling pills they knew would cause an OD, so their victims would be incapacitated at the time of the theft, and maybe that syndicate had come to Chicago? Their disdain for New York was palpable. When Carson calmly said she was from the city, they recoiled, looking at her anew, as if this anodyne middle-aged woman might stab them with a syringe.

It was clear to the women, hearing comments pointed, paranoid, and plainly wrong, that no one knew Miles had been in rehab. The women didn't correct the record, but clocked the cluelessness for later discussion. For years, they'd been supporting Hillary supporting her husband and his struggles with addiction; these dudes thought the big tragedy of Miles's last few years was the Bears. But who were they to judge their fellow mourners? Friendship meant different things to different people; maybe these guys were good friends to Miles, if willfully ignorant; maybe Miles had pulled the wool over their eyes too. The men's lack of understanding, their eschewing of the truth toward something more palatable, wasn't necessarily malicious. It only probably was.

The circulating women also sensed, unspoken but present like stage directions in a script, a resentment for Hillary. If she hadn't . . . put him out. Kept Roger from him. (The men seemed to be speaking about the interim custody arrangement—Sunday afternoon supervised visits, on the advice of both of their lawyers—like it was and forever would be the Koenigs' policy; they didn't know how much Hillary had hoped to shift toward a fifty-fifty split once Miles had cleaned up his act.) If she hadn't . . . given him an ultimatum to find a new line of work by x day. They didn't realize that x had slipped into x plus three months, six, twelve, that at some point she'd shouted that he could volunteer at a soup kitchen, take classes in macramé for all she cared, she just wanted him to do something more than stare at their son and cook fancy cuts of meat and think about using.

The women found this critique of Hillary's wifehood confusing, because they picked up on another, contrary current coursing through the attendees. It was this: If only Hillary had been tougher on him. If she hadn't tolerated Miles's bad behavior, if she'd been more of an enforcer when he tried to sneak this or take that, he'd still be alive. Like, in some way, through her patience and grace, she'd enabled his tragedy. She'd given him a sharps box, one man whispered (knowing nothing of her gestational diabetes and the needle receptacle's original use), and if that didn't give the guy mixed signals, what did?

By the women's third circuit, a prevailing refrain emerged. To Miles's family and friends, Hillary couldn't do anything right. She was wrong with her patience, her persistence, her support. Wrong to be paying down both their med school loans (the loan servicer didn't care if his degree had been made moot). Wrong to be supporting the three of them on her income. Wrong to be doing the larger share of the child-rearing, even though Miles had the larger share of free time. Wrong to have forgiven him when he'd come crawling back, and wrong to have punished him when she'd had enough.

Bella bit the inside of her cheek as a doctor from Des Moines monologued about Miles's jump shot. It was like a loose wire pulsing with electrical current, how the mourners' judgment zapped this way and that. Could they hear themselves, recognize their hypocrisy? Apparently not. She noted how Gregg and Carson seemed to be bearing it all with poise (Gregg was habituated to BS from strangers, and Carson's affect was reliably flat), but Bella wanted to scream. She was having a tough time keeping everyone's faces and names straight—all of Miles's friends looked like paunchy frat brothers (she had hoped, in the spirit of *The Big Chill*, there would be at least one Kevin-Kline-in-his-prime look-alike, but no dice); she was having some difficulty controlling the volume of her voice. But maybe she wasn't the only one struggling? Gregg was nodding too much—she looked like one of those drinking bird toys—and when Bella next glanced to Carson, she seemed agitated, her face a burning flush.

Then Bella noticed an older, unfamiliar man—ah, that must be the rabbi—crossing the room. A door opened on the side of the hall, and the family entered, Miles's parents and his brother and his sister-in-law. A beat later, Hillary, in a staid black dress. As the family settled into the first row, the women, along with the rest of the mourners, found their seats.

49

Wed, Feb 1 at 10:55 AM

Reba:

On our way sorry sorry!

Reba and Terrence had not meant to cut it so close, to arrive at the venue after Bella and her flight delay, but they'd done a morning session and had some difficulty finding a cab, and so they stepped into the hall as everyone was getting seated. Was this like a wedding, where there was a bride's side and a groom's? Reba wondered. No, that didn't make sense. It wasn't a his-and-hers situation, there was just the one person, a dead person in a plain wooden casket at the front. But she didn't want to accidentally sit next to Miles's brother, with whom she'd hooked up at the wedding—shorter and pudgier and probably nicer than the groom; even so, she'd known theirs would be a one-nighter already as he unzipped her bridesmaid's dress.

Reba scanned the room, then saw Carson's head and Gregg's; she could recognize her friends from the front, back, or slice of the side, from the very tips of their noses. They were sitting up and to the left. And there was Hillary, right ahead of them, and was that Amelia and Bella, shoulder to shoulder? Reba did a double take, uncertain what to make of that. But seeing that her people were indeed on the left, she pulled Terrence's sleeve toward an empty stretch of pew behind her friends.

The rabbi did some perfunctory prayers in Hebrew and English, then came a series of speakers—father, brother, best friend . . . but not stoic Hillary, even as people kept glancing in her direction, waiting for tears or a tribute. The way the eulogizers spoke made it sound, to Reba, like they'd not known about his SUD, or they had and hadn't thought it was so bad. Or they had thought it was so bad, but they'd still believed Miles was close to getting clean. His NA sponsor stood up—from the look on Irene Koenig's face, he was not on the schedule of events—but rather than saying something uncouth about Miles's addiction, he spoke about his exemplary character, how committed he was to his sobriety. Delusional or gullible? Reba pondered this, and as he droned on about the importance of fatherhood in Miles's recovery journey, Reba nearly took off her boot and pulled a Gregg. She wanted to shake these people out of their complacency, she wanted them to understand that they were wrong to believe that Miles was innocent in all of this. Terrence had sussed it out in ten minutes, Hillary had been fighting it for more than ten years—why couldn't the rest of them see what Miles had been doing? Yes, Reba knew he'd been suffering, understood that addiction was a disease, recognized that she needed to offer him more grace . . . but for fuck's sake! These people needed to get a clue.

After the poor-him, good-guy speeches, there was a quiet beat, eyes again turning to Hillary. Would she say anything? At the least, she should express her thanks, because weren't they all munificent for being here, for being Miles's friends and colleagues, for letting him lie to them too? Oh no, they couldn't have possibly known about the other Miles, the one who had drained his and Hillary's joint checking and alarmed their neighbors and occasionally wet the bed. That wasn't their Miles, that was only Hillary's, and he had wrapped himself around her shoulders like a mantle made of lead. Reba wanted to scream.

Bella popped up and was moving before she wholly realized what she was doing, and that was striding to the front of the room. Reba almost stood up to chase after her, but Terrence put a hand on her thigh and that held her down. "Let her go," he whispered, not because he knew all the messy dynamics of Reba and Bella's friendship (he had heard the top-level summary of their bond, and had been inconvenienced when Reba pushed out her move to help Bella after her first

C-section), but because he recognized a determination on Bella's face. She reached the lectern and the rabbi stepped back to make room.

"Hi, I'm Bella." She looked out at the group and remembered that she hadn't spoken before a crowd in so long. When was the last time she was in court? Not Zoom court, motions on a laptop, but standing in front of strangers, willing her knees not to shake? And the last time she'd made a speech . . . was it Gregg's wedding? (Or more precisely the rehearsal dinner, to which 150 guests were invited; the wedding itself, with its celebrity appearances and pyrotechnic toasts, was too much of a production for speeches from commoners.) "Some of you might remember me from Hillary and Miles's wedding. I was the bridesmaid who made the sloppy speech about when Hillary stitched up my knee on a Saturday night because I'd tried to compete in our campus's 'drunk decathlon' appropriately intoxicated."

The friends all remembered the wedding speech and the bloody knees, but where was she going with this?

"While it was a good example of Hillary's tenderness, her unflappability and steadfast friendship—and, pro tip, if you ever need first aid, this woman has you covered, Neosporin in every one of her handbags. But it, well, the decathlon and my recollection of it were not my best moments. Right, Mrs. Koenig?" The older woman nodded. She recalled it, Bella could tell from the press of her lips. And she could also see that the room was leaning forward, rapt by this short woman in a black suit.

"For all the laughs, those intended and the unintentional ones, for all it said about Hill—her Florence Nightingale instinct, how good a friend she was and how good a wife she'd be—would you believe that it wasn't my best speech of the day? Most of you don't remember, just one or two of you could even know"—here she looked back at the casket, then to Hillary, then her eyes flitted to Amelia—"that Hillary almost didn't marry Miles that day. Thirty minutes before the ceremony, she locked herself in the bridal suite bathroom and refused to leave. Scared shitless, pardon my French. She loved him, but some *stuff*—we could call it *baggage*, or if we're being blunt, and at this point, why not, his *addiction*—was already present. He'd recently been expelled from his residency, which we weren't supposed to talk about. We're probably still not meant to mention it, and for that, Irene, I also apologize." The woman dipped her head again.

"Because, whoever said it, and several of you have, you're right. He'd have made a great surgeon, if only, dot dot dot. But here's the thing. There's no *if only*. There is only the cold, hard fact of addiction, and how Hillary and I both knew, crouched on either side of that door, that she was going to marry that too. It would be a challenge they'd face, every day. I didn't try to convince her it would be easy, or suggest that their love would conquer all his demons, because we both knew that no amount of love could do that. Addiction is a disease, as clinical as cancer of the throat." Bella could feel her closing statement adrenaline, that old friend, coursing through her veins. But there was something else. Had she taken her meds that morning? It had been so, so early, she couldn't recall reaching for the cluster of vials on the dresser. She couldn't recall anything before arriving at the airport and the sharp smack of that flight delay.

"But even as we were staring down that elephant—and drug addiction is a muddy and mad pachyderm, folks, no way around it—I also got her counting the things she loved about him. How Miles had let her cut out the heart of their cadaver in anatomy lab, even though it'd been his day with the scalpel, because he knew she really wanted to see how it, quote, 'hooked in.' How Miles, who could have taken his ambidexterity to any orthopedic surgery residency in the land, picked Chicago. Still a good program"—she looked toward one of the blowhard doctors she'd talked to earlier—"but not the most prestigious. He wanted to be with Hillary, who liked the ENT surgery program here and wanted to be within driving distance of her mom. Let's see, also on the list . . ." Bella made a pondering face, drummed her fingers on the lectern's wood. "He was gorgeous, we can all agree. Funny. To adults, but he also was a hit with the preschool set—my son went crazy for his Daffy Duck." Her heart was racing. She definitely hadn't taken her meds.

"Anyway, crouching in that bathroom, Hillary went on a tear, listing the ways she loved the guy. We got up to something like one oh three—his French toast, his Scorsese impression—the two of us whispering through this stupid keyhole, before I got her to unlock the door. We were very late—many of you probably remember that part. I heard those pews were hard! I had my girlfriends"—she pointed over to the women, all watching with wet eyes—"spread a rumor about a wardrobe malfunction, which seemed to calm most everyone down. But, glancing into the sanctuary while Hillary was getting her veil re-placed, it was the one time I ever saw Miles truly frightened. Wondering if she'd show." Bella made an overdone wince, tugged at her neckline as if she were wearing the groom's purple bow tie. "Praying that she would."

Bella's eyes found Hillary's in the front row. "And we all know, she did. That's what I want to leave you with. Because I think we're all glad she did, that Miles chose to make his life bigger by welcoming Hillary into it. They had some great years. They made a home here in Chicago—gourmet meals in its tiny kitchen; he'd say thanks again for the wedding crockery. And if you were visiting them in the summer, you could always tell whether the Cubs were winning. Hill told me about their blissful beach days on the lake, and there's a great story about going to see his favorite band at the Liar's Club and Hill accidentally crowd-surfing."

Bella paused, trying to calm her pounding heart. "They became parents together, and learned a new love." She didn't mean to look at Reba then, but she did, and the woman's face was screwed up in sadness. "I loved seeing them with Roger, how happy that kid made them."

Bella took a slow, big breath before going on. "I could probably count up to one hundred and three myself, listing the ways their life together was beautiful. But I will stop there, with gratitude for Miles, and for Hillary, trying their best, each and together."

50

Wed, Feb 1 at 12:14 PM

Gregg:
Is it kosher to Uber to a burial?

Reba:
Doesn't matter it's a mitzvah

The service ended and the mourners headed into the chilled-over day. Out on the street, the immediate family slid into waiting limousines; the rest of the guests hailed cabs or called Ubers or got their cars from the parking garage around the block. The four friends, plus Amelia and Terrence, split two Ubers and started north, toward a Jewish cemetery in Forest Park. Bella smiled to her fellow passengers (Terrence and Amelia; where was Reba?). This was the first time she'd met Terrence, and she knew she should be offering gently prompting questions, but she was so discombobulated by her waning adrenaline and a mounting headache that she pulled out her phone to check on things at the office. Terrence also sank into his phone (LinkedIn); as did Amelia (a dating app; she was staying in Chicago for the night and had updated her location in her profile—why the hell not?). Frankly, they were all grateful for the pause in the performance of sadness and sociality.

In the other car, Carson received notes from three anxious parents, to whom she replied with something that sounded like an automated out-of-office message but was just her typing and retyping a handful of stock phrases. Reba replied to her mother about a grocery order, and Gregg updated Zeke on her new ETA back to Texas. She would postpone her flight home until Thursday because she was "feeling fluey," which was a euphemism for feeling like she'd recently had her insides scraped out and was bleeding more than the doctor had said she would. In the back of her mind, a disquiet whispered; she hoped it was nothing, but if it was something and she flew home, she'd have to get right back on a plane because no doctor in Texas could help with an abortion-related complication. That was too much to text, in length and emotion, so she pinged, "How are you holding up with the cold snap?" She'd seen on the news that the temperature was twenty degrees below normal and dropping another twenty tonight. Tomorrow, it'd be colder in Texas than Chicago, and what a weird thing that was.

At the cemetery, the pallbearers were the other five of Miles's three-on-three basketball game, plus Terrence, because he was there and looked strapping and the original sixth, a middle school friend, had gotten lost en route. The graveside portion of the service was mercifully short—another round of farewell blessings—and then they lowered the coffin into the ground.

Reba had sent a group text while they were driving about what would happen at the grave. At the end of the ceremony, everyone would drop some dirt atop the coffin, and the women could—no pressure—participate; it was a mitzvah to chuck a handful on the departed. "Wait till after his family and the med school bros go," she typed. "But don't go very last—that's the rabbi, with a pinch of soil from Israel."

"From where?" Bella was incredulous, and whispered at her phone. Reba, in the other car, may as well have heard Bella's utterance, as she sent another message. "I know, it sounds complicated, but just watch me."

And so they did. On her cue, they approached the squared-off pit. The exhumed dirt, prepped into a mound, had frozen over since the gravedigger's rounds, so extracting a clump was harder than it looked. (One of Gregg's indestructible magenta nails finally did break.) The upside of the icy soil was that when it landed on the casket, it made the most satisfying *thunk*.

One of the women's Uber drivers, extending sympathy for their loss, had closed his app and was waiting at the cemetery gates—he'd drive them back downtown gratis. (The other had places to be and was long gone.) So, after the burial, half the group piled into the kindhearted Chrysler—this time it was Reba and Terrence and Amelia—while the others waited for a new ride. Another of the pallbearers felt sorry for the three women huddled against the cold and offered them a lift back to the funeral home. This required, because of the other passengers, that Bella (the smallest) sit on someone's lap. Gregg had more room in the back seat and across her lap, but Carson was insistent that Bella pick her. Once Bella was astride her friend, Carson cupped her shoulder and whispered into her ear, "You did so good today."

The cars unloaded on Michigan Avenue; there would be a reception in the funeral home's social hall. The women wanted to leave as soon as the event started, but they didn't, doing more interference and peacekeeping and outreach, for Hillary and young Roger's sake. Reba even had a brief, awkward conversation with Miles's brother—and how convenient it was that he'd "found" her precisely when Terrence left for the bathroom. The twerp was happily married in Omaha, three children. She murmured pleasantries as he showed her pictures of his girls on his phone, even as what she really wanted to do was drop the device in the coffee urn.

Everything was going fine, the energy level moderately uneasy, until the pretty, young PA—the woman who had, Hillary suspected, been responsible for Miles's escape—came up to her to offer condolences. Hillary did not yet know the entirety of what had happened (in the future there would be a formal review by the facility, a redacted version of which would be shared with the family), but she'd had misgivings about this PA already at intake, and further suspicions when the woman had wailed audibly during the service. It now looked like Hill might hit this young woman, and Gregg, quickly at her arm, swept into de-escalation mode. She greeted the girl, then created distance between her and Hill with her body, did some put-on gesticulating with her arms. Reba noticed this and swiftly ushered Hillary and Gregg to the coat check, where they bundled in hats and gloves and scarves and coats, then rushed out into the snow, leaving the PA speechless and perplexed and in the middle of a sentence. (Carson and Bella had spotted Reba's hustle and were not two steps behind.) Not knowing what else to do but keep moving, Reba directed them lakeward, toward the park and its big metal bean, which looked silver white and glowing in the day's light snow. The thought of Terrence, alone at the funeral hall, passed through Reba's mind, then floated right back out. He'd done two deployments into war zones, he could manage himself in Chicago for the afternoon.

The women, now reassembled on the plaza, approached the sculpture tentatively; the flagstone was slippery with slush. With a last cautious step, they were stretched and squished in the sculpture's high-gloss reflection. Their black and gray coats were smooshed into dense lumps of coal; the curved light squeezed them so tightly that they might have, if they'd taken one more step forward, become diamonds or disappeared. In any case, they looked diminutive against the big teeth of the city, the steel-blue skyscrapers, the endless sky. "There we are," Gregg said. The women reached for one another, held hands through their gloves. Except for Bella, who'd misplaced her mittens. Her fingers were chapped red with cold; Carson tried to warm them as best she could.

"Here we are," Carson said. This funeral had not been as bad as she had imagined it might be. It was, in any case, much easier than her last, which had been her mother's. There had been losses between then and now (old professors and young musicians, a tutee who died in a bus crash), but she'd become very adept at dodging funerals, memorials, wakes, and unveilings, always ready with the excuse of inflexible travel or contagious ailments (always burying the real reason, which was absolute terror of her own mortality). Except for this time. This time was for Hillary, and for Hillary, she'd endure the empty eye sockets (Miles was an organ donor, Hill had mentioned when they chatted on Tuesday, and although the closed casket saved

Carson from the gore, she knew they were missing under there) and that spooky cold breath whistling around her shoulders. The cold breath was death, reminding her of her own inevitable conclusion.

No, it wasn't death. It was just a wintery gust. Chicago was staggeringly cold. She watched her reflection. She'd made it through another funeral and the world hadn't collapsed in on itself. Carson was silently relieved.

"That was awful," Hillary said, her voice warbly. "But Bella, thank you. What you said was—"

Bella swiveled her head toward Hillary. Her brain throbbed like it was ready to burst and her fingers felt numb. Where were her mittens? Had she left them in the cab? "You're welcome."

Hillary looked at the five of them in the big shiny fava. "Seriously, thank you all for being here." She hadn't wept yet, not during the stiff-armed hug with her in-laws or by the icy grave when the rabbi chanted the Mourner's Kaddish, not at the reception when that twit came up to her like they were friends. But her eyes brimmed now, and a single tear ran down her cheek.

"We'll always be here for you, Hill," Gregg said. "And now it's done, right? You made it through." She clasped her friend's hand through her woolly glove. As she did, she had the distinct sensation of a drop of blood slipping along the leg of her tights.

51

Wed, Feb 1 at 3:15 PM

Hillary:

OMW home. Roger burn down the house yet?

Hillary contemplated a cab (she could take one, but she'd already bought the monthly L card, so the train would essentially be free), contemplated that it was messed up to be debating the cost of a car fare. She was forty years old, a doctor, on the way home from a *funeral.* But it was also messed up to pretend that big numbers didn't come from small ones, so she walked toward the station, fishing through her purse, fingers passing emergency fruit snacks and Band-Aids, her hospital ID—why had she brought that today?—until they found her wallet and fare card.

She hated how money was constantly on her mind. But it had been that way for ages, maybe since she and Sheila had moved out on their own, or maybe it started with the cognizance of class among her college friends, how much less she had than Bella (who felt poor, but was only broke in comparison to her richer Scarsdale neighbors) and Reba (very affluent, by any measure) and Gregg (whose family was middle class, but who had learned to carry herself like a Boston Brahmin way before she'd met Zeke and come into serious wealth). Hillary had more resources than Carson, then and now, but that was saying hardly anything. The disparity among friends had been underscored when she'd come home at breaks and seen how her mother struggled with the bills, now that Hillary's father's court-mandated child support had ended. Hadn't her mother asked for alimony? No, Sheila reported, she'd been too proud for that. Hillary had felt enraged at her hubris then (not yet realizing she'd inherited the trait). Her father helped with college tuition, but he'd lost his shirt in 2008; from then on, Hillary was on her own. Or on her in-laws' tab, which was maybe worse.

She found the platform's heated section, where the snow had melted into a gray puddle and her crown felt like it was being baked. She liked the sensation, and tilted her face up. For one idyllic breath she was back in Palm Springs, that warm winter sun . . . until a commuter's racking cough brought her back to the present. Bad cold, she thought, maybe a sinus infection. She stepped away from the cougher and the heat; in the cold she watched down the track. At least Miles's parents had covered the funeral bills, which were not insignificant. Jewish funerals were modest in some ways (the simple coffin); other rituals (the rabbi flown in from Omaha, the rush-job grave dug into frozen ground) were more expensive. And being beholden to her in-laws' largesse was not new. They'd paid for the wedding, all but the dress (Sheila's gift), and with their generosity, Hillary had conceded to a hotel ballroom in Omaha. There had been three tables of Irene's society friends; if Hillary had not been dressed so conspicuously (at the time her dress had felt princess-ish in a good way, but in retrospect, when she deigned to look at the wedding album or a "memory" showed up on her socials, she found the taffeta tacky), she doubted they could've picked her out of a lineup. That's how uninterested they were in anything beyond Irene and her charming son.

Even so, Hillary had too much pride to ask the Koenigs about funds at present. Not because of the burial bills but because of an oblique and mildly aggressive comment that Irene had made while they were waiting for the service to begin. It seemed that Miles had suggested to his mother that he'd been supporting Hillary, rather than the other way around. No, Hillary had wanted to yell, her mother-in-law's monthly account transfer had not gone to childcare, or to their rent, or to their ballooning student loan payments. Hillary had thought of her dead husband then, and whether his body, resting in the next room, might twitch or turn or somehow respond to having been caught in the lie. The older woman was staring at Hillary; she could feel her glare's bore. Did she seriously want Hillary to *thank* her right now? For what—birthing such a deceptive son? Ignoring his struggle for literal decades? Or did she want Hillary to compliment the ugly floral arrangements, which were just as fusty as the flowers she'd picked for their wedding? Hillary had excused herself to the restroom then, and as the hand dryer roared, she opened the room's frosted window and yelled onto the building's back alley, a big guttural scream.

The train arrived; she boarded. It rumbled along, stopping every couple of minutes, the midday ridership quiet and patient. This was a route she'd taken hundreds of times, but it felt different today. When the doors opened at a stop, there was a moment during the pause when Hillary questioned whether they would ever close again. Was this what it meant to be in mourning?

She'd not had time to ask herself that. She'd been back from the morgue for twenty-seven minutes, and had said nothing to anyone in the office, other than to cancel her afternoon appointments, when her boss appeared at her doorway. How had he found out so quickly? Was that guy in the morgue a snitch with a photographic memory (that quick flash of her hospital ID), or had someone in the ER seen Miles, cold and blue, and recognized him as formerly one of their own?

She had listened to the older doctor bumble through telling her how sorry he was to hear the news, saying that she should take the week; then, as she scowled, he shifted to "as much time as she needed," by which he meant a second week would be acceptable. And it would be great if she could start the leave on Wednesday, he added, because Tuesday's surgery couldn't be moved. Generally, she liked her boss, who had a reputation as one of the nation's top surgeons of the nasal cavity, but typically she had to beg for any shred of time away, and now he was coming to her hat in hand with bereavement time... How did that work? She looked down at her watch. Vacation was generous on paper but made inaccessible by their relentless surgery schedule, and she was still low in the seniority rankings. Sick days were discouraged unless it was virulent—and if it was, you were supposed to find your own coverage, which meant whenever Roger got sick, or when Roger got her sick with his preschool cooties, she'd have to find a sub or reschedule her patients into epic twelve-hour makeup days, which caused major headaches for the anesthesiologists and operating room nurses. None of this *We'll figure it out*.

She was livid, but also wasn't about to look a gift horse in the mouth. So instead of pointing out her boss's hypocrisy, she'd just said, "Roger." By which she meant she had to get Roger; she was already late, and the doctor was blocking her exit. But he took it to mean *okay*, and was glad to be so affirmatively dismissed. She told him she'd write that evening with details, and when she did, she'd typed, "One month." She imagined the email had made him guppy-mouthed in disbelief, but he'd replied five minutes later, with one word: "Approved."

Now the train pulled into Addison. She rose and exited, walked down the familiar salted steps. Hillary had thought this would be their first neighborhood, their starter apartment, but a decade later, here they still were—no, here *she* still was, she had to get used to that—spitting distance from Wrigley Field. It had been novel to know when someone'd hit a home run by how the windowpanes rattled, sort of fun (when they were childless) to absorb the game-day energy of the bars and restaurants along the strip. But try navigating a stroller with twenty thousand people on the sidewalk; try keeping a baby asleep when any long fly ball sent the crowd screaming. Proximity had become a nuisance.

She crossed the lobby and climbed the stairs (a walk-up, which had been a disaster with baby gear). The place was starter on the inside as well, furnished with the beat-up pieces they'd lived with since the start of residency. A new slipcover over the couch (Roger was like a heat-seeking missile with upholstery, ready with grubby hands and fruit juice), another tablecloth to cover the gouged and scorched dining room table. They had beautiful pots and pans (wedding gifts), not that she would use them much now. Miles had been the chef in their household.

Inside the apartment, her mother—who had made it clear upon arrival that she would not be venturing to the funeral—and Roger were on the floor, surrounded by a scatter of Legos, which had been discarded for a thing Hillary could not see behind their hunched-over bodies.

"How'd it go?" Sheila asked, glancing up. Roger was too focused on whatever they were doing to greet his mother or see her face shift with the question.

"It went." Hillary took off her boots by the door, surveying the spread of good things and bad. The bad announced themselves first: her mother-in-law's barbs, Miles's friends' blithe oblivion. That harpy PA from the rehab facility. She couldn't be sure what had happened with Miles, but the woman was his type: sweet-seeming, Midwestern, too young to know better (which could have also described Hillary, for a time). But then, there were the good. That her college friends had come and so skillfully dealt with Miles's people. What Bella had said at the service, the unprompted kindness she had offered them all. The five of them, lined up before that shiny bean.

Bzzzz. Hillary stepped gingerly forward, and soon saw the cardstock abdomen, the red-nosed patient offering a dopey grin. Operation. Roger's tweezer tool hit the edge of the chest "incision" again and the game's alarm rang out. That rib was so hard to get. The boy held the tool against the sensor a third time, as if he savored the sound. The nose lit up.

Who had given them this game? It was a baby shower gift or a toddler birthday, in no way age appropriate, a spoof for the parents that ignored the choking hazard (high), the amount of storage space in their apartment (minuscule), the grating noise (loud). She should've donated it immediately, but instead she'd stowed it high in a closet. She'd thought that she'd hidden it well enough to keep it out of Roger's line of sight. Had he found it anyway, or was this her mother's fault?

"How's surgery going?" Hillary leaned down and kissed his head; he wriggled from her touch. His forehead was damp, warm. If he was getting another cold, she didn't know what she'd do.

"How's Irene?" her mother asked. *Bzzzz*. Maybe the batteries would die soon.

"How do you think?" Hillary stretched out on the sofa. Her mother-in-law wanted to see Roger while they were in town—they were, she said, disappointed he hadn't been at the funeral. Hillary hadn't decided yet if she'd make a visit happen. From what Reba explained, while shiva wasn't a happy occasion, it was not as morbid as a pine box. It wasn't that Hillary didn't want the Koenigs to see their grandson, but she was still so mad at Miles. Could she pretend for another hour that she wasn't? The performance today had left her drained.

"And how's Carson and Gregg and all them?"

"Be quiet!" the boy demanded. "I have to concentrate." They had tried, several times, to talk about death with Roger: Hillary on that first day, when they got home from school; Sheila, when she arrived that night bearing a book about when Grandpa goes to heaven, though this had only confused Roger more, because Miles's father was alive and well, and Hillary's dad, while alive, was so estranged that Roger didn't know he existed.

The alarm rang out again. The women exchanged knowing glances; Sheila's showed an apologetic cast. So Hillary *had* hidden it; Sheila was the one to pull it down from the closet shelf. But Hillary could've warned her too.

Roger looked up with his jack-o'-lantern smile. "Did you have a nice day today, Mommy?" He posed this question every day; it was a script between them. He knew today she was saying goodbye to Daddy, but seemed unfazed that she had. Had he forgotten he was supposed to be sad? How do children process grief anyway? That had *not* been in her pediatrics unit all those years ago.

"Yeah, bud. It was good."

"Let's make a video." Even after she explained that Miles was gone, Roger had wanted to keep making videos for Daddy. On Monday it was jumping on the bed, yesterday was him play-eating carrots like a rabbit. (It was as close as he'd been to a vegetable in weeks, so she wasn't about to discourage it.) Today, he wanted to show Daddy his surgery game.

She'd have to stop this eventually. But not today.

Hillary opened the camera app and pointed her phone at her son. "Action!" The boy leaned over the game board again and, miraculously, removed the broken heart without even the briefest buzz. He cheesed for the camera, showing his prized plastic knot. Hillary, off-screen, said, "Nice work, bud."

She stopped the camera, and the boy sprang up. "Did you send it? Did you send it?" He hugged her knees. She tapped at her blank screen with what she hoped looked like concentration. She didn't have the heart to say anything but yes.

52

Mon, May 19, 2014 at 8:06 PM

Reba:

OMG remember that guy I dated soph yr? He is on The Bachelorette!

Sometimes, whole months of the women's lives would go by without remark. Sophomore year of college, for instance, felt like a mild interregnum, a quiet span between 9/11 and the chaos of their junior year (Carson's mother's illness and death, followed by Bella's summer breakdown and Gregg's first real part, supporting but at Steppenwolf). There were midterms and term papers, a new Britney single, shopping at the local vintage store (Carson finding that beloved cardigan that she still wore every winter), all of them procrastinating and pulling all-nighters in the campus's brutalist library. They turned in dozens of critical essays, but aside from Carson, who was born with an aptitude for sentence construction (her mother once told her she'd started using adverbs correctly at eighteen months), none of them wrote anything especially good that year, though they were all getting better. At coursework, at life, at negotiating disappointment and regulating hope. Which is not to say there wasn't screaming and jumping and laughter so raucous that someone passing by on the street paused at the shrieking outburst—there was, there was—but as the women grew up and grew closer, they also learned how to use the dimmer switch.

Of course, those nine months weren't an actual pause, neither calm nor cool nor collected—there was a war going on in Afghanistan and another one in Iraq, the mind-bend of *Adaptation* and all those airlines running out of money. But for the women, in general, the year was blissfully boring. Snow flurries and warm cookies, gossip and karaoke at the local dive bar, the leaves falling off the trees and then the trees growing leaves again. Carson read Victorian literature (back then she was both fascinated and repelled by the marriage plot; now she was mostly bored by it), and Gregg was in the campus production of *Guys and Dolls* (made contemporary by its gender-blind casting; Sergeant Sarah Brown was a brawny six foot three). The world was quiet, but it was different from the stretched-out, flickering hush of Hillary's bereavement time, unlike the expanse of silent days during that first fall together, in the immediate aftermath of the towers. Then, everyone moved around campus like they each were carrying a dozen eggs, and not in anything as sophisticated as an egg carton—eggs in the crooks of elbows, set into that dip behind the clavicle. Eggs delicately balanced on the tops of heads, in belly buttons, against eye sockets, cradled in the hollow at the back of the knee. Students, contorted with care and wincing pain, moved slowly and spoke quietly and arced wide around one another. Despite everyone's best efforts, eggs were always dropping, cracking, sluicing on the sidewalk.

By sophomore year Sonja was already dying, but Carson didn't know that yet, and Bella was already settling into the illness that would be her lifelong companion, but she thought skipped meals were why she felt like the world was thrumming against its axis. Hillary worked diligently in her premed labs and lagged behind on dating; she still wasn't letting boys take off their boxers, nor would she remove her underclothes (plain briefs and unadorned bras that could all but disappear into the woodwork of her skin), but when she looked into the eyes of her entreating young men, for the first time she saw more than the colored cells of their irises and the narrowing black apertures of their pupils. She saw the pinprick of a person floating in that black space, and it terrified her. When this happened, she reminded herself of what her friends had taught her: Keep your heart open. Planes crashed and we could all be dead tomorrow and despite such threats, some people went their whole lives without love, withholding it, protecting it, and for what? Safety was no longer a viable argument, a reason to keep oneself closed off. That interminable loneliness could be Hill's . . . it *would* be Hill's, Bella threatened, if she didn't make herself keep staring into the dark.

• • •

Another quiet stretch for the women was 2014. In the eighteen months prior they had all turned thirty (Reba, with her basketball gap year, was the first across the threshold; Gregg brought up the rear). They had each encountered the occasion differently, some running into their fourth decade as if it were the last hundred yards of a marathon, some fighting against its arrival as though they were being dragged toward a not-cartoony cliff. So even as thirty itself had been eventful—they rented a place in the Hamptons, spent what felt like an inordinate amount of money on a long, cloudy weekend during which they caroused, ate many lobsters (rolls, then halved and buttered, then in eggs Benedict), and sang the same karaoke songs they'd been belting since age twenty—the time after was a snooze. New chapters in domesticity for those who were settling down; the ones still on the road upgraded their luggage. Reba reached Delta's million-mile club—she was told she was among the youngest to achieve the status—which unlocked a handful of mollifying perks. Occasionally she'd intercept Gregg at an airport, Dallas or Denver, and the women would drink martinis in Reba's VIP lounge.

Hillary was doing her residency in the state of Illinois, and kept her long coat at work so Miles wouldn't feel bad about not having one. Bella was at last and officially a bar-approved lawyer in the state of New York (it'd taken her three tries to pass the exam) and had hung her license—and diploma, and a picture of her and Bill on their Venetian honeymoon—on her cubicle wall so everyone would see the accomplishment (also so she could remind herself of Bill when her eye strayed toward a hot paralegal or the hunky FedEx guy). Carson was already a writer, but she was often being asked to prove it, like a hardback edition and a *New York Times* review were required credentials. Were words not valid, sentences irrelevant until they were typeset between greyboard covers and assessed in the paper of record? Carson seethed at the narrow-mindedness and channeled her frustration into her characters' sharp-elbowed evaluations of one another. She wrote one character, a good-looking young lawyer who was some version of every young professional Bella had brought out on their Saturday nights, and had him fail the bar again and again until he, emotionally trounced, jumped off the Fifty-Ninth Street Bridge.

Reba cut 20 percent of the workforce of a surfactants processor in Ohio; Carson wrote and rewrote pages of her first novel, her drafts growing until the stack of sheets reached high ankle, then mid-calf. She thought about her father, and thought about her mother, and did nothing about either. In 2014 the US went after Syria and it snowed mightily in the mid-Atlantic and Gregg wrecked her carbon count on flights to LA, multiple callbacks for a recurring role on a broadcast sitcom that ultimately were for naught. Bella and Bill both had sanctioned extramarital affairs (again: no one in their bed, and don't get too attached), but they found their secondary partners so predictable and ditzy and in the end unsatisfying that it caused them to redouble their efforts with and affection for each other. (And hadn't that always been the point?) Hillary and Miles had already had the shock of their decade in 2012, his unceremonious dismissal from the hospital, and the joy of it in the guise of their wedding, but 2014 was a series of LinkedIn job adverts, the re-reformatting of his CV and résumé, trying to ideate a new vocation, a new life if ambidextrous orthopedic surgeon was not in the cards (he was a lefty, but all the surgical tools were designed for the right hand, and so he'd made it work). He cooked ambitious recipes from the newspaper in their wedding pots and rubbed Hillary's feet after work. She'd been the one to suggest he cook so they could save money, but his meals, elaborate and delicious and becoming more so with each passing month, just increased the grocery budget. He'd spend all morning sourcing ingredients—exotic vegetables that were more expensive than most meats—and all afternoon prepping multicourse menus. As soon as she stepped in the door: *Taste this, what do you think of that? More cumin?* Even when it was too salty, or spicy enough to make her eyes water, she'd invariably say, *Almost there, honey.*

She wanted to encourage him because that year, when Hillary looked into the dark dots of her husband's eyes, she saw something different—not the unbridled desire of their early days, or the despair that would cloud them later, but some kind of concession she did not totally understand. Was that when he realized his addiction was like an allergy? That getting high did not make him happy, but he could not be happy when all he thought of was his next score? He never articulated anything so dire; he only said he'd try harder. And he was trying, she saw that, tasted it, heard it too, as Miles kept clanging in the kitchen, improving one recipe after the next.

• • •

The year 2021 was calm for the women only in relation to the previous one—the election was over, the vaccines were coming, no bother that it was unclear if their children might ever get pricked, at least their aging parents could be protected (or in the case of Bella's folks, could *refuse* prophylactics and get walloped by the virus again). Carson read about the spread of Covid-19 in prisons, the failed isolation strategies and botched attempts at compassionate release, and as she did, she was frantic to know what was happening at Monroe Correctional. But she'd told herself to wait until her draft was done; she didn't want to be shoved off track, not while the manuscript was still an unsteady and knock-kneed foal. And the story was coming—still far from done then, but she'd arrived at a smooth stretch of progress, a thousand words a day. She was the pilgrim walking to Santiago de Compostela; if she just stayed the course, at the end, a cathedral.

In these sleepy stretches, the women's text chain might go slack or be filled with inanities. They updated one another on inconsequential college paramours (he'd gotten fat, he'd gotten famous, he was running for Congress in Connecticut), minor medical annoyances, Britney news (none of it good, until, miracle of miracles, the conservatorship was done!), and foreign policy (none of it good, and everything getting worse with Bibi's and Putin's and Orban's returns to power). The women would guess at who was getting laid (everyone, unless Carson was going through another celibate stretch) and who was getting pregnant (in 2014 it was Reba, with a vice president of sales for a major Midwestern retailer, the workforce of which she was halving; but even then she was not *staying* pregnant, her uterus already doing its six-week eviction thing), and who was embarrassing themselves. Bella picked the wrong door during a hookup and got locked out of a stranger's apartment in her underwear, which was funny once she realized she wasn't getting robbed. Gregg had a very awkward on-screen kiss with an aging heartthrob, someone they'd all grown up pining over, and he had horrible halitosis. There was that one time Hillary peed in the kitchen sink (this she didn't share on the text chain, and it wasn't her embarrassment so much as Miles's). He'd locked himself in the bathroom right before nodding out, which had terrified her, but then she heard him snoring so knew he wasn't dead. That didn't change the fact that she really, really had to go, that it was snowing, that most of the Addison Street bars were closed by that time of night. In the end it wasn't so difficult. Theirs was an old kitchen with a deep porcelain washbasin, a faucet spout that swiveled to the side. She ran the hot water for a long time afterward, then went to press an ear to the bathroom door again, then went to bed.

53

Wed, Feb 1 at 5:15 PM

Hillary:

Thank you for being there, ladies. I really appreciate it. Safe travels home. ♥

But these first months of 2023 were not a dull stretch. Since the women had convened in the desert, a father (Carson's) had heard from his daughter for the first time, and another (Reba's) had fallen on several occasions, downplaying the severity and the frequency of these tumbles. A dozen states had, since *Dobbs*, banned access to abortion care, and a handful of progressive lawmakers, inspired by Gregg's statehouse outbursts, had vociferously protested on their own statehouse floors. Their conservative-leaning legislative bodies had reacted in similar fashion to the senate in Austin: boot and reboot, the offending lawmakers removed and reinstated, with a fawning press cycle and on-the-fly fundraising campaign in between. Gregg would've been chuffed that her ad-lib performance had become a solid growth strategy, if the whole thing hadn't made her so sad.

In the time since their desert reunion, under a month, Gregg had ended a pregnancy and Reba had let Terrence ejaculate inside of her thirty-seven times. Hillary, suddenly and inarguably single again (the unsigned divorce paperwork still folded in the dining room hutch), could not determine if she'd spent fifteen years of effort (and *effort* was the right term; being with Miles had required a real heave-ho) in a good way or a bad one, though Roger's morning mattress trampolining was like a slot machine flashing *good good good*. Also in that four-week span: Terrence had lost his job and Zeke had lost millions of dollars on his exploded rocket and Bill had started an affair with a young woman in his office, accelerating the flirtation into something more, because life was short and Jill was sexy and even though Bella had stopped her extracurricular activities, she had not made hooking up against the rules, and Miles had died.

Miles dying was worse than peeing in the sink, worse than being locked up with a life sentence and not even knowing, for the first forty years of it, that you had a daughter, worse than being four years old and tongue-tied. Dying was worse than disloyalty or addiction or poverty or violence or the repercussions of all the above. What was that line from *Crime and Punishment*? Carson thought of it so often, something about how it'd be better to spend a lifetime on a scrap of wind-whipped land, to wedge oneself onto a crumbling ledge on the side of a cliff and endure the most miserable of conditions—all of that would be better than a flame extinguished. "To live and to live and to live!"

Or had it been "to live!" four times? She'd have to check the text, except her translation was gone, lifted or lost while she was out of town. (That she chose to blame her roommates' friends rather than entertain the idea that she might've forgotten it in some coffee shop, left it on a park bench, or dropped it on the train said more about her embedded skepticism than about her roommates' friends' capacity for theft.) Whatever the case, she liked to believe that somewhere, someone was picking up that dog-eared edition, staring at the manic marginalia, and asking themself, Why had Raskolnikov's fever dream meant so much to the prior reader? What did all those marginal references to "dad" mean? Someone was wondering, Carson had to hope. So long as it wasn't moldering in a Staten Island landfill, she'd be okay.

Miles was no longer living, and that was worse than shorebird habitat destruction, worse than the future unavailability of a caffeinated alcoholic beverage. It was worse than two young boys in Austin crying about how much they missed their mother (with a Tibetan gong and a kind-sounding instruction, they would stop their wailing and settle into a sniffling lotus pose). No, they could not yet fully comprehend hours and days, the *soon* of the nanny's reassurance, but at least they knew, in their kid-sized hearts and the marrow of their growing bones, that Mama would be coming back.

Because Miles was not coming back, not to narrate Cubs games in his announcer voice, making up a box score on the basis of Wrigley's *oohs* and *aahs* and *oh nos!*, the applause that rattled their windowpanes. *It's going, going, gone!* Or, *It's going, going, caught on the warning track! The Cubbies win! The Cubbies lose! The Cubbies exist in this precious and fleeting universe!* He was not coming back to pass out in the bathroom again, to avoid looking for work again, to offer to mind Roger when he really shouldn't be in charge of a child again. When he was sober, Miles had doted on his son with ferocity and enthusiasm; Hillary loved him for this. But he'd also watched Roger while he was high—and that was closest, in Hillary's mind, to unforgivable. He would not come back to see Roger's shtick as a clumsy board game surgeon (it had been Miles's brother, with his well-behaved daughters, who'd thought gifting the Koenigs Operation would be a hoot), to witness Rog devour French toast (Miles's secret ingredient was cardamom), to track his becoming a more humane human. Because behind the biting impulse and the unpredictable bellowing and the side-eye he'd shoot when he set the Operation board buzzing, Roger Koenig was a decent kid, and poised to become a good one. He might still make it, but now the incline of his route had been notched up a tick or two or ten, to the sort of steep grade that required four-wheel drive.

Miles was dead, and per Jewish custom, he had been washed, guarded, and prayed over until he could be placed in the frozen ground. It had taken three days to make the arrangements, rather than the customary two, but did the first day really count? That Sunday afternoon and evening, when the rehab facility thought they might still find him, when the young and swooning PA thought Miles might still come to her house (she'd written out her home address for him, then stayed up late, then gone to bed with her apartment door unlocked), no one knew he was dead. Or, the train station bathroom attendant who first saw his blue lips did, as did the security guard who called 911 while shoving Narcan up Miles's aquiline nose. The responding EMTs (more Narcan) and the emergency room docs who received him on his gurney also knew, but none of them could say who was attached to this cooling, lifeless body.

Now, across town from Hillary and Sheila and Roger and their heartless cardboard patient, a group of Miles's family and friends were sitting shiva in a hotel suite. Reba offered to go on Hillary's behalf—her hotel was down the block and she knew what to do, having sat for aunts and uncles and elderly cousins, her grandparents. A part of Reba was bracing for her next shiva, her mother's or father's, and when, as her mother forewarned, Reba, too, would become an orphan. She did not feel at all ready for orphanhood, but she knew that if she prayed for motherhood, she was truly asking for them both. That was time for you—a real cocksucker, so keen to giveth *and* taketh away. (The women ended up going together that Friday, Reba whispering explainers of the religious aspects and suggesting social cues into Hillary's ear throughout the hour as Roger climbed all over his grandpa.)

No, at this point in the women's lives, things were going so fast, changing so rapidly, it was remarkable they weren't thrown into the sky. But they were held down by gravity, in the Newtonian sense and in the sense of the weight of their obligation, their hand-forged balls and chains. In Hillary's case, it wasn't a ball made of lead but a forty-pound sack of bones and flesh and boogers and sharp teeth, that would soon be a fifty-pound bag; a few years more and he'd be one hundred, then a full-grown man whose teeth (somewhat ground down with use) had stopped biting the hand that fed him, but who still could not fully appreciate his mother. How could he?

Even as each day (especially these bereavement ones, without the relief of day care) felt endless, Hillary knew her time with Roger was only ever shrinking. Just as gravity was unavoidable, shrinking was undeniable too. Everything was dwindling: Florida's landmass (Bella's parents seemed nonchalant about how their not-waterfront property was nosing closer to beachside with each storm), the women's remaining time on earth, their biological capacity to ovulate, the time when their young humans still thought they were gods (or if not deities, then at least all-important, all-knowing giants). The amount of clean oxygen left in the atmosphere, the amount of clean water pooling in underground aquifers, the amount of arable land that was not sprouting genetically modified seeds or being overtaken by kudzu. The number of shorebirds on the Gulf Coast of Texas, the number of healthy corals under that gulf's waves. Their memories may have been growing—that oblong rearview mirror was getting more and more crowded with faces and names, things they might've done differently . . . but their capacity to remember was also shrinking, heading toward the shriveled pea that was everyone's end.

And how was Miles's end? Hillary thought about it often in the days after they laid Miles into the ground. She imagined it was a long moment of stupendous bliss as the chemicals hit his blood, hit his brain, hit those neuroreceptors that had been pining for this very thing. Then the diminishment began, the world going smaller and smaller until it was tiny enough to roll across his palm.

And after the pea of death, what next? A vast black space? Clouds and harp music? Reincarnation or desiccation, and what if he needed those donated corneas again? In the morgue she had vacillated for under a minute about the donation—he'd had such sharp vision, better than twenty-twenty, to go with his meticulous hands. Someone else deserved that gift, though it was disquieting to imagine his irises and pupils, those portals she'd studied so closely over the years, being installed in another human. What would she do if she passed them on the street? Burst into tears or scream or buy their new owner a cup of coffee? Or did the surgeons just take the cornea itself, skimmed off the top of the eyeball like so much milk fat from a cup of shaken cream? Hillary wanted to know the mechanics of how it happened, and she didn't. Because the idea of those glorious irises being denuded, then discarded into a bin of medical waste wasn't any more comforting than the prospect of seeing her husband's eyes in the face of a stranger.

54

Wed, Feb 1 at 5:15 PM

Bella:

Any time

What I mean is hopefully never again but... we love you

Sorry srsly sleep deprived

Things that February were not dull and were getting not duller still. Because during the week that Miles had died and they all gathered in Chicago to bid him adieu, Reba and Terrence's concerted coupling would hit its mark (though they wouldn't know as much until Reba's period was weeks past due and she at last allowed herself to pee on a stick), and Gregg would lose a lot of blood, way more than last time and more than anyone at the clinic had cautioned her she might. That week would prove that Carson was right to think she'd nailed it with her latest manuscript—as she stood looking at her icy reflection in *Cloud Gate*, Tina was at last reading her new draft and thinking the book was a weird one for Carson but very, very good.

And elsewhere in the universe, as those old friends watched their reflections in Kapoor's polished stainless steel, more things were happening to them, the details of which they could not yet possibly know. In Brooklyn, a piece of mail addressed to Carson, the return address from the state correctional complex in Monroe, Washington, was being sorted at the local post office to go out in the next day's delivery. And back in Austin, Zeke, who had just wrapped up a midday workout at their home gym, was doing one more lift—of the kitchen's large potted ficus, with which he blocked the doggy door to the backyard. The animals would be fine outside for the afternoon. The evening too. He'd heard it was going down to the single digits tonight, but they had so much fur. Glancing out the window, he noted that two of them were on the shallow steps of the pool, congregated like so many one-eighth-sized sea lions, panting and proud; maybe they'd still be wet when the temperature nose-dived later, but their splashing in the saltwater pool was all the more reason not to let them come inside, trailing puddles and wet-dog smells across his kitchen. Wolves lived outside all winter, and they were related; the furry cast of *Saved by the Bell* could deal with staying outside until Gregg came back. They had food and fresh water available from automated dispensers, shade under the cabana, their agility course (though so far, no one did anything but sunbathe on top of the ramp), and one another for body heat.

Three years ago, during the pet purchase negotiations, when he said he was interested in one hairless, hypoallergenic cat, Gregg had started crying (he couldn't tell what was disappointment, what was pregnancy hormones). She'd promised him the dog would be mostly outdoor (she'd also promised *the* dog, one, but come back from the breeder with four matching puppies). Back then, Gregg had gotten her way—she'd even named one Zack, when she *knew* he wanted that name for a future son!—and he'd been sneezing ever since. Now he listened through the door. The corgis mewled and nudged, kept trying the custom-made flap and finding it blocked.

It felt marginally wicked, blocking them out, but after what she'd done, *retribution* was like a loud gong clanging in his ears, tolling on the hour, the quarter hour, practically on the minute. How could she have made this decision without him? He heard her, and he saw her almost desperate attempts at playing the part of working mom (how she clung to bedtime, story after story even as the boys were dropping off, her voice animating the plotlines with an actor's élan and a just-restrained mania). But he also spotted the contradiction, her glaring hypocrisy. How short on time was she really if she managed to make a girls' trip to Palm Springs, to spend the whole weekend in New York, and now most of the week in Chicago? That she was even considering Washington meant she had some other source of energy, a hollow leg of vitality. Did she really think he'd not notice her paradox?

If he had to simply solve for Gregg and her hypocrisy, that'd be one thing (that's why she'd signed the prenup), but this was their life. His life, and he didn't like the way it was heading, with her one-sided decisions and absenteeism. The dogs nudged some more, barked a few times. Maybe several times, but Zeke had put on his noise-canceling headphones and joined a call with his product team. The dogs would be fine. Or they wouldn't, but that too would teach Gregg a lesson about unilateralism.

And on the Upper East Side, as the friends in Chicago were holding hands and staring at *Cloud Gate*, maybe waiting for a cosmic gate to swing open and welcome Miles's soul, a woman named Jill was walking into the Winstons' apartment, one Winston boy clutching each of her gloved hands. She'd done such a good job with her cover story for these weeks, having taken enough lit classes as an undergrad to sound like a first-year grad student in the same. But she wasn't. She was a paralegal with Bill's firm, and she was feeling glad to be "reassigned" from filing to babysitting, flirting to fellatio. She recognized that it was highly strange that her boyfriend was the guy who was paying her, the one to linger over her desk at various times of day and tell her to stop what she was doing—*You can't possibly be that busy*, wink wink—and go pick up his kids from school. But the boys were so cuddly, and he was nice-looking and talented (legally, but also in the sack). She'd had to pick up poop once (how had Bill Jr. managed to do it in the hallway, when the bathroom was right there?), but accidents happen. "He was trying," she'd insisted as Bill cursed his namesake. "Mistakes happen." Her excuses had mollified the elder Bill, or maybe it was her hand on his chest, that same hand sliding down his front, toward his dick. He'd calmed, in any case.

Weeks into the affair's escalation it still felt funny to be carrying on as they were—he was married, these were his kids—but he was insistent, emphatic that it was fine. Or mostly fine, or fine enough. To Jill he was quick to explain that it was Bella who'd been the one to cheat first and flamboyantly, back when they were dating; it'd been Bella to beg forgiveness and propose an open relationship. Now, the rules they were following and those they were maybe breaking (he had hemmed enough for her to sense something was amiss) . . . Jill felt knowing less was advantageous in this situation. Besides, *she* had not made any everlasting vows to anyone, not on the altar or anywhere else.

When Jill walked in that afternoon, Bill was home, and smiling, pleased as punch with his ingenuity. Calling her "the babysitter" was a great cover, but it also solved a real problem of logistics. Jill did pickup and drop-off, coordinated the snacks and gloves and winter hats he could hardly keep straight. Jill also took care of him. With her, sex wasn't a negotiation, a chit to be offered in exchange for some other favor. Maybe she even liked his requested sixty-nines? Either way, she wasn't anywhere near as irascible as Bella had become. That woman's glower could send a thousand ships screaming. Such a far cry from where they had started, with horny, glowing Bella and her endless appetite, Bill unable to keep up. He missed that Bella and wanted her back. He sensed such a return was not feasible, but Jill, with her Zara blazers and sexy underwear, was a balm for his disappointed heart.

In the past week, Bill and Jill had become bolder with their midday trysts, their late-night couplings, their morning romps, because Bella was too wrapped up in the future of that ridiculous caffeinated alcoholic beverage to pay them any mind. (Before bargaining her Brooklyn party for a blow job, she hadn't touched him in weeks, maybe months.) Today, she was even farther away than pretrial cramming on Sixtieth Street or a caviar party in Sunset Park; she was in Chicago, staring at a corpse. She wouldn't be home till midnight, she'd said over her shoulder as she departed that morning. And so

Bill put on the television, knowing that the boys—who had run to him screaming, delighted at his unexpected afternoon appearance—wouldn't budge from the living room rug when there were cartoon Australian shepherds available, and took Jill into the bedroom to undress.

55

Wed, Feb 1 at 8:15 PM

Zeke:

Holding down the fort. Boys are fine. Sleep well.

None of the women knew about any of that, not yet. Not that afternoon, and not later that night, as Zeke watched out the kitchen window at the dogs shivering and whimpering and nuzzling themselves together, and Gregg tucked herself into bed in Chicago none the wiser. She texted with Zeke—she didn't quite want to talk to him, and from the clipped tone of his response, it seemed he didn't want to talk to her either. He was right to be mad, but he'd come around. They both had, and they both were, finite resources, and ultimately he had to respect that, to respect her, her body, her decisions. She checked her email. In her work account was a draft document that outlined next steps in a legal action against the rocket company, if and how the state might sue for environmental damages. Even if it went nowhere in the courts, the case's existence, its publicly available evidentiary attachments (documentation of those barbecued birds), would cause the rocket company to pump the brakes, to slow down and think for a minute before they lit their next fuse. (It would also wipe out several million dollars of market valuation for her husband and his friends. She knew that, but thought of the crass ice sculpture, how casually confident they'd all been.) She looked on the internet, scanned some medical sites, and decided she probably wasn't dying any faster than usual. She still felt like she'd been pummeled, but the bleeding had let up; she thought she should be safe to fly in the morning.

And there was Bella, who had already realized her brain was slipping its moorings as she delivered the best closing argument of her life, who'd hightailed it to the airport (the wrong one, but it didn't matter—Midway had flights to New York too) as soon as she could slip away from the group in Millennium Park. She talked her way onto an earlier flight (okay, it was not a negotiation; she just purchased a new ticket), sprinted through the terminal, arrived seconds before the boarding doors closed. By the time she made it back to Manhattan and her neighborhood and into the clanging elevator, by the time she rustled open the heavy door of their apartment, Jill and Bill, hearing her keys, were hurriedly getting dressed, and the boys, still splayed before the TV, were five hours into *Bluey*. The children, Bella saw upon entering, were slicked with the orange grease of a pepperoni pizza, which annoyed her, but at least they were wiping their hands on an old picnic blanket rather than the rug (what a smart hack—why hadn't she ever thought of that?).

Then the young woman, Jill, was there in the hall, smiling warmly at Bella, welcoming her home. She thumbed back toward the laundry. "Just put in a load, didn't think you'd mind," and Bella didn't—instead, it vaulted the young woman into a new level of regard. She was now an ad hoc housecleaner, Olivia's backup.

Bella said "Oh, thanks," pounded straight to the bedroom, swallowed what she needed, and came out again. When she returned to the living room, her children were degreased, her husband was grinning like he'd gotten away with something, and Jill was cleaning the counters in the kitchen. How had Bill found such a heroic young woman? Bella flitted from that question to feelings of familial love. She hugged her boys, she kissed her husband. Then she marched into the kitchen, gave Jill a twenty, and told her to scram.

The woman departed, chancing one last longing look at Bill. Bella, watching the children squirm on the carpet, did not see it. She was thinking about bedtime, how this thing that had been a tedious chore was, by its recent absence, again a treat to be relished. "Another ten minutes of play, then it's time for bed, okay boys?"

Finally there was Reba, who for this month could only hope on her ovulation app and the cycles of the moon, who could just pray that something was pointing her and Terrence in the right direction. It was the app that had suggested she bring him along to Illinois to mourn this guy he'd barely met, the app that had her pack a suitcase of sex toys. It felt crass, but timing was timing, so along with her black wool suit, which she'd not worn since she fired a third of Wexford Manufacturing's staff, she packed a see-through, crotchless leotard. The app advised an upgrade to a nice suite, in which they would stay through Sunday (by then, the egg would be fertilized or expired, there were only two outcomes), the app encouraged they fuck like bunnies and eat aphrodisiacs from room service (chocolate-dipped strawberries, artichoke dip). They left the hotel for the funeral, for a short stay at the Koenigs' shiva, and for an afternoon at the Art Institute, during which Reba stood in front of that great big Georgia O'Keeffe painting, the one with the horizontal bands of perfect white clouds, and begged whoever was up there, Georgia or God or one of Gregg's celestial sprites, to let things work this time.

• • •

Carson was the first to feel the impact of how the universe was shifting, the first to sense that what the women were facing wasn't some moon phase or set of coincidences but a major planetary realignment. Because when she got home from Chicago, late that Wednesday night, there was no mail for her, and her heart sank. But the next day, as she was hours into staring at another blank document—thinking about narrative POVs and getting nowhere—a note from Monroe Correctional Complex was pushed under her door. Zariah, home early from a shoot, had found it in the mailbox, bundled in among her DSW coupons.

Carson stared at the envelope on the scuffed hardwood floor. It came! She felt as dizzy as Bella without her pills, as hopeful as Reba in the promising glow of her ovulation app, nearly as sad as Hillary, because the forty years lost with her father were not equal to the infinite years lost with Miles, but edging up toward it. What would the letter say?

Hopeful as she was, she also felt almost as scared as Gregg should have felt, if, instead of waking peaceably in a Chicago hotel, she had had the capacity to peer back into her Austin life. If she could have, she would have seen, in the back corner of the yard, as the sun rose but the temperature scarcely budged from its twelve-degree low, her once happy dogs in a heap, frost-lipped and lethargic. She would have seen how they tried to lick warm their clumps of wet, now frozen, fur to no avail, how they sought—and did not find—liquid in their frozen-over water bowl. But Gregg was not there to see them, to save them, to put them under high-wattage heat lamps. And by the time she'd return to Texas, later that afternoon, the offending ficus would be returned to its normal, un-incriminating spot.

56

Thu, Feb 2 at 1:10 PM

Zariah:

Dunno if yr home but dropped off some mail under yr door. You never told me you had a prison penpal. Abolition now!

Why had she taken so long to write? The answer had shifted over the years. First it was out of deference to her mother, her deathbed commandments that Carson have nothing to do with her father, not ever. Carson was so mad, wanted to spit at how hypocritical it was that *she* had to stay away, when her mother demonstrably hadn't. Sonja had kept copies of the arrest records, fine, but also saved cheesy rhyming poems, and receipts of cash transfers to the prison commissary up through 1999! (At this point in the argument Carson had waved the binder in the air, the damning evidence glowing radioactive.) "Why do you get to know him and I don't?"

A mother's favorite, most efficient rebuttal: "Because." It was ludicrous, but she was also dying in increments visible to the naked eye—here came the bedpan, there went the last of her appetite, now her skin was going sallow—and so Carson acceded to Sonja's demands and shoved the scrapbook back into the box with her school yearbooks, pushed the heavy cube into a corner. There would be plenty of time to study it later.

Then, the inevitable *later*: her mother gone, the grass over her grave sprouted, grown, and mowed, and Carson still hadn't retrieved the scrapbook from its banker's box (which was stored, along with Carson's childhood relics and her mother's most meaningful effects, in the back of her Brooklyn closet). It had taken years for Carson to admit it wasn't exclusively her mom's ultimatums and her nosy ghost that were keeping her from opening that lid; it was her own dread at what she might find. How could someone commit such an awful crime? A burst of violence was one thing, but there was premeditation, there was relish. And she was half him. She had nightmares of epigenetics and Hannibal Lecter, waking dreams about generational trauma and the *Halloween* film franchise; she sometimes caught, in the corner of her eye, the glint of an imagined blade in the moonlight and blanched. (Reba's conniption in Palm Springs had set her back in this regard—then, she hadn't been imagining it, there *was* a knife coming at her.) She recognized that pop culture violence skewed her perspective—why was murder so entertaining?—but when she got around to systematically studying the history of violence, from the Bible's bloodshed to the Bobbitts' domestic disturbance, she thought: Maybe not so skewed. Maybe violence was closer to life, more prevalent than she'd ever be comfortable with.

Carson was twenty-eight when she marshaled the courage to look again at her dead mother's scrapbook. And from the first day she properly combed through the binder, she knew that she would write about it. Because whether it was personal history, societal present, or humanity's future, she wrote about everything she didn't understand, trying to sort not only how she herself felt, but how others might feel as they confronted the same sheer rock face. Her approach was one of radical empathy, an experiment in possibility: to stare down the hardest questions in life and come up with . . . She typically tried to elucidate a half-dozen answers, all of which were valid. From the wall of inscrutability emerged handholds; the handholds connected themselves into multiple routes up the rock face, routes that she studied and slowly ascended.

That was the idea. But after sketching out some clunky scenes that felt more like a novelization of the movie adaptation of the memoir *Dead Man Walking* than any sort of literature, she realized she was not ready for the climb. She had a good vocabulary and superb sense of rhythm; already in undergrad writing workshops she was praised for her spare but cutting use of dialogue. But her upper-body strength, her capacity to reach and pull, the depth of her empathetic reserves and her regret reservoir just weren't there yet.

So Carson had shelved it and begun writing that initially mean and ultimately generous book that became her first novel. Then, with the soft wind of its success at her back, she returned to her earlier prompt. Now she was better at writing scene, now she knew how to seamlessly move between a character's interiority and his external interactions, now she understood more about the world and its fuckery, full stop.

And now, maybe, she was ready to face her father.

She'd opened the scrapbook for the first time in years, wanting to imagine a world in which she was wrong about her first impressions. What if her father hadn't been such a vile criminal as he'd appeared to her then? Or maybe he had done something awful, planned and gratuitous, but there was more below the surface—perhaps she didn't understand the *why*? And what about time? At twenty-eight, she hadn't been able to think beyond the next week, and absolutely couldn't grasp the epochal time frame of someone spending decades in one compact cell. Was his sentence sufficient for atonement, for rehabilitation, maybe even for fundamental change? Maybe he'd gone through more gates of understanding and turns of transformation than she could count. Perhaps whoever it was who had stabbed those lady hikers to death, who had cut off their pinkie fingers as tiny trophies of his crime, was long, long gone.

At first she thought she would need her father's voice and vision to begin the project. She wanted a vocabulary sheet of prison slang, a daily schedule for his cell block. Verisimilitude as procrastination. But then, she encountered a welcome development. His voice came to her, as clear as a bell. Well, not *his* voice, not Erik Gustavsson's, but her protagonist's—she called him Anders—and she was as certain of it as she'd been of any character she'd ever drafted. And in this way she'd found a route up the rock face, one that would not only give her courage for herself and her epigenetics but from which she could also, she hoped, throw a lifeline to a society that had been entirely fractured by violence and an overly punitive, unproductive system of incarceration. She found herself drafting a portrait of male friendship, telling a story of atonement and indefatigability. It wasn't fantasy, she told herself as she climbed. And she definitely didn't feel fantastic, fluctuating from a generosity of spirit to the utter difficulty of transformation (for her characters, for herself, for America and its obsession with retribution and "justice"). It was turning into an abolition novel, she realized about halfway up the wall, and that scared her. Not because she didn't want abolition—she did—but she didn't want her art to morph into a screed. If she'd wanted to write about politics she'd have penned a manifesto, gone into left-wing media. But feeling scared also made her keep going.

She took some liberties with location, moving the prison from its real site in Eastern Washington onto an unpopulated island in the San Juans, because she liked describing the lushness of old-growth forests and because winter storms on the island, with their wind and crashing waves, felt more perilous than those east of the mountains, where winter often arrived as steady, quiet snow. She tried writing an unexpected alliance with a warden; she struck it, too saccharine. She experimented with an unanticipated return to faith, which felt encouraging enough that she started attending the local Baptist church. She wanted to absorb the pastor's cadence, wanted to see the parishioners' faces as they embraced the word of God. She didn't gain faith on those Sundays, but she believed some people did, and had a better sense of why.

It wasn't all smooth sailing. She got herself stuck often, was caught clinging to the stone face without a handhold in sight. Times like these, she thought that maybe she wasn't ready after all. Maybe she never would be.

But then she'd done it. She'd finished.

With caveats. She had a running list (nine pages, single-spaced) of questions that she wasn't able to resolve from her reading and research, the dozens of documentaries and two weeks she'd spent at the Washington State Archives. But she sensed that to ask her dad would also be to break a seal, or open a dam, some metaphor evoking liquid redirection. She did not want to interrupt her imagination with authenticity (how the tables had turned!), because she knew that as soon as she wrote to him, or more precisely, as soon as he wrote back, the book would change. Its voice, its horizons, the dimensions from the front end of the cell to its back. She did not want to cede any vertical gain to this person who had sparked the project. Her story came first.

She'd put her writing before so many other things in her life . . . why not this, as well? She was just a few reaches from the top, and then, at last, she pulled herself over.

57

Thu, Feb 2 at 1:25 PM

Carson:

Thanks, Mx Postman.

She'd resolved not to start with her queries, the questions that sorted themselves into two lists; those for the book ("How hot is the hot water in the showers: Tepid, scalding, or just right?" "Do you have friends?" "What is the best meal in the mess? The worst?" "How has your incarceration shaped your opinion of retribution?") and those for herself ("Did you know I existed?" "Might we become a family, and how?" "Do you have any hereditary illnesses?"). She'd introduce herself first, for heaven's sake, before subjecting him to her grilling.

She'd written a draft of the letter on her computer, then cut it back significantly, reconsidering its balance of enthusiasm versus overwhelm. She wanted to stay on the right side of the ledger, and her initial, long-winded version had made her sound unhinged. Then she'd written it out by hand, because who wrote to their dad on a computer? Typed-up pages felt formal, so cold.

She had waited for the postscript—trying to sound breezy even as her heart pounded—to see if he might share some family "history" of the "medical" variety. (The color for her novel could wait, but it turned out she didn't have the stomach to postpone news of another inherited health threat.) The casual way she phrased it—and it had taken many attempts before she found the right words—was a friendly, open door. “Anything I should know?” She was suggesting that . . . was wondering if . . . should she prepare herself for more cancer, heart disease, high blood pressure?

Written in ink, the query felt brazen, but she reminded herself that there were plenty of legitimate reasons she might pose the question. Maybe she was pregnant, trying. Or she was dying and needed a donor; that was a good reason to write out of the blue. He didn’t need to know that she was afraid she’d inherited any among the list of disorders his lawyers had trotted out at trial. Was she a psycho killer too? She weighed the stone of asking against that of more waiting, felt how each sank into the meat of her palm. She chose inquiry and dropped the other rock.

The likelihood of a joyful or irate response was a coin flip, but as she’d been waiting for a reply, she did not allow herself to imagine anything other than the profile of George Washington. Heads was how her protagonist would have felt upon receiving the news of a long-lost daughter and how, she’d told herself, her father would feel too. The reply she expected was warm and wide-reaching. Maybe the reason he’d taken weeks to write was that he’d not only read her book but analyzed it across second and third readings. In his reply he’d offer exegeses on her characters, a lucid commentary on the novel’s tone. To hear him say that he liked the work—even imagining it made her heart beat faster. It’d be as gratifying as the endorsement of a literary hero.

She had asked, innocuously, for “stories from childhood,” and he’d be generous with his recollections about happy times, but also candid about formative, painful ones (embarrassments on the playground, an unrequited first crush). There’d be stuff about his parents and siblings (she’d found birth records; his parents had met while Lars was in the service; Erik had one older brother, deceased). He would talk about how good a cook his mother had been (unless she wasn’t), how she’d learned recipes from her mother-in-law (unless she hadn’t, the older one too skeptical, too stuck in her ways). Every morsel would be a gift; her research had turned up very close to zilch. She sensed she’d come by the scarcity honestly: They were a boring family. Nothing happened in their lives, until, with Erik, it did.

He'd also talk about his routines in prison. She wanted to believe he had friends, maybe a lover, that he'd been taking correspondence courses or that, like the protagonist in her novel, he was becoming one of those prison lawyers who got compassionate releases and reduced sentences for scores of guys on his block. Or maybe he'd immersed himself in creative writing and was working on a novel (and what a good story that would be: father and daughter, separated before birth, both launching their literary careers). Mercifully, he'd put her health concerns to bed—no cancer, some heart disease but not till later in life, and the claimed mental health disorders were just a defense lawyer's Hail Mary.

Then, in the letter he was supposed to write, the one she'd assured herself was coming, he'd have his own cagey PS, addressing the crime. His crime. The way he would describe the *why* wouldn't be as Carson had imagined it—and she had envisioned so many permutations of motive, had drafted version after version of the crime (some accurate, some less so, all of them taking place on that same desolate stretch of trail) as potential sparks to light her narrative's fuse. Maybe his real reason was "better" (more compelling, more complicated) than the fictional one on which she'd landed. Would she revise toward his truth, or accept that there were many starting points, and hers was also satisfactory?

One might ask why Carson was this hopeful. What made her so convinced of what he'd say? Maybe it was because she was 50 percent him, and despite her insecurity and low-grade self-loathing, she sensed she was a foundationally sound person. Or because, ignoring the villainous picture the media had painted of him during the trial and the nasty things her mother had said from her hospice bed, Carson believed Erik Gustavsson was basically a good man who had had a bad day. Or maybe he hadn't actually been good back then, but she believed the end of *Crime and Punishment* to be true: All people could atone; with enough patience and penance, anyone could reform. He'd had forty years! An unconscionably long sentence in her abolitionary mind, but also enough time to make things right.

And the envelope from Monroe, when it at last arrived, was very thick, which she took to mean long, which she equated with expansive. It had to be.

58

Thu, Feb 2 at 1:40 PM

Tina Trimble:

Carson, did you get my email? Good things come to those who wait! Call me!!

Carson pulled the letter from its envelope. The paper was bright white, lined with aqua-blue rules, three-hole punched. As she unfolded the sheets and started reading, she quickly understood that the letter would not be as she'd imagined it.

For starters, it was written in the big, brick-like block letters of a child—what had happened to that looping cursive of the love notes in her mother's binder? Had Erik suffered a brain injury, did he have rheumatoid arthritis or a degenerative disease? (She thought of what Julian had told her about environmental factors for memory loss—isolation, repetition, bad diet, lousy sleep . . . prison had all of those.) Or might he simply no longer care? And while the letter did go on for pages, his thoughts were not the organized, coherent narrative she'd envisioned; the prose neither capacious nor kind. She noted misspellings toward phonetics; grammar mistakes abounded. And maybe the most crushing: It was clear that he had not read her book. Or rather, he had started it but found it boring. "Too much talking." He spent a fair deal of pencil lead dissecting her author photo and every attribute of her face, claiming her nose and eyebrows and the sticking-outness of her ears ("They called me Dumbo when I wuz a kid") as his. He thought she was nice looking, he wrote, but she'd be prettier if she put on some lipstick, wore a lower-cut blouse. (That he was commenting on her cleavage made her skin crawl, and she grabbed closed the sides of her cardigan.) He'd read her bio—if she went to *that* school, she must be rich ("Ha!" she barked). Could she send some cash? He must've mentioned his commissary account four times.

In his lines, and in the spaces between them, he sounded mad. Angry with his treatment in the prison, angry that Sonja had stopped sending cash. (Did he not realize that she was dead? Carson had written as much in her letter, so the question became, did he not understand what she'd told him, had he forgotten it, or did he not care? She thought of Alzheimer's again.) Angry that his lawyers had not pushed more for an appeal, that the continuing ed classes were too dumb or too hard, that the food they served was disgusting. (That answered one of her questions, at least.) Angry that a dozen guys from his unit had died of Covid, that the guards were all pricks, that he hadn't made a single new friend since Rick got out seven years before. "And did that asshole come back and visit? Not once!" He was angry that she'd not found him before—why'd it take so long, if she was so smart? She noticed points where the pencil's force had torn through the paper.

She read the letter once, then started it again, her hand trembling. To acknowledge the things she had hoped would come for the two of them, what she thought might grow from this exchange—her zhuzhing questions, but also the parole boards and manuscript swaps she'd dreamed up, his restorative justice campaign and her prison book club—now seemed absurd. Had she really thought that with some random letter—*Hello, remember me? Jk, you can't, but I'm your daughter!*—she might unlock a new and magical universe? She was so foolish. What she'd actually done was open herself up to an unstable person who now felt he had some leverage over her. A new source for candy bars and cigarettes, a new ear for gripes.

She shouldn't have sent the letter, and would not write again, not suggest a Sunday phone call or, in due time, a Saturday visit. At least she'd done one thing right—she hadn't mentioned anything about her new book, how she'd based so much of it on his life. And now she would not.

Her mind was racing, already back to the book. How could she spin this? She'd have to come up with some other genesis story, were anyone to wonder about the petri dish of how she'd arrived at such an inventive, vivid premise. She could talk about Dostoyevsky—it wasn't a lie that she'd been obsessed with his account of crime and punishment. She could talk about Ted Bundy; he was butchering people in the same years and the same part of the world as when and where her father had committed his double murder. Maybe they'd even think she was clever, to transmute that well-known criminal into a long-lost cousin, a man who enters as cipher and leaves as sage. She could say she conjured a character specifically to contain her message of prison reform, wanting to make readers understand, like a blow to the forehead, the inhumanity of our carceral state.

As she read his letter over again, her stomach turned sour. She thought about scanning it, so she'd have the record of its existence, a document of his decline, but decided: No. She wanted no trace that this had happened, that she'd been so wrong. And so, Carson gingerly folded the letter back into its envelope, then used a glue stick to reseal the flap. She wrote in a shaky cursive, the letters quivery with her upset: "Return to sender, addressee unknown."

She stared at the envelope. Maybe he'd get the hint, maybe he wouldn't. Her phone pinged; a text from her agent. She thought she'd been waiting these antsy weeks for Tina's evaluation of the manuscript; she understood now she'd been waiting for this letter, the answer to the question of whether she'd have a new family, or if, moving forward, she'd be even more alone. She glanced at her phone and clicked into her email, steeling herself for another reveal.

Outside her window, a bird was singing. It sounded very lonely to Carson, but she realized that perhaps she was just projecting again.

59

Thu, Feb 2 at 3:20 PM

Gregg:

Hi Gis pls keep the boys OUT OF THE BACKYARD thx

Gregg landed at the Austin airport Thursday afternoon and came home to four very cold and torpid corgis. Two of them rolled their eyes slowly toward her approaching footsteps; the other two were unresponsive as she stepped into the backyard. But still alive? Gregg felt the faintest of pulses, but none came to her when called, not even when she jiggled their tub of biscuits.

She loaded *Saved by the Bell* into the back of her car and sped to the vet's. She called her husband in tears as she drove. "They seemed fine this morning," he said, trying, she thought, to sound perplexed. Hadn't he noticed they were nearly frozen to death when he left for work? And why hadn't he brought them in last night, when he knew the weather was going to be so cold? He said they had seemed happy outside, and as he did, she could imagine his *not my problem* shrug on the other end of the call. (She could not, however, imagine the ficus.)

Usually the dogs loved a car ride, were a squealing swirl in the wayback of her hybrid SUV. Today, they were unmoving, very quiet. Their silence made her want to wail.

She pulled up to the vet's emergency bay and two techs helped her hurry the dogs inside. Once they were in triage—each wrapped in its own heated blanket, with an IV drip of warmed fluids and heart-boosting electrolytes—she was called into the vet's office to discuss prognoses.

Vet degrees and pet art were mounted salon-style, all over the walls; the room seemed much happier than the news it held. Which was that Zack would lose his tail (it'd been a point of pride for Gregg that she'd not cropped them for breed aesthetics); and Kelly had frostbite on her ears; the dead tissue would need to be clipped. Screech had ice burn on his snout, which was different from frostbite in a way she couldn't understand; it required a special skin treatment. Slater seemed physiologically fine but was showing some cognitive symptoms? Maybe his inner ear had been damaged; the animal audiologist was out today but tomorrow they would investigate.

Upon hearing that none of her dogs would die, Gregg felt a surge of relief so strong she cursed. Then, reading the stern-faced room, she followed up with a more restrained "Thank you."

When the vet asked if she had any questions about the dogs' care plans, Gregg said she didn't right now, that she was just very, very grateful for his team's diligence and skill.

In that case, he continued, he had some questions for her. Namely, "How did this happen?" He sounded scornful.

Gregg considered how best to answer. Because while this was absolutely Zeke's fault, they were, ultimately, her dogs—she'd strong-armed her husband into them, buying a boatload of Claritin and sending him Lassie GIFs until he'd folded. As part of the negotiation—and the debate had gone on for weeks, into her first pregnancy's second trimester—she had said that she'd take care of them fully by herself, and had sworn on Charlene's best book of poems that they'd be "mostly" outside dogs. Zeke was guilty of blatant inattention, but she'd abnegated her responsibilities; they both were culpable. But also: Neither, at this point in their careers, could comfortably weather an animal endangerment charge made public.

She decided to try to thread a needle, claiming a he-said, she-said oopsie-do. She thought, she started, Zeke was taking care of them, he thought she was on pet duty. She'd had a flight delay, some wires were crossed. It was an honest misunderstanding.

The vet cleared his throat. "Now Senator, I understand you're under a great deal of stress right now, and I am aware of and grateful for all your good and valuable work on behalf of your constituents."

So he was pro-choice, she thought. Good, but she didn't want to be a state senator right now. She just wanted to be told her fur babies would be all right, just reassured that this mistake could be undone. She was still shuddering in the shock wave of seeing their half-frozen bodies, of feeling the pain in her own abdomen, still reckoning with the spleen she felt toward . . . "Just Gregg, please."

"Okay, Gregg." The vet shifted his weight. "You understand the responsibilities of pet ownership, correct?" He was glaring now.

She blinked at him stupidly. Was he about to report her for neglect? "I do."

"Now, I know mistakes happen. Miscommunications, as you said, and things like that. And mercifully, the dogs will be all right, if a little worse for wear. Another hour out there, and I don't know if we'd be having the same conversation. But please, Senator—"

"Gregg."

"Right. Gregg. Don't let this happen again."

She bowed her head. "Understood."

60

Sun, Feb 5 at 7:30 PM

Gregg:

Making grocery list are you eating this week or just 🥕??

There were several days of avoidance—Zeke at the office all weekend, Gregg catching up from her time away, both of them dreading the inevitable confrontation. The children, sweetly oblivious to the mounting tension, asked about when the dogs would be home from their "vacation" (she'd told them they were away at the doggy spa, rather than recovering from surgery at the vet's . . . she didn't want to explain amputation to her toddlers) and used her as a jungle gym, which in her fragile state felt more like a game of Operation, every blow to her chin or kidney or kneecap electric and buzzing. Each night she read them six stories to make up for lost time, and when those were done, lights out, she'd read reams of constituent complaints and staff emails before sleep. Zeke would still be absent as she drifted off, working or plotting or sticking his thumb up his ass elsewhere, and in the mornings, finding him mummied in his mask and earplugs all the way across their California king, she didn't have the energy to wake him and rage.

But even in that big house, with those opposite schedules, they would eventually have to cross paths. They arrived at that intersection the following Monday night, in the kitchen, and it was a big fight.

She asked him first if he noticed the dogs were missing; he'd not mentioned them once since her teary call on her way to the vet. He glanced around the room, inspecting the corners as though they might've been lurking quietly behind the wine fridge, and when he found no corgis, he shook his head. Maybe Giselle had taken them to the dog spa? They did get regular baths and blowouts to keep their fur smelling nice, but he'd never acknowledged these efforts before.

"They're not at the dog spa."

"Are they still outside?" He looked at her like he was a sweet and dumb cow.

"That's rich. You left them outside, remember? They nearly froze to death!"

He shook his head in objection. "What are you talking about? They could've come in." He pointed at the doggy door.

"Why did you do it?" She was trying to keep her voice down, but it was barreling up and out of her control.

"Do what?"

"Leave them out in the cold?"

"Because you did the same." He didn't raise his voice, which was more unnerving than her escalating volume. Its flatness made her knees go weak; she braced herself against the counter.

"I didn't try to kill four living, furry things in an ice storm."

"I didn't kill them. And it was a polar vortex. No precipitation."

"You neglected them. They were on death's door!"

"I'm sorry that happened, but you said they'd be fine outside. Remember?" He almost smiled. "Outside dogs?"

"How could I know it'd go down to twelve degrees? They cut off Kelly's ear!" She pulled on her own earlobe to emphasize the point.

"Like I said, I'm sorry that happened. But also." He shifted his weight, puffed up his chest. "Now you know how I feel."

"How is this the same? *That*," she said, looking down at her middle, "wasn't anything, anyone yet. These are my dogs!"

"It was the size of a lime! It had a heartbeat and fingers and the nub of a kidney!"

"What?" Her mind was spinning. Had Zeke been reading mommy blogs?

"It was my future child. And you got rid of it."

"That doesn't mean you can get rid of something else I care about."

"Doesn't it?"

"No. This isn't *Spy vs. Spy*. I am your *wife*." Her creature was out from its hiding place and thumping on her lungs, turning her voice boomy. "Don't you realize that if I said I couldn't manage another, it was because I really don't think I can? That I am overwhelmed, unhappy, in over my head? Don't you care how I feel about anything?"

"Explain this to me, Gregg. You're overwhelmed, but you have time for Palm Springs, and Brooklyn, and Chicago?"

"It was a funeral!"

"It was one funeral, fine, though you've been gone two weekends in the past month. But that's not the part that bothers me. Live and let live, fly to the moon and back for all I care. Run for Congress even! Go ahead. What pisses me off is that you don't listen to me. You don't listen when I say 'No dogs,' don't listen when I say 'More kids.' You don't care what I think, what I want."

"I listen to you!" she shouted, but she was thinking, What was he saying about Congress? She hadn't told him she was running for anything yet. She was waiting on a feasibility study by "Anne-Stylist" because they both liked empirical data.

"Well, then, listen to this." He stalked to the other side of the kitchen island. "I'm ready to talk about surrogacy."

Her eyes narrowed. "What?"

"It's when another woman carries—"

"I know what it means, Zeke. I mean, no fucking way." They glared at each other. She watched his anger smoke, saw that smoke thicken into a hovering cloud, then begin to dissipate.

"Fine. But if you don't want to delegate, you better think about becoming more efficient." He stomped off.

"I hate efficiency!" she yelled after him. She was one of the most efficient people she knew, but Zeke took the mandate to new levels. He rarely did fewer than two things at once—even as they argued, he had been making himself a celery-rich smoothie.

"It's a mode of self-respect, Gregg!" he shouted over his shoulder. "If you were more efficient with your time, you could be president by now!" That seemed ludicrous (and exhilarating), but she wasn't about to go chasing him down the hall to ask that he explain his thinking. She was too hung up on how he was still telling her to go faster, when all she wanted to do was slow down. It was as if he hadn't heard a word she'd said.

"I don't want to be president!" she cried down the hall.

"Good!" He slammed the door to his office.

"Just a congresswoman," she said to the now empty corridor. She went back into the kitchen, gathered Zeke's celery trimmings for the compost, and for dinner fried herself an egg.

• • •

An hour later, determined they not go to bed angry, Gregg knocked on the door of his study and let herself in. He looked peeved at the interruption, but she was expecting a skeptical audience, and so started into her monologue without delay. They'd both hurt each other, she ventured, because they were feeling hurt and unheard. He nodded a tight nod of assent. They'd let their anger get the better of them, she added; Zeke spun around in his chair and looked up at her. They were both hotheaded, but that was part of why they loved each other so much. She pressed a hand into his shoulder (thicker, stronger than she remembered) and suggested they should've talked more about how they were feeling, unpacked the *why* and *what next*, been candid about how their bodies and their ambitions were growing or wilting, what they wanted to speed up and where they were dying to hit the pause button. His hand found her waist. She said that, moving forward, they should both try harder to meet in the middle, to see things from the other person's perspective, to share how they were feeling before what they were feeling was blinding fury. His grip tightened, and she stiffened before he could pull her close—the doctor had told her to refrain from sex for two weeks; her body said no touching below her waist until March.

For now, she offered that they could both make an effort to spend more time with the two kids they had, and when the dogs were back from the pet hospital, she'd keep them out of the bedroom. She would be happy to think about ways to be more efficient with her time, and maybe they could both work at being more patient, with each other and themselves? Did all that sound okay?

He gave her another silent nod. She leaned down and kissed him quickly on the crown of his head before slipping out of his grasp.

Gregg slept in the guest room for the rest of the week.

61

Mon, Feb 6 at 8:25 AM

Bella:

Here I go! Thx for putting up with a wild few months

Bella, after the oops of Chicago, was back to her regularly scheduled meds, but they hardly helped against the surges of adrenaline and exhaustion that careened through her days like a loose pendulum. Thursday, back at Cushman, everyone watched her closely, because she was the case's lead counsel and they had ninety-six hours to go, but also to double-check she wasn't still sick—they'd taken her stomach virus story too seriously, perhaps? Though after 2020, everyone was, and rightly, fearful of contagion. Their client was scheduled to arrive Friday midday, and Bella was caught off guard when the beverage conglomerate did not send June, the chummy, hard-charging woman with whom she'd been working for what felt like decades, but Timothy, someone she'd only ever talked to twice. This Timothy had appeared quiet and pale on Zoom, and was even more pallid in person. He offered that June was "indisposed" at present, no more. As he observed them putting the finishing touches on their strategy for jury selection and what they'd say coming out of the gates, he seemed moderately withdrawn, maybe jittery. Bella figured he was, like her, just nervous.

In the handful of hours she was home during this final stretch, Bill knew to stay out of her way, the boys flinched at the sharpness in her voice, and the babysitter slept in the maid's room. Bella, noticing her family's avoidance and their recoils, checked herself. Was she using her litigator voice at home again? She tried to keep the two versions of herself separate, but this close to trial, with so much on the line, she allowed one Bella to overpower the other. She barked and paced, grimaced and guffawed. Her litigator voice and pretrial demeanor pissed Bill off, but seeing his annoyance, she also knew she was close to her target, the way she needed to sound on Monday morning. "Just a bit longer, babe," she said with hope, stroking his thigh. His thigh was hard and sinewy, and did not respond to her touch.

Over the weekend, Bella practiced her opening statement in front of her bathroom mirror as she dried her hair, hoping the loud, blowing air might drown out her words. She practiced it whispering in front of the napping Gus and Bill Jr., who did not stir at her breathy declarations. That Sunday—and they were all in the office Sunday, the conference room teeming, more like a war room than a Midtown office on the Lord's day (not like Bill had taken the boys to church; he was watching the Pro Bowl, letting them destroy the living room's hardwood with their clattering train sets)—Bella kept at her OS. She repeated it in front of the office bathroom mirror (briefly thinking of the pregnant associate, how she was feeling), then in front of Darcy in the office kitchen (who was clutching her mug like she was very hungover), then in front of her co-lead in the hallway, and lastly in front of her practice group lead and Timothy in Conference Room B. All were encouraging, offering actionable, straightforward feedback. Swap adjectives here and there, smile not so big (she looked a trifle crazed?) but also don't look angry. Litigator Bella nodded resolutely, then reminded herself to turn her present frown upside down. She smiled with teeth, made appreciative eye contact. "Got it, thanks."

Jury selection went fine, faster than anyone expected, so that it was still Monday afternoon when they had their twelve, with alternates. Tuesday morning, Bella felt like she might vomit, even as she pumped herself up, splurging on a black car—no wild card of the subway today, no thanks—blasting Britney in her headphones as she walked up to the courthouse. She was stronger than yesterday! Now there was nothing but her way! So what if the song was about a breakup, today it was also about being a *boss*. And Bella was one: Her hair looked great (the salon had opened early, just for her), her shoes were awesome, her statement was memorized, even where to put in the breaths. She'd started paying attention to her breath in her high school girls' choir (marking little commas on the sheet music where her inhalations should go); in the years since, she'd channeled Gregg channeling her mom channeling those old hippie poets. Her pants fit, her meds were on track, and her pits were soaked but she was wearing one of those fancy undershirts that sopped up all the sweat.

She had this.

• • •

Except, except. Isn't there always an *except*? A curveball or a wrench, a wrenching curveball that slips from the pitcher's grip a nanosecond too soon and catches the meat of the batter's bicep, the unprotected bone at the side of the knee. A place that should be tougher than it is, and when the hard sphere hits, it strikes like pure white pain, like crumpling. (Gregg may not have understood baseball, but Bella's brother had played, and she was his backyard catcher from an age far too young to be gloving seventy mph strikes. She knew from a beaner, that throbbing heat.)

Baseball. The only sport where the defense has the ball, and she was the defense's lead counsel. But no. That morning, pacing in front of the jury box, delivering her perfectly polished opening statement, Bella only *thought* she was on the mound. In an instant—that instant being lunch, an old-school diner around the corner from the courthouse—she was swapped, with no warning, into the batter's box and given the cardboard tube of a toilet paper roll as her lumber. Because Timothy, that reserved stand-in client rep, was giving off a weird vibe as he ordered his soup and salad. Honestly, things had felt off all day. He'd arrived at court in a tan suit (Bella had considered sending him back to the hotel to change; June would never have donned something so egregious), and he had listened to the plaintiff's opening statement, then to Bella's case for freedom, with an inscrutable pout.

And now, during their lunch break—before they'd even received their soups—the man announced that the corporation, which also had a chips division and cookie company under its control, wanted to settle.

"What?" Bella asked because she couldn't understand what he was saying, which sounded a lot like *I quit*. That couldn't be right. After that one instance in the fall, June had never again mentioned settling—she also wanted to fight to the end. This guy wasn't June, but over the weekend he had duly signed off on Bella's statement, and after she'd delivered it in court that morning, given her a literal thumbs-up. She replayed his words, slower, until they made meaning, then blurted to the table, "We can't." Her colleague winced. "You said I did a good job," she added, mimicking his approving thumb.

The man looked at her the way she looked at Gus when he put his shorts on backward. She had, he said. But they could settle. They would.

Oh, how Bella tried to talk him out of it! He was being shortsighted. The plaintiffs had such a lame strategy, no strategy at all. She listed the defense's expert witnesses like they were the batting order of the Yankees—a reliable leadoff hitter, then more and more power, then the taper of the utility guys, the speed and tricksters at the back of the order. She spoke about liberty again. The man seemed unfazed, blowing on his freshly delivered chicken noodle soup.

Bella did not pick up her spoon. She could see only one kind of cutlery—the blade of a guillotine just above her, swinging in the winter wind and poised to drop on her neck.

When it seemed clear, his soup mostly drained, that Timothy could not be swayed, Bella let free her last shred of dignity, and asked: Was it something she said? (Her co-counsel, across the table, made a sucking noise.) The client replied it wasn't her, not the firm's qualification or its line of defense. Her statement had been brilliant, her shoes were fabulous. And those earrings—big enough to make a statement, but not so big as to make the wrong statement. (She began to sense Timothy wasn't so oblivious to style in his bad-colored suit, which was, she now saw, well tailored, more camel than tan.) But what? Bella pressed. Under the table someone kicked a table leg—the table bounced—then kicked her leg. She swung back, missed. Had they thought the AG's open was that much better than hers? Had she not appropriately managed their fear and risk and fear of risk? Had they heard an update from their company actuary or corporate psychic that they weren't sharing with the team? (This was the case—an actuarial update, not medium—but Timothy was not keen to say so, or to discuss what had really happened to June and her supportive leadership. Fortune, it turned out, didn't always favor the bold.)

There went the soups, here came the salads, and Bella was still trying to convince him to stick with the trial. This decision was supremely important to the future of the brand, to the future of the industry, to the future of free and open commerce, and wasn't that the bedrock of America, that consumers continue to be able to consume as they see fit? Alcoholic caffeinated beverages were freedom! And freedom was imperiled. She realized she was repeating herself; the bedrock line was straight out of her opening statement. But it was also true.

Bella was also imperiled, and worried she'd hit max saturation on her fancy sweatproof undershirt. She felt her makeup sliding around her face, her previously well-set hair frizzing. Her despair might as well have been written in lipstick across her forehead.

But the client could not be dissuaded. He mentioned P&L for this brand and a dozen others (one jack on the table); that they'd realized a straightforward reallocation of resources would more than cover the loss in product and settlement costs incurred (laying down two more). Bella's mind raced. She had memorized every stat sheet that June had provided, the beverage conglomerate's development costs and distribution expenses, the price of ingredients and depreciation of machinery. And yet Timothy's numbers were new—nowhere in their tables was a zeroing out. Also new: They didn't fundamentally *care* about this product? June had been adamant, had persuaded Bella to feel similarly. If they could let this drink go like a scarf in the wind, why hadn't she seen her boys in a month? Timothy revealed—"Between us, because I like you, Bella," and here he patted her hand—that they were launching a line of boozy seltzers. Vodka, rather than grain alcohol, and market research suggested consumers would love that. (He set down two sevens next to his water glass.) It turned out that people valued a night's sleep more than they'd anticipated; those who still wanted a buzz-buzz and a buzz could have an espresso martini or that old staple, a vodka Red Bull. They were confident, he said, it'd all come out in the wash. Her co-counsel, Timothy added, would handle the settlement talks.

Bella's colleague smiled smally, like this news was no surprise. But it was! To get this information was to see the client's full house (three jacks, a pair of sevens), face up on the table. Bella, holding queen high and until now feeling good about it, was stupendously beat.

They filed back to the courthouse, past security and through the courtroom and into the judge's chambers, Bella willing herself to keep her head high, even as the jury looked curious and sleepy in their box. After ten minutes of talking around the judge's desk, everyone sitting like they'd been called into the principal's, the case was dismissed.

It was all over: the trial, her work with this client, her future at Cushman. If her sole client no longer believed in her, what, pray tell, was her value to the firm? Fifteen years of effort, and she had such a negligible amount to show for it, just a long string of settlements, actuarial wins rather than winning arguments. She wanted to asterisk the timeline with her mat leaves, star it again with the pandemic, when everyone had taken a wait-and-see approach to litigation. To put one of those dagger-shaped symbols on the years she'd worked with the first assholey group leader, who'd given her so few opportunities for growth. Her second boss had been better, but that wasn't saying much. She was hardly a mentor.

When did a striving but stationary lawyer become obsolete—was it at age forty or fifty, or a specific number of years past licensure? She tried, as she stomped to the defense's table and started grabbing at papers, to do the arithmetic, but then quickly decided a concrete number didn't matter, because her obsolescence was here. Hello, failure! Nice to meet you, dead and dark end! She called herself a litigator, but after being a gofer and grunt and assistant counsel on so many cases, after being assigned supporting roles for years because she had to "think of her family," she'd at long last had a chance to show herself, and they'd settled. Behind her back! She wasn't sure what she was shoving into her briefcase, but also didn't care.

The judge announced the news to the jury, and Bella couldn't help but notice their relief. (She also spotted the stupid prosecutor looking pleased, and wanted to scream.) What next? As her colleagues packed up their files in a more measured way, Bella imagined going with them to the office, stepping out of the elevator onto the forty-first floor, and facing her boss (who would already smugly know what'd happened, or wouldn't and would make Bella go through the excruciating process of describing the day, or she'd know but would *still* make Bella stand up and announce her failure). But Bella could not imagine it. The elevator said 41, but in her mind the doors opened onto a big, blank space. Her office was a place that no longer existed or, more pointedly, one in which she could no longer exist. She couldn't take its bland carpet or her glorified cubicle, the anonymous conference rooms or her boss's skepticism, which had slowly curdled into a round, dense ball of disapproval. She couldn't, so Bella asked Darcy to schlep the case files uptown and told her co-litigator to deliver the bad news solo. She had a family emergency, she lied, glancing at her phone.

"Whatever you need." He bit his lip; his eyes held more gloom than those of a sad puppy. He'd only graduated (Yale Law) a few years back; they both knew he had far fewer red marks on his tenure file. He'd ride another day at Cushman, his empathetic green eyes said, but she, Bella Winston, she would not.

62

Tue, Feb 7 at 12:35 PM

Bill:

How'd OS go?? Sure you slayed!

When Bella arrived home, the building's lobby was quiet. The resident children were in school, the adults were at their offices, and the old biddies had gone down for their afternoon naps. Bella gathered their mail from the mail room: a package (a pair of sneakers, another Instagram impulse buy; it was remarkable what she could purchase on days when it felt like she didn't have time to chew, much less swallow), a letter from Bill's former and Gus's maybe-future school (a prestigious all-boys prep ten blocks up Park); it did not feel thick enough to be a welcome packet. She stepped into the elevator with the shoebox and her fistful of envelopes. Below the school letter was a bill from Gus's speech therapist. They didn't take insurance, none of the best places did.

The elevator opened on her floor, and she fumbled her way into the apartment, set the shoebox down on the kitchen island. Third in the mail stack was a quarterly newsletter from Bill's firm—the stodgy logo, a group shot at some leadership retreat. Bella did a double take when she saw Bill and his colleagues gathered around a big stone fireplace, because . . . it couldn't be, but there was Jill the babysitter, in a trim gray skirt suit.

Bella set the newsletter on the counter, rubbed her eyes, and lifted it again. She must be hallucinating, imagining, paranoid. But no, it was Jill, confirmed by a second shot, on the pamphlet's page 3, a different day and different suit, in a column that announced the company's internal promotions and external accomplishments. Paralegal Jill Smith (NYU '20) had been studying diligently for her LSAT, and with thanks to her mentor and manager William Winston, would be attending Columbia Law in the fall with a partial scholarship.

"What the actual fuck," Bella said to the stand mixer. Because one, it was her Jill, the nanny, smiling up at her, and two, Bella never could've gained admission to Columbia Law.

There was a noise at the front door; Bella turned. That same Jill Smith was opening the door, Bella's children streaming in around her legs. This could still be some mix-up, she thought, a convergent evolution. Maybe this woman had committed her life, or at least most of her twenties, to the study of Edith Wharton, and she just looked strikingly similar to Bill's assistant. Smith was such a common name; there must be dozens of Jill Smiths in the city.

Bella watched the woman as she retrieved her keys from the door. She had a freaking house key, and several nights a week was sleeping in their guest room. What was happening? Was this a very long con, and if so, toward what end? Bella tried to think it through, rewinding the tape to when this woman had entered their lives. Seeing Jill pull off the boys' boots and then work on her own, she wanted to yell, *Tell me the themes of* The House of Mirth*!* She wanted to whisper: *I know you're lying to me.* She wanted to burst into blubbering tears and confess: *You tricked me and I don't like being tricked.*

Bella thought back to the night Jill had done them the favor of washing their sheets. Maybe that was no favor at all? Because of the surprised look on their faces when Bella came home early, because of the black panties that she'd later found in the dryer. Bill had sworn to Bella they were a gift for the upcoming Valentine's Day, which he was prewashing for her comfort and safety. Bella had said okay, but the next morning, once she'd gotten some sleep and was already on her way down to Cushman, she thought she should've asked, *But where was the tag?*

"Oh, you're here!" the young woman chirped and smiled amiably. From where she stood, Jill could not see what was in Bella's hand. If only Bella could start this confrontation, tell this woman that she'd been caught. But after the morning's heavy use of her litigator voice, after lunchtime's mortal blow, Bella, breathless, found she could not form her mouth into words. She tried again, squeezing her lips, shoving her tongue against her palate, gulping air. No, no. It was gone.

"I need," she started a third time, pushing through the strange mushiness of her mouth, "time. Could you, uh, take them to the playground? Or if it's cold, get them hot chocolate. Whatever." Her tongue, though thick, was working again, but she could not catch her breath. The fact of the affair was one thing—she'd slept with plenty of guys other than Bill, though she hadn't for so long. But what about rule number two? Bill had trounced it. Jill hadn't just come into their bed; she'd washed their bedding!

"Sugar!" Gus crooned with delight.

Jill nodded. "No problem. We'll come back in a while." The woman returned the boys' tiny shoes to their feet and reversed them into the hall. "Buh-bye!" Bill Jr. screamed. Bella silently watched them go.

63

Tue, Feb 7 at 3:25 PM

Bella:

Wouldn't u like 2 know

Yes, Bella and her girlfriends controlled their own destinies. They had opportunity, ambition, a strong enough sense of self to reach and stretch, and not just in yoga class. They might've had difficult parents and hard pregnancies and dimes-on-the-dollar pay disparities with their male counterparts, but they were net-net fortunate, all things considered.

However.

Hillary couldn't control Miles's cravings, and Gregg couldn't control her husband's determined drive, and Carson couldn't control becoming an orphan—she could try to control *un*becoming one, but even that had raced from her reach. Reba couldn't control not becoming a mother, regardless of her attempts to circumvent or outwit nature. Sometimes, receiving fertility treatments in a medical wing that bore your grandmother's name didn't do squat; the rigid chief nurse could not make herself into a baby-granting fairy, she could only be urged to be more polite to and patient with the anxious VIPs. Bella couldn't control her clients' decision tree, not without a graphing calculator and a surveillance device.

Said another way: No one could stop the hands of time from blithely swinging around the clock face; no one could stop the hands of erstwhile compatriots from delivering sharp and unexpected and life-altering slaps. You could want the best of everything for yourself and your dearests, and you should always work toward that, assume and presume and cross your toes that your earnest efforts would be duly rewarded. But in doing so, you also had to acknowledge a simple fact: Sometimes you—yes, even you, Bella—might draw the motherfucking short stick.

Bella stomped back to the bedroom. Rather than swallowing one golden pill, a quick-acting sedative her psychiatrist had prescribed in case of the very type of emergency that was currently unfolding, she took all the golden pills, and a whole bottle of anti-anxiety meds. She swallowed all her morning pills too, the ones responsible for her brain's daily back rub. And she took some meant for muscle inflammation; nothing like twenty extra-strong ibuprofens to set the cerebellum right. She downed Bill's more powerful muscle relaxants for good measure, his Prozac and Viagra, because: Screw you. She poured the syrup of ipecac down the toilet and flushed the coated bowl so she wouldn't get any ideas. She padded back into the living room—was she floating, or simply light-headed with hunger? She couldn't remember eating lunch, only the sheen and steam of that awful, ominous soup. But rather than drumming up a snack, she opened the liquor cabinet and started in with Bill's whiskeys. The one in a bottle in the shape of a baseball (from Cooperstown, which could have been a sweet family outing, except the boys were too young to enjoy or even really understand the concept of a hall of fame, and he'd taken them to a *distillery*, while she was breastfeeding), the scotch from when he went golfing in Scotland. Had it been legal to travel internationally then? His mother had flown him—him, not the family—out on a charter; maybe they were more lax about health mandates at Westchester County Airport.

Bella next made herself a pint-sized semblance of a vodka martini, dirty with pickle juice because they were out of olives. She drank it down in gulps. Her phone buzzed and she ignored it. Her phone buzzed and when she couldn't ignore it like she wanted to, she dropped it in the toilet and flushed. This did nothing except stir it around, but she left it there—that'd keep her from scrolling—and glided into the bedroom, where she settled in for a nice long nap.

64

Tue, Feb 7 at 4:35 PM

Jill:
Is it ok to come in now? Bill has to pee.

Bella had the most expansive dreams. She was playing soccer with Abby Wambach and Megan Rapinoe, except Bella was the one with purple hair, and she sent the stands—a crowd of young girls in matching jerseys (hers)—screaming. *Bella, we love you! Destroy, destroy, destroy!* The three athletes sprinted down the pitch, the thud of defenders' cleats diminishing in their wake. One glance up at the panicky keeper, a quick flash of a self-assured grin, and then, *She shoots, she scores! Bella the Destroyer for the win!*

When was the last time Bella had run a full-out sprint? When had she stretched her short legs to their longest stride, but also run so fast and easy she hardly registered contact with the ground? She often dashed across the playground to prevent Bill Jr. from putting something foul in his mouth, but that didn't count. Now it felt like she'd never *not* been running, and she was not at all winded.

She was running down another field, alone, and with each step her legs lengthened, until she was tall, taller than basketball-dunking Reba (it'd taken some cajoling to get her to divulge her vertical, which was very impressive), taller than tall Bill. Bella, from her new height, saw the top of his head and his bald spot, which she'd suspected was there, but between his ball cap collection and the way he burrowed into the pillow at night, she couldn't exactly inspect his dome. Now she saw his exposed pate, and felt positive it was a portal—functioning much as Hillary believed pupils did—to his inner being. Through his bald spot and temporarily transparent skull, she could see into his mind, and there they were: her and Jill in a head-sized version of the Winstons' apartment. In one room, tiny Bella sat on a mini version of a couch she'd admired at Ralph Lauren, which Bill had said was out of the question, too expensive. (She'd made a case for fabric quality, implored him to consider its solid construction.) Shrunken Jill, in her adjacent room, pranced around in sexy underwear and a Columbia beanie, humming to herself.

Bella stared down into his brain. Did he think that she and Jill could share a wall in his head, a bed in his life, and she'd not figure it out? Because she'd found the thong among their clean sheets, curled into the corner of the fitted. *What are these?* She'd held them by the narrow hip, waved them like a lacy pennant. His stammered excuse about the upcoming holiday had been implausible but possible.

If she hadn't been so exhausted, so sad (Miles was dead!), so distracted, she might have added it up right then. But that night, she couldn't keep track of anything except the time until the downbeat of the trial (T-minus 102 hours), and how many minutes she might sleep before she had to start sprinting again (315). And so, as Bella fell asleep that evening, Jill returned to her teeny West Village apartment (not far from Reba's old place, in fact), her slacks swishing against her bare crotch.

No—Bella kicked her legs against the duvet—she wasn't chasing that bad thought now. Wrong way! Don't harsh my mellow! This wasn't the time for sneaky twenty-four-year-olds, this was a time for soccer stardom and gamine legs. She had entered a land where children stopped growing right after they'd learned the power of possessive pronouns (*mine* and *yours* and *ours*) but before they started to flaunt it (*mine!*). This was Bella as Perry Mason—what was happening to her eyebrows? They were growing like caterpillars, but in a hot way, and she was wearing shoulder pads and the smartest double-breasted suit she'd ever seen and the court was eating out of the palm of her manicured hand. Here she was her getting her sex drive back, but not so back she wanted to bang the hot UPS guy, just back enough that she and Bill could couple regularly. This was staying sexy for decades without any Dorian Gray-ish compromises (look, Carson, a literary reference!), just a tough-but-doable ab workout and two jogs a week.

(In her reverie, she had time to jog, and her sleeping face smiled.)

In this place, she could eat whatever she liked, as much as she wanted. She started with Carson's fish and pink onions from that Venice restaurant. Then she was in the other Venice, eating seafood risotto, telling Bill it was the best thing she'd ever put in her mouth, no offense. (Their honeymoon had been lovely, even if Piazza San Marco was flooded and she'd brought such cute shoes.) Next was one of Bill's massive porterhouse steaks, then it was an oozy cheeseburger like she'd had in Palm Springs, then she remembered the tiny mushroom chocolates and their ensorcellment. She was still running, and eating, and without any side stitches. A pepperoni pizza, with olives, which her kids hated but she loved. An ice cream sundae—no, a banana split. With her movable feast she swallowed drink after drink, some matching her real-world beverages—the baseball whiskey and her filthy martini (too much pickle juice, but she'd muscled through)—while others were just conjured. In her dream, she chugged alcoholic milkshakes and sipped alcoholic coffee, slugged weeknight merlot and special occasion merlot. She had some oyster shooters, like the ones on Martha's Vineyard, that place they'd gone when she was pregnant with Gus and couldn't have vodka or raw shellfish, but Bill could, which was annoying but okay until he had started slurring his words and suggesting a throuple for the weekend. When she'd said no, he'd called her frigid, which he, with his booze-tied tongue, had mispronounced. Was that where Gus got his speech impediment?

Wrong way!

More oysters—these she could eat—at the party they'd hosted, pre-kids, where raw oysters and martinis were all they'd served, which had felt Gatsby-ish (Carson, catch, another literary pop-up!), until everyone was altogether wildly drunk, because oysters could barely soak up any booze. And Bill had blamed her for the collective catastrophe, a whole guest list gone woozy with drink. *Why didn't you think of baguettes? Garlic bread?* he'd shouted. Bella dream-screamed back at him, years too late: *Why didn't you!?*

After recalling that bacchanal, one of the first (and last) they'd hosted at this apartment, back when the kitchen was done up in its former avocado tile (the renovation had been a nightmare), she sat up and was spinning, the room familiar and strange at once. She realized it was her same old bedroom but with a new smell—a different detergent?—and a new shadow blotting the doorway. The babysitter. No, not the babysitter, the paralegal, the woman who was as familiar with Bill's holes—his mouth and ass and the opening at the tip of his dick—as she was. But did Jill know about the aperture at the top of Bill's head? She had to know, or, Bella meant, she had to be told. They must escape his skull if they were going to survive—quick, through the bald spot!

"Do I know about what? A hole?" The shadow approached.

Bella did not realize she had spoken aloud.

"Bella, what's going on? I saw the bottles in the kitchen and—"

Bella was listening to this woman until she wasn't—she was falling, falling, falling fast off her own private cliff.

65

Tue, Feb 7 at 5:02 PM

Bill:

She did what???

Bill came to the hospital straight from work, arriving not long after the ambulance. He sent Jill and the kids back home in a cab, no reason for them to be more traumatized than they'd already been by the stretcher barging into the apartment, the barking medics, the incapacitated Bella, to say nothing of the other patients incoming at the ER. Why had Jill let the medics drop Bella at Bellevue? he wondered. Bellevue was for indigents and ODs and kids from NYU.

Oh, right.

Bella didn't note Bill's presence until much later, when she stuttered awake around midnight. He looked scared (for her or for himself? given how bad he was with all things medical, it was a coin toss) and kept one hand in contact with the wall at all times, save for when he sprang forward to give her a chaste kiss on the forehead. Then he left or she passed out and when she woke again, a nurse was checking her vitals in the blue light of predawn, and Bella didn't totally remember his visit, only an ashen-faced, Bill-shaped shadow.

She did clearly register him at the foot of her bed the next morning—the sun was bright and strong through the window—and he looked ghastly, wan and jittery. He said that she'd made him promise to bring her her medicines and her phone, and he asked that she please not be mad that he came bearing neither. She wasn't, and she didn't remember logging any such request; her New Year's resolution was reduced phone time and the doctor said they could fill her prescriptions in-house. But now, as Bill was explaining how he'd failed to fulfill her requests, he was shaking his head like she was the one that had done the disappointing. Why, he wanted to know, had she put her phone in the toilet? And all her prescription bottles were empty, she must've realized that when she asked him to retrieve them? Bella shrugged. There was a big blank spot where Tuesday had been.

He told her he would talk to Cushman, explain the situation in the vaguest, most couth of terms. By implication, Bella realized there was something *un*couth about her situation. What had happened? The last thing she could remember was a bowl of soup, a creeping sense of devastation. A thing must've happened after that. Or had she been the uncouth happening? Sorting between the possibilities gave her a headache. There had been something in her mailbox, but what was it?

She remembered and narrowed her eyes at her husband.

"Do you want me to call your mother?" It seemed like a silly question (why would Bill call her mother?), until it turned into a scary one (what had happened to her mother? her mind rushing to Florida, her last spiking fever)—until she realized that the bad thing had happened to *her*, Bella, this time. Then Marianne's features came into focus: her scowl and perpetually skinny, always tan legs, the judgment she dispensed like thrown lightning bolts.

Bella couldn't tell what face she made, but in response to it, Bill said he'd make the call. Hopefully she could come up, he added. Bella doubted she would. She'd never told him the particulars of that college summer, the Mediterranean cruise that absolutely could not be interrupted; how Doris Boaz-Becker, not Marianne, had come to the rescue with her bossy inquiries and a surfeit of mothering. Bill was only recalling how it'd been such a negotiation to get her to visit for Gus's baby shower (she'd ultimately come), or while Bella was recovering from the emergency C-section (she'd declined: "I'm no good with that nursing stuff"). Even Gus's baptism had been like pulling teeth. (She'd accepted the invite only when Bill told her Katie Couric was a parishioner—not like the TV personality would show for some random baptism, but Marianne always liked a proximity to fame.)

Bella studied him fidgeting at the foot of the bed. So he didn't know that this was her second time at Bellevue, but could he really still not know that she knew about Jill? There were only two rules, and he'd broken at least one of them. The way he looked back at her, like he was the magnanimous one in this hospital room, she thought, No, he doesn't. "And we're working on a transfer," he said. Bellevue was, apparently, not a place she should be. "But," he added, "Jill didn't know any better. She's not from here, doesn't have a clue about hospitals in the city. She told the EMTs to take you 'wherever made sense.'" Bella's mind pushed through the facts of this, its unfacts. Her mind was like a hamster wheel, but underwater, the hamster burdened with scuba gear, tanks and flippers that made wheel spinning hard. Maybe Jill knew nothing of Bellevue's reputation. Or maybe the girl knew just how dire this place was, and as the emergency crew asked her about insurance and preexisting conditions and said that if Jill didn't know about either in Bella's case, they'd take the writhing woman to the public hospital . . . maybe Jill had brightly agreed to that course of action.

As if on cue, a blood-curdling scream carried down the hall and into Bella's room. Bill flinched. Hospitals were rough for him, full as they were with blood and gore and visible illnesses. (He'd needed medical attention in the delivery room, even as she was the one getting sliced open.) That he'd endured the psych ward this long this morning, and had spent hours by her side in the ER last night, was a real testament on his part. He was scared for her.

"The boys?"

"They're fine, with Jill."

"Good." This was the opposite of good—in the last twenty-four hours the nanny had morphed from innocent assistant to a clear and present danger . . . but danger of what? Bella looked around, halos of morning light or migraine light emanating from the window and the light fixture and her husband. The underwater hamster hiccuped and a big air bubble floated upward, popped at the water's surface. The thought of halos and bubbles and other round things made her look to her hands, an unfamiliar sensation there—where had her wedding ring gone? That big rock of an engagement? The proposal had been so predictable—Tavern on the Green, the ring box next to a piece of cheesecake—but she'd been thrilled anyway. (No one celebrated Bill for his creativity—it was his jawline, his tush, his appealingly preppy demeanor.) She lifted her left hand close to her face, examining the ring tan that lingered from her weekend in Palm Springs. Had that really been a month ago? It felt like a year ago, a decade gone.

"They had to cut them off," Bill said solemnly. "Some circulation crisis. Did you know you had an adverse vascular reaction to the Viagra?" She did not know that, but Bill wasn't done. He wanted to tell her how he'd collected the sawed-off jewelry from the surgeon, right outside the operating theater. "You never can be too careful, especially not around here." He glanced suspiciously left and right like these same doctors and nurses hadn't recently *saved her finger*. Bella pursed her lips; she'd have criticized him if she weren't so tired. He would get them repaired, reengraved if needed, he said. After, of course, he fixed her phone and called Cushman and contacted her mother and obviously took care of the kids. With his long list of unplanned-for tasks, things he'd have to manage on her behalf, he sounded exhausted. I've done this to you, Bella thought, with a feeling close to regret. Then she paused. Did he realize—and more importantly, did she—that the inverse was also true?

"Thankfully, Jill could help out extra this week." He said this with a straight face, and Bella watched to see if he'd shudder or twitch. He did not.

She tried to make her expression match his, even as she was pondering how they'd gotten here. Her tongue felt thick again, but she managed to slowly push out the words. "What luck."

66

Sat, Feb 11 at 11:08 AM

Carson:

Happy weekend, B. How was wk 1 of trial?

Bill, on his next visit, was full of updates. Her medical leave had been approved; everyone at Cushman wished her a full recovery. She noticed his omission of *speedy*. Was she that far gone? Or were none of them in a rush to break the bad news of her dismissal? There were probably rules about mental health and employment discrimination, and Cushman was biding their time so that no one could accuse them of causality. He reported that her mother would not be making the trip north; Bella's father was in a charity golf tournament. (Since moving to Florida her dad had become a bad but self-serious golfer, treating his bogeys like major accomplishments.) Bella asked Bill if he'd told Marianne she was in the hospital. Bill nodded gravely, he had, and Marianne had said she hoped Bella felt better soon. Her mother's rejection stung less than Bella had braced for—maybe she'd expelled all her disappointment already, a tube of toothpaste thoroughly squeezed.

She asked about her phone. It was still broken, Bill reported. She resented this; it turned out that accomplishing her New Year's resolution wasn't as important to her as regaining access to her messages, her apps, and especially her pictures of Gus and Bill Jr. There were thousands of photos at this point, milestones and the unbelievably cute things they did day in and day out. How could she have flushed them away? She had not been in her right mind, that was clear.

Bill pointed out that even if her data couldn't be recovered, they still had plenty of snaps of the kids. But hers were the best, she argued, even better than the studio shots they'd gotten for Christmas. He frowned. If they were so precious, why hadn't she uploaded them to the cloud? He knew why (Bella didn't trust the cloud, not when some of the pictures showed the boys in the bathtub, their wee-wees flopping around), but the question was rhetorical. As she tried to explain her aversion to cloud storage, her voice went from litigator confident to wavering, and so Bill softened. (The doctor had told him to be gentle; she was in "a fragile state.") No, he hadn't had a chance to see about rescuing her data, but he would get around to it.

Maybe, she suggested, Jill could help with the phone, while the boys were at school? This was the first time she'd said the young woman's name since she'd known who she was. "She has her studies," Bill sharply replied. "She's already working overtime. We can only ask her to do so much."

Bella imagined the woman "studying" in their apartment, wearing one of Bill's dress shirts and those black panties and nothing else. Had she reclaimed them from Bella's drawer yet? Or maybe Jill had rifled through all her intimates, judging Bella on the stretched-out sports bras, the saggy boy shorts. (Bella had not completely stopped trying, but since the kids she hadn't been trying very much.) The idea of that woman snooping made her enraged. So what if Bella had snooped when she was Jill's age and playing the part of the other woman? This was Bella's home! "Right. She's busy."

• • •

Two days later, Bella was transferred to a private facility on Sutton Place. The pastel walls were more tastefully hued (less boiled-pea undertones), the locked-from-the-outside doors more inconspicuous, and the patients wore their own pajamas and puffy robes instead of scratchy hospital-issued gowns. Bella requested her flannel jammies and cashmere eye mask, which Bill dutifully retrieved. He looked relieved the first time he showed up at the new facility; was this because she was getting perceptibly better, or because illness here was swaddled by luxury bedding and monitored by a three-to-one patient-to-care ratio? With proper resources, everything was made more reasonable.

The first time her boys visited, they were frightened by her frailness but enthused by the river views and the endless supply of chef-made chocolate pudding. They returned the next Saturday, and the next. The staff endured the boys' energy, their hallway sprints and high-pitched shouting, because of the therapeutic benefit to Bella, and because patients paid a lot for the privilege of good pudding. Here, the customer could not always be right (some were delusional, a few hallucinated regularly), but they could always be treated with deference that was rooted in respect or a fear of retributive litigation.

Bill's visits were shorter than his sons' but wholly courteous. Several times a week he brought takeaway containers of her favorite foods from around the city (places he'd only ever complained about), delivered books that had sat untouched on her nightstand for years. He was far from amorous on these visits but very conscientious, kind and careful as he updated her on Gus's speech therapy and news from Cushman.

Bella appreciated his efforts, but why hadn't he fixed her phone? She was like a broken record about it. She wanted her pictures, to be in touch with her friends. Not the acquaintances, she clarified—she'd be fine to not see any preschool moms for the rest of the school year, to never again go to a Cushman happy hour. But her real friends, Carson and Reba and Gregg and Hillary—she wanted to let them know what was happening. "I don't know if you're ready for that," Bill said the first time she brought it up. The second: "The doctors suggest we wait, until you're feeling stronger." Had any of them called? she asked the third time, and a flash of impatience crossed his face. How could they, her phone was broken, remember? Dead as a doornail. "No, called *you*," Bella clarified. She wasn't an idiot, only impatient. "When they couldn't get a hold of me."

Bill's face was blank. "Why would they do that?" Bill didn't have many close friends. Or he did, but they spoke by phone maybe twice a year. More often they ran into one another on jogs in the park or at the low-lit tables of Bemelmans or crossed paths on the resident beaches in the Hamptons. He had a group text too, but it was mostly about fantasy football.

Because they're worried about me, Bella thought but did not say. In the days before the trial, she'd received a steady stream of "You got this" GIFs, and she'd promptly replied "TY" to each. How might her friends interpret her abrupt silence? Perhaps they thought things were going poorly and she was being pissy. Or things were going well and she was too superstitious to say it. Both had happened in the past—and those cases had been much lower stakes. Might any of them note her silence and envision all the pills she'd chomped down like a bunch of Skittles, the pickle martini and the gallon of whiskey, her present six-week confinement?

No, that was impossible to imagine, even to Bella. She would never do something like that, toss in the towel and say, *Enough*.

But she had. Almost. Tried to.

In her exhaustion, in the silo of her own crisis, Bella couldn't stretch her imagination to reach for another idea, the truer one—that her friends might all be occupied with their own lives and too busy to think about her for the time being. Because across the East River, Carson was receiving a deluge of letters from Monroe Correctional, each in a determined, angry hand ("return to sender" had decidedly not worked), while in San Francisco, Reba was feeling funny (equal parts optimistic and uneasy) and worn out by her parents. In Texas, Gregg was eating a lot of iron, working like a maniac, reading board books, and helping her ailing dogs recuperate. (She also hired a fleet of vet students to watch them round the clock until their wounds healed. She'd never be accused of animal endangerment again!) And in Chicago, Hillary was in the middle of a long argument, the short version of which was no, Sheila couldn't move in with them, even if it was the best way forward for them both. Hillary wasn't ready to acknowledge their codependency, how much easier her daily life with Roger was when Sheila was around, or conversely that her mother might need a guiding hand; Hillary assiduously avoided asking about her mother's credit card balance or most recent lipid counts. Hillary also refused to acknowledge that with her truculence she was insisting on loneliness for them both. But was there anything quite so sad as a forty-year-old who needed her mommy?

As Bella sat in the posh psychiatric ward, trying to discern if Bill was lying, her friends' silence seemed suspect. But if she were totally lucid, she'd recognize and admit that the starts-tiny-but-snowballs negligence of friendship happened among them all the time. It had been happening since college, when they were living together and so present in one another's lives that their cycles synced up. Back then, the women were too frazzled by finals to travel to Carson's mother's funeral (though they did, with their parents' credit cards, buy the headstone and plot). Now it seemed unconscionable to have skipped it, but at the time they didn't know how to negotiate for alternate test dates, how to explain to grouchy professors that no, it wasn't their mother, not a friend of the family, but the family of a friend and it was important. At the time, they didn't realize what mattered most. How could they have? They were just big-eyed pups.

Lower stakes, but similar: how casually indifferent they'd been when Hillary got an STD from a guy who went MIA soon after their liaison. Hillary was prescribed a course of aggressive antibiotics, pills as big as fava beans. Watching her swallow a dose at dinner one night, Bella had mused, "What are the odds?" Not of an uncommunicative twenty-year-old guy—those odds were high—but of catching something on her second run around the block. Had she used a condom? Bella asked. She had, Hillary replied, sounding offended and stabbing at her vegetarian lasagna. Bella had thought that, between the horse pills and Hill's fact-of-the-matter reply, the whole issue was done and dusted. But while the pills had cleared the infection, Hill was far from okay. Her capacity to try new things had been punched in the nose, and none of her friends had noticed.

Sometimes it was an active dismissal of another woman's plight, and at other times, the women were simply left unawares. They didn't know about Gregg's casting couch close calls (how would they, unless Gregg dished, and she found them so demeaning she'd rather not say a word), not about the times (two) Carson got mugged on the subway (she couldn't mention it to Bella; if Bella knew, she'd never go underground again). Reba couldn't talk about her parents' frailty and her worry, because Carson's parents were already gone and Bella's were basically emotionally abusive. Bella hadn't talked about her college breakdown because, well, she didn't have a good, solid reason, but a feeling that she shouldn't. Was that feeling stigma? Shame?

"Well," Bella said, scrutinizing her husband now. What had the question been? Oh, right: her friends. "Let me know if you hear from anyone. Or convince Nurse Ratched out there to give me internet." (Her sons were permitted on the premises once a week; the internet permitted never. The place's web-free, no-phones policy made her cell phone inquiry moot; even a functional iPhone would have been verboten. That didn't mean Bella would drop the point—they were her friends!)

"You could always put out the bat signal." Bill made a shape with his hands that was more like a butterfly, and hooted.

"That's an owl sound," she said.

"Of course." He dropped his hands to his sides.

Sat, Feb 25 at 11:11 AM

Carson:
Morning. Has anyone heard from Bella?

Reba:
I haven't but things have been busy over here

Gregg:
^^

Hillary:
Ditto

The contrast between the women's responses to the news of Miles's death and how they all treated Bella's hospitalization, which stretched from one week to two weeks and into a third, is not intended as some illustration of thresholds. The women were all very busy with site-specific, time-sensitive tasks, but it's not like there were clear tiers. If the death of a spouse happened, the group came running. If a child was coming, a shower was thrown, or at the least a gift was sent (Carson was spotty about remembering to do this, but the others, the mothers and aspiring parents, were as reliable as clockwork with their Zulily orders). If a dog nearly froze to death by the pool, if a child nearly broke his neck on the stairs, it went unacknowledged. (And how could they have known about the canine amputations, about

Roger's stairwell acrobatics and how many times he'd close to cracked his skull on the way up to the Koenig apartment?)

No, there was not some baseline below which the women rolled their eyes and told one another to handle their shit; there were infinite variables. The strength of the sun and dew point in their cities on any given day. Where in the sky the moon rose, and how full—not only Gregg believed in lunar forces, even if she was the most vocal about the moon's pull. Children were a factor—when babies arrived, days shrunk—but kids didn't make their mothers instantly or irrevocably thoughtless friends. The moms were just able to allocate fewer minutes to each act, and to act on fewer non-kid concerns in any given twenty-four-hour period. It wasn't only true of the relationships they had with one another, it was true of everything under the sun.

Nor is it a comment on hierarchies, the better friend or the woman most deserving of support. They each had relationships with the others—the women by twos and threes at a time, the all-but-one text chains. The sum of the permutations was not an infinite number but a big one, which Hillary could probably compute in a snap but Carson categorically could not (each woman had her strength, and Carson's was not math). When and how and whom they helped was more arbitrary and random than that, including the variables of:

If and when and how the supplicant asked for help.

If and when and how the universe amplified the sound waves or stifled them (under traffic noise, thunderstorms, the slamming of doors, the wail of a child).

And consequently, if and when and how the invited ears heard said entreaties.

Sometimes they were literally in the waiting room, on the edge of their seat, jumpy as an alley cat when the phone pinged, and the response came just as fast. *I'll be there.* Other times they were moving too quickly to feel the vibration of a silenced phone trilling against their ass.

On some occasions the woman in crisis said nothing, but there was something discernible in the pitch of the silence that cued her friends to her plight, like those high-frequency whistles only dogs can hear. In these cases, a woman might pick up her unringing phone and dial into the void.

And then there were the instances when the non-pitch was a non-pitch was nothing.

What was their track record on medical emergencies? Well, the women hadn't had to think about such situations too often (knock on wood), but their performance with hospitalizations was only so-so. When Bella had been sick in college, she'd wanted to keep it a secret; Reba had had to know—she was the one who'd found her, barefoot and raving in Tompkins Square Park—but why bother Gregg and Hillary and Carson with her temporarily outrageous behavior, the scary-sounding diagnosis? Reba had promised her friend she'd respect her wishes of privacy; mum was the word. Gregg had taken Carson to Planned Parenthood, but no one went with Hillary to get that STD treatment, even if she could have used some moral support. When Bella had had her first emergency C-section, she'd not had time to share with the group what was happening, but Carson had figured it out (across four months of museum meet-ups they'd discussed her birth plan, the forking conditionals) and tracked down the hospital and ward; she and Reba appeared in Bella's recovery suite to coo and cluck over their friend. For Bella's last birth—during Covid, Bill Jr. giving her such a run for her money, more blood loss than the first, if that was possible?—the women couldn't visit owing to health and safety protocols. But they were in touch, blowing up her phone with so many memes of encouragement, Britney clips, and outpourings of love.

And in this hospitalization's case too, if they could have supported Bella, they would have. Carson even got close to sussing out the situation. She had been miffed by Bella's nonresponse to her last few go-get-'em texts, then more annoyed by the continued mute when she, one-on-one, asked about the trial, then concerned when her friend never did reply, not even when she sent the can-you-believe-it?! news of so many people wanting to buy her book; she was being courted by several houses. She thought it so strange that she called Bill at work. The assistant who patched her through, Jen or Jill or Jackie, had sounded huffy, and then, only when Carson questioned Bill with an urgency that would've impressed Gregg, did he explain what was going on—or not what was actually going on but what he wanted Carson to believe was happening. Bella was "dealing with some personal issues" and their family would appreciate it if she, Carson, and the rest of them (so Hillary had Facebook-messaged him, the social dinosaur that she was) respected their privacy during this trying time. Bella was fine, but she needed a minute. (That was another variable: how much a husband deflected the women's outreach, how often he told them to mind their own stinking business.)

It was all Carson could do not to call bullshit right then and there, but instead she asked if he could say more about the situation. He declined to do so. In his calculations, he (correctly) knew that if he told Carson anything, she would tell the whole group, and all would start in on some full-court press, Power Rangers or storm troopers or whatever it was they did. Unrelenting in any case, and there was no way he could handle their deluge. And so, after listening to his heavy breath for ten seconds, Carson thanked him for the update and asked him to please pass on the message that she'd been thinking of Bella and sending her well wishes. Bill said he'd do it, but obviously, he did not.

68

Wed, Mar 1 at 1:04 PM

Carson:

Talked to Bill. Bellas ok but something smells 🐟y.

While Bella was working her way through group therapy and one-on-one therapy and therapeutic craft projects, Bill and Jill played house in the Winstons' apartment. Every morning Jill would rise and rouse the boys, dress and feed them, get them off to school—Bill was either still in bed or already out the door to some gossipy, meat-heavy breakfast meeting (in this, Bella's assessment of her husband's modus operandi had been correct). Jill and Bill met again at the office. No one noticed, no one cared that Jill was coming in an hour later than normal, that Bill always seemed to dispatch her to some off-site errand, be it research at the law library or documents that needed to be hand-delivered by midafternoon. (Meanwhile, he off-loaded a good deal of Jill's real work onto an intern, who was grateful for the boss's attention, and only a hint suspicious.) Jill would collect the boys, Bill would select the takeout or maybe choose a meal from the grocery that'd already been two-thirds prepared; he wasn't above admitting he needed the head start. He'd oversee dinner and bath time and bed like it was a huge accomplishment, like Jill wasn't washing the dishes and setting out pajamas, doing the shampoo when Bill Jr. splashed out of Bill's reach. (In this she was different from Bella, who was so judgmental of Bill's deficiencies that she all but blocked him out of daily parenting. No wonder he didn't know how to do it; she wouldn't let him try.) Once the boys were asleep, they'd wrap their bodies together on the king-size bed. Some nights, they went at it for hours, some nights Bill was done and dozing in under ten minutes. Always, it was different from what had become the norm for him and Bella, which was largely ignoring each other.

Postcoitally or first thing in the morning, before the boys awoke, the lovers sometimes spoke of the future. Jill let Bill take the lead on these conversations; when replying, she used hypotheticals and qualified conditionals. She'd never tell Bill to leave his ailing wife, but *if* he wanted to leave his ailing wife once she got better, because really it sounded like their marriage had been limping along for a while, Jill would entertain the idea of continuing this "thing." *If* he and Bella got divorced morphed to *when*; *if* Jill moved in became her not renewing her West Village lease. As it was, she went downtown once a week to check the mail, water a plant, and grab a few blouses. *Thing* became *affair* became *relationship*.

Jill let these evolutions unfold organically, even as, in her head, she was engineering a plan for the months ahead. She could definitely, happily slide from faux babysitter to steady presence to stepmom—the boys liked her so much. And she was as good as—maybe better than?—Bella at managing their needs, their squirmy tantrums; she'd never throw up her arms, drink a fifth of vodka, and announce, *I've had enough*. Jill could look into postponing her law school start, maybe take classes part-time to accommodate the kids' schedule, because Bill had a whole team to keep afloat, a company to protect, such responsibility at the firm. She recognized and appreciated that, way more than Bella did. (Bill had mentioned how mean Bella'd been when he'd left Cushman . . . she had called him a pussy!) Anyway, Jill was in no rush to become a lawyer, not if what Bill was saying about moving in together, about seeing what came after that, could be made true. He was still using conditionals, but she heard the hope in his voice. Her mind raced toward Easter egg hunts and Memorial Day picnics, summer weekends on the beach and cozy chalets in the wintry woods. It was convenient not to think of Bella in these sandy or snowy environs, even as Jill knew she wouldn't be locked up forever, just six or seven weeks. And when she was free, where would Bella go? Not to Jill's imagined vacations, and not back to the way things had been.

Across their pillow talk, they also manufactured a backstory to tell Bella, creating a new timeline for their courtship. Jill could still go to law school in the future; while there were more plausible routes than her switching from the Victorian novel to vice law, the way they'd tell it—that she was an internal transfer, from one side of Columbia's campus to another, because after spending so much time with Bill and the boys, she was so *inspired*, and found a real sense of purpose in the practice of law—held enough water. And speaking of spending so much time with Bill and the kids, did they mention they'd fallen madly in love? They hadn't meant to (this part was true, if mislocated along the timeline—Bill, who'd had nothing to do with the hiring of his paralegal, had been bowled over when Jill first sat down at the desk outside his office), and didn't know where it was headed (this was maybe still correct, though Jill had been pausing at the window of the jeweler on Madison, looking at their rings with growing intent), but they had to listen to their hearts, to follow them. Bella would let them follow their hearts, wouldn't she?

This phrase was deliberate, as Bella had hung a similar credo (second person, follow *your* heart) in the hallway that led to the bedrooms. It was one of those cursive gold leaf-on-wood-block things, and while Bella had known it was tacky, that she should have purchased a piece of challenging contemporary art or featured a valuable antique from her mother-in-law (someone might visit and she wanted to be ready to show off their taste and investment strategy), to see the directive each day gave her a jolt of affirmation. Or it had, until she looked at it and saw a crock of shit. Was that the week before the trial? The night she found the thong? Something had changed, some switch had been flipped, and she wanted to throw the wood block out the window, drop it down the garbage chute. But Bill and Jill couldn't have known that, not as they were nakedly figuring the lines of their argument, practicing their opening statements and rebuttals. They decided that Jill's opening statement would be to smile quietly at Bill's side.

That was their half of the equation. Next, they waded into the question of Bella, and what to do with her upon discharge. Sutton Place required a six-week minimum to work their magic, but then what? Bella could hardly move back in, not when it was clear she found life with Bill so unsatisfactory as to try to snuff out her own existence. (It didn't occur to Bill that breaking both rules of the marriage—letting Jill into the marital bed, and also the more sacred one, allowing this young woman to supplant Bella in his affection—might have contributed to her hurt. Bella hadn't acted like he mattered to her for a long time.) Bill and Jill talked about taking over an adjacent apartment—the next-door neighbor was getting increasingly frail. Maybe they could do a co-living thing? A nesting agreement? Jill wanted neighboring townhomes downtown, not understanding that as rich as Bill was, even he couldn't afford that until his mother died.

They landed—and it was a real stroke of brilliance on his part, Bill thought—on a house. For Bella. In Scarsdale, close to where she grew up. It'd put some distance between them, because did they really want to share a wall? She'd get the space she'd been bitching about since approximately five minutes after they'd moved into their classic six, which had been a real point of contention. Was a six-room apartment on Park Avenue really not enough for her? (Bella would make the point that he grew up with *ten* rooms, across the street from the park, but he still thought she was ungrateful.) The house she grew up in, that her folks had sold with little compunction in 2018, was unavailable—he'd cold-called the new owners and made a persuasive offer, even as he'd always regarded the Gomez home as a little dumpy—but another house, a similar vintage but recently renovated, was on the market, with a pool and a hot tub and proximity (close but not so close as to be a nuisance) to the commuter train. Metro-North would be handy; eventually, the boys might travel up there without an escort. (Jill stared at him. Was he looking ten years into the future right now? He was, and that futurecast, with Bella in another county, Jill by Bill's side, made her want to squeal.) Bella would get her bulbs and hydrangeas (every spring, she whined about how much she missed her childhood yard's perennials); she could practice law from the mother-in-law apartment—it was already zoned commercial, as the last resident was some kind of interior architect. Or maybe she'd get a tidy office facing the village green, a couple of blocks away. She'd be comfortable sliding from corporate courtroom battles to resolving small-scale arguments, clean-cut divorces and neighborhood property disputes, wouldn't she? Or if that didn't suit, she could abandon litigation outright and make a decent income in estate planning. After all, with her streak of settlements, she hadn't exactly proved herself to be a maven litigator. Going to court was performance anxiety and blowouts and shapewear and shoes that looked great but in which she could barely walk to the bench and back. Bill wouldn't say all that aloud, but what he meant was that maybe Bella the Destroyer just wasn't cut out to destroy.

69

Thu, Mar 2 at 10:56 AM

Carson:

Bella this is getting ridiculous & Bill is no help. Call me back!

Bella listened to their pitch from bed. She was hardly convalescing anymore, and felt the center's minimum stay was excessive—three weeks in, and she was fine! Good as new. Better, if they'd only give her the internet. She and Bill and Jill could've met in the common room, or sat on patio furniture on the blustery roof, but Bill advised that they might want "some privacy" for this conversation, as it was "delicate." So here they were, Bill and Jill groveling at the foot of her bed, Bella propped up with a stack of fluffy pillows.

They delivered the story, about how, during her recuperation, they'd fallen quickly in love, how it'd astounded them both in its speed and ferocity. Bella tried not to roll her eyes. And not only did they love each other, Bill continued, but Jill loved the boys, so, so much. Maybe the universe had some bighearted mode of co-parenting in mind when it brought Jill into their lives? Maybe the world meant for Bella to be responsible for the boys only three days a week? Bill reminded her she'd talked about the prospect of monthslong summer camp already when Gus was a baby, and told her this was so much better than camps or Swiss boarding schools; she'd get regular breaks from parenting, but no painfully long absences. Didn't it sound nice to have nights off without the need for a sitter? Imagine the sleep! Jill started talking—up until that point she'd been silent, grinning like a goon—about the upsides of part-time parenting. What did she know about it? Bella thought. Maybe Jill liked the boys, and could manage their needs okay, but this young woman had never experienced the feral love of motherhood, the mountain lion fierceness that Bella had for her sons. Getting more sleep sounded nice, but she'd only been joking about boarding; it was merely a thought exercise in how much one could delegate. Now, joint custody, and not seeing them for weeklong stretches, sounded far-fetched and painful, like stomping on her heart . . . until she realized she'd managed their six-day separations for nearly a month now, and mostly she just felt a lot calmer with the new rhythm, the syncopation of not-mom, mom. Was that messed up of her?

Bella zoned out as Jill explained her household-management systems for school day snacks and after-school sports and Gus's speech therapy, talking like she'd invented the Gregorian calendar, when really she was just moderately organized. Then Bill cut in. "Did we mention we'd buy you a house?"

Bella squinted at her husband, his forehead sweat visible from seven feet away. Had she heard him right, a *house*? She thought of the portal in his scalp, the well-furnished rooms in his brain. Did this mean she would get out of her compartment in his head, or would she move from an apartment to a freestanding building within his skull? She crossed her arms, "Tell me more."

Bill pulled a sheaf of papers out of his briefcase. She almost snorted at the formality—he'd brought his briefcase, like this was some adjudication—but accepted the printout without comment. It was a property listing, an updated Cape-style in Scarsdale. She noted he'd blacked out the price—ridiculous, but true to his Waspy roots.

She thumbed through the color photos, the shots of the elegant dining room and four bedrooms (one for each boy, plus a guest), the porches and the yard. She noted its mature trees and great natural light, the subtle but sophisticated landscaping. That pool. A kitchen that, while older than her kitchen, was bigger and probably better.

Bella gestured for him to continue, because even though he'd broken rules one *and* two, a part of her had seen this coming for ages.

He talked about the new boiler and newer roof, the school district that was good but also moot, as the boys would be going to his alma mater. Jill, who'd gone back to mutely staring like a serial killer, added, "Bella, look at all those closets." Bella looked. There were many, and a basement, and an attic.

Hadn't she always wanted to have a yard? Bill pressed. She crowed so often, every spring, about daffodils and tulips. Well, she countered, what she'd wanted was ready *access* to a yard, a regular place to go. Not the responsibility of actually owning one. "We'll get you a yard service!" he all but shouted, he was that wound up.

When they were through with their pitch, Bella told them to wait in the lounge, where she knew the weekly bingo game and its enthusiastic participants were likely to unsettle them, "while she considered." She let them wait a long thirty minutes, after which she called them back in and accepted Bill's proposal, with caveats. One, it'd be an all-cash purchase, with two, a decade's assistance for property taxes, and three, he'd provide alimony until . . . She made a hand gesture that suggested it was too soon to guess if she might find love again. She let that thought linger a second, then snapped back to business. Four, assuming the boys went to Bill's prep school, she'd get them on the weekends, Fridays inclusive, but five, there needed to be a clause that schooling and the incumbent split in custody would be reevaluated annually, as their children's educational needs evolved. Bill nodded like he would humor her but was certain of their academic paths. (She didn't know if he'd missed Gus's pre-K rejection letter in the hubbub of the last few weeks, or if he'd seen it but thought he could sway the school to reconsider.) The idea of being without her boys for such a large portion of the week did two things at once. It made her feel like a piece of gum on the sidewalk, squashed and filthy and without its intended purpose. But it also made her feel floaty, a helium balloon whose line had been cut. All that time to herself.

Child support, alimony, the house—those were fairly straightforward terms, presupposed by Bill. But Bella, still in her pajamas and bolstered by designer pillows, was not through. She shifted into litigator voice, and continued with the fingers of her other hand. Six, he'd cover closing costs; seven, moving costs. Eight, the house would be furnished, with her selections, at his expense (that meant the overstuffed RL sofa she had long coveted). Nine, he'd pay for housecleaning, yard work, and pool service. He began to hem on this, but she pointed out that it would be his boys swimming there, and did he want them to be burned by chlorine or to get some weird fungus? Presumably not, and she was an unemployed lawyer, not a chemist—how might she keep the pool's pH safe? Ten, a modest tab at the Carlyle, for when she wanted to come in for parental duties: recitals, soccer games, parent-teacher conferences, and the like.

She knew—and he knew that she knew—it was not his money she was gouging from him, but his father's, by way of that sour woman, and she loved the idea of Bill having to go to his mother to request an advance against his inheritance. The empire strikes back! That wasn't the right metaphor, but her heart was thrumming with the prospect of just deserts. That old shrew hadn't been nice to her once.

The following week a friend of theirs—the best man at their wedding, ironic as that was—drew up the paperwork. Bill rushed the house's closing (it was amazing what an all-cash, no-contingencies offer could do), and everything was ready by the time she was released.

• • •

And so, after six weeks of intensive talk therapy, which aimed to amend her restrictive tendencies and curb her addictive ones, which tried to bash the whack-a-mole of Bella's Helen Gurley Brown complex (Bella's therapist had told her that Brown hated the title *Having It All*; Brown had only intended to coach normal women into assertive professionals, not turn them into conquer-the-world titans), six weeks of delicious nights of ten-hour sleeps, busy but not hectic days of group sessions and arts and crafts and bundled-up tai chi on the facility's caged-in roof (they claimed it was to protect the rooftop pickleball court, but Bella knew it was also to deter jumpers), of catching up with *The Bachelor*—which had hardly seemed salutary, but as she liked the show, she did not complain when it was broadcast in the community room—Bella was set to be released from the facility on Sutton Place. Bill had done the kind or controlling thing of taking the boys away for the week—it was their nursery school's spring break and he said he wanted her to focus on herself. She could come back to the apartment if she wanted (though he had already done the best he could to pack and move her things; she thought maybe this meant he had gone through their belongings carefully, sorting on the basis of sentiment, or maybe it meant he'd hired Olivia's nineteen-year-old niece to box up her half of the closet, plus everything in the house with a floral print). They'd collected the new house's keys, her furniture was ordered (and hadn't that been a fun day, going through the phone-book-like Restoration Hardware catalogue, circling yes and yes and yes again?), and Jill had hired a housecleaning company to scrub the new place, bottom to top.

Bella, as she packed her little suitcase at Sutton Place—mostly jammies and toiletries and undies and loungewear, only one real blouse—tried to get excited for her new life. She was getting a porch, ready access to a yard. Her floor would be no one's ceiling, and while her bedroom windows might still look into someone else's bedroom, it would be from a far greater distance, with some bushes and trees in between. Moving out of New York wasn't about the city being too tough for her—she and her therapist had been working on this and related concepts of self-worth for weeks. It wasn't that she'd not been able to cut it at Cushman either; her relocation was about acknowledging her preference for a different pace of living, a different price-per-square-foot lifestyle. She wanted—she *deserved*—rooms that could hold oversized furniture, days that could hold downtime. They'd also discussed how young boys shouldn't have to wear matching miniature blazers; how the food at Tavern on the Green wasn't even that great. (No, it *was* delicious, but it wasn't the only yummy meal available to her—the world held so many restaurants, some with even better views than that glassed-in atrium.)

There was also the task of deprogramming herself from work. She had to face the billable hours (the billable *minutes*, the billable *seconds*) issue—she had to decouple herself from this as a marker of accomplishment—but also that Cushman's insistence on winning was, if the therapist could be frank, a small-dick problem, and one Bella shouldn't feel bothered to solve. Because sometimes settling was the smartest move, and Cushman's brass (even her boss; just because she was a woman didn't mean she couldn't perpetuate the patriarchy) were dummies not to see that and recognize her worth. But no matter. There was a whole world beyond Cushman and their forty-first floor, a whole universe outside the city, and it contained, her therapist promised, fewer and less aggressive rats.

Bill had bought her a new phone and dropped it off, along with her laptop and her keys (old apartment, new house), at Sutton Place's admin office before he left town. He'd told her about his phone victory, how he'd found some iPhone forensics guy in the Diamond District who could transfer her old phone's images onto an external hard drive. Bill had also—maybe thoughtfully, maybe because he'd figured out that she knew the truth about Jill but was as fed up in their marriage as he had been—loaded four hundred of those salvaged photos onto a digital picture frame, which he'd set on the mantel of her new home, a housewarming gift that would, when she later spotted it, remind Bella that he wasn't always, or only, a prick.

As soon as the reception desk handed her her electronics and she turned on the phone, a torrent of messages came pouring in.

What was happening? The phone buzzed and pealed. Someone—coincidence or Bill's idea of an homage?—had set the ringtone to church bells, and the phone chimed like it was a saint's day or a royal wedding. Bells for Bella! "Please," the administrator said scoldingly, "not inside the facilities. You might disturb the guests." Bella silenced and pocketed the phone, feeling glad to no longer be considered one of the guests. The device kept purring against her leg.

Outside, freedom! And retrieving her phone, she discovered that none of the arriving texts were tied to contacts; apparently, her address book had not migrated. (But at least Bill had gotten the pictures, and thank God for that.) She could soon tell which were from work. It seemed her assistant had quit while Bella was inside; consequently, Darcy's texts went from buttoned up to gleefully surly indictments of Cushman and the work they'd spent years doing together. The 917 of the boys' school notified her of each of Bill Jr.'s accidents, even though they'd been told that Jill should be the emergency contact for the semester. A West Coast prefix was her big brother, checking in with his standard nonchalance. "Haven't heard from u for a while. How's my baby sis?" (This was accompanied by a picture of him surfing, because while he didn't have the homing device of worry that Carson possessed, he did have a tendency to humble brag.) It was easy enough to figure out, from area code and context, which messages were from Carson, from Hillary, from Reba and Gregg. There were dozens, there were hundreds, and doing the backward and hurried reading of them made her confused. Restraining orders? Polar vortices? A picture of a picture in a museum, a painted pink horizon spanned with puffy white clouds?

She looked up long enough to cross the street—she didn't trust the wide white lines of the crosswalk to be honored, not in this city—then dropped her nose again. She'd comb through them later, figure out what everyone had been yammering about. She saw something about a deal. Holy shit, had Carson sold her book? And something about Reba's parents moving. Again? No, only her dad, around a hedgerow to . . . assisted living? That didn't sound good. But first, she tagged the women's four numbers and opened up a new group chat.

"Bitches, heyyyy. Sorry to be MIA. What did I miss?"

70

Fri, Mar 24 at 1:02 PM

Carson:

. . .

Gregg:

. . .

And what had Bella missed? Most of the daffodils in Central Park and those rimming her new yard had bloomed and withered, but it was okay because the tulips were, on that spring day, just reaching peak pretty. She'd missed Carson receiving so many letters from her father that she'd texted to see what legally constituted stalking. (Actually Carson had sent Bella a series of texts, at first vague, later more distressed and direct. "What do I have to do to get a federal restraining order? Pls help." She never explained it, who it was who was harassing her, but she made it clear it'd become a problem.) Without Bella's guidance, Carson had found the number for the warden of Monroe Correctional and had almost worked up the nerve to call. But did she want to punish her father? She had started this, after all, and he hadn't done anything really wrong—well, of course he had, but what he'd done to her, so far, wasn't that bad. Just annoying, kind of creepy, mildly threatening. She also thought that any additional contact might tip Erik off to the new book. Some people would be glad for her appropriation (she'd read a quip by an author of romans à clef that once you turned plums into plum pie, who really cared about the genus of the tree?); however, she suspected it would only make

Erik Gustavsson more pissed. In the karmic arm-wrestle of Carson's psyche and that which she imagined to be her father's, the conflict between *This was not yours to take* and *You were not here to stop me*, who would slam whose fist onto the tabletop? She'd always had crappy upper-body strength, but she had to continue pulling. She'd defend her book to the death!

Speaking of the book, Bella had missed Carson's group-text updates on the merry-go-round of shopping the novel. She'd kept it vague but vaguely optimistic for a month, her dance card full of lunches of beautifully prepared pieces of fish (none as lovely as that meal in Venice, but she was getting her omega-3s), a passel of editors making entreaties for why they should have the privilege of publishing her book. The purchase prices they were tossing about wouldn't catapult Carson into Gregg or Reba levels of wealth, but they did suggest a changed set of circumstances. When Sonja died, Carson had twenty-seven dollars in her bank account, Sonja's held forty-eight, and rent was due. Back then, Carson had allowed herself some *if only*s: If only Sonja could've died a week sooner, and she'd cleared out quick. If only her friends had sprung for a more modest cemetery plot or a thinner piece of stone, and given Carson the balance in cash. She had pushed those thoughts down—she was grateful for every minute of those last weeks together (except for the minutes they were arguing over her father). And she was glad for the burial plot, the impressive view (while it lasted), the thick marble headstone. She'd found a way out: off-loading their dinged-up furniture on Craigslist, selling some clothes and an early Pearl Jam album that had, for reasons inexplicable to her, become a collector's item. She'd paid the last month's rent, put her plane ticket and shipping costs on credit, and made her way east to finish up her incompletes.

Bella had also missed the March day that Carson made her decision, picking an editor and signing the electronic contract, texting her friends a picture of Britney at the 2000 VMAs, body bedazzled and face exultant. And that was how it had felt to Carson, after several agonizing days, talking pro and con with her agent, with her writer friends, with her jade plant. (Donny and Zariah heard Carson on the phone or elsewise talking one-sidedly for hours; at times her voice was raised high enough that they could hear a handful of words: "crime," "punishment," "what I deserve.") Ultimately, she went with the editor who offered the smartest editorial note by a mile, and the second-best amount of cash. She felt good about the decision as she'd clicked through the Docusign with her eSignature, clocking a growing elation and mounting relief (she might've whooped). And a moment later, documents executed and celebratory text message sent, as she stood from her desk and opened her door, thinking that she should apologize to her roommates for the days of dour moods (plus the door slamming, the stomping, the railing on the phone), she felt a very loud amount of astonishment because Freddie Mercury was there on the living room speakers, sing-saying that he'd paid his dues, and Donny and Zariah were waiting, with champagne and smiles and Julian, who was also grinning at Carson. The music played on—Carson's brain snagged on the line about serving a sentence for no crime. For her it'd been the other way around, but her crimes hadn't been so bad: a fling with a guy a few years younger, some heavy borrowing from the life of someone who wasn't there to stop her. Were those crimes or more ethical concerns? And who was truly ethical these days? It was all gradation, no one wasn't at least 10 percent duplicitous or 15 percent hypocritical. Then the song was on to kicking sand and going on and on and on and on—that part was applicable to her life; she was nothing if not relentless. Then, they arrived at that rousing chorus. The champagne popped, and the four of them danced around the living room, waving their arms and shout-singing about their champion status. When the song was over, the champagne poured, Carson asked Julian why he was there. He had a poor excuse of "wanting to catch up with his old pal," but how auspicious that he was there on such a consequential day. He hung around for the whole bottle of champagne, for dinner at the local Malaysian restaurant (the four of them), for a nightcap of her nice smoky Japanese whiskey (three; Zariah had turned in), for whatever came after that (Donny peeled off as well).

Bella had missed a lot in Texas too. Gregg never told the group about her abortion; she was mindful of Reba's fertility journey and Hillary's grief journey and Bella's unfulfilled longing for a daughter (Gregg didn't know the sex in her case, but it could've been a girl), and didn't want to hurt any feelings. And she didn't tell them everything about the dogs, because she saw Zeke's point about the outdoor thing, and the he-okayed-one-but-I-got-four aspect of their disagreement, and because Zack the dog didn't seem to mind his missing tail—he was home from surgery and killing it on his backyard obstacle course. Also, she didn't want them to sour on her husband, because he was a blowhard but he was *her* blowhard, and now, to show his devotion, he was planning her a big birthday blowout.

At first, she tried to quash the idea as too much—couldn't he just make a donation to Planned Parenthood? But then she backed off—she could see Zeke was fixated on the idea, because why? Because he loved her so much, even if he wasn't always good at showing it, or because he wanted everyone to know she was getting old, or because he wanted to create, inadvertently but so conveniently, the perfect place for her to announce her congressional run? She flipped through the options and landed on: because he was still (and forever) a narcissist, but perhaps they'd turned a corner in the relationship. The dogs would trot again, the boys were happy and healthy and not crowded out, and their marriage would be okay. When she accepted the party plan and told him she was glad to see he'd chosen to move past what she'd done, he looked at her beatifically. "I've been working on doing better, I'm glad you noticed." He added that he was trying to be more Christlike, by which he didn't mean more religious but more forgiving. And loving. And he was growing out his hair. She looked at her husband, and she wanted to believe him. Not about the Christ part—she'd never call him *all-loving*—but the part about doing better.

"I'm glad," she said after a beat. She was doing better as well—not up to mega-multitasking like her husband, but she delegated more constituent requests to her staff, didn't hem and haw over decisions as much as she previously might've. When Giselle did something for the boys, rather than getting jealous, she tried saying *thanks*. She was hopeful there was a middle ground between that director's lackadaisical patience and Zeke's ruthless efficiency that would not just satisfy her husband but make her happier too.

Zeke, it became clear, had his heart set on throwing the party at the base of the moonlight tower in Zilker Park. It seemed unnecessary to Gregg. Why not just rent out a bar, or pick somewhere with indoor plumbing? But he was committed to the grand gesture, to letting her (and the city) know how much she meant to him. The spindly, fourteen-story towers were such an iconic part of Austin, he argued, his eyes twinkling like they were at that moment catching the arc lights of one of the same. Of the thirty-ish original towers (and this was their big selling point; one moonlight tower could illuminate a dozen blocks, whereas streetlights required poles and power every hundred feet), a dozen rusty relics remained. Depending on whom you asked, they were the embodiment of Austin's late nineteenth-century optimism—talk about innovation!—or a wind hazard; people loved their bright, moony light or the glow made them wish they had thicker drapes. The tower in Zilker Park was the best known of the remaining structures, seasonally famed for being the trunk of the city's big Christmas tree. By late March and Gregg's birthday, however, the strings of holiday lights would long be packed away, the holiday tree's trunk back to being a fifty-meter monolith.

Getting the permits for a major private gathering in a prominent public space wasn't easy, but Zeke acted like it was. He was doing it for his wife on her big day; he was doing it to publicly demonstrate his magnanimity. Did he also hope it would be a countermeasure to the rocket's environmental damage, which was starting to be picked up by local and lefty news media? Gregg didn't want to be cynical, though she couldn't help but wonder. In selecting this location, he also got to use that beloved clip from *Dazed and Confused* in the e-invite: He embedded a GIF of Matthew McConaughey driving up, smiling, and saying, "There's a new fiesta in the making as we speak," so recipients had to click through to realize it was a celebration of Gregg and not just a chance to indulge in Austinite nostalgia. "It could be both," he'd said when his assistant rolled her eyes. Even she, who was paid handsomely to facilitate Zeke's antics, was getting tired of him walking around the office saying, "Full kegs, everybody's going to be there, you ought to go." Of course there would be full kegs—she had ordered them herself!

As Zeke (mostly his assistant) booked talent and procured fancy tequila and hired the bartenders to pour it, Gregg kept thinking about Congress. That expert political consultant, "Anne-Stylist," had run the numbers and felt good about Gregg's odds for taking over the octogenarian seat warmer's seat; in 2022 she'd not had the curb appeal, but now she was practically a household name in Travis County. The old legislator had given her his and the state Democratic party's blessing, if in a somewhat patronizing way; he talked to her like she was in fourth grade and not about to turn forty. And Gregg reasoned that her family, now that its growth had been capped at four, could manage it. No one was on the boob, and her boys were reaching an age at which they could communicate their needs without always and only wailing. She was worn out, but without another on the way, she could make space, find time for the campaign. Adopt some of Zeke's hacks and she'd get hours on the day back, right? It was important enough to try. It was the future of America!

She couldn't help but flash forward to a successful election night, thinking about a life in Washington. Would the boys stay back in Austin, or would she bring them (and Giselle, of course) to DC? That Zeke might come did not once cross her mind—how could he leave his company, his rockets? She reminded herself that this type of thinking was putting the cart before the horse. For now, she needed to think of her campaign and its kickoff, to focus on the kismet of already having a party being thrown for her, with all her friends in attendance. Zeke was even flying in her college besties; apparently he didn't resent them as much as previously indicated. He explained to her that even this was an efficiency hack. With a dose of largesse and a few plane tickets, they'd all come to her, rather than requiring hours of travel time on her part.

After she scuttled three attempts because of cold feet—she was imagining scenarios wherein he threw the "too busy, too tired" line right back in her face—one night in early March she summoned the bravery to tell him she was thinking of running. Fine, she was more than thinking about it. She had a feasibility study, she had T-shirts and buttons at the printer, she had a website that, while still beta and buried in a password-protected corner of the internet, was coming together nicely, and no, she wasn't ready to share it with him yet. But she thought the party would be a great time to announce her run, and didn't he agree? Everyone would be there, her staff and his, plenty of supporters who thought they were attending as friends but would be, she wagered, delighted to become supporters anew. As she made her pitch, she was proud of her enterprise, of how she'd managed to think outside the box, but then she looked up and saw Zeke's blank face.

She had been ready to argue against vociferous charges of hypocrisy, poised to jump in and say that while, yes, she saw the catch of being too taxed for some things but not for others, that these two possibilities were far from equivalent! One was furthering her commitment to the public sector, the other was the most self-involved and resource-intensive thing she could think to do. Outside of the British royal family, there was no public interest in an infant.

Instead he was silent. She wasn't prepared for that.

"Zeke, are you following?" He was not in Zilker Park with her, not planning the party that had been his idea, with its throwback *Dazed and Confused* theme that she'd thought dumb but abided because they were trying to support each other more, and more often. He was somewhere else, spaced out or scheming, and she snapped her fingers in front of his face. His eyes came back to her, and he grinned.

"Announcing a run for Congress? Sounds great."

71

Fri, Mar 24 at 1:02 PM

Hillary:

...

Reba:

...

And that was the slim side of what Bella had missed. As she was enduring her device-free convalescence, in Chicago Hillary couldn't stay off the search engines. She didn't have the same strictures against WebMD as Bella—she thought the site was poorly designed, but that was beside the point—and she didn't have a problem regulating her screen time. At least she hadn't, until she started Googling "deaths of despair." She was searching not because she knew what was happening with Bella and her recent dip into the deep end of despondency; she was trying to get her arms around her nascent widowhood, what had pushed Miles off his precipice. Had he even known he was at a ledge? This question led to her reading up on the potency of fentanyl and accidental ODs; every text used the analogy of table salt (thirty-two grains to kill a person; a shaker to get a whole city stoned). Then she was Googling "five-year-old grief," which yielded grown-up people who were slow to recover from their losses; "childhood loss" drew results about the loss of one's childhood in the coming-of-age sense. When, at the end of her patience, she typed "What do I do when my son's father dies, kindergarten," the hits started becoming more relevant.

Before Miles was gone, Hillary had worried about a Miles-shaped hole in Roger's future, but she had not contemplated the inverse: that Miles would start showing up everywhere. Every time she ran the kitchen sink and heard the water plinking on the enamel, she thought of him. She thought of him in the chipped plates that once bore his opulent meals, and she saw him peeking from behind his tower of boxes in the corner of the living room. (When she'd asked Irene if she wanted any of Miles's things back, the older woman recoiled like Hillary was offering up Miles's sweat socks—which she was, but also his short coat, his record collection. "Roger might want those someday," Irene had said, like that day might be tomorrow, like they had access to attic storage.) Hillary considered other options—maintaining the stack, splurging on a storage space, throwing it all out. Sheila was pro tossing—she'd read that tidying book and thought no old band shirt could spark joy. But Sheila hadn't seen Miles at that Baroness concert, the way his eyes closed in bliss at the surging chorus. That face he'd made . . . That was happiness, and this worn T-shirt brought Hillary back to it.

Was it possible to enjoy bereavement? *Enjoy* wasn't the right term, because Hillary was sad and hadn't figured out what to do with Miles's things and still felt bad about how lumpy her convertible sofa was, though Sheila never complained. But that month, the three of them slept in and went to the frozen-over zoo to watch the pleased-as-punch polar bear; they visited the science museum and the Field Museum and the Art Institute. It was at the art museum that they paused in front of that big O'Keeffe painting of puffy clouds. While Reba had stopped before this same oversized canvas and thought of storks amid the cumulus, Hillary saw heaven, saw Miles. Not her husband with angel wings, but the floaty feeling of their pairing, the full-body rush she'd only ever encountered with him. She'd not heard of sex being described as oil on canvas, but when it went right, it was just like this artwork: a pink horizon, an endless parade of clouds, the calmest blue in the universe. She understood the brain chemistry, knew what she'd felt after sex was a drip of neuropeptides cooked up in the hypothalamus, but it was also, or could be, *Sky Above Clouds IV* (1965).

Slowly, steadily, Hillary saw her city anew, saw her son and her mother freshly too. Not as responsibilities to navigate, places to show up and do what had to get done, but more like dance partners who, unassuming as they'd seemed while shuffling onto the floor, had surprisingly graceful moves. Not that she waltzed through the Field Museum, but to take Roger there on a weekday, with enough energy to relish it, made her value the ritual more than she'd thought possible. Her mom commandeered the kitchen, which would've been annoying except that she made delicious, vegetable-laden meals. She was not the culinary artist that Miles had been, but very good, and Roger ate all her dishes without complaint.

And after their days of museums and errands and the tedious process of unknotting Miles's measly but complicated estate, after dinner and Roger's chaotic bath time (which was easier with two adults, Hillary had to admit), the two women would settle into conversation. In that nightly quiet—the stadium still snow-covered, the strip of sports bars in the doldrums after the Super Bowl and before March Madness—Hillary felt things were as they'd been twenty-five years prior, her and her mother at the table, talking about the future. About Hillary's future because, while Sheila hadn't meant to make Hillary feel bad, Hill was her life, the best thing she'd ever done. Hillary had resented the guilt and pressure Sheila mindlessly heaped on her shoulders—whose fault was it that Sheila had put all her eggs in one basket? Hillary had never asked to be doted on—and these many years later, Sheila was able to acknowledge her smothering hope. She had thought, for a long time, there would be more baskets in her life—a long and happy marriage, friendships that carried on through the decades, work she liked. She'd never pursued a career, not like Hillary's dogged exploration of the sinus canal, but Sheila had thought she'd happen upon something, anything to hold her interest. She hadn't.

With enough mint tea, the dimensions of Sheila's situation were revealed. A dwindling bank account, the looming rent increase—even Watertown, Wisconsin, was getting expensive. The bad blood sugar test (*tests*, plural; it'd been going on for two or three years) she'd thought she'd turn around with her diet but hadn't. Maybe couldn't. Not on her own, at least.

"Jeez, Mom. What was your plan?" Hillary wanted to know. Her life was difficult, but Sheila's problems seemed intractable.

Her mother shrugged. Her plan was no plan. The women watched each other, both quiet, as their teas cooled between them.

And Bella wasn't aware of the volume of flowers Reba had been ordering over the past month and a half. None for Bella—as previously explained, Bella's radio silence was normal, then annoying, then distressing, but Bill had told them, via Carson, to back off. And so Bella's situation had not moved to the level of floral arrangement. No, Reba's bouquets were for Doris's house and her father's room. For her father's room again once the first batch wilted, and Doris's house again, because Doris was so acerbic these days. She should be relieved—Hans was getting better. But instead, she was dour and snappy, except for moments like this one, when she lapsed into dejection. In the silence after Bella's long-awaited text came in, Reba looked from her phone back to her mother, and saw a woman whose face had taken on an absent cast, her eyes sad and searching.

Reba had been anticipating this, dreading it, for a decade or more. In some ways, it could be traced back to when Hans was a septuagenarian and cruising on two wobbly wheels, not taking his advanced age seriously enough. Or it could be pinned to that first Monday in February, when she was just getting back from Chicago—impregnated (not aware yet) and sore (very aware; she hadn't been so achy since her basketball days, though that had been the fronts of her thighs and the back of her ass, not the space between, the core of her being)—and her mother called midmorning.

"I'm not late yet," Reba had protested that day, because she wasn't. She was glad to fulfill this filial obligation of Monday lunches, but that was different from liking it.

"I know you're not," her mother had replied, sounding snippy.

"I'll be on time," Reba said, even as she doubted she would, not if she dried her hair and did her makeup and dressed in a smart outfit, the way Doris expected. But at the point of becoming late (still in the future, though Reba could see her mother waiting in the cottage window, alternately glaring out the glass and glancing at her wrist), Reba could blame traffic, a wreck on the bridge.

"I'm not calling about that," her mother had continued. "Your father—"

Is dead, Reba thought, completing the sentence in a heartbeat. She hated that she'd thought of that first. She tried again, hoping to finish the phrase in a more innocuous way. Your father . . . would like one of those donuts from that place on Fulton. Your father . . . needs a new tube for his trike. Your father . . . told me that he thinks Gavin Newsom will run for president in 2024, and we'd like to start a PAC. Please bring your checkbook.

"Is missing."

"What?" This hadn't been in Reba's carousel of maybes. Did Doris mean abduction or desertion or another, worse fall, a tumble into the sea like a geriatric Icarus on a winged and melting trike? Reba listened to the dead air between them. Were they waiting for a ransom letter or court papers citing irreconcilable differences or a call from the morgue? "When did he leave?"

"Yesterday. After lunch."

"And you're just calling me now?" Reba recalled from her crime procedural binges that twenty-four hours was the threshold for filing a missing person report, but what about a missing octogenarian? They could rightfully panic after eighteen hours, couldn't they? And what about campus security? The senior community didn't require ankle bracelets, but didn't their outrageous monthly bill include keeping tabs on the residents?

"I tried you last night." Her mother had sounded defiant a minute before, but Reba now heard a hint of despair in her voice, the warble of oncoming tears. Had she been up all night fretting?

Reba looked down at her phone to see if there were texts, missed calls, voicemails. None, though her phone had been off while they flew, and when they'd landed she discovered her battery had drained to zero; she'd plugged it in and gone to bed. "Did you leave a message? Send a text?"

"Why would I do that? You'd see that I called. Doesn't your phone have that caller ID thing?"

Reba huffed a huff that rustled the leaves of the potted philodendron across the room. "Not if my phone was off. I was in the air, and that's not—" She stopped herself. This was not the time to explain how cell phones worked or lecture Doris on phone etiquette for the twenty-first century. But why did her mother have to be so old, so clueless? It wasn't the time to ask that, either.

She started again. "Where did he go? Or, where did he say he was going?"

"For a bike ride."

"In this rain?" Another round of atmospheric river was gearing up, and the sound of it on the windowpanes would've been comforting if it weren't so menacing.

"It wasn't raining then."

"Right, right. Okay. I'll be right there." Reba hung up and Terry was unceremoniously roused from bed, because he had more upper-body strength than her and Doris combined (two decades after basic training, and he could still do a hundred push-ups in a go), and Reba thought they may need to do some hefting. Or they may need to do some crying, and if that was the case, she'd need Terry for that, as well. The two of them raced out the door—Reba barefaced, her still-wet hair dripping onto her shirt, Terry in his pajama pants.

They found Hans two hours after that, curled in a ditch—Terry's upper-body strength had come in handy. At the hospital they learned Hans was concussed, had a broken femur (the other one, and they couldn't advise whether this was better or worse than breaking one bone twice). The bone had snapped, probably by the blunt force of his handlebars, the trike's hard stop upon encountering what Hans insisted was a sleeping, then spooked coyote. The animal had been right in the middle of the path, in midafternoon? His audience was incredulous; rather than a coyote it was more likely a marmot, a big house cat, or Hans making a face-saving excuse for his unassisted gaffe. In any case, he would need a humongous brace and round-the-clock care while his leg healed; given his age, he might not ever walk unaided again.

But he was alive. Smiling, either because he felt good on his painkillers or for his family's benefit.

In the hospital's waiting room that day, Reba had made some calls. There was a bed available in the campus's assisted living facility, right around the hedgerow. Her mother acted like this was akin to putting Hans into a kayak on the River Styx and giving him a shove, despite Reba's and Terrence's and even Hans's cajoling. They'd won out in the end, but hence the stream of flower deliveries, the many nights that first month that Reba had stayed over, sleeping restlessly on her parents' old, familiar couch. She was in her mother's powder room the morning she finally allowed herself to pee on a stick (two, because she'd been here often enough to know she'd never trust a single positive), and that was where she got the first double stripe of good news, then duplicated the results.

"Constipated?" her mother had asked when Reba stepped out of the bathroom. Ten a.m. and Doris was still in her bathrobe. No makeup, her roots showing. She looked like she'd aged twenty-five years in five weeks.

"Something like that." Reba would tell her about the test, but it needed to be her secret for a while longer. She wanted to be selfish, but she also wanted to protect her mother from another sadness, if it were to come to pass, because there was still a high possibility of the ejector seat. For now, they got dressed and took their daily walk across the complex, down the boulevard, and around the bushes to a building that matched the others on the outside but inside was so aseptic as to look like the inside of an egg.

In those days with Doris and their short walks to the care wing, watching her father's incremental improvement as the child inside her grew and grew, Reba could see into the future, to when he stabilized and plateaued and eventually, inevitably began backsliding again. She did not believe in anything so woo-woo as reincarnation—if she did, the embryo inside her would as likely be taking its cues from a player on the Bulls (they'd been watching a game in the hotel room at the moment of conception)—but she did allow herself to question if some of her father's energy was being pulled out of his circulatory system and into this new life. And if these two, grandfather and grandchild astride their seesaw of being, might hit some equilibrium and *pause* for a moment. She wouldn't be so greedy as to ask that they overlap for a decade, not even until the baby's first words or its incipient memories. But oh, how she wanted her father to meet his grandchild.

72

Fri, Mar 24 at 10:03 AM

Reba:

What the fuck

Reba, in California, called Bella's number, but it went straight to voicemail. (In New York, Bella's thumb hit the reject button before she realized what she was doing, but what she was doing was protecting herself—she wasn't ready to speak with anyone, not yet.) So Reba typed out what she was going to say, and it arrived on the Upper East Side and Bella's screen a split-second later: "What the fuck." Reba expressed it first, but it could've been any of them, texting from anywhere in the country. "Not cool, ghosting us like that," Reba added in a second text.

"Bill's a dick btw," Carson responded. Bella was confused—the women didn't know about Jill and the divorce. Until suddenly, she wasn't. When she'd queried about her friends, if anyone had gotten in touch with him while she was inpatient, his coy "bat signal" reply. Bill had denied their concern, acted like she was the narcissist for thinking someone might care about her enough to reach out. But her friends had been freaked out! And they would have been even more alarmed if they'd known what, exactly, he'd done. Or, for that matter, what she had.

"Where were you?" Hillary added. She had ten minutes between consults and was reviewing an X-ray of a recently shattered nose. Her boss had given her a hard time about taking the afternoon off so soon after her return to work, to which Hillary had muttered something about "the estate," and then he'd offered to cover her patients. (To avoid rousing further suspicion, she'd stowed her weekend bag with a friend in Rheumatology.)

"Where are you???" wrote Carson. She was presently in Brooklyn, unpacking and repacking her suitcase, as she'd forgotten that the shirt she'd planned to wear to the party had previously belonged to Reba, and she'd rather not face that *nice blouse* wink. She had three hours until her flight, which would've been cutting it close on the F-train-to-A-train-to-AirTrain route to JFK, but she was splurging on a car. She could splurge on a car now, thanks to that lovely advance. "Are you coming?"

Bella was confused. "Coming to what?" she typed.

"Uh, Gregg's birthday party?" Reba wrote. "Zeke bought us all tickets. Didn't he get you one?" Back in California, Reba was buying two last bouquets before she headed to the airport. One to atone for the trip to Texas; Reba had assured Doris it would be short, way shorter than Chicago, but her mother was newly clingy. And one for Gregg—how could her fortieth already be tomorrow? She clicked "purchase."

"Apparently half of Austin is going to be there."

"Two-thirds."

Bella chewed her lip. "Dunno. I've been MIA."

Gregg chimed in, Bella's phone, unsilenced again, literally pealing with churchy chimes. "Duh. Check your texts, girl." So the guest of honor, their host for the weekend, was reading the chain. Shouldn't she be voting on a budget or bill? No, Gregg was typing. "Z's assistant probably bought you one anyway. She is A+++. 512 area code."

Carson again: "I told her you prefer LaGuardia. You prefer LaGuardia, right? I know you come out to JFK for me."

"Um," Bella started, "either's fine. Not Newark."

"Obvs."

She looked back through her texts and found a long chain from a 512 number. A flight confirmation code, preceded by questions about preferences for aisle or window, preceded by another about whether she liked flying in the morning or at night. Her birthday was October 11, 1982, correct? Was her legal name different from Bella Winston?

Not yet, Bella thought.

"Got it," Bella typed to the group. This elicited four thumbs-ups.

"So we'll see you there?" Hillary asked.

Bella scanned through the flight details again. The plane was leaving in three hours. Could she make it?

"Are you coming?" Reba added.

"I'd love you here, if you could make it," Gregg wrote.

"C'mon, B, we're rolling deep!!" Carson, normally loath to use an exclamation point, text-shouted, then added, "Any way, you have a LOT of explaining to do."

Bella thought of what was waiting for her otherwise: a familiar Metro-North ride to that pretty, unfamiliar house. There was plenty of work to do; she'd need change-of-address forms and had to figure out homeowners insurance, then do that first grocery run, a cart full of boring staples, condiments and pantry powders and a jumbo box of those fish sticks the boys preferred. She'd have to come back to the city next week for the awkward uncoupling from Cushman; she'd have to go to the apartment and see what Bill had missed in his packing. But all that also felt like nothing. All of it would remain unreal and inconsequential until she could see her boys again. But they were in Disney World or Disneyland, screaming on the teacups or harassing a cartoon mascot (Gus had a thing for Goofy). And until they got back, until they were standing in front of her, she would not feel complete.

Bella stopped her walking. This was *not* what her therapist had taught her. Family, in whatever configuration it happened to be, was very important, but her ailing relationship with her mother, her suffocating need to be very close to her sons, her imploded marriage—none of that defined her. She defined herself, and could redefine herself, again and again, as many times and as much as necessary. The people who cared about her would give her that grace. Even Bill, offering her the quiet and calm space to get settled, was showing her a measure of care. This was time for her to begin again, but not without acknowledging where they'd been. That digital frame on the mantel, the fridge and pantry that he'd already stocked with her preferred brands (and that'd be another jolt, when she walked into her new kitchen and saw it full), said as much. Maybe he was sad about their dissolution, he just showed it differently. By breaking rule number two, then buying her a gallon of her favorite imported EVOO.

"Whatever, we're just glad to hear from you," Gregg wrote.

The other three replied with up-pointing arrows, "dittos," "same same" GIFs.

Bella considered her suitcase, with its face creams and pajamas, her toothbrush and underwear, one pair of jeans (the rest was loungewear), a paperback Carson had recommended years ago but that she was only now getting through (and duly enjoying; Carson knew her so well). "Gregg, can I borrow some clothes?"

"What's mine is yours, you know that. You need shoes too?"

Did she? She looked down. After six weeks in slippers, she was wearing stylish sneakers she didn't totally recognize. Brightly clean, very comfy—were these those last ones she'd bought on Instagram, just before? Had they ever touched city streets? She could not remember if they had.

"We'll see," she typed as she did an inventory of her present possessions. She had her phone, her wallet and ID. She had a new life waiting, but she could push out the start date by a spell. For once, she wasn't up against a deadline, didn't have a preschool pickup or dinner or brief waiting impatiently for her attention.

Except she *did* have one deadline: this flight. Could she make it?

At First Avenue she hailed a cab. The driver nodded when she told him LaGuardia and turned toward the bridge. In the comparative privacy of the cab's back seat, she pulled out her new phone and opened up her voice memos. These, inexplicably, had migrated, the titles a series of dates—dates that she knew corresponded to recordings of Gus and Bill Jr. singing, to notes to herself about caffeinated booze. To Gregg, reciting one of her mother's poems, and to Carson, reciting another. What had they been doing that night that had turned it into an impromptu recitation? Bella could remember only the vaguest shapes of the evening, the diminishing candles and copious wine, Gregg's corralling them downtown after her meeting with . . . was it the Society of American Poets? It might have been psychosomatic, but even a few beats of Gregg's warm voice, ten seconds of the squeals of her boys, were like happy-time elixirs, and Carson, talking about anything in her flat affect, was a soothing balm. Anyway, Bella would go through these later, deleting the ones that made her sad, keeping those that milked her serotonin in tiny tugs.

Because for now, she had something to say, and she wanted to say it only once. No questions, no clarifications, no exceptions. And so she tapped the phone's red record button and spoke into the device, starting with the first day of oral arguments but doubling back to falling asleep during the caviar party, Gus's lisp, her forever deficit of sleep. She explained how things with Bill had devolved, not into acrimony, but so impersonal, their once-a-month dinner dates at the same stupid steakhouse, his fantasy league, the blow jobs she doled out like casino chips. She hadn't meant to put her boys above him, and he didn't intend to resent her for it, but she had, and he did, same as he resented that she worked so hard for a job that he didn't think was worth fighting for—it hadn't been worth it for him, and therefore, it needn't be worth it for her. Not that she was apologizing for him, or finding excuses for what had happened next . . . but she wanted to be clear that she wasn't the victim, or not only one, that she had gently ignored him for years now, taken him for granted when he was helpful, chewed him out when he was not. One thing she'd learned in her daily therapy was that, apart from the crisis of the affair and its deception, there was a good chance she didn't want to be married, at least not to Bill. They liked different foods, they liked different footballs, they voted for different candidates (Bella had never said it aloud, but now she admitted into her voice recorder: he was a Libertarian), and they had different definitions of success. On top of all that, she had pretended she didn't care that he was going bald, when he and she both knew that she really, really did.

She was saying all this as context for what had happened that first Tuesday in February, the brilliant opening statement and the steaming soup and the heartbreaking corporate newsletter. The rageful feeling she felt, the despondency that was like nothing so much as a boulder, tied around her neck. She'd been tricked by Bill and Jill's ruse, and she did not like being made the fool. No more than she liked it when the opposing team's offense slipped by her screen on the pitch—but in this case, instead of sprinting toward the soccer ball with every ounce of her energy, what she'd done was sit down in the grass and declare that she was toast. She noticed the driver's eyes darting her way in the rearview, but the phone recorder kept speeding through its milliseconds, and so she pressed on. She wasn't proud of it, but she had been so tired of being tired, of knowing that that immovable boulder was stony-faced and gloating by her side. She felt like no one wanted her to thrive, no one cared if she could or couldn't move the rock. Well, the four of them cared, and the boys cared (or they would, once they'd figured out the foundations of empathy). But that support, that belief, didn't feel accessible, not when her case had just guttered out and she'd seen Bill and Jill staring up at her from the page. Just then, she'd forgotten she was loved.

She *almost* made it through what she had wanted to say without crying, but then, as the car cruised past one of those cemeteries on the Grand Central Parkway, a sob slipped from her lips. Because she was so sorry to have acted in a way that might have hurt them, to have done something that discounted what wonderful and kind friends they had been for so long. Not that she was their responsibility, but they'd brought such richness, such joy and strong hallucinogens, so much fashion inspiration and sane medical advice into her life. Because she was sorry to have not been better able to recognize what she did have, which was a lot of privilege and opportunity and a life that, battered as it was, could still be a good one. Just not as she'd imagined.

The cab was rising along the big arc of an overpass, lifting toward the terminal. Bella didn't know how to end her confession, so she hurried through the plan for her Westchester relocation, which sounded, as she recalled it, not like a failure but like a golden parachute. "You guys have got to come out and see me. I'll have plenty of room to host. But if any of your brats poop in the pool, swimming privileges are revoked. Okay, I'm here. I gotta go. No questions about this, again, and please, and thank you. When I get there I'll request a stiff drink and some hugs, and Gregg, I'd like to borrow that pink sparkly late-Elvis jumpsuit you were wearing in Palm Springs if it's available." The recording continued as Bella paid the driver, as she refused any change, as she slammed the door of the taxi and walked into the airport. Then she stopped the tape and hit send and looked for her gate on the monitors.

73

Fri, Mar 24 at 5:45 PM

Hillary:
I'm by Cinnabon. You??

Everyone listened to Bella's voice memo as she made her way to Austin. Everyone freaked out, and recovered, then freaked out more when they realized how close they'd come to disaster.

As their flights' Wi-Fi capabilities allowed, Reba and Hillary and Carson texted with Gregg in Texas, the four women going forensic, searching for the fingerprints of warning signs and cries for help. Hillary said Bella had seemed moderately high-strung in Palm Springs, but when was she not?

"I thought she was just being teary again about not having a girl," Gregg wrote.

She'd seemed to appreciate the mushroom chocolate, Reba added. "Kinda a lot."

"She was being funny about food, but not as bad as she used to be," added Carson, thinking of the pink onion rings, her friend's yearning eyes, the times, when they were younger, that she'd been too skinny. "She was worked up about looking good at trial."

What about Chicago? someone probed. She'd been fine in Chicago, they said, or as fine as any of them could have been in that situation. The women replayed the funeral via pinging text. She'd arrived late, remember? It'd been snowing, right? She was distracted, but she was under so much pressure. ("Did anyone think she was going to win that case?" Hillary asked. Radio silence.)

And what a speech. "The performance of a lifetime" was high praise coming from Gregg, but that was how she felt about the eulogy. "Sorry, poor choice of words," she added. "She's not dead!"

"And thank God."

• • •

Hillary arrived to Austin-Bergstrom International Airport first, then Carson, then Reba. They gathered at the gate of Bella's flight and waited anxiously. They were famished; someone bought soft pretzels. Hillary told a joke about getting Cinnabon on the way out of the airport, which made them chortle, despite themselves. The LaGuardia flight arrived, taxied, and docked.

Coming down the jet bridge, Bella appeared the same as always or irrevocably changed; her roots were showing silver but her skin looked amazing, the dark circles under her eyes all but disappeared. She was, again, sporting that powder-puff tie-dye sweat suit; she'd worn it for most of the six weeks at Sutton Place, having determined it was the most comfortable thing she owned.

Upon entering the terminal: She had never been hugged so hard.

74

Sat, Mar 25 at 12:34 PM

Reba:

Alright, ladies! Car is here. Let's go celebrate us some Gregg!

The party was as parties are. The weather was kind, low seventies and plenty of sun, a smattering of clouds on the horizon. The park swarmed with tech bros and friends from the statehouse, Xavier and Zack's playgroup pals and the Thomas-Graveses' neighbors, the last group grateful that the celebration was taking place in a public park and not drawing guests to their street, where inevitably partygoers would have blocked multiple driveways.

There were several bands, because Gregg was worth it (and Zeke was indecisive on the day his assistant did the bookings). First bluegrass, then mariachi; he told Gregg there would be a huge (size or fame? Zeke wouldn't clarify) rock band later, after the big reveal. The music and the open bar were for the grown-ups, while for the kids, Zeke had gone beyond bouncy house to a bouncy *village*, a short street of laminated canvas castles and forts and slides. They'd hired a sitter for their sitter; Giselle was attending as a guest. There was an ice cream truck and a grill station, a booth for temporary tattoos and another for non-temporary ones. A showy astrologer—sporting a silky turban in a velvet-draped tent—was giving tarot readings, while Gregg's regular astrologer (also velvet-draped, but in a billowy dress) mingled with a group of health policy people. At least she was mingling until she saw the women talking in a clump; she hurried over and introduced herself. As soon as they were through with names, the woman turned to Reba, stared straight into her eyes, and said, "This time will be different." They all laughed uncomfortably. The stranger asked Carson about her book, which was also eerie, because the publishing deal hadn't been announced yet. Had Gregg said something, or was she able to divine secrets from the waning shape of the moon?

The feathery woman departed in a swish of velvet. Soon Gregg approached the group, looking amped up and luminous. The women did a round of applause for the birthday girl. Reba squeezed her arm.

"Three times in three months," Carson said. "It's like we live together again." She thought fondly, they all did, of those dogpiles on the sofa, the *Before Sunrise / Before Sunset* double-feature movie nights. Now there was a third film in the series, and while they'd not seen it together, the filmmaker was at this party. If that wasn't the universe folding in on itself, she didn't know what was. The multiverse was real, and it was collapsing into central Texas.

Hillary crossed her arms. "Like we live together again, or the world is ending."

"The world is always ending." Bella's speech was calm and slow.

"But extra."

"True." Bella's head lightly bobbed in agreement. Hillary wondered to herself: Was Bella sedated or was she better?

"But special," Gregg said conspiratorially, then her face burst into a not-so-discreet grin. She pulled something from her pocket—pins, "Thomas-Graves 2024" emblazoned on them. She handed one to each woman. "Don't put them on until after my speech."

75

Sat, Mar 25 at 3:12 PM

Zeke:

T minus 3 min darling! See you onstage 😉

Kegs were drained, more were tapped. Reba stuck with fizzy water, which all the women noticed but no one commented on, because they knew about the ejector seat.

The bar order had underestimated the crowd's taste for tequila (the assistant worried: Was this a fireable offense?); a busser was sent to the closest liquor store to buy another dozen handles of the store's best brand. A bouncy house sprang a leak and was quickly, skillfully patched. The mariachi band finished their set and the DJ played Queen while another band's roadies shuffled gear onto the stage.

Behind the stage, unbeknownst to most, there were stacks of unmarked boxes, containing campaign T-shirts and buttons like the ones the women were clutching, pens and envelopes and palm-sized stickers with QR codes that linked to Gregg's live-as-of-ten-minutes-ago donation page. Gregg's capable campaign team had kept it so quiet—spy style, because why distract the rest of her statehouse staff from the work at hand? They had so much to do yet in this session, and Gregg didn't want anyone to think she was about to cut bait. She wouldn't; she just had to see about this extra thing, what might come of it. Because she could fight against the draconian decisions of the Supreme Court as they, one by one, rolled into Texas, or maybe she could get herself into a position from which she'd have a say on the *composition* of that same court and could prevent them from being idiots in the first place? Proactive versus reactive, moving her game from whack-a-mole to Battleship. She knew it was the Senate, not the House, that voted on court nominees, and that US senator was still several squares down her game board, were she to be so blessed, but getting elected to the House of Representatives was one step closer, and more useful, societally speaking, than getting scolded by the lieutenant governor every few months. Whom she'd invited to the party, because she was the bigger person. (He'd graciously declined.)

Consequently, most of her staff still thought they were there to celebrate a big life event and acknowledge their own mortality, to get sloshed on the boss's husband's dime and startle one another with how they looked in weekend attire. They partook readily, because who didn't love Gregg? She was such a good boss, thoughtful all the way down to the detail of selecting local, organic meat for the grill station. (They'd hired the place from which she'd ordered that quarter cow.) There was much to celebrate, and plenty of steam to let off. If accepting mortality felt this good, they'd do it every Saturday.

The techies were also there to lap up Zeke's benevolence, but were doing so more aggressively—already as the second band was heading offstage, some were staggering; every few minutes you could hear, over the general crowd noise, a stray and slurry shout. Where the politicians were glad for a blazer-free afternoon and the relief of a cold beer, the tech attendees felt they'd earned their heavy pours, because Zeke was a brilliant leader but an erratic one, who had taken Peter Thiel's advice to run his company like a cult to heart. The mostly Gen Z staff acted like they were too smart to lean in (those poor elder millennials had been sold a bill of goods!), but even if they didn't advertise it, everyone was still grinding, because Zeke was charismatic and no one wanted to see his mad side, because the stock options and the IPO were always dangling just out of reach. Today no one cared about their future stock holdings; if they could only look as good as Zeke's wife when they turned forty, well, something would be going right in the universe.

The lawn settled into another his-and-hers setup. They weren't so evenly divided as to be split down an invisible center aisle; some in the tech team were tipsy enough to venture over to the legislative part of the grass and start conversations with the prettier among the senate staffers. These efforts were humored patiently.

Zeke's right hand and consigliere, a grizzled executive in a yellow playsuit, stepped onstage. She tapped the mic and shh'ed. The mingling, the chatter dutifully stopped. "Do y'all want to hear from our hosts?" She made a *c'mere* gesture, and the crowd came forward. Give them a couple of margaritas and engineers became so pliant.

The four friends, too, came closer. They found an oblique enough angle that they could see the microphone stand at center stage, but could also watch Gregg, waiting in the wings, pacing nervously in her now signature cowboy boots. She had smiled at the passing CTO and was now considering her hands, her new manicure (it matched the campaign colors), her golf-ball-sized engagement ring. Then there was Zeke, bounding up the stairs. He briefly put his palms around Gregg's shoulders, he quickly pushed his lips into her cheek. He said something in her ear that the watching women would never know, then he stepped out onto the stage.

The crowd roared. Not like Wrigley after a walk-off win, but loud.

"Thank you for being here! As you know, we've come together to celebrate my beautiful wife's, your state senator's . . . twenty-ninth birthday." He paused for a laugh, for clapping, some hoots. "We're also celebrating this beautiful community, this beautiful city with its rusty, obsolete, and very tall infrastructure." He gestured upward.

Someone in the crowd shouted, "Moontower for the win!"

"Bingo! I don't know how many times I've quoted McConaughey over the years about making a fiesta, but this one has finally been made good! Thanks to everyone who helped set it up. And thank *you* for being here." Zeke looked out over the crowd, then to his left—to Gregg, waiting with an almost anxious smile. "It's so nice to see you all."

He pulled the mic from its stand and started pacing. He was good at this part; he could make the inanest script sound like a TED Talk. But he wasn't spewing tech jargon today; today was from the heart—that was apparent from his first stage-right pirouette. "You know, witnessing Gregg's hard work at the capitol over the years has been so inspiring. I've been moved by her drive and her passion, and . . . by her footwear." Bella had noticed earlier that Zeke was wearing bespoke boots himself; he now did a heel-toe tap that got some whistles. "Being so progressive in this state is not for the faint of heart, I think we can all agree."

"Woo, Gregg!" The cheer pinged around the crowd.

Zeke paused patiently, waiting for the noise to dim. "Woo, indeed. Which is why I'm here today to wish my wife a very happy twenty-ninth birthday, wink wink—and to share some special news. Gregg and I have been thinking about how we can help our city, our state, and our country. What can we do here in Austin? What might we be better suited to do somewhere else, say, maybe, in Washington?"

Someone screamed, and Gregg turned toward Zeke, ready to step out. From her resolute expression—Carson recognized it from years of running lines with her friend, watching her make so many entrances onto so many stages—it was clear that this was the cue before her cue. Next he was supposed to say something like, *Here comes the birthday girl, the next congressperson from Texas's thirty-seventh district . . .* Gregg inhaled deeply, lifted her boot, and—

But instead of saying whatever it was that he was supposed to, Zeke held his hands in the air, palms pressing down, the universal sign for *please shut up*. On the side of the stage, Gregg set down her foot, and her face slid into vexed. "Now, Gregg has thought about it, extensively, and ascertained that she—*we*—still have a lot of work to do here at home. It's an uphill battle in that building, but somebody's got to push the rock up the mountain. That, and I know she didn't want to be away from our kiddos when they were so dang small and adorable. Zacky, Xavier, where are you at?" A high-pitched cry came from the back of the crowd; someone lifted Xavier onto their shoulders. The boy raised his arms and the crowd cooed at his cuteness.

Zeke continued, "Well, if she's there"—he indicated toward Gregg's side of the stage—"and I'm here, well . . . I assume someone is supervising those two." A few people laughed. Zeke's face turned serious. "Now, I respect Gregg's decision, I do—a mother *should* be close to her sons, am I right? But I told her, 'Gregg, that's why God—I mean, Steve Jobs—made FaceTime.'" Several snickers lifted from the crowd and floated over the women. Where was he going with this? "Anyway, she—and me, supporting her—thought long and hard, and decided that now was not her moment, not the right time for her to make a peregrination to DC, even if this new congressional district of ours is heaven-sent. Family first, no argument from me." He pointed at his chest. "But we put our heads together, and came up with a very solid plan B, if I do say so myself." He stopped pacing, planted his feet, and stared into the crowd. "Me."

The women, in their clump, collectively stopped breathing. That wasn't in the script! Gregg was ready to go to Washington, she wanted to take advantage of this once-in-a-generation open door. Why, why, why was he lying, and with such a straight face?

But his was not a straight face. Zeke was suddenly grinning like a cat with a bird in his mouth, and blocking their view of Gregg. What was she doing? The crowd was too thick to shift their position.

An uncertain clapping started from somewhere in the audience; it was quickly building. Zeke spoke over it.

"Me! I want to take Gregg's vitality and good ideas and implement them on the national stage, to make the country pay attention to Texas! I know my wife and I don't have the exact same agenda—she's a dog person and I'm more of a hairless cat kind of guy. I'm more techy and she's more into the arts—did y'all know that before she became an elected official, Gregg was on *Law and Order*? No, not a regular detective, but Dead Body Number Two in SVU season nine, episode seven or eight, look it up. She's creepy as fu—fudge. Fantastic acting."

Now he was just being mean, Reba thought. She and Terrence had happened upon the rerun some weeks back. Gregg had two lines before being murdered, and spent the rest of the episode in gray lipstick, lying on a slab.

"And only one of us has made a big financial investment here in Texas, but it's not Gregg's fault that she didn't 'come in with capital.' She knew where to find it." He thumbed at his own chest again, then resumed pacing, a new spring in his step.

"When it comes to me and Gregg, I'm more live free or die, though we both feel that living free encompasses the freedom of choice, so you can bet your next round of VC funding that I'll keep fighting for a woman's right to choose!"

The crowd erupted in cheers. Gregg's friends stopped caring about whether they might jostle their neighbors—they wriggled and pushed, trying to get eyes on Gregg. But she had vanished from her post at the side of the stage—had she run off to drown herself in Barton Springs or imploded with astonishment? This was supposed to be *her* announcement. Gregg for Congress!

Back at center stage, Zeke beamed ear to ear.

So this was it, Carson thought. The final comeuppance for what Gregg had done. Gregg had a very good reason for her decision, and it hadn't been so Zeke could kick her in the teeth in front of most of Austin, so he could take away this thing she'd been hoping for and working toward so doggedly. Carson watched him bask in the applause and felt briefly frightened.

"Now, I know I'm a bit of an underdog, something of an outsider to this whole 'politics' thing, but Gregg could've said the same, and look at how well she's done. That's thanks in large part to a great many of you—folks who were willing to take a gamble on a new gal in town because you believed in what she had to say. We rely on our friends around here, new and old"—was Zeke looking right at them? Bella was flabbergasted at his gall—"and Gregg and I will be calling on you again with this campaign, and asking that you call on your mama, and your kids, and your kids' mamas, to help us make this happen. Because Texas deserves better. We all do." He paused, looking up at the moontower for an awkwardly long beat. His eyes snapped back to the crowd, and the blues of them had a new, sapphire glint. "So, now let's get to work! The first order of business in my campaign to represent Texas's newest congressional district in our nation's capital is to sing a rousing rendition of 'Happy Birthday' for my beautiful wife. Gregg, darling, come on out here."

• • •

Gregg hadn't run away or atomized—she'd crouched behind a monitor and put her head between her knees, because the world was spinning. How could he do this? This was supposed to be her day. This was more sickening than the wooziness of her first trimesters, more embarrassing than being kicked out of an audition after thirty seconds, more devastating than getting dismissed from the senate after all she'd done was try to help. This was the worst.

But in that moment, the crowd shouting her name like it was two syllables, *Gre-egg, Gre-egg!*, she drew on her training, she remembered her breath. Her whole body felt crushed, her soul and spirit squooshed, but she started inhaling, more and more and more, until her chest filled and her spine straightened, until her neck lifted from her shoulders. She kept inhaling as her chin rose, as her eyes lifted past the crowd and reached the sky, until she could see only the pale blue afternoon, and then she drew in another big breath. There was nothing left to do, she knew, but respond to Zeke's summons with a smile. And so she strode forward, one step, then two, those beloved cowboy boots clomping right up to her husband.

The crowd clapped and yelled and whistled at her arrival. And then, at Zeke's big, arm-waving cue, they all together started singing.

76

Sat, Mar 25 at 3:34 PM

Bill:

Just met Goofy.

Bella:

👍 can't talk bye

Zeke had told Gregg there'd be a "huge" band next, but as the couple stepped toward the front of the stage, Zeke holding up his arms like he'd already won the primary, as the rigger dropped a banner from the moontower that said not "Thomas-Graves 2024" as Gregg had planned but "*Zeke* Thomas-Graves 2024," as the women were picking their jaws up off the lawn, questioning how he'd gotten the color scheme and font so close to her campaign's materials that the boxes of buttons and shirts behind the stage would still work for his purposes (he must have had a plant, paid off the designer, sneaked into Gregg's server somehow?), there was no giant stage show. It was just one man, with a guitar, who emerged from the wings.

Carson gasped at the sight of the familiar musician, who was the front man for Spoon. (Another romance of her twenties had been with a guitarist who'd been in the opening act for Spoon's 2008 tour, and she'd tagged along for the Eastern Seaboard dates.) The crowd applauded for the hometown rocker, and when he started playing, the noise doubled, everyone ecstatic at the recognizable opening strums. At the front of the stage, Zeke kissed Gregg on the cheek, waved once more to the crowd, took his wife's hand, and, pulling somewhat assertively, led them offstage.

The crowd kept hooting, thrilled at the news and the song, which was an acoustic, solo version of the band's biggest hit, "The Underdog." Likely they were thinking that Zeke, despite his billions, was the race's new underdog, and, as neophyte and outsider, it was he who would prevail in 2024. Carson knew the happy throng was wrong, at least about the song's meaning. On that long-ago tour, she had listened to the song night after night and remembered the tricky turn of the lyrics. It wasn't only about an underdog triumphing; the first verse was sung to another person, an unnamed *you*, a second-person asshole who wouldn't cede any ground or listen to the messenger or try to understand ideas that were beyond their comfortable comprehension. The song was a lot more vindictive than its poppy handclaps might suggest, and to play it now, presumably at Zeke's request, pointed toward this: Today, that *you* was Gregg, and she was summarily fucked.

The screaming had hardly let up when the rest of the band filtered onto the stage. The drums drummed, then the trumpets came in, followed by trombones, the brass building toward the song's catchy chorus. With the surge of the refrain, swarms of Zeke's staffers emerged from behind the stage with cut-open boxes of Gregg's T-shirts and pins (her QR-coded stickers and pledge envelopes conspicuously absent). The crowd, already earsplitting, got louder. Someone had a T-shirt cannon, and at the temporary tattoo station, a new design was revealed. Five hundred arms could be adorned with Zeke's spiffy campaign logo.

The women were dumbstruck, frozen in place. The nerve! *Chutzpah* would be too kind, this was demonic. Gregg was supposed to run, and instead he'd flipped the script, pulled the rug. Did he want the job, or did he just want to hurt her? Because while no one, not even Carson, knew all the particulars of the couple's back-and-forth, they all knew the two of them were cutthroat competitive, with the world and sometimes with each other. Historically, Gregg didn't complain about this, though this year she had started to. But how had some inconsequential asides about his work ethic led to this betrayal?

The four friends' anger thawed enough that they could turn their heads again, move their arms at last. But despite their craning and squinting, they couldn't get eyes on Gregg. Was this when she'd run, Ophelia-like, to sink herself in the springs, or had she, like them, turned into a pillar of salt and disbelief? All these thoughts flitted through their heads as they maneuvered and twirled around anxiously, searching. Finally, tall Reba spotted her. Gregg was a few feet from where she'd been, now tucked behind a stack of monitors on the far side of the stage. Whereas before she'd looked on edge, unsure of what was afoot, now there was no doubt in how her hands were clasping, how her shoulders heaved.

Bella was the first to bolt, a hot-pink flash jumping a hip-high barrier at the side of the stage—that borrowed jumpsuit was ideal for motion, even if, short as Bella was, she'd had to roll up the cuffs. The rest of them followed fleetly behind. Security approached, and Reba quickly dispatched the large man—"Back off! Best friends of the birthday girl!" He let them pass, and they ran up the stairs, ducking behind the drummers and backup brass (all except Bella, who ran right across the front of the stage, a neon streak). As they reached Gregg, who was now openly sobbing, the crowd sang along, so merrily, to the song's chipper hook: "That's why you will not survive!"

77

When the women climbed into the bouncy castle, the children present, unsure of how to share the squishy space with five forty-something women, one of whose face was streaked with tears, quickly departed. A staffer, among the few who'd known about the announcement and how it was supposed to go, who was on the verge of tears herself, posted up at the inflatable entrance, telling anyone who came near: "Closed until further notice."

Inside the castle, the barefooted and socked women jumped and screamed, their *goddamnits!* and cries of *cocksucker!* drowned out, sort of, by Spoon's set across the lawn. How could he do this? What was he thinking? He didn't even pay taxes, and now he wanted to run for Congress!? How could he want to be an elected official when his last goal was to leave the planet—there are no congressional districts in space! None of them had seen it coming, none of them could believe it true. Or they could, but they didn't want to. Someone jump-shouted about filing for divorce, another sprang a somersault and suggested he might find himself involved in a very unfortunate "accident." They laughed at the idea of Gregg as a young, becoming widow—think of the sympathy vote!—until they saw Hillary and remembered they already had one of those.

Once they'd tired themselves out with jumps, screamed themselves hoarse with well-earned profanities, the five of them lay down, heads together, faces pointed toward the sky.

"What just happened?" Hillary was the one to ask.

To answer, Gregg had to tell them the whole story, not redacting the part about the abortion (she touched Reba's hand, she put her cheek on Bella's shoulder), not omitting the rocket, the dogs, the Christ comment.

"Wait, he *froze* your dogs?" Reba, who'd made a career of hatchet jobs, could not process the raw violence.

"Only almost," Gregg clarified with a sigh. "And they're okay. I had promised they'd be mostly outdoors." She told them she'd thought they had apologized to each other enough, that it was all water under the bridge, or that, if all was not totally forgiven and forgotten in their marriage, they'd at least resolved to build a new bridge to span their respective banks, several hundred yards downstream. It turned out she'd been right about river construction, wrong about the structure. Apparently Zeke had quietly been erecting a hydroelectric dam around the river's bend, intent on harnessing the energy of their marriage's quick-flowing water for his own purposes.

Not theirs. *His.*

"I thought I knew what I was getting into," Gregg said, shaking her head. Zeke's ego was not unknown, even back at the cast party their first flirty night—she'd read a magazine profile about him, seen him once on *60 Minutes*. "I did know. I walked in, willingly. Eagerly." Because while Zeke had arrived at his position of power by being rash and retributive, the flip side of that coin was big-feels devotion and a propensity for going to the mat for the things he cared about. These were attributes that made him a good partner, or at least a good partner for go-get-'em Gregg. They were going to take over the world!

Until, that was, they'd turned on each other. Gregg's metaphors shifted from bridges and dams to war zones and minefields, all the deadly springs that Zeke had just set with his big surprise announcement. If she brought up the shorebirds, he would say something about her abortion; if she mentioned his unpaid engineering interns, he'd let slip the recent almost animal abuse. Whose trespasses were worse did not matter; it was mutually assured destruction. Because if they attacked each other, knocked the other down or even just lowered them a peg or two in public opinion, there was a good chance they'd explode the Democratic ticket, ruin the new district's chance of liberal representation in 2024, and maybe for a long time after that, momentum and incumbency being what they were. Austin had always been weird, but it was getting weirder in a new, unsettling way. As she spoke about demographic shifts, her voice climbed to an agitated octave, and she registered her creature climbing out of its lair. It hopped from her breastbone to the castle's red vinyl and did a first, tentative cartwheel across the soft floor.

Maybe, Gregg wondered aloud, she could run out the clock? Maybe Zeke's maneuver was only the last word for *now*. They could get quietly divorced on November 6, 2024, hours after the election, and she could start rebuilding. Or perhaps she could let the hands spin a few more times around the dial, wait and see? Knowing Zeke and his magpie attentions, he might well be onto his next project by 2026. If she remained in good stead, she could then reclaim the congressional district that was rightfully hers but make it look, to the voting public, as easy as a ball pass. *Zeke, I'm open!* In 2026 she would be a spry forty-three, still a generation younger than the congressional average. And wouldn't that be a nice outcome?

The creature did a complicated roundoff back handspring in the style of Simone Biles and stuck its landing with a big *ta-da*.

Carson listened carefully to Gregg's pretzeling logic. It made no sense; her friend was spinning out scenarios in which what'd just happened wasn't the end of the world. Carson watched Gregg's face. Was she in shock? Delusional?

Bella was listening closely too, and said, "Gregg has a point. At this rate, maybe he'll be on his way to Mars by 2026." Bella, on this day, was not beyond magical thinking. She had read in the news about the rocket development, had seen Zeke's name as a lead investor, but had not heard about the burnt birds, the environmental impact complaint that quietly had Gregg's fingerprints all over it. Bella didn't care about the future of wetlands, she cared about separating her friend from this toxic situation. A flight to Mars would do the trick.

"Or maybe he'll be headed for Uranus," Hillary added. This got a smile out of Gregg, a groan from Carson.

Then Gregg's face curled back into a grimace as she remembered the director in Culver City, her sobbing on the street, the patience she did not have then. Did she have it now? Could she really wait three years? "That feels like so long," she whined to the group and to herself.

Carson patted her thigh. "It'll be here in a blink. If that's what you want." Carson did not add, although she was thinking, that she'd done it, achieved her New Year's resolution, and had even turned the corner from not having enough patience to being the one pumping the brakes on life's insistent forward motion. Now, she wanted things (her father's correspondence, the book publishing process, the besotted courtship with Julian) to slow down, because when things went so fast—in any direction; good, bad, or sideways—it was overwhelming. Could she transmit some of her new patience to Gregg, transfer it like an AirDrop? The woman sniffled, and Carson backed away from that idea. "You could also burn it all down and come back to New York with me. Try that whole acting thing again." It sounded wild coming out of her mouth, but Carson figured it was worth a shot. "You've got a platform now."

"Very funny." Gregg blew her nose. She had thought she could control her destiny, but she was wrong. Not wrong for trusting her instincts and her reasoning and her star chart, but wrong for forgetting there was a whole universe out there, and some constellations looked different from the other side of the galaxy. Maybe, she told herself, from where Zeke stood, what he'd just done wasn't retribution, or not only that. Maybe it was also a way of giving her what she'd said she wanted—more time with her boys—and maybe it was him joining the fight, if in a supremely self-aggrandizing way. Because even as he'd pulled the carpet out from under her, he'd not cut her down completely. There had been singing, a big public declaration of love, an oath to keep fighting for what she believed in, because maybe he did care about a woman's right to choose, he just didn't like Gregg's own choice. He'd left a big door open for her, one he could've easily slammed shut, given the stakes of their disagreement. But he hadn't. "You guys think I should wait?" she asked her friends. "I mean, what is time, really?"

Her friends rolled their eyes and moved their heads and twisted their necks around until they'd all made meaningful eye contact with one another, looks that affirmed their mutual feeling. Then they all, to a woman, turned to look at Gregg. Their eight unblinking eyes, staring at her, suggested she was talking crazy talk.

"Alternatively," Reba said calmly, "we can drive you to the marriage bureau on Monday morning and pull off this Band-Aid real quick."

Bella placed her hand on Gregg's arm. "I know a guy, if you need him."

• • •

How long did they stay like that, collapsed together in their inflatable fortress? It was hard to tell, as the quantitative and qualitative aspects of time had decoupled again. The two parts unzipped from each other like a jacket opened, then that jacket was torn in two, split apart along the seams, ripped to swatches, and shredded into so many palmfuls of time-flavored confetti. The women were eighteen and twenty-five and thirty-two, they were laughing at one of Hill's quiet zingers or clapping for Gregg's curtain call or touching Reba's belly, five months from now, as the baby kicked. They were all piled into a car, reading aloud off Carson's cell phone, grateful for the good fortune of being together when her sophomore novel's first review dropped, or they were swimming in Bella's pool, or they were in the desert, letting those bitter chocolates dissolve on their tongues. They were clapping at Roger's high school graduation, crying at Doris's funeral, holding one another's hands in front of a piece of installation art. And again, and again, and again, they were holding one another, squeezing Gregg's hands, telling her it would be okay, because it would be. They would get through this; they would get through everything in one solid piece or shattered to smithereens but with enough glue and fortitude to reassemble the shards. Because for every Zeke in the world, for every monkey wrench in the shape of a pinch-hitting beverage company rep or a young mistress or a pill bottle . . . they had their own culpability in how things fell apart and their own wherewithal to put things back together again. For the women to move forward, from this and from every one of life's unexpected chutes, they were going to have to embrace their agency too.

The confetti of time was scattered in the air, then it drifted downward, because gravity. Maybe those torn-up pieces were the best way to measure time's passage just then—not anything as precise as the Newtonian equation for falling, but the touch-feel of accretion, how many tiny specks of it landed on the friends' supine bodies. It was a while. At some point, someone adjusted the celestial dimmer switch and the sky sank into a deeper blue. And then, not so long after that, that old moontower, tall and tired, its own exemplar of patience and rickety pride . . . well, it flickered to life.

Acknowledgments

A tremendous thank you to Jin Auh, Abram Scharf, and everyone at Wylie; to Masie Cochran, Becky Kraemer, Nanci McCloskey, Beth Steidle, Nathalie Ramirez, Anne Horowitz, Allison Dubinsky, Tiffani Ren, Laura Schmitt, Julia Talley, Molly Stern, and everyone at Tin House/Zando. I'm thankful that you believed in this book and published it with such care. Thank you to the Thiebaud Foundation for allowing *Supine Woman* to grace the cover.

This is a book about the power of long-term friendship. I couldn't have written it without the meaningful relationships I've lucked into and worked at keeping afloat over the years. Gale (Orcutt) Darling takes the prize for longest (since 1988, forged on the soccer pitches and lakeshores of Seattle), but the friends I made in Seattle, in Rhode Island, in Madrid, in New York and Louisiana and New York again . . . thank you for being you—and thank you for tolerating the little flints of our friendship that flash up from these pages.

A thousand thanks to Alyson Pomerantz and Marc Kristal for reading early versions of *Clutch* and giving me such astute notes. Garnette Cadogan, Jennifer Croft, Olivia Clare Friedman, Alan Grostephan, Diane Mehta, Mark Powell, Vijay Seshadri, and Craig Morgan Teicher: thanks for cheering me on when I needed it most. Thanks to Abby Rapoport and her family for hosting me in Austin, to Brian Dice and Amanda Uhle for helping me track down rights, to Rhian Sasseen for the astrology fact-check, and to Lauren Kane for the Sutton Place one. Charise Castro Smith and Faye Reiff-Pasarew, thanks for a million things, but specifically here: checking theatrical and medical details, respectively. The "plum pie" line is by Mary McCarthy; I am grateful for it and her novel *The Group*. It, along with works by Rona Jaffe and Sarah Jaffe, offered me such guidance.

I'm grateful to the Picador Professorship in Literature at the University of Leipzig, the Rachel Rivers-Coffey Distinguished Professorship of Creative Writing at Appalachian State University, and Bennington Writing Seminars, which have given me the opportunity to teach while providing community and the gift of time to write. Thanks as well to the Hermitage Artist Retreat and Hewnoaks for the beautiful environs and focused time with the manuscript.

Ellen Steinbart and Dan Possumato, David Nemens and Karen Sloss, Jessi Nemens and Brian Maier, and all the Gehebers: thank you for rooting for me as I went hither and yon figuring out *Clutch* (and every other writing project). Keel and Willow: thank you for offering unconditional love, the reading recommendations, and, of course, the family walks.